The day dawned cloudy and unexpectedly cool for the last week in August. The feeling of fall made Philip suddenly more aware of Vivienne's coming departure for college. What would his life be like next year without her?

He sat despondently under the tree at their meeting place. What if he absolutely rotted as Romeo tonight? Vivienne was going to be a marvelous Juliet. What if he spoiled it all?

He was considering jumping into the river when Vivienne's hand touched his shoulder. He bounced back, startled. Vivienne kissed his cheek and sat down.

"What's the matter?" she asked. "Are you worried about your part? I'll help you." She lay down and looked up at him. In the cloudy light, her pupils seemed enormous and her lips were pink and curving. He knelt beside her and touched her face with his hand.

"Say 'I love you'," she said.

Philip had never said those three words to her before. He drew a breath. "I love you."

She smiled and pulled his body down against her.

"Philip, I love you too," she said. And as he watched, scarcely breathing, she began to take off her clothes.

Tonight their performance of Romeo and Juliet would be electrifying. Everyone would know, she said to herself, that Vivienne Dane had everything it took to be a great actress!

SUMMERBLOOD

by Anne Rudeen

WARNER BOOKS

A Warner Communications Company

WARNER BOOKS EDITION

Copyright © 1978 by Anne Rudeen
All rights reserved

ISBN 0-446-82535-2

Cover art by Elaine Duillo

Warner Books, Inc., 75 Rockefeller Plaza, New York N.Y. 10019

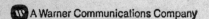 A Warner Communications Company

Printed in Canada.

Not associated with Warner Press, Inc., of Anderson, Indiana

First Printing: March, 1978

10 9 8 7 6 5 4 3 2 1

SUMMERBLOOD

Prologue

Philip

The women sitting at the roulette table were often beautiful, but Philip did not look at them or at the lavish furnishings of the room surrounding him—only at the numbers on the table before him and at the spinning wheel and the whirling ball; the units of time in those hours were not minutes, the blocks of time in those years were not months like February or May, he often had to be reminded of the date at the end of the night when he wrote out his check to pay . . . his psychiatrist cost him almost as much per hour as his gambling habit, he complained, but he saw the doctor every day and together they worked to find a pattern, something that might explain these two lost years . . .

. . . there was a pattern; he would put one chip on 9 and two chips on the lines above and below 9, and then at the last minute before the cry "No more bets!" he would place three chips on 8 . . .

"What do those numbers mean to you?" his doctor asked, and he remembered that in school he had thought 9 was a weak number, because it was easy to learn the 9-times table, the mirror-image of the answers—18, 27, 36, 45/54, 63, 72, 81—aiding memory in a way that

8 never did . . . he hated 8: it was always hard remembering what 8 times 7 was, and once he had been severely caned for not knowing . . .

"Then 8 could be—"

. . . they had talked about his parents, who lived in America, and when the doctor paused, he finished the sentence,

". . . My mother";

"And 9 is—"

"My father";

"And there is a number you never bet—"

"Yes, 7";

"So 7 is—"

"Me. Philip Alexander . . ."

. . . the third row on the roulette table, 7, 8, 9; the doctor and he worked it out—unconsciously he guarded his father by placing the chips above and below 9 and symbolically at the last minute he attempted to blot out his mother by smothering the 8 with chips . . . the result of the analysis was that Philip didn't use the pattern any longer, but he still gambled all night until morning and four A.M. and time to settle up, collect winnings, pay losses, walk out into the London streets and wander in the dawn; how can one's life take such a turn? or not a turn but a spiral, a spiraling downward and inward, until there's nothing but the accelerating spin into the center where at last one is gurgled down like bathwater—and it would all go down with him: his brains, his business firm, his cool nerves, his contempt for weakness, all he possessed that was circling with him on the periphery of disaster and awaiting the final plunge down . . .

. . . but these were the thoughts of exhaustion; Philip worked hard during the day, he went to his doctor and sincerely tried to find a way to halt the slow descent into the abyss; then night would come and with it the draw, the pull, the tug to the center, and again he'd find himself beside the spinning wheel and again life would be—

"Yes," the doctor said, leaning forward with interest, "go on, would be what?" and they always hung up at this point, hung on the edge of discovery; Philip could not put into words what it was that made those gambling hours so completely interesting, so stimulating, so addicting that he had to have them, to feel stingingly alive, alert in every sense, the way you feel—

"When you make love?" the doctor asked with his eyes on Philip's face, and so then they took that tack, but the solution wasn't that simple: Philip always made love whenever he wanted, with many girls on many nights, and the physical thrills of those encounters bore no comparison to the regular satisfactions of the roulette table—the gambling was not a substitute for sex . . . it couldn't be that simple: the key to it lay deeper, lay buried under layers impenetrable to him; doctors could not help him, priests could only pray for him, strangers give him sympathy, friends watch in sorrow as he came closer to the final four A.M., the last check—"Do you know the date?" he asked, as always, and was told, "Why, yes, sir, Mr. Alexander, it's Saturday, June fourth . . ."

. . . someone stood beside him, one of the beautiful women, and unlike him, she had won; but then, she was from Land's End, and didn't the damned Danes of Land's End always win? Whereas he, Philip Alexander—

Book One:

Vivienne and Mab

I

Two things brought Vivienne Dane to New York City that Wednesday the eighth of June.

"Just don't drop entirely out of sight," her agent Tom Clancy kept saying. "You're tired, and I want you to rest. You must rest. But you know where you are right now, Viv. You've got it all. Don't let it slip. At least appear now and again on a talk show. Don't let people forget Vivienne Dane."

Clancy was clucking like an old hen, she thought. From February to June she had made no appearances, but finally, to please him—when she found she had to go to New York anyway—she accepted the offer to appear on Sally Berman's show.

Clancy met her plane; he had arranged for her to arrive at Kennedy airport without fuss, and he whisked her into a limousine so quickly that she didn't have to sign a single autograph. Tom Clancy was an excellent agent; the best. He was more, he was a great friend.

"Clance, how are you?" she asked.

Clancy looked at her closely as the car left the airport; he did not answer, and there was a worried expression on his thin white face.

"Are you sure, Viv, that you want to appear with this babe Cherie Dillworth? I told you Sally was surprised. She thought you would want to be on the tube all by yourself."

Vivienne smiled, a slight warm smile, and shook her head.

"I would, Clance, if an interview were the point of

the show, but I thought we were supposed to be discussing pornography on the stage and screen. How could I do that all by myself? I've never even taken off my socks in anything. I can't sit there for half an hour repeating that I think nudity is shocking and that I thank God nobody's seen my boobs because I'm kind of flat-chested anyway."

Clance grinned. "You are not. And let me tell you, you're looking wonderful. South Carolina must be a vast health spa. I've never seen you so pretty."

"What does Cherie Dillworth look like?"

"Well, huge tits of course, fat bottom, stringy blond hair and an operated-on-looking nose. In fact, she's styrofoam all over."

"Um-hum, and nineteen, I'll bet. I think I'd trade."

Clancy laughed. Vivienne made him nervous when she referred to her age. Vivienne was nearing thirty-nine. Clancy wondered to himself sometimes, in the dark of night, how long she could sustain her superstar position in show business. But that was absurd. Vivienne's fame was based on her acting ability; it wasn't just her face or body, gorgeous as they were. She could act. Her voice gave you goose bumps with its rich, husky tones. She could express any emotion. When she wanted to, she could look more vulnerable than anyone in the world. She could pull a rage that chilled you, or let her heart break right there in front of you while old men and young girls wept in sympathy. When she made love, people had orgasms in the dark watching her. Her range was incredible, he felt. It was ability; more, it was *genius*. Vivienne knew what she was doing, and her core was steel.

"I've got some scripts for you, honey," he said. "Mike Nichols wants you in the fall, as I told you. Meanwhile—"

"Not now, Clance. You know I have to go up to Havenfield. That's enough for this trip. I'll take the stuff back to Land's End and read it. You can come down. It's time you saw Land's End, anyway. The house is almost finished."

"Sure, honey, sure." Mention of Havenfield depressed him and he fell silent.

They turned into Fifth Avenue. Viewed from the air-conditioned comfort of the limousine, the trees of Central Park looked wilted under the hot sun. People walking on the sidewalks still hurried despite the heat, unlike southerners, who sauntered when the sun was hot. Vivienne always noticed the difference in pace—it struck her even more forcibly today, fresh as she was from home.

"First things first. I thought I'd spend the afternoon getting beautiful to combat this Cherie," Vivienne said. "Wonder what she'll wear? What do porn stars go around in?"

"A sequined caftan slit to her navel?"

Vivienne smiled. "Not on Sally's show."

The limousine slid to the curb beside a white and gold canopy, and a doorman instantly opened the back door.

"How do you do, Miss Dane. It's good to have you back."

"Hello, Charles," Vivienne said, getting out. She hurried into the coolness of the long marble lobby of her building and Clancy followed her as she entered the elevator.

Her apartment had been dusted and aired and filled with flowers. Jeanne, her secretary, was there waiting for her, and there was also a young girl whom Jeanne had hired to unpack the suitcases and press her clothes.

The moment she saw Vivienne, Jeanne complimented her on how remarkably healthy she looked.

"Yes, the rest has been wonderful," Vivienne said. "Fix a drink, Clance, if you like. Jeanne? I don't want one."

"Lunch is ready for you here, Vivienne. Just what you ordered." Jeanne gestured toward the dining room.

Excusing himself, Clancy said, "Honey, I'm due at

Twenty-One to eat with some heavies from MGM. I'll pick you up at four-fifteen, okay? The tape session begins at five."

"Better make it four o'clock, in case of traffic," Jeanne advised.

Vivienne wandered into the dining room. A bowl of chicken salad stood on the glass-topped table. As Jeanne brought her coffee, Vivienne took a plateful of salad. It was tasteless. She wasn't too hungry, but she ate a little. It was strange to be back in New York; she felt as if she were in a stranger's apartment.

Jeanne chattered on, consulting her notebook as she went along.

"Jackie called you; something about a friend of Caroline's from Radcliffe who wants to act, and could they arrange for the friend to meet you? She knows you're on the Radcliffe consulting board. Oh, and Mrs. Paley called. Something about Mab, actually. She wanted to get Mab's opinion on a painting. I gave her your sister's telephone number in Chicago. I hope that was all right. And—"

Vivienne only half listened to her. The air-conditioning was on, but she still felt sticky.

"When's Jimmy coming?" she asked, interrupting Jeanne's commentary.

"At one, okay? Any minute, actually." Jeanne looked at her watch.

"I'm going to take a shower."

As Vivienne undressed in the bathroom, Jeanne tapped on the door and told her that Jimmy, who did her makeup, and Omar, her hairdresser, had arrived. Vivienne climbed into the sunken white marble tub and used the massage-sprayer to run lukewarm water all over herself for several minutes. Then she sprayed her feet for a while and finally toweled herself gently. She felt much better. Grabbing a full-length rose-colored cotton bathrobe from the closet in the bathroom, she wrapped it around herself and went out to

16

meet the boys. Jimmy and Omar both declared that she was looking "radiant, beautiful, divine."

"What are you wearing on the show?" Jeanne asked, opening the closet where the maid had hung her clothes.

"Oh, could you have the girl press it first? That white sundress. I bought it down in Eyreville."

"I love it," Jeanne said, taking the white cotton dress out of the closet. It was made of thin handkerchief cotton, delicately embroidered over the bodice with pale flowers and leaves; it had a narrow sash, and the bodice tied over the shoulders with narrow ties. Vivienne liked its innocent air. It made her look young.

"Hair up or down?" Omar asked.

"I don't know, with that dress. What do you think?"

"Let's try up," Omar said. "Up, but falling down at the sides. I'll show you."

Before they started on her hair, she had a twenty-minute wet pack on her face while Jimmy gave her a massage. Her dermatologist continually told her, "Skin cells are water and protein. Give them protein from your diet, and water from your faucet." He was right. The combination worked. The twenty minutes left her skin plumped up and softened. Her fair complexion was one of her best features; its whiteness contrasted vividly with her dark eyes and hair—her skin seemed to gather light to itself the way white flowers shine in the dusk.

The shampoo came next, and Omar gave her a last ice-cold rinse and a treatment with henna dissolved in camomile tea. When he blew her hair dry it glistened. He pinned it into a knot on top of her head, sweeping it severely back from her brow. Vivienne's brow was her greatest asset. It had a high curve, giving her a queenly look, and thanks to hot needle treatments it was not even faintly lined.

When Omar had pulled her hair back and emphasized her brow, he drew out tendrils on either side and let

17

them fall, curling them with a curling iron. Both he and Jimmy admired the result.

But Vivienne wasn't sure, "You don't think it's too dignified? Maybe down?"

"No, darling. If you wish, I'll pull more out." Omar coaxed more tendrils out of her topknot and curled them. "There. It's perfect. Don't you think so?"

She agreed and Jimmy took over.

He worked on the famous Dane eyes for a long time, murmuring compliments to her as always. Her eyes were beautiful, large eyes with a naturally heavy row of dark lashes. Vivienne had never used false eyelashes. In fact, she used few tricks. She didn't need the cinch some actresses tied under their hairline to lift their eyes. Her eyes had a natural upward tilt. And she had no use for the French eyedrops that accounted for the amazingly blue eyes of many an actor and actress. Her irises were dark amber brown, and because her pupils were unusually large she actually appeared black-eyed except in strong light.

Jimmy brushed a smoky-colored eye shadow on her lids with spectacular results. He contoured her face expertly with clown white and umber, applied a smooth liquid makeup over all, painted her lips, and she was finished. Vivienne added some Aliage and they helped her into her dress.

Clancy reappeared, punctual as usual. It was exactly four.

"You look ravishing!" he said. "Watch out, Cherie."

"You don't think I look too dignified?"

"You look sexy. When women wear their hair up, men always want to take it down," Clancy said. "Watch out for me on the way to the studio."

Vivienne grinned at Clance. Theirs was an easy-going relationship that had never been physical. He was good for her morale.

Sally Berman and Cherie Dillworth were already in the studio when they arrived. Sally rushed up to greet them. Vivienne liked working with Barbara Walters

18

better; Barbara had a hard intelligence, whereas Sally seemed to have only a kind of wistful intuition. But she got along with Sally well enough. They exchanged compliments and Vivienne turned to Cherie Dillworth. Cherie was wearing black Bermuda shorts, a white blouse with a Peter Pan collar, and she looked all of fifteen, except for her huge breasts. Vivienne felt sorry for her; it must be hell to have your breasts full of silicone. She gave Cherie an encouraging smile, and the girl returned it with a grateful look.

The talk show went well. Their discussion of skin flicks was just surface chatter. Obviously Clancy had briefed Sally; she made no mention of Alec Markowitz. Not mentioning him left a big hole in things, a hole they all carefully skirted and tried not to fall into. Cautiously, Sally brought up Vivienne's movies; she asked if Vivienne had ever undressed in films or on the stage.

"No," Vivienne said. She looked over at Cherie. "Not that I wouldn't, if the part required it."

Cherie, whose entire performing life had been spent naked or in boots and pasties, looked surprised.

"You don't disapprove?" she asked.

"People make compromises," Vivienne said. "All life is a compromise of one sort or another. I didn't have to make that particular one—nobody offered me money to take off my clothes." The corners of her lips quirked.

"On that note I'm afraid we have to leave you," Sally said into the camera. They filmed a few more minutes, as background to the credits at the end, and then took off their microphones.

"You were wonderful, Vivienne! You too, Cherie. Sort of sisters under the skin, if you'll pardon me for saying so." For a moment Sally looked as if she thought she had said the wrong thing, but Vivienne smiled.

"Actresses have to stick together," Vivienne said. "Acting is like childbirth. There are different methods for delivery, but everyone goes through the same pain."

"I never thought of it that way," Cherie said in her breathless baby whisper. "It's been such an honor to meet you, Miss Dane. Would you sign my book?"

The girl had actually brought along an autograph book, and Vivienne wrote a few lines in it. She thought, judging from the accent, that Cherie must be from Texas. When she asked, Cherie admitted that she was.

"My folks are dead," she added. "Otherwise you can bet I wouldn't be in this line of work. I hope I don't meet them in heaven."

Vivienne nodded, a bit nonplussed at the girl's remark, and Clancy rushed up and hustled her away.

"You looked sensational on the monitor," he said in the car on the way back uptown. "Your hair was just right, and those eyes—Jimmy outdid himself. The Dane quality came through perfectly, sexy but graceful. There's nobody in the world, nobody like you, Viv." He looked at her fondly.

"What are you doing tonight, Clance?"

"I'm yours. Is there anywhere you want to go? Dinner, the theater—want to catch Mikey M. in his hit?" She considered.

"I think I'd like to stay home and get drunk."

"Come on, honey. Is it Havenfield? You shouldn't go to Havenfield at all tomorrow if you feel that way. Let me call the doctor and cancel you out. I don't want you upset."

She looked directly into his gray eyes.

"Clance, don't overdo it. It's all very well never to mention his name. But you know as well as I do— Alec was much more than just a ladder you climb up and then kick away. I owe him something. A lot. Maybe everything."

"Poor bastard. If that were true, Alec wouldn't be at Havenfield."

Clance's words silenced her.

When they reached her apartment, Vivienne had a glass of Jack Daniels on ice and then another. Eventually, Clancy gave up trying to get her to go out for dinner, and went home. Jeanne ordered some hamburgers sent in for them, and stayed until Vivienne went to bed. The whiskey worked; after a while she fell asleep.

Vivienne had been to Havenfield before, on a bleak day in December when she and Clancy and Alec's parents had driven up with Alec. On that day Alec's father had signed the papers necessary to admit Alec to the exclusive Westchester County sanatorium. Mrs. Markowitz, trying to look on the positive side, mentioned the indoor swimming pool and the huge gymnasium and nine-hole golf course that were part of the facilities. Alec and his father remained silent. Their little group stood in the reception hall of the large gray stone mansion. Patients were housed both in the mansion and in another long stone building overlooking a rose garden, now covered with snow. A fire burning in the fireplace made the scene less depressing than it might have been. Havenfield was mostly a drying-out place frequented by the rich and the famous. It was also known because it employed an excellent staff of psychiatrists, and every patient was seen daily.

The doctor who was taking Alec's case, a calm, middle-aged gentleman named Cipes, met them in the reception hall. Vivienne had not talked much with the doctor that day. But he had called Land's End last week and asked Vivienne for an interview. "Interview" wasn't the right word, Vivienne thought; she shouldn't always think in professional terms—"consultation," or something. It seemed that in six months Cipes had made no progress with Alec's case, and he hoped Vivienne could fill in a few blanks.

The car turned, past brick pillars and the discreet *Havenfield* sign, and started up a winding drive lined with dogwood trees just losing their pink and white blossoms. The drive was a quarter of a mile long. On either side, rolling lawns with carefully cut grass stretched to the woods. Vivienne hoped the patients at Havenfield were tended with half as much care as the lawns.

She was nervous. She had turned down Jeanne's and Clancy's offers to accompany her. She hadn't wanted to make them sit and wait for what might be hours, but perhaps she should have let them come. She hadn't known she would be so nervous. She swallowed hard.

Her driver paused under a stone portico and Vivienne stepped out of the car. He drove on into a parking lot. For a moment there wasn't a sign of another person about. It was a nice morning. Vivienne walked out from under the portico and inhaled the country air. She was observed, though she didn't know it, by four secretaries and three nurses looking out of an upper window. The word had spread that Vivienne Dane was coming to see Dr. Cipes, and the staff was agog. They were accustomed to celebrities, but Vivienne Dane was special.

The women agreed that the actress looked marvelous. She was wearing her hair down, and it glinted darkly in the sunshine. She had on dark pants, a yellow shirt, and a gray-and-white checked vest with a matching jacket slung over her shoulders. As they watched, Dr. Cipes hurried out.

"Miss Dane! I'm so glad to see you. We're honored."

The doctor was very polite. He escorted Vivienne inside, up a winding staircase and into a large, book-lined office. She sat down in a comfortable leather chair beside his desk and politely refused his offer of coffee or tea. As he seated himself behind the desk, she regarded him silently with her dark eyes.

"I won't waste your time. We'll get right down to it," Dr. Cipes said. He had firmly shut the door of his office. No sound from the outside disturbed them. In the room, a grandfather clock ticked softly.

"How is Alec? You said he wasn't any better."

"That's why I called you. He is the same. We haven't made any progress." Dr. Cipes stopped, and the ticking of the clock filled the silence. "His parents have been here several times. He still doesn't know them, or won't admit to recognizing them."

"From what Alec told me, he never knew them," Vivienne said. "They're very nice, you know, but they're —ordinary. Normal. I think the only way Alec could relate to them was as characters in some fantasy of his."

"Oh, I agree. Absolutely," Dr. Cipes said.

"Alec must have been an easy son for them to have. I mean, while his mother danced and his father imported wine, they hadn't a single worry about what he was doing. From age five, he spent his time looking at old movies on television, or new movies in a theater, and that was it. His father told me that he had just one problem with his son, to get Alec past Loew's Theater on the corner and into school." Vivienne stopped. "That's the sum total of what I know about their relationship," she added.

Cipes looked at Vivienne for a few moments in silence, trying to gauge her mood. She seemed like a mature person. She had impressed him in December as very well-balanced, especially so for someone in show business. And she had agreed to come here to help him. He could see why Markowitz adored her. Her combination of beauty and strength of character was irresistible. And those eyes!

"But you want to know about our relationship, Alec's and mine, don't you?" she asked, looking directly at him.

"Yes."

"All about it?"

"If it isn't too painful for you, I want you to start at the beginning. The first time you ever saw Alec Markowitz."

"It was at a party."

Dr. Cipes settled back in his chair. He said nothing, and after a moment Vivienne continued.

"It was in 1972. People were wearing all sorts of

23

crazy outfits to parties, at least the sort of theatrical parties I went to. I'd gone shopping that afternoon in a thrift shop and I'd found a sort of gypsy outfit, yellow and green and black, with fringe. I decided to wear it to the party. I didn't ordinarily go around looking outlandish, but that night. . . . Anyway, when I arrived at the party this slim boy with curly black hair and big brown eyes started staring at me and following me around asking 'Who are you?' I told him my name, but it didn't mean a thing, obviously. I mean, for ten years I had been simply a typecast actress. I played Ophelia for Joseph Papp in 1961 and that did it. I'd walk into an audition, and unless it was a classical play or Shakespeare, I'd walk out without the part. I didn't mind; it's better to be a classical actress than no actress at all, but I certainly hadn't made much money or become famous.

"Anyway, I told him I was an actress and he said he wanted to see me act. He actually came up to Stratford to the Shakespeare theater a couple of weeks later to see my Lady Macbeth. He came backstage afterward and told me to pack because we were going to Hollywood."

"Just like that."

"Just like that. I told him he was insane—he *was* insane, you know—but he had a connection with a producer who made B movies out there. Actually, the man had proposed that Alec make a movie for him. I guess the producer figured anyone so obsessed might really have the goods. I mean, all Alec could think about or talk about or eat or sleep or breathe was movies. He'd been writing movie reviews for a paper on Long Island and was still living with his parents, though he hardly ever saw them.

"The decision was crucial for me. Up to that point, I hadn't really worried about breaking out of my mold. But I was depressed—there were personal reasons: an affair had gone sour—and right then I wanted out, all of a sudden. It was strange. Alec caught me at just the right moment. I tore off the gown I wore in the last act and threw it into the trash basket and said okay. I asked him, Why me? and he said he could see me as the heroine of the thriller he was going to direct. So we took off, me with only my clothes and Alec with his television set, so that he would never have to miss the late-late show. We drove across the country in an old Dodge. Of course my friends all thought I had gone over the edge. My sister Mab had moved to Chicago; otherwise, she wouldn't have allowed me to do such a crazy thing."

Vivienne paused, a quizzical expression on her face. "Is this the sort of thing you want me to tell you?"

"Was there a personal relationship?"

Vivienne shook her head. "Not at that time," she said. "I was surprised at first. I thought he'd—he'd want to sleep with me, I was prepared for it. I didn't really mind. My life's been—rowdy at times. But he didn't relate to *me*, either, then. I meant no more to him than his parents. It happened only after he saw me on film, after we made *Quits*."

Dr. Cipes's eyes narrowed with interest.

"Of course," Cipes said, "I've seen all five of Alec's movies. I saw them the first time around, but I've also had them screened for me again recently. The studio sent me the films. They are fascinating—except the last one. Before that he did what he wanted to do so beautifully."

"Yes," Vivienne said. "He wanted to make one movie in the style of every great director; he used to say that a conductor of an orchestra must be able to play any music, and a movie director should be just as versatile. That's where he got the title for his last movie, *Play Any Music*. You know, there was a song in it, 'Play Any Music and I'll Dance.' "

Vivienne's dark eyes filled with tears that threatened to run over. She looked toward the window, struggling to regain her composure. Her hands clenched into fists in her lap. The doctor was surprised by her sudden emotion. "But there are tunes you can't dance to," she murmured.

While she dabbed at her cheeks with a handkerchief, Dr. Cipes tactfully looked over the notes he had made on Alec's movies.

Quits, Alec's first attempt, had proved an excellent investment for all concerned. Alec had brought it in for less than his allotted budget of one hundred seventy-five thousand dollars by using an unknown as a script writer and Vivienne Dane as his star. Vivienne played a go-go dancer involved with twin brothers who hated each other. One brother was a professional football player. The non-player brother kidnapped the player and held him for ransom on the eve of his team's Superbowl appearance. There was confusion about which brother returned to play in the game; only the go-go dancer knew for sure. It was a Hitchcock-type thriller, and audiences loved it.

Once launched as a director, Alec followed *Quits* with his greatest success, the winner of seven Academy Awards including Best Dramatic Actress for Vivienne Dane. *Turn of River* was a beautiful and affecting drama set in Kansas in the nineteen-forties. Its story concerned a young boy growing up on a farm with a brutal father. The boy had an excellent voice and longed to become a singer. Vivienne played a doctor's wife who taught the boy to sing and also introduced him to sex. He betrayed their relationship in the end, under duress, to his father, and the doctor's wife was ruined. The last scene was haunting: Vivienne at the train station waiting for the Santa Fe Flyer, leaving in disgrace. The boy came to say good-bye, and audiences sobbed out loud while they watched Vivienne consider for a moment throwing herself under the train as it pulled in. Then she gave the boy a kiss, a smile, a look that said she would always love him, and climbed aboard. The train was in sight for a long time as it crossed the prairie horizon.

Next came Alec's Bogart-type tough guy movie,

26

Johnny Nassau, which won Best Picture and the Best Actor *award* for the star in the title role, Robert Redford. Johnny Nassau was Alec's strongest male creation, a gutsy wise-cracking sports photographer whose flashy wife (Vivienne again) left him for a millionaire speedboat racer whom she met while on assignment with Johnny at a championship race.

The fourth movie was the classic *Return of the Native.* It was a big artistic success but less popular at the box office. Vivienne played the lead, Eustacia Vye, and gave a stunning performance, but she lost out in the Academy Awards to an English actress who played a psycho killer.

Dr. Cipes liked *Turn of River* best. Now, as Vivienne looked at him with wet eyes, he was shaken—it was unbearably like being at that train station. He looked down and rustled his papers. She straightened in the chair, recovered herself, and the moment passed, leaving the doctor with a glimpse of her dramatic power.

"Can you tell me why you weren't in Alec's last film?" he asked. He made the question as mild and gentle as possible.

Vivienne drew in her breath. "We quarreled over that. It was partly a question of pride, my pride. For so many years I had been typecast as a Shakespearean actress. Then people said I was Markowitz's actress. Of course, I was. Without Alec I would never have made a movie, never have broken out of the mold. But after four movies, Alec was obsessed with me. It was embarrassing. He didn't let me out of his sight. He wanted me to go everywhere with him, and I had no life of my own. He wanted us to marry. Most of all, he wanted to keep on making movies with me in them. But Los Angeles—"

Vivienne had been speaking in a rush, and suddenly she paused. She pushed back her dark hair and looked out of the window, then let her gaze travel back to the doctor's face.

"I guess I had the Coast blues. The movie colony, the pace of life out there was getting to me. I was tired, and I began to miss the theater more and more. When I was offered the lead in a new play for Broadway, I accepted."

"And that was *Rivers to the Sky*?"

Vivienne nodded. "I told Alec that it was exactly what we both needed, to be apart for a breathing spell. But he was deep into plans to make a musical and he was absolutely beside himself that I didn't want to be in it. Even though I couldn't sing a note. We had a knock-down, free-for-all fight."

She paused for a moment and then gave a faint chuckle.

"Alec said I would stink without him. He said I'd mess up the part, muck up the show. He never dreamed that he would fail and I would succeed. I wasn't too sure myself, but when I stood on the stage of the Music Box and heard the applause—"

Vivienne's eyes were fixed on Dr. Cipes's face, but she seemed to be talking more to herself, trying to put her feelings into words.

"When I read Clive Barnes's review," she went on, "I was truly happy. I felt free; felt that I had proved myself. But Alec wasn't speaking to me. He didn't come to opening night or even send a wire. Nothing. There was a rumor that he came to a matinee—but I don't know. I hadn't seen him since our breakup in L. A. I wrote to him, though. I felt so ungrateful. I said I would make another movie with him, but he never answered."

Vivienne's gaze wandered across the bookshelves on the walls and then to the window again. She swallowed and continued.

"As you know, Dr. Cipes, late last fall Alec's movie *Play Any Music* opened and got panned by the critics as the biggest bore since *The Great Gatsby*. And in our business, when you're down, you get stepped on. Alec had made enemies. Now they were delighted to say that he had never had anything but good luck and me. It was so unfair! They said that with the exception of *Johnny Nassau*, which had Redford, I'd carried every movie. It made me furious to hear it—that sort of talk. But what could I do?" Vivienne stopped, frowning.

"And then?"

"Well, you know the rest."

"I'd like to hear it again, if you don't mind," Dr. Cipes said. "Everyone was so upset last winter when you brought him here."

Vivienne looked troubled. Cipes wondered if he were pushing her too far. He offered her a glass of water and she accepted. She took several swallows and put the glass down.

"Well," she said, "I hadn't seen Alec since I left California, or heard from him. Then one night he just walked down the aisle and jumped up onto the stage. It was the middle of the first act. Everyone was stunned. Alec looked terrible—unshaven, shaky. He called me Sarah. That was my name in *Johnny Nassau*. There was a scene he had rehearsed with me a lot. In it, Johnny realizes that Sarah has just been using him and he's still in love with her. Well, Alec went into that scene . . . I mean, he started saying the dialogue. There was pandemonium, as you can guess. Some-one—"

Vivienne paused and took another swallow of water.

"Someone from the wings came out and pulled him off the stage, and he was struggling, and I had to watch and then just—try to go on. It was terrible. But the audience had paid their money and they wanted to see the show. After the first act, I rushed back to find Alec. Someone had called my agent, Tom Clancy, and he had Alec in my dressing room; Clance gave me the strangest look when I came in. Alec was sitting there. When he looked up, he started that scene all over again: 'Tell me Sarah, tell me about how the kid is mine—' "

Vivienne paused. The clock ticked. "I had betrayed him, you see. That was the betrayal scene in the movie. Alec was like a broken record—he just kept repeating the lines.

"I had to finish my performance on the stage. Clance got the Markowitzes to come down to the Music Box. No one knew what to do; somebody mentioned having heard of Havenfield, or being here, or something—somebody's shrink recommended it. I sat up with Alec all night and then we brought him here the next day."

Vivienne stopped and took a breath. "Is he still Johnny Nassau?" she asked.

"As much as he is anybody."

"He felt close to the character when we made the movie. He thought Redford did a good job, but he liked to take the role himself and rehearse with me. He did that with all our movies."

"Do you agree that Johnny Nassau was the strongest man in any of Alec's movies?"

"No, there were Diggory and Clym Yeobright, in *Return of the Native*. They were both strong characters. But Johnny had a camera in his hands. Alec related to that."

"Yes, it's easy to see how Alec would identify with Johnny. What I'm searching for is some clue as to how to restore Alec's real identity—his talent, his creativity, his desire to make movies. It's all gone."

Vivienne shook her head. "You told me on the phone that Alec doesn't even watch the movies on television—I can't believe that."

"He doesn't seem interested at all."

Vivienne was silent for a moment. "Didn't someone say, 'You are who you pretend to be, so be careful who you pretend to be'?"

Dr. Cipes looked interested. He made a note on his pad and then looked up.

"You mean," he said, "Alec was just pretending to

be a movie director and doing it well enough to convince everybody?"

"Dr. Cipes, I was no closer to Alec than anyone else —no one was close. When Alec screened the movies and watched me on film—*then* he believed I was there. It was eerie. He wasn't really ardent. In fact, sex meant very little to him, as far as I could tell—he didn't really care enough to pretend. Now, if he's lost interest in movies, it's the same thing. He doesn't care enough to pretend. And that's all I can think of to say."

How garbled that all sounded, Vivienne thought. Cipes must think she was babbling. But he looked down and wrote more notes on his pad. When he looked up, he smiled.

"That was helpful," he said, putting his pencil down. "It was wonderful of you to do this, Miss Dane."

"Dr. Cipes, may I see him?"

"I was hoping you would want to. He may not know you. Are you prepared?"

Vivienne stood up. "I'll be all right," she said.

The doctor led her downstairs and out a back door into the rose garden. The scent of a thousand roses filled the air. In the center of the garden was a stone fountain in the shape of a woman with a jug that poured water endlessly. The large square of lawn was crisscrossed by gravel walks, and on all sides the roses bloomed, rows and rows of every color and shade.

"We have a place called the Glasshouse, a summer house, over here," Dr. Cipes said. "That's where Alec has been sitting lately. Let's see if he's there."

A young boy passed them as they walked toward the Glasshouse; two elderly women pacing on the path called out cheerily to the doctor. Cipes returned their greeting. When he and Vivienne reached the Glasshouse door, he looked inside.

"Yes, he's there."

Cipes stood back and Vivienne walked in. There were rustic chairs scattered about. Alec was seated near the glass wall on the far side. He looked well. He had a little color, his hair was neatly cut, and he was clean-shaven. Vivienne was relieved at first glance. But Alec sat very still, looking fixedly out of the open casements.

Dr. Cipes stayed behind Vivienne as she approached Alec's chair.

"Alec? How are you?"

He looked up, slowly, but he seemed to have trouble focusing on her. His lips trembled.

"It's me. Vivienne." She pulled a little rustic footstool up and sat down beside him.

Alec's eyes rested on her face.

"Can't you say anything, Alec? Or don't you want to?"

"The kid," he said softly, with no change of his blank expression. "You said it was my kid."

"Oh, Alec, don't!"

"You said it was my kid, Sarah, but I was getting the business all along, wasn't I? You weren't going to come back. I was just bait, like you bait your hook and throw it in, and who cares what happens to the bait so long as the big fish is caught—let the bait be swallowed, right?" His face was still expressionless, but somehow his voice sounded like Robert Redford's voice.

Vivienne's dark eyes flashed wildly to Cipes's face and back to Alec.

"It's Vivienne," she cried. "The gypsy girl at the party, remember?" She spoke the words with such passionate entreaty in her voice that Dr. Cipes felt his skin break out in gooseflesh. "Alec, darling. Please. Come back to me."

Alec's dark eyes stared into hers. Cipes held his breath. A woman walked in the Glasshouse door, saw them and stood frozen with surprise.

Vivienne knelt beside Alec, looking him straight in the face. She spoke coaxingly.

"I saw *Swiss Miss* last week. You weren't watching? It was on in the afternoon. Remember Laurel and

Hardy as mousetrap salesmen in Switzerland? Remember that song, 'I Can't Get Over the Alps?' And—and *Streetcar Named Desire* has been on. Remember how you asked me, when we first met, whether I was related to Vivien Leigh? Because our first names were the same? You screwball. Remember, darling?"

Her tone was caressing, and she looked earnestly at Alec as she spoke. That look would have melted stones, Cipes thought.

"Yeah, that was it, Sarah, get yourself a big sucker. Get the biggest. Get Johnny Nassau."

"Oh, Alec!" Vivienne stood up, shook her head, and ran out of the Glasshouse. Cipes found her leaning against a stone wall, weeping, her hands to her face.

"How can I leave him here?" she said into her hands.

Cipes touched her shoulder.

"Miss Dane, don't. Please, don't cry. You've helped me by coming here. I'm convinced now that you're not really involved with Alec's condition at all. He wasn't reacting to you. He says those things to the attendants, all the time."

"Really?" Vivienne looked at the doctor in disbelief. Was Cipes just saying that to make her feel better?

"Until today I couldn't be sure," Cipes said. "But now I'll try a new line with him, a new approach. I'm sorry if it was hard on you, but it was enormously helpful to me."

"I hope so. I hope he gets well. I have to—"

Suddenly Vivienne wanted out of there, out of that place with its storybook house and grounds and kindly doctor.

Cipes escorted her to her car. They were observed from above as before, but there was no one in the parking lot except her waiting driver. Dr. Cipes thanked her again.

In a few minutes she had left the dogwoods behind.

Vivienne squeezed her eyes shut as the car turned onto the Sawmill River Parkway. She let her head fall back. Just relax all over, she told herself. It's over now. Come on, Vivienne. You did everything you could to help.

But it was her fault Alec was there in the first place.

Vivienne hated to look at the situation in that light. But if you put the worst construction on it, she had given herself to Alec, and although theirs had been a pale, strange love, not satisfying to her except as it involved her career, still she had used him and gone on. She had let Alec direct her to fame, and then she had left him. It was all so complicated! But she felt like a mother who had taken her child on a subway ride and then jumped off the train at Forty-second Street and let the kid go rattling on alone, to God knows what fate—

To Havenfield.

But she wasn't Alec's mother, or his keeper; she was just his movie star, she argued back. All right, his sort-of lover. But you could leave people, you *could*, without blame or censure. You had to protect yourself.

She seized that thought. It had comforted her many times since last December, when Alec cracked up. It was only logical.

A little voice inside her went on saying, Ah, but you're strong, Vivienne Dane; you were tempered long ago with pure steel, *you* need protection? But she ignored the voice.

She would put Alec behind her, firmly, and look the world in the eye, and belong to herself alone. She repeated that several times, and then opened her eyes. How about going somewhere and washing Havenfield off? She felt as if the place were sticking to her. It would be dreary to go back to the empty apartment. An idea struck her, and she tapped on the glass partition.

"Carlos," she said when the driver slid it open, "When we get into town, take me to the Omega."

She would have a massage and a Turkish bath and a facial and everything in the whole chic expensive

34

place. The works. Maybe that would put her back together again.

"Miss Dane! How nice to see you. You haven't been here in a long time. We heard you were in the South."

The pretty receptionist who greeted her wore the Yves St. Laurent peasant dress uniform of the private beauty salon on Fifth Avenue. The Omega had a clientele of famous New Yorkers from all professions. The only requirement for membership was wealth—the hefty fees paid for privacy, for the lavish art deco furnishings—swirls of bronze and gold covered the walls and the furniture was gold kid—and for anything the client wanted in her pursuit of health and happiness.

"I'd like a private room. I want a massage and a facial, and afterward I'll have the Turkish bath," Vivienne said.

"Do you want David for your massage, as usual?" the receptionist asked. "I think I can get him for you." Tactfully, she did not mention that Vivienne had not made an appointment. For Vivienne Dane, she would juggle schedules.

"Yes, fine," Vivienne said.

Another attendant led her down the hall, past the door to the large gymnasium and the small, private gold-carpeted exercise rooms, and into a rose-pink room with mirrored walls, a bed, a dressing table, chairs and a rubbing table. Rose lights glowed in the ceiling. The attendant turned the lights down, and in near-darkness assisted Vivienne to undress, wrapped her in a pink sheet and helped her onto the table, giving her witch-hazel pads to put over her eyes.

"David will be right in," she said in a low voice.

"Could you do me a favor?" Vivienne said. "My agent and my secretary are going to wonder about me. Could you call my answering service? Tell them to get in touch with Clancy and let him know I'm here. I think they have the number at the desk."

"I'll be glad to. Here's David."

Vivienne took the pads off her eyes and said hello. David was a young man of about twenty-two who had an extravagantly beautiful body, like the statue of a Greek athlete come to life. He came in wearing a white tee shirt and white pants; even in the dim light Vivienne could see that both were skin-tight. Vivienne wondered whether he kept his trim physique by using the devices at the salon. He had a pretty face, and long curly chestnut hair.

"Hello, Miss Dane," he said in a whisper. "I'm glad to see you again. How are you?"

Vivienne sighed and turned over onto her stomach on the padded table. "I've been better," she said.

"You look in wonderful shape." Expertly David bared her legs, draping the sheet up around her torso. "I think you've lost weight." He ran his hands over her legs. "Good muscle tone. What have you been doing?"

"Ballet," she said. "I've been home since March, and my old ballet teacher is still in town. She comes over to give me a class every day."

"Wonderful. Yes." David began on her right leg, patting it all over briskly and then massaging with his strong fingers. He didn't talk and Vivienne relaxed a little in the dark room. There was no sound but that of his hands softly stroking her skin. It was soothing. He worked on her legs, her feet, and then her buttocks. Finally he bared her back.

"Do you want anything special?" he whispered to her.

"I'm just coasting right now," she said. Maybe later, she thought. She didn't feel up to sex at all, despite the sensations his hands were creating. He said nothing and continued his gentle ministrations, working down her arm and then down each finger in turn.

There was a tap at the door.

David left her for a moment and went to consult with someone. When he came back he whispered, "Your agent is calling. Do you want to talk to him?"

"Clancy? Oh, yes. Bring me a phone." Vivienne sat

up on the table, pulling the sheet around her. David turned up the lights and plugged in a pink telephone.

"Viv, are you okay?" Clancy asked.

David began to massage her shoulders.

"I called Cipes when I didn't hear from you in the early afternoon," Clancy went on. "He said you two had a very helpful session, but I thought from the way he talked that something happened. You okay?"

"It shook me," she said. "I saw Alec."

"Jesus. What did you feel?"

Trust Clance. She certainly couldn't complain that he didn't have her welfare as his sole concern. Instead of asking how Alec was, he asked how she felt.

"What did I feel?" she said. "I felt regret, sweetie. Incidentally, the name of the only filly ever to win the Derby."

"What does that mean? Wait a minute—that's a line from *Johnny Nassau*!" Clancy's voice rose in alarm.

"Two can play the game." Vivienne paused. "God, Clance, it was awful. Alec is so corny and pathetic, you don't know whether to cry or laugh."

"And you felt—"

Vivienne sighed. "To be honest, I felt afraid."

"What do you mean?"

"I can't tell what's real and what's sham anymore. Alec becomes a character in his own movie—even our nervous breakdowns are stagy in this business. It gets to you. I mean, what if it could get to me?"

"Nonsense." Clancy sounded uneasy. "A tough customer like you? You're about as likely to crack up as a"—he paused to think of an example of stability—"as a bank vault."

"Oh, that's what I am to you." Vivienne chuckled.

"That's a girl." Clance sounded relieved to hear her change of mood. "Have a drink and forget the whole thing. You know, honey, you shouldn't have gone out there alone. I almost drove out myself and waited for you beside the road. I was worried sick something would happen."

"That's sweet, Clance. Oh, you just reminded me, I didn't have any lunch." Vivienne looked around at David.

"Do you want something to eat?" David asked. "I can get you anything you'd like."

Vivienne thought a minute.

"How about ice, some glasses, some carrot juice and a fifth of Jack Daniels?"

"Coming right up." David departed.

"Sounds like a party," Clance said. "I think I'll come over."

"I'm going to have a Turkish and the whole works. I'll call you when I'm a new woman."

"Promise."

"Sure," she said, hanging up.

David came back with carrot juice, Jack Daniels, a bucket of ice and two glasses. They each had a Jack Daniels. As the warming liquor crept from her stomach out into her arms and legs, David lowered the lights and continued her rubdown.

"You're much more relaxed now," David whispered after working on her back for a while. "Your muscles were tense before."

She was about to suggest that she have a little special massage when someone tapped on the door again. David answered, came back and whispered, "There is a long distance phone call for you from your sister in South Carolina. Will you take it?"

"Yes, of course," she said, and picked up the pink extension phone again. "Cypriana? How are you? That's all right, I'm just having a rubdown. David, could you hand me the carrot juice? You've been where, Cypri? London with whom? *Philip Alexander*?"

Vivienne waved aside the carrot juice David was offering, turned over and sat up. Her sister's voice went on, and Vivienne stared straight ahead of her at the mirrored wall. She didn't appear to see herself sitting there. The sheet slowly unwrapped, coming open over her breasts and sliding down onto the table and the floor, leaving her naked, but she didn't notice. David stared at her.

"I see," Vivienne said finally. When she spoke, her voice had its usual decisive tone. "Of course, Cypri. I'd love to have you all at Land's End, if Philip is coming over. Sorry I haven't been in touch lately—I didn't know you'd gone to England. Oh, I see—in a hurry, yes. Well, a house party is fine. The guest house is almost finished; the house, too. And a ball is fine; you make out the guest list, invite anyone you'd like. I'll call you when I get home—I may fly back tomorrow. Mab? Oh, I'll call Mab. I'm sure she'll come if she can. Yes, well, good-bye."

She handed David the pink receiver.

"Were we finished?" she asked, looking around in a dreamy way as if she was almost surprised to find herself there. David was puzzled. He didn't want to gape at her, but she sat there with her beautiful breasts and stomach bare and he could hardly take his eyes away.

"We were almost finished," he said, "but if you'd like some more massage, I'll be glad—"

"No. That's all right. Oh." Vivienne noticed that she had come uncovered. She slid off the table and picked up the sheet. "I think I'll skip the facial and just start the bath."

David thought she looked shaken, but she spoke normally enough. He went out to get the bath attendant.

"Watch her," he said to the girl. "She seems a little on edge today."

Back in the pink room, Vivienne poured another Jack Daniels and drank it. The attendant brought a pale lavender silk kimono, wrapped it around her, and led her to the steamroom. For fifteen minutes, huddled on a bench in the middle of the hot white mist, Vivienne could scarcely get farther than just repeating the name Philip. When was the last time she had thought of Philip? She always thought of Philip when she acted in a passionate scene, thought of *her* Philip, the one who

39

had loved her when she was young. But the real Philip, the one living in London and getting richer and richer —she never thought of him at all. She didn't ever picture him to herself.

Vivienne began to sweat and she felt a little dizzy. Maybe it was from the Jack Daniels. Or the news Cypriana had just given her. Philip was destroying himself—that was how Cypriana had put it—Philip was gambling heavily and destroying himself. Something had to be done to save him, and—

It was unbearably hot. Steam rooms always gave her claustrophobia.

She made her way out and the attendant, her arms full of sheets and blankets, joined her. They went into a dark glass-sided room off the pool, where the girl wrapped Vivienne up like a mummy in two sheets and two layers of blankets. After settling her in a full-length steamer chair, the girl added another two layers of blankets and placed cool pads over Vivienne's eyes. "The pack" could last as long as one liked. In the silent, dim room, two other wrapped-up bodies nearby were motionless. Muscles relaxed, lulled by the soft gurgle of water from the pool, people often fell asleep there.

"Ring the bell when you are ready for the hot room and the scrub," the attendant whispered. Vivienne heard her tiptoe out.

The cool pads felt like kisses on her eyelids. *Philip*. Her mind couldn't seem to go forward at all, could not move past that word. Destroying himself, she thought; destroying himself. She couldn't think back, either, at first. Then she glimpsed his face; she was in a tree, and Philip, naked, was looking up at her.

The image flickered and faded. If only you could reach the truth, the whole truth of the past . . . , but it would take more than her power, because the past belonged to Philip too. Did he ever think of it? Of her . . . Vivienne . . . ?

II

While Vivienne was growing up at Land's End, the house on Curzon's Neck, Philip was in Cambridge, England. He had told Vivienne about his past in such detail that it was easy to picture the narrow streets of his town, the bustling corridors of his school, where he brawled to gain respect and save himself from the taint of being a poor poet's son. He was always tall for his age; a strong boy who punched his way through life from the beginning.

Philip's father, Thomas Alexander, was a thin, pale American whose paid profession, tutoring, and unpaid profession, writing poetry, led no one to admire him. The tutoring brought in a small amount of money to support Thomas, his English wife Mary Clermont, and Philip; the poetry brought a large amount of scorn from everyone, Philip's classmates included. Mary Clermont was the daughter of a don at the University, but Mary failed to add a plus to the Alexanders' situation. She had a waspish tongue and only a tiny store of patience for either the great clumping boy growing up in her crowded flat or his thin and sickly father.

Having so far failed to publish any poetry, Thomas could boast only a slightly better record at saving students from failure in the humanities. Failure pervaded the Alexander household. It shook from the folds of the worn blankets they slept under and accompanied the greasy boiled beef to table on a cracked platter. Its reminders were all about. Rejection slips arrived for

Thomas in the mail even as anxious-faced young men rushed up the stairs in the dark afternoons clutching assignment books; returned manuscripts piled up on Thomas's desk beside his pupils' essays marked in angry red ink, "Parse these sentences!"

Mary had wanted a second baby, but as Philip grew up she was fond of pointing out that God knew best, and she thanked Him fervently for her failure to conceive again. At thirteen years of age, Philip was an only child.

One brisk fall day, Philip came home to tea to find the kettle cold and his mother and father arguing with their voices raised. When he asked what was up, his mother replied with a furious smile, "If your father has his way, we're going to live in America."

Philip was amazed. Mary shouted that she hated the idea of leaving England for a world full of wild Indians, and stormed out. Later, Philip heard her tell a neighbor that she despised the very thought of South Carolina, because it was the state that had produced her husband, he who as a graduate student at Cambridge had possessed shining blond hair and a soft drawling voice and cloudy gray-blue eyes which looked soulfully into hers while he told her lies. Rotten as her life was, she said, here at least she had her friends to share her sorrows, and she could go to visit her family for a taste of civilization. She had only consented to marry Thomas when he swore to live in England for the rest of his life!

Thomas simply presented Mary with the facts; he had inherited the family grocery store due to the unexpected death of his older brother. The grocery store—in a tiny place called Crosstree, near Eyreville, South Carolina—the rooms above it, and his aging mother were now Thomas's to look after. Thomas wanted to go home. He could write poetry in the evenings, Philip would have the country to run in, and Mary—

"And I can pack groceries! I see it exactly," Mary cried.

Mary finally consulted with her family. The Clermonts at first were shocked. Her father was doubtful that a move would better matters. A poet here was a poet there. Her mother thought that she should try it. Charleston, Mary's brother, sided with her mother, and Mary valued his opinion the most. Charleston was doing very well for himself in London as a partner in a firm in the financial district; he had broken from the family's academic, university-centered life successfully, and he thought Mary should do the same—break away and try something new.

With very bad grace, Mary Clermont packed to go.

Philip had a dim sense of one thing. In England his father was the one with the funny accent, the one a bit awkward with local customs, the outsider. Over in America, his father would be the native and he, Philip, would be the odd one. He reserved his opinion about the change.

Eyreville turned out to be a small town full of green lawns and large houses, none of them attached to each other. Philip got only a glimpse of it before the local taxi took them to Crosstree, which turned out to be a crossroads out in the country; only the white Alexander store gave it the right to a name. There was nothing else there.

They were met by Philip's grandmother, a kindly, smiling lady who smelled very old. She took Philip upstairs, through the rooms above the store that were to be his new home, and into a large kitchen where she pointed out a wooden cookie jar that she said she always kept filled.

Philip took some chocolate cookies. He thought his grandmother talked awfully slowly. Her words seemed to melt and run together. He had to listen carefully to understand what she was saying.

The next day, in a place called the Junior High, Philip was assigned to a class and he looked over the boys in the room. Some of them were as big as he. They stared at him. The teacher spoke to him, and he had to answer back. At the sound of his elegant English, he saw the boys kicking each other under the desks. The girls giggled.

During recess that morning he knocked down two boys. He was taken, struggling, to see the principal. When he returned to the room he could hear a general whisper of approval.

The day did not end so well. He got home to find that he had become a delivery boy. In the afternoons his father expected him to go along in the panel truck and help take orders out to the houses scattered up and down the shoreline. Philip didn't mind loading and unloading bags of groceries, but as the afternoon progressed, something about the deliveries began to bother him. His father drove the truck up long, winding driveways and around to the backs of the big houses and they went in at back doors and into kitchens. Usually, there were only servants in the kitchens.

"This was what I did when I was a boy, help my father deliver groceries," Thomas said to his son as they stopped at the tenth house. Thomas looked happy. He was glad to be home again. Mary had many scathing things to say about her new home and its lacks, but even she had to admit that the climate was far better and the country life bound to be healthy.

If his father didn't mind going into the back doors of houses, why should he? Philip wondered. He shrugged to himself. What difference did it make?

Everyone on Curzon's Neck knew that Thomas had taken over the Crosstree grocery store. His absent-minded scholar's reputation had preceded him; and Vivienne's mother, China Dane, sighed when her cook, Ella Browning, came in to report that the grocery order from Crosstree had been all mixed up. Ella added that the sugar to make Mister Bascomb's birthday cake for that night was among the missing items.

"Well, I guess that's what happens when a poet runs the grocery store," China said in her gentle manner. "I'll call him up."

China got Thomas Alexander himself on the telephone and explained the problem. He would be right over, he said.

Thomas hung up the phone, grabbed a bag of sugar, and left Mary in charge of the store. He had personally delivered the groceries to Land's End that morning and he wondered what the deuce had gotten confused. On his way to his truck he saw Philip coming home from school and told him to come along.

"You haven't seen Land's End yet, have you?" he asked Philip. "It's a beautiful place. The largest around here, about a half-mile away. Belongs to the Danes. Mother says they buy all their groceries from us."

Thomas drove quickly down the dirt road. Past a stand of woods, a very large brick house, perfectly square, with six dazzling white columns rising to its roof, suddenly came into view. The house stood in the middle of rolling lawns, with flat fields stretching away on all sides. It was very grand in its country setting, and its beautiful proportions made it seem a natural part of the landscape.

Thomas wheeled sharply into the driveway, and the truck rattled up past the side of the house and around to the back.

Philip got out of the truck and stared up in surprise. The back of Land's End was exactly like the front. It was a perfect duplicate, six white columns spaced across the long first and second-story porches, each porch with two enormous windows on either side of large centered square doors. The only difference in the back was that a raised walkway ran from the right end of the back porch to a big two-story white house behind.

"That was the cookhouse in the old days," Thomas said. "The servants would cook out there and bring the food into the dining room through an outside door around on the side."

"Why is the back exactly like the front?"

"Oh, it's a type of architecture they fancy around

45

here, or did when it was built. Georgian. The house is two hundred years old, I think."

As he spoke, they climbed the nine blue-gray stone steps up to the wide porch. It was the first house Philip hadn't minded walking into the rear of, and he wondered what sort of people lived in such a house.

The day was warm and the back door stood open. Thomas knocked and entered, Philip behind him. They could see straight down the wide center hall and out the open front door that led to the front porch.

Thomas turned through double doors on the left and led Philip into a big square room with high ceilings that turned out to be the kitchen, although it seemed too imposing to be a kitchen. There was a huge fireplace in the far wall, with a black cast-iron stove on either side of it. Twin refrigerators stood in the corners, and the wall opposite the windows to the porch held a long counter and a triple sink.

"Mrs. Browning, I'm sorry about the mix-up," Thomas said to the large black woman who turned to face them. He put the bag of sugar down on a counter. The black woman smiled.

"Well, I don't know. I wouldn't complain, but we have to make the cake this afternoon. And Miss China didn't order any Miracle Whip salad dressing, not for sure. The girls hate it. We did get cottage cheese, but—"

She went on in her liquid tones detailing the things wrong with the order. Philip looked around. Near one of the long windows overlooking the porch, at a round table, sat a girl about his own age. The late afternoon sunshine fell on her heavy long dark hair, making coppery glints in it.

The girl looked back at him with the largest and darkest eyes he had ever seen. Their darkness was startling against the whiteness of her skin. She didn't smile, but regarded him steadily. She was wearing a nondescript brown skirt and a man's white shirt with the tails out. Her slender legs were wound around the

46

legs of the chair she sat on, as if she needed to be anchored there or she would float away.

Since she didn't smile, he didn't either. She saw him, though. She didn't just look through him the way several other people in kitchens had before, saying, "Put the groceries over there," as if to the air.

His father collected the things the cook declared hadn't been in her order, promising to straighten everything out and wondering whose groceries Land's End got and who had gotten theirs. Philip wasn't listening. The rejected items were placed in a paper bag and handed to Philip. He realized he was still staring at the girl, but he couldn't take his eyes away. She hadn't moved. She kept looking at him, too. He felt prickly all over.

"Now, we can tackle this cake, Miss Vivienne," the cook said, picking up the sugar.

Repeating apologies, his father started out. "Come on, son," Thomas said, touching Philip on the shoulder.

All the way down the porch steps, Philip resisted the impulse to look back up at the big kitchen windows. At the bottom of the stairs, he couldn't resist any longer. Something forced him to turn his head. He drew in his breath sharply. The girl was standing at one of the windows, looking out at him. He could see the gleam of her white skin and her white shirt through the square panes.

Quickly, Philip jumped into the truck.

"Who did you say lives there?" he asked his father.

"The Danes," his father answered. "They have two daughters, I believe."

Philip had been in school only two days, but he was sure he would have spotted that girl if she were there.

"Does the Dane girl go to school?" he asked, trying to sound uninterested, as if he were just asking for the sake of saying something.

His father didn't answer. He had decided to tour all the houses on that morning's route and find the rightful owner of the Miracle Whip.

Philip asked again.

"Huh? Oh, the Dane girls. They probabaly go to the private academy in town. Now, how do you suppose those two bags managed to get labeled wrong?"

Their quest ended at the third house. They retrieved the items that were intended for Land's End: a dozen oranges, a box of Tide, and two boxes of Kleenex.

Philip hoped they would return; he wanted to see the dark-haired girl bent over a bowl of cake batter. He wanted to see her move. She had sat so still. If they went back and found her beating a cake, red-faced and flour-covered, she would seem less special.

The cook had told Thomas simply to send the other items with their next order, however, so his father drove straight back to the store to accuse Mary of marking the bags wrong. It turned out that he had done it himself.

In fact, if Philip had returned to Land's End he would not have seen Vivienne beating the cake. Her part in the process was to put on the fancy decorations after the cake was baked and Ella had loaded the pastry tubes with colored icing. Her sister Mab came in from dance class before the process was finished, and together they executed a vine with green icing leaves on top, and added icing violets, their father's favorite flower, and yellow bows on the sides. Mab was three years younger than Vivienne, but she had a steadier hand, and she added the yellow bow knots.

"There's a new boy at Crosstree," Vivienne told her, licking violet icing off her fingers as Mab put a graceful "Happy Birthday Daddy" in yellow icing on top.

"How old?"

"Fourteen, maybe. Big."

Vivienne did not add to that description, although she had looked at the boy so fixedly that she had memorized his features. He had a handsome face. And there was something interesting in the way he stood and looked at her. He didn't shift and look away like so many boys would have.

She wondered if she would see him again. Crosstree wasn't far.

On Saturday Philip found he was to deliver groceries all day. He and his father took five bags into the big kitchen at Land's End early in the afternoon. The cook was there and spoke pleasantly to them, but there was no sign of the girl.

On Sunday Philip's grandmother produced a large noon meal: fried chicken and biscuits, as she called them—they were rolls to Philip—and something terribly slimy called okra. His father fell on this dish with joy. He hadn't had any okra for fifteen years. The green pods made Philip shudder to look at them. With awe, he and his mother watched Thomas finish the whole dishful.

After a dessert of canned peaches, Philip was free. The grown-ups went into the front room and talked of taking naps. Philip stuffed his pockets with cookies and said he was going out.

"Don't get lost," his mother called after him as he hurried down the stairs and out the door.

The afternoon was clear and very warm, with a sky that looked especially blue at the horizon. The road was dusty, and dust hung in the air, covering the pale-colored leaves of the trees and coating the slightly-browning grass.

Philip walked in the direction of the river. He wanted to explore its banks until he found the bottom of Curzon's Neck where the river emptied into the sea.

He passed a few houses, came to the bridge and climbed down under it to the river bank. The river twisted along, bordered with rocks and fallen trees, which made the going hard in some places. Clambering over branches and boulders for fifteen minutes or so, he came to a place to where the river took a bend to the left. There the water ran more slowly; the river widened out. Philip came to a large flat-topped boulder at the river's edge and saw with excitement that it formed a natural landing-place. He could go swimming. He was hot from the exertions of climbing, and he bent over and stuck his hand into the river. The water was chilly but not unbearable. He looked around. At that point, the river was completely secluded by pine woods on either bank and it was silent on both sides. There couldn't be anyone around. Birds weren't even singing.

He shucked off his clothes and dived in from the rock, gasping as he surfaced. The sudden, shocking cold made him numb. He struck out swimming fast to warm up, doing a crawl and kicking hard. The water seemed to tug him along a little when he reached the middle of the stream. He swam on, beyond the bend, where the river made another curve. For a moment he stopped to tread water and test the current. It was stronger—the river narrowed here.

His blood suddenly felt as if it were at zero degrees. He turned to swim back. After a minute he realized that he was getting nowhere in spite of his vigorous crawl. The river was actually carrying him away. Alarmed, he started swimming sideways, toward the shore. He made some progress, at first, but then he was caught by the current again.

"Catch the rope," a voice said.

He looked up. Directly ahead, a tree slanted out over the water, and dangling down from it was a rope swing. Even as he spotted the rope, the river smoothed out again and the water against him went slack. He took a couple of strokes and easily caught hold of the dangling rope's end.

Catching his breath, he shook the water out of his eyes and looked at the rocky bank. It was empty. Had he dreamed he heard a voice? He hung onto the rope and looked up into the tree above him.

A pair of dark eyes looked down at him. A shock went through Philip. It was the girl from Land's End. She was stretched out full-length on the overhanging branch, and her long dark hair hung down, mingling with the twigs and pale yellow leaves.

He was still gasping. The current had frightened him. As he hung on and shivered, staring up, he noticed again the girl's extraordinary stillness, her trick of holding herself motionless as she looked at him.

She must have been the one who called to him.

"Thanks," he said finally.

She regarded him with a grave expression on her face.

"You shouldn't swim out there," she said, her eyes indicating the river beyond. "In here, it's safe. It's sheltered and deep—we swing off the rope from that rock." She moved her head to indicate a large boulder at the edge of the water ten feet away. Philip didn't take in what she was saying. The sound of her voice was all he heard. It was deep and throaty; it made what she said sound important.

"Aren't you cold?" she asked.

"Yes."

She could see gooseflesh on his arms and shoulders. As he spoke, a tremor ran over him.

"You can climb out on the rock," she said.

He made no move to do so, but hung dangling and shaking with cold instead. His teeth began to chatter.

Vivienne looked over at the rock and back down at him. She made her face stay perfectly straight, although she felt like laughing aloud. She could see that he didn't have any clothes on. She examined the muscles bunched in his white arms. He had wide shoulders and a full chest that sloped down to a very slender waist. Below that there was just a glimmer of white beneath the dark water.

He looked at her rather wildly and then back toward the bend he had come around.

"I wouldn't try to go back," she said. She had to struggle to keep her expression solemn. "And you can't go on. The current gets really strong. You'd be swept out to sea."

51

If his blood hadn't been frozen, he would have blushed furiously. He was too embarrassed to see the expression on her face.

"I—uh—" He stopped as a tremor shook him. The water was shaded, but the rock was in the full sunshine and looked hot and inviting.

"Get out," she repeated.

He considered asking her to shut her eyes or something, but it was more than he was capable of. With a desperate plunge he let go of the rope and took three strokes to the rock. He climbed out as fast as his numbed limbs would move, grateful to feel the hot rock under his feet, and without looking back he rushed up the bank and into the pines. Once, his wet foot slid on some mud and he almost fell, but in a second he recovered and plunged on.

His clothes lay on the rock where he had left them, and he pulled on his pants with shaking fingers.

In the tree, Vivienne laughed to herself. She had enjoyed the sight of the boy's bare white buttocks—how small and narrow they were—and she had glimpsed something even more interesting swinging between his muscular legs as he raced off.

Philip thought to himself that she couldn't have seen anything, really. He shook the water out of his hair. He had run so hard he had warmed himself. He wiped his arms off with his shirt and pulled it on. By the time he tied his shoes he felt remarkably good. His whole body glowed. He stood in the sunshine and considered. Should he go back to the tree?

She was only a girl, of course; but somehow she didn't seem like only a girl. She seemed like a spirit or something. Like something powerful. He wanted to hear her speak again.

If he went on in his exploration, she would be right in his path.

He picked his way along the bank toward the slanting tree, wondering if any boys lived around here. So far he hadn't seen a one.

The river bent, and he saw the tree with the long rope swing. Its pale golden leaves trembled slightly, reflected in the dark water below. For a moment he couldn't make the girl out. Then he saw that she was stretched stomach-down on the branch, staring into the river.

He hesitated. The tree had two main branches, which parted close to the ground; one limb stretched out over the water and one slanted towards the woods. There was room for him in the crotch. He swung himself up. The girl turned and sat up, drawing her knees in. She was wearing blue jeans and a man's white shirt. A pair of loafers lay at the bottom of the tree. She swung her leg over, straddled the branch and let her bare feet dangle down, wiggling her toes.

He straddled the far branch.

"I guess this tree saved me," he said.

"Did your whole life flash before your eyes?"

The girl did not act silly or giggle or mention that she had seen him nude. He didn't think she would. She looked at him intently, apparently only interested in the question she had asked. As before, the tone of her voice was so surprisingly melodious that it took him a minute to translate her words. Life flash before his eyes?

"Oh—no," he said. "I wasn't *drowning*. I just couldn't get over to the shore."

"Remember," she said, "in here it's safe. But don't go out yonder."

He fingered a cluster of small red berries growing on a twig of the tree. He squeezed them. They were fleshy inside.

"This is a witch tree," she said softly.

He stared at her. She looked back somberly. Her eyes were deep black mysterious pools.

"What?"

"It's a rowan tree. Here they call it a mountain ash. But in Europe they call it a quick beam—the first tree of the world, the tree of life."

"Really?" He looked at her intently. When she talked, it made him feel funny, somehow.

She nodded. "It's rowan wood that you use to make stakes to drive through vampires' hearts."

Now that was interesting. He looked down at the brown-gray bark under his hand.

"But there are no vampires here," she said.

He picked some berries and skipped them one at a time into the water.

"You're English, aren't you?" she asked. "I like to hear you talk. What's your name?"

"Philip. Is yours Vivian or something?"

"Vivienne," she said, stressing the last syllable slightly.

He realized suddenly that clouds had appeared and covered the sun. The air felt heavy and close.

"Maybe it's going to storm," he said, looking around. "So?"

Was she going to stay in the tree? Everything Philip had ever been told about lightning and water and trees indicated that their perch was perilous. However, he wouldn't move if she didn't.

Rapidly, the clouds built up. They were darkest where they covered the sun. The air seemed to turn yellowish. A bird flew over, calling raucously.

"I go to the barn," she said at last; "I always go to the barn in a storm. Want me to show you?" She glanced up at the sky. "If we hurry we can make it."

He jumped down immediately and she followed him. She slipped into her loafers and began to run. A path led them through the woods and to the edge of a wide, flat field. Land's End rose beyond, its white pillars gleaming starkly. To one side, in the back, was a long rose-colored barn. White shirttails flying, Vivienne ran straight through the field toward it and he sprinted after her. Thunder rumbled in the south and a few raindrops hit them. Just as they reached the barn door a jagged streak of lightning tore the sky overhead in half. The livid glare etched Vivienne's upstretched arm with light.

She pulled up the door, and in a second they were safely inside, dropping onto hay bales to gasp for breath. A tremendous clap of thunder shook the barn. Rain began falling.

"I didn't count—did you?—but that was a close one," Vivienne said. She climbed up over the bales, which were piled high on one side of the barn. At the top a loose board gave a view of the outside.

Philip crawled up after her. The barn smelled good—a scent of dry grass and dirt, and a faint cedary odor that came out of the beams. With the door closed, it was dim inside. He knelt beside Vivienne to look out at the wet fields and the woods.

She smelled good too; a smell he couldn't place exactly. Actually it came from the vinegar rinse she always gave her hair when she washed it, and the generous amount of her mother's Chanel Number Five perfume that she borrowed whenever she went into her mother's room.

He could feel her breath on his cheek. The landscape outside was turning a purple shade, and the willows behind the house lashed violently. The clouds overhead darkened to black, and curtains of rain swept across the field below.

"The rain won't last long. We get storms like this when it's too hot for the time of year," she said.

Turning away from the scene outside, Vivienne lay on her back in the hay. Rain drummed heavily on the roof above them.

Philip settled himself beside her. He had never been so close to a girl—at least, not to one who made him so aware of his nearness. He was embarrassed to look over at her, but as if he saw with a third eye he was conscious of the curve of her breasts under her damp shirt and her small waist and smooth stomach under her worn blue pants. She lay very still, hardly breathing. His body felt flushed all over; he felt a stirring between his legs, and suddenly instead of being flushed he was burning hot.

"Do any boys live around here?" His voice cracked a little as he spoke.

She turned her head, looked at him, and smiled. Her curvy pink mouth parted and he saw the white teeth inside. She had a dimple in one cheek. As he stared, she closed her eyes, and he saw how long and curly her dark lashes were. She didn't answer his question, but sank deeper in the hay.

Thunder sounded again, and Philip found the strangest image fleetingly in his mind—a window pane with two drops of water running down it, their erratic paths suddenly joining into one stream that raced quickly down and disappeared. Could it be that his life was mixing with this girl's in that way, merging to go on as one? He felt confused, and he whispered her name. "Vivienne?"

She made a sound in her throat, not a real answer. As the rain drummed loudly, he pushed his right arm under her slender body. She turned her head toward him and opened her eyes. From only an inch away, her eyes were huge. He put his other arm across her body and pulled her against him, and their lips met. They kissed for a long time. Vivienne had read about such kisses in books. Several times, boys had grabbed her at odd moments around the academy or in darkened rooms at birthday parties. So it wasn't her first kiss, as it was Philip's, but it was the first kiss that counted.

When they parted both of them were breathing hard, and she could hear Philip's heart pounding. He pulled her back to him, pressing his body against the length of hers.

"It's stopped raining," she said.

He didn't want to move. He was living in a strange new country—he should expect strange new experiences. But the strangest new country was his own body. He was bewildered by all the parts of it which felt new sensations. His arms wanted to hold her and hold her, to feel the soft flesh so different from his own. His legs wanted to tangle up with hers, to press against her thighs. His forehead and his cheeks were burning, and his lips wanted to touch hers again. He wished they were naked together. He wanted to probe into her with the part of him which was most urgently different of all.

She put her hand up to his face, touched his nose and smiled again. "I like your nose," she said in a whisper.

At the same time, she drew back a little. She wanted to think about the way she felt. It was all right. The boy was a part of the mystery of the day. He had swum to her down the river and now he was hers, the same way her own body was hers. She didn't so much want him as *have* him. She was glad that he was so handsome and strong, since he was hers.

Vivienne lived her life believing that everything that happened was fated. She did not worry about changing things. All her energy had always gone into presenting herself to the world, giving herself fully to her experiences. The barn and the hay bales around her were just the background for what was happening, and for all Vivienne knew or cared, they vanished as soon as she went into the house, and the house was new-built for her every entrance. She, Vivienne, contained the universe within her. Not a tree in that universe lost a leaf but it was fated, and nothing that happened to her was without a reason. She never questioned nature; the Celts who thought they conceived from trees had much the same relationship with the forest as Vivienne with fate.

Her heart raced now, as she looked at Philip.

"I like your mouth, too," she said.

The sound of the rain on the roof had stopped. The barn door was raised and a voice called, "Vivienne?"

Vivienne sat up and let her body coast down the bales to the floor. Philip drew in his breath, checked to see that his clothes were arranged correctly and

57

the swelling unnoticeable, and slid down behind Vivienne.

A small girl stood by the barn door.

She looked at Philip curiously, and he returned her
scrutiny. In the dimness of the barn she semed more
an elf than a girl. She had nut-brown hair and skin
and eyes. Since she wore a brown dress, too, she
reminded Philip of a book illustration all in one color,
a sepia-tone page. He peered closer at her. She wasn't
really so brown; her skin was a honey shade.

"I saw you come in here before it rained," she
said, looking from one to the other.

"This is Philip, Mab. This is my little sister Mab.
She's eleven." Vivienne made the introductions.

"The new boy from Crosstree?" Mab said.

Philip chinned himself on an overhead beam that
formed the door of a stall. "That's right," he said.

"You promised to make paper doll clothes with me,"
Mab said to Vivienne.

"Want to come in?" Vivienne asked Philip.

Philip dropped to the floor. "I should go along
home for tea."

"Come on," Vivienne said.

He followed them out of the barn and up the stairs
to the back porch. "You talk funny," Mab said to him.
"You *really* talk funny."

They wiped their feet on a woven mat at the back
door, and Philip followed the girls inside.

"Come meet Mother," Vivienne said. Philip wanted
to hang back, but she led him into the front of the
long gray-green hall and to the right, where open
double doors led into a large drawing room. The room
was full of velvet and satin sofas and chairs, in shades
of rose and blue and silver. The walls and the woodwork were white, and white strips of marble were set
into the design of the imposing fireplace at the end.

As he walked in behind Vivienne, Philip felt his
feet sink into a thick carpet woven in an intricate
pattern of cream and blue. He had a confused impres-

sion of tables scattered around, full of silver and glass objects and flowers. Several large gilt-edged oil paintings, landscapes, hung on the walls. The ceiling seemed very high, and the windows—which rose to almost the height of the ceiling—appeared enormous. Their square panes were still wet from the rain. Outside, the sun came from under a cloud just as Vivienne led him up to a woman sitting at a small desk beside a window.

"Mother, this is Philip Alexander."

The woman smiled at Philip, and her sparkling dark eyes reminded him of Vivienne's. She sat very erect at the desk. She had been writing, but now she put down her pen. Her "How do you do?" was uttered in the softest voice Philip had ever heard.

He stiffened and made a bow, as he had been taught to do. He was too embarrassed to look closely, so he got only a glimpse of her dark hair, pulled back in a chignon, and the pearls at the neck of her light-blue silk dress. His eye fell on her hand, lying in her blue lap, and he thought it was the softest, whitest hand he had ever seen.

China Dane gave a look of gentle inquiry to her daughter Vivienne. Why, she wondered, was Vivienne bringing the boy in here?

"Philip is from England," Mab said. She had tagged in behind them.

"Oh, yes, that's right. I hope you will like it here." China's eyes traveled from the boy to the girls' faces. "Wasn't that a hard thundershower? I was worried about you, Vivienne, until Mab told me she saw you run into the barn."

"The barn's a safe place," Vivienne said.

"You must be careful in there. There's sharp equipment lying around."

Philip was struck with Mrs. Dane's gentle manner of speaking. He wondered what it would be like to have her as a mother. She was certainly nothing like his own, whose raised voice issued angry orders all the time.

Vivienne's mother glanced out of the window. "I think the weather will grow cooler now."

Beyond the white pillars of the porch, where she was looking, the green lawn, its grass sparkling now with raindrops in the sun, stretched down a long way, out to the road.

"Oh, a rainbow!"

Mab and her mother exclaimed the words at the same instant. Philip and Vivienne, who had been looking at each other instead of out the window, saw it a moment later.

"Let's go outside."

Mrs. Dane led them out onto the front porch to get a better look. The immense rainbow stretched across half the sky, glowing brightly against the clear blue now in the east again. Mab ran to tell her father about it.

Philip drew a deep breath. The air was pure and fresh, and in it was a faint whiff of salt from the sea, mixed with the smells of wet ground and grass and, because Vivienne was standing next to him, Chanel Number Five perfume. The air seemed charged, vibrating. The nerves in Philip's body felt the same way; they had throbbed ever since the embrace in the barn. He was acutely aware of Vivienne standing beside him. What if he got hard right there! In a sudden panic, he murmured something about having to leave. Vivienne's dark eyes swung to his face, and a small smile turned her lips up. He thought she guessed why he had to go. She had been standing very close to him while her mother's back was toward them. Unobtrusively, she moved away as China turned from looking at the sky.

"It's fading fast," she said.

China preceded them back through the big front door. Philip went inside with them, since he felt that it would somehow be too bold to take his leave by walking down the front steps and the front path. Vivienne accompanied him, leading him under the great staircase that swept up and across the hallway. Sunshine was streaming through the fanlight and the panes of glass around the back door. Vivienne's mother followed them, turning into another pair of doors, opposite the kitchen. Philip suspected that from there she might be able to see them, so he ducked his head, keeping a respectful distance from Vivienne.

"Thanks," he said in a low voice.

Vivienne said nothing, but smiled, and her dark eyes looked closely at his face. He felt the blood rush up into his cheeks, and his palms grew clammy.

"Well, cheerio," he said.

"Cheerio," she replied softly.

Quickly he turned and plunged out across the wet porch and down the stone steps. He cut through the woods on the south side of the house, hoping this was in the direction of Crosstree, and after a minute he began to run. He reached a road that looked familiar and ran the rest of the way home, where his mother scolded him for being late to tea.

The Alexanders, it turned out, had spent the afternoon to great effect. During their postprandial nap, with Philip out of the way and Thomas's mother sound asleep, they had conceived a baby, although the knowledge of this was months away for Mary, who, when she finally did accept the truth of it, declared herself dumbstruck. But she could recall that there certainly had been something in the air that day—the crazy thunderstorm that had come out of nowhere and waked them up, the magnificent rainbow that had followed it. *Something* had made her usually passionless husband urgent and his seed fertile—something in the air . . . or could it have been those strange green pods called okra that he ate for lunch?

Philip lived in suspense the next week. Land's End was on Thomas's morning route, and by the time Philip was home from school they had to deliver in the other direction. Philip counted the days until Saturday. Friday night he looked at the order slips. There was one for the Danes.

Philip woke up early on Saturday and went downstairs to pack the Dane order himself, wondering which orange of the twelve Vivienne would eat. And what were hot tamales? They had ordered six cans of them. "Wrapped in real corn husks," he read on the label. This did not enlighten him. He packed the box of "Kotex, Regular" thoughtfully.

"Be careful now. The eggs go on top," Mary said.

Land's End was the second house on their route. It was only nine-thirty, and on their first trip in, the kitchen was empty. Some blue breakfast dishes stood on the table, one with an untouched piece of toast, heavily glazed with honey. Philip looked down the hall as they went out. No one was around. His heart sank. One bag was left to be carried in.

"I'll get it," he said quickly. His father climbed back into the truck.

When he went back in, Vivienne had materialized beside the fireplace in the kitchen. She was wearing a dark blue robe that covered her from chin to toe. The robe was disturbing to him, with its connotation of bed and sleep and——her hair was tousled. He put the bag down and stared at her. He cleared his throat.

"I have to work today," he said. "But tomorrow, will you be at the river? In the afternoon?"

His heart beat hard. She looked solemnly at him.

"In the ahhf-ternoon," she repeated, mimicking him. "If I can," she added.

She spoke softly, and he thought that perhaps she didn't want anyone to know about their meeting. He could see that it might be difficult for her. Another week of walking through back doors had further impressed his class-conscious British soul with the wide social difference between the people who serviced the great houses and the people who lived in them. He'd asked around at school and learned that the Dane family was very old, very respected, very distinguished.

Also very rich. Still, Vivienne seemed to belong to herself.

Philip was standing beside the counter where he had placed the last bag with the others, and Vivienne walked over to him deliberately, passing so close that her robe brushed his foot. She glanced into the bags and took out an orange. As he watched, she bit it to start it, peeled back a strip of skin with her thumb, and then glanced sideways at him. It had the desired effect. He hastily said good-bye and fled.

He thought about her all day, falling into such abstraction that Thomas thought he might be sulking.

"Have you had a fight with your mother?" Thomas asked. A tongue-lashing from Mary could get a person down, he knew.

"What, sir?"

"Have you been fighting with your mother?"

"Oh, no, sir."

"Everything all right at school?"

"Yes. I'm learning football—what they call football here."

"And"—Thomas hesitated—"do you like America, then?"

"Jolly good," Philip said with warmth.

Thomas was glad to hear it. As far as he was concerned, he was home for good. If Mary wanted to go back to cold England, she could go back alone. His sciatica was better, and his poetry flowed night and day. Just yesterday, he had jotted down, on a paper bag, a line that had come to him while he swept the floor of the grocery store. It might have been the best line he had ever written. Unfortunately, he'd never know—Mary had packed someone's order in the bag before he remembered to copy the line off; he had probably delivered the line himself to some kitchen. But anyway, the poetry was flowing.

The next day, after the usual Sunday meal of chicken and biscuits, Philip was down the stairs and off. The weather was cool and crisp, more like a fall day, although by English standards still very mild. Instead of clambering along the bank of the river, Philip cut straight through the woods bordering it. When he saw the rose-colored barn and Land's End on his left, he angled down toward the river and found the path that led to the ash tree.

Vivienne was already there, sitting out on her branch wearing a brown tweed riding jacket with leather patches over the elbows. He swung himself up and inched out until he was close to her and again conscious of her special scent. She didn't speak, and at first he didn't know what to do. She was sitting sideways on the branch, and her right hand lay on her blue-jeaned thigh. He looked at her slender fingers. Without stopping to think, he picked up her hand and raised it to his lips. He closed his eyes and kissed it over and over again. When she raised her other hand to his cheek, he caught it and kissed it, too, turning it over and putting his lips on its palm. He could hear her breathing and feel her breath tickle his ear, and suddenly he almost lost his balance and fell backwards. She laughed and caught his arm, and he opened his eyes and put both of his arms around her and squeezed her, jacket and all, close to him. She gave him her mouth to kiss, and this time her lips parted under his. As he tasted the sweet cave inside her mouth, it made him think of the other red cave inside of her and he had his usual problem. After several more kisses she drew back slightly.

"Let's get down," she whispered.

He jumped out of the tree and held his arms up to her and she half fell down into them. They were locked in another embrace for a time; then she showed him a spot where they could lie down by the river's edge, a place where the bushes were thick enough to hide them. They lay close together, inhaling the pungent odor of the pine needles on the ground. He slid his hands up her back under her jacket and felt the slender

64

curves of her shoulders. They didn't breathe so much as gasp between kisses. He kissed her eyes and her face and gathered her hair all up in his hands and kissed it, too; it was silky and smelled freshly washed and perfumed.

Vivienne ran her fingers through his thick brown hair in turn and let her hands feel the hard muscles in his shoulders and arms. When she touched his hair again, his body tensed all over and trembled, and she smiled and looked up at the blue sky overhead, a patch of which she could see through the pods hanging from the witch-alder bushes. Her eyes went back to scrutinizing the face so close to hers. She felt glad again that he was so handsome. Her sense of ownership of Philip was total. His eyes were closed and she kissed them.

"Don't," he breathed, but it was too late and something had happened. She felt his arms quiver and his cheek grow hot as flame. Vivienne could guess exactly what was going on, thanks to her best friend Deidre Parker. Deedee had found her parents' marriage manual hidden below a layer of stockings and garter belts in her mother's drawer. Vivienne and Deidre had read it together and found out many amazing things.

Vivienne hugged Philip closer to her as his body shook convulsively and he cried out her name and kissed her mouth wildly. What was happening to him seemed to last for a long while. He had to stop kissing her to gasp for breath. It was exciting. Philip must be having what was called an orgasm, although according to the Parkers' book this usually happened after the man "entered" the woman. There was a section on inducing orgasms with your hand, and something fantastic called "oral sex," but nothing that said that just kissing could lead to it.

Philip opened his eyes and looked at her, and she wished that he *had* been inside of her when it happened. She would have liked that, except that the book was specific about the danger of it. You had to obtain something called a diaphragm, first, and fit it inside you. If you relied on a sheath for the boy, the book said, you were playing Russian roulette, because the sheath could break. Vivienne wondered if Philip knew any of this. She felt his heart pound under her right breast, which was pressed hard against his chest.

Philip's face had a worried expression.

"It's all right," she said softly. "I know about it."

He swallowed. "You do?"

She nodded and touched his cheek where a muscle still throbbed.

"I have to go pretty soon," she breathed into his ear.

A strand of her dark hair had fallen over her cheek, and he pushed it carefully back with his fingers.

"I wish we could just lie here forever," he said. "Always." He caressed her hair, thinking that her eyes looked dark gold so close.

"And the birds could come and cover us with leaves," she whispered.

"I thought about you all week," he whispered back. "You're so beautiful, so much—better than anyone I ever knew. I'll wait here every Sunday, and when you can—"

He broke off to kiss her again, his hands touched her breasts, and she had lots of strange sensations this time. Sensations that almost seemed to be leading up to the same thing that had happened to him. Almost—almost —She drew a long breath and then it began, like a roller coaster ride, going up and up and finally plunging down over the lip. She cried out, pushing her tongue into his mouth, and Philip strained her to him, trying to help her. Her body arched up convulsively, over and over again, and finally relaxed totally in his arms.

"I think I blacked out," she said in wonder, opening her eyes a minute later. She felt glowing and sweaty all over. "Wow."

Suddenly she sat up, turned and knelt beside him.

"Philip, I really have to go," she said. She kissed his cheek.

He caught her hand. "Wait. Will I see you next week?"

"I don't know," she said.

Philip was afraid he had done something wrong, and he was stricken. He stared earnestly at Vivienne. In a moment she gave him the sweetest smile he had ever seen on anyone's face.

"If I can," she said, and she was up and off through the woods before he could get to his feet. He went back to the rope swing and the tree, and sat on the rock for a long time staring at the river.

III

China eventually found out that Vivienne sometimes played with the Alexander boy from Crosstree. She didn't approve, strictly speaking, but not because she worried about what they did together. She didn't dream of that. Vivienne never heard the slightest word from her mother on the subject of sex. Sexuality was not something China Dane could bear to discuss, either early or late in her girls' development. Certainly their father, Bascomb, would never bring up the subject. What happened between him and China at night in bed was never even discussed between them. When Mab and Vivienne joined their father in his library, they read Shakespeare and discussed art and nature—botany, not biology. And the time they spent with their mother was devoted to gentle pursuits, to making valentines or May baskets, or listening to stories she would tell them about her own childhood, or taking trips to see relatives or going on shopping expeditions for party dresses. Mother was never cross, never scolded them—or scolded anyone, for that matter. She saw the good side of every situation and every person, and there was no end to the good she saw in her own girls. She adored them and believed them capable of no wrongdoing.

China simply thought that Philip's station in life was not what she would prefer in a friend of her daughter's; on the other hand, this was in no way the boy's fault, and her nature was far too gentle and mild to allow her to point this out to her daughter. She let matters go along by themselves; the children would tire of running over the fields together in time, she was sure. China had heard about the Alexanders' new baby, a boy they named Beauchamp; too bad there were so many years between the two sons, she thought. The three years' difference between Vivienne and Mab was about right. The two girls were friends but not rivals, as children very close in age sometimes were.

China's satisfaction with her family did not change when she learned that she herself was pregnant. Bascomb was vastly surprised at the news, and China was delighted. She loved babies. Mab and Vivienne were scarcely children at all any longer. Now there would be someone around who believed in Santa Claus again. China hoped for a boy, for Bascomb's sake, but when the baby turned out to be a girl she was thrilled. Girls, with their hair ribbons and frills, their daintiness and quick intelligence, were all that she was used to. No two daughters could have turned out more beautiful than Mab and Vivienne, and here was a third to join them.

All China's friends and relatives came to see the baby, and declared her the prettiest thing they had ever set eyes on. Each morning China examined the baby's eyes to see if they had turned from their initial deep blue, as she expected they would. All her family, the Austins, were dark-eyed, and most Danes. But the baby hung onto her blue eyes. They seemed to grow bluer. "She's going to be a beauty," people predicted.

China tried not to neglect her other girls for the enchanting new one. Vivienne was at an interesting stage in life. Boys were noticing her and calling her on the telephone every night. There were dances at Trinity Academy and at the Eyreville Country Club "for the younger set," and Vivienne always had a date. Two boys in particular vied for her: Julian Royal, who was remotely related to her through China's mother, Elizabeth Royal Austin; and James Hastings, the richest boy in the school.

Philip hated both boys. He knew exactly who they were. Julian lived in a palatial mansion called Southwind, next door to Gardens, the Royal estate; and James's house, up a mile-long drive of crushed oyster shells, had been designed to be a small replica of Versailles. Philip sometimes caught sight of Julian in the Royal kitchen. At James's house they delivered the groceries to the butler's pantry and never laid eyes on James, but Philip knew what James looked like, because in order to watch the star halfback on the Eyreville High School's freshman team, Vivienne asked James to take her to a game. The freshmen played on Friday afternoons, and Philip that day could clearly make out every detail of the ugly red-haired boy sitting next to Vivienne in the stands. Philip played the game in a fury, scoring two touchdowns and setting a record for yardage gained. The coach was delighted, and predicted the varsity would be glad to get Philip next year.

"Did you kiss him?" Philip asked Vivienne. She laughed. She would never give Philip any details of her dates. He was tempted to twist her arm behind her back and force her to tell him the truth. It drove him wild; he trusted Vivienne, and yet she was so tempting —he couldn't see how either boy could refrain from trying to kiss her, and it made him hate them. He didn't tell Vivienne, but in an alley behind Trinity Academy he came upon James having an illegal smoke, and without a word he plowed in and beat him up. James was startled by the attack, but he retaliated vigorously and turned out to be no mean slugger. James got some bruises, but he left Philip pretty sore all over, too. They parted with a certain amount of mutual respect. James never told; in fact, he didn't know who Philip was, except some low creature who went to Eyreville High and hated rich kids.

Philip went onto the varsity squad the next year, and Vivienne was considered hands down to be the most beautiful girl who had ever attended Trinity Academy. Things between them were sometimes tense.

Vivienne tried to have mercy on Philip, but because it was so fascinating to see how jealous he became at the mention of another boy, she couldn't help teasing him sometimes.

Philip was the heartthrob of Eyreville High, but the spirited, short-skirted cheerleaders and the strutting baton-twirlers flung themselves at the handsome halfback in vain. Philip was completely true to Vivienne. He looked at other girls only to remark how superior Vivienne was. The hours he could spend with her, which were strictly secret now from the whole world, were the only hours in his life that really mattered to him. They had worked everything out. They knew how to give each other intense pleasure without risking pregnancy for Vivienne. Philip minded not going all the way; he longed for actual union with her. Sometimes his frustration grew until he could scarcely live with it, but he managed. And someday, he promised himself, she would be his completely.

"She possesses a *brilliant* talent," Laura Beltane said to China over the tea table at Land's End. "Brilliant!"

Miss Beltant had scarcely waited to be seated and handed a cup of tea before she made the dramatic announcement.

"You mean Vivienne?" China said, offering her the plate of petits fours.

"Of *course* I mean Vivienne!"

China smiled, pleased. Laura Beltane was someone to pay attention to on the subject of dramatic talent. Miss Beltane herself had acted on the stage, in summer stock companies, and had toured with the road show of *Oklahoma!* before she turned to teaching. The resume of her feats that Miss Beltane had sent to Trinity Academy had just managed to counteract the impression she made in person. A theatrical soul, Miss Beltane had played her first scene at Trinity with her reddish hair swept up in a wild beehive, bits sticking out all around so that it was more like a haystack. She was in full makeup including green eyeshadow, and she wore a dress of burnt-orange that fit a bit too snugly over her girdle—weight control had always been a problem—with many gold bangles jingling on her wrists, and long blood-red fingernails.

Mr. Grayson, Trinity's headmaster, glimpsed her getting out of a taxi and had to sit down. Miss Beltane swept into his office, with perfect diction declared herself ravished to meet him, and immediately mentioned her cousin Wallace Hastings, a wealthy alumnus and major contributor to the school. She then declared that she had come to *do* something with the dramatics at Trinity. Wallace had told her that this year's senior play had been *Arsenic and Old Lace,* read from *scripts!*

"Why not do Shaw and Shakespeare?" Miss Beltane waved her red-tipped hands gracefully and her bracelets jingled.

Faintly, Mr. Grayson asked what her plans were for her class in senior English.

"We shall write novels, plays and poetry. I shall make English *interesting.*"

She fixed burning green eyes on Mr. Grayson. Having learned from her cousin Wallace that the teacher whose place she was taking had been as dull as a five-hour sermon and that many a student had left Trinity despising his native tongue, she emphasized the "interesting."

On the first day of the fall term Miss Beltane donned a lemon-yellow two-piece suit with a frilly cream blouse, put on gold high-heeled shoes, and achieved a "chemise" style of hairdo, which looked as if she had combed her head with an eggbeater. Vivienne walked into Dramatics class, took one look at her teacher and muttered, "Wow!" This was certainly the year to take Dramatics.

One look at Vivienne was all Miss Beltane needed as well. *Who* was this dark-eyed witch-child? *Here* was material. Miss Beltane was instantly aware of Vivienne's trick of holding so still, of looking at you so fixedly. It was the stuff of drama. Before Vivienne picked out a desk and sat down, Miss Beltane had cast her. Vivienne would be a star.

"Vivienne's beauty is a tremendous asset," she said now to China, waving a petits four. "That skin. Those *eyes*. But the greatest plus is her voice. I couldn't believe the quality of it when she spoke. With training, there is nothing Vivienne couldn't do."

China looked at Miss Beltane with wide eyes. Miss Beltane was certainly living up to her reputation. All winter Vivienne had told her mother about her exciting Dramatics classes. Dramatics was famous at Trinity now. Miss Beltane declared that *anyone* could sing, tone-deaf or not, and to walk past the auditorium during Dramatics class while she was proving it was to subject oneself to stranger sounds than ear had heard before. Vivienne's case proved particularly stubborn. Miss Beltane was reduced to pleading, "Now, dear, you sing notes *you* want to hear," and as Vivienne croaked away even Julian and James had to leave the auditorium before they died.

Miss Beltane declared she would *never* give up on Vivienne's singing voice, but it was her speaking voice that she praised to China. There was no necessity for Vivienne to sing when she could speak so thrillingly. She would make a great dramatic actress. "The greatest of the great," Miss Beltane now declared firmly. "She projects beautifully and has natural stage presence. There is but one thing we must work on. Do you know"—Miss Beltane bent forward and fixed her green eyes intently on China's face—"Ava Gardner, who's from North Carolina, had to make her first screen test completely silent? They just did dreamy close-ups of her face—because she couldn't be allowed to open her mouth until she got rid of her thick southern accent! The same thing would happen to Vivienne. Now, next summer I am taking some pupils to work with, and since Mr. Grayson has been so kind as to give me use of the stage at Trinity, I shall produce a play."

By the end of their tea party, China scarcely needed any more convincing. Vivienne begged to stay home from camp the next summer and join the Youth Drama Circle, as Miss Beltane called it, and the hundred-dollar fee China paid for the privilege helped provide a scholarship for Philip Alexander. Vivienne took Philip to meet Miss Beltane, and Miss Beltane was in raptures the instant he said, "How do you do."

"*Listen* to him, dear," she said to Vivienne. "*This* is how we should all speak. Say *M-I-R-R-O-R*, Philip."

Philip, who had consented to this meeting under extreme duress, obliged.

"You see? *Mirror*, not *mirrow*. Listen to him."

Miss Beltane immediately offered to let Philip study free with the group. He was surprised. His greatest liability, his ineradicable English accent, had become an asset. The Drama Circle was to meet in the afternoons. Philip spoke to his father. Since the unhappy advent of a new Winn-Dixie supermarket in Eyreville, the grocery delivery route had been steadily dropping. For the summer, Thomas agreed, if Philip worked in the mornings, he could be spared in the afternoons. Philip had no great interest in acting, but he had a great interest in being with Vivienne. He accepted the scholarship.

Philip's personal attributes and handsomeness and magnetism were not lost on Miss Beltane. She cherished a romantic idea about young boys being introduced to ardor by older women, as the civilized French did it. She made Philip go up on the stage and read from *Hamlet*, eyeing him speculatively.

Late in August the Youth Drama Circle presented *A Midsummer Night's Dream*, with Philip as Oberon and Vivienne as Titania. China, who had a great fondness for the theater, and Bascomb, who revered Shakespeare, were delighted and surprised. Miss Beltane actualy got excellent performances from the children, and the production was also quite creditable. Miss

Beltane's cousin Wallace was thanked in the program for his contribution to the sets-and-costume fund.

That fall Vivienne began her senior year at Trinity. She had Miss Beltane for senior English; it was really an extension of Dramatics, because novels and poems went by the boards, and they chiefly read plays and acted them out. Philip was lost to Miss Beltane during the school year, because he was a junior at the public school, but the next summer Philip came back on scholarship. The Youth Drama Circle was now "in," the chicest group for young people in Eyreville. James Hastings and Julian Royal joined the ranks—for the same reason he was there, Philips suspected: to see Vivienne.

Miss Beltane assembled everyone in auditorium seats on the opening day of the Youth Drama Circle's second season, and then climbed up on the stage. For the hot summer day she had put on a lime green chiffon dress and tied her hair up with a green ribbon. Only one stage light was on and, unfortunately, it backlit her, clearly outlining her ample figure through the taffeta slip under the chiffon. The dramatic effect of her opening words were somewhat spoiled by the younger boys' poking each other.

"We," Miss Beltane announced, "shall give *Romeo and Juliet.*"

A murmur ran through the group below. Miss Beltane announced that auditions would begin tomorrow. "She's got it cast already," Deidre whispered to Vivienne. "You'll be Juliet and Philip will be Romeo."

Miss Beltane went on to say that she was obtaining real foils for the fencing scenes, and her cousin Wallace would teach the boys to use them. Wallace was a master fencer. The swordplay, Miss Beltane announced, would be real.

Philip began to be interested.

"I want to make it a performance we will all be proud of," Miss Beltane concluded.

In Miss Beltane's own high school days, she had

played Juliet. She could clearly remember the romantic aura that surrounded that entire production; it evoked an erotic mood in the participants. Miss Beltane had happily given up her virginity to the boy who played her Romeo. Now she saw Philip in the part.

Auditions the next day went well. Wallace might have liked seeing his nephew James get the lead, Miss Beltane thought, but she trusted when he saw the play Wallace would agree that Philip simply *was* Romeo. Red-haired James became Tybalt, and his fatal duel with Romeo was to feature vigorous swordplay. The first day at the Drama Circle James got a feeling he knew the boy sitting next to Vivienne. Finally he remembered—the fight in the alley! When his uncle Wallace turned up with the fencing foils, both Philip and James were ready to lay on.

Philip was able to kill his other rival, Julian Royal, as well; Julian was cast as Paris. Philip began to like *Romeo and Juliet* better and better.

The thin, sullen Cunningham boy nicknamed Hellraiser was assigned the part of Mercutio. He was taking the summer course at his mother's insistence, to keep him out of trouble—his nickname was no idle one. A fat ninth-grader named David Churchill was picked to play the friar, plump Deidre got the role of the nurse, Ginny Royal became Juliet's mother, and Cordie Parker got the one line of Lady Montague.

Miss Beltane abridged the play and began rehearsals with the last act. If the actors were secure in that, she said, they wouldn't feel during the performance that they were going toward the dark. Vivienne learned to stab herself realistically with a letter-opener and Philip to choke on the bottle of Dr. Pepper the stage manager supplied him for poison (promising to substitute brandy on the night of the performance).

At Land's End the Danes were delighted with the choice of play. Vivienne as Juliet! Her mother agreed to let a dressmaker produce a red velveteen gown for Vivienne. Miss Beltane had decreed that the boys must wear long underwear, dyed black, but she relented and allowed their white tunic tops to cover their hips. It was too bad in Philip's case—she was sure he had perfect male equipment—but anyway his legs would show and she bet herself they'd turn out to be handsome.

The headmaster, Mr. Grayson, dropped into rehearsal one day and was impressed. The sound of swordplay rang from the courtyard, where the Montagues and Capulets perfected their clashes, and the gymnasium contained party guests performing a dance to the stately measures of Mozart. The stage was held by a chubby boy loudly declaring, "These violent delights have violent ends." In a deserted classroom, unseen by Mr. Grayson, Romeo and Juliet practiced kissing.

Philip loved rehearsing in private, but he was having trouble kissing Vivienne on stage. He felt constrained, making love to her in public, even though he meant every word he recited. Vivienne, on the other hand, had a purely professional attitude about it all. When she got into the spotlight, she *was* Juliet, and Miss Beltane could have given her runny-nosed little Scat Honeychurch for a lover and she would have loved him as well. Vivienne, as Miss Beltane was fond of saying, could *act*. Philip wasn't capable of such an attitude.

Working backward through the play, they reached the balcony scene. Miss Beltane had cut half of it, but what was left was so suffused with poetry and emotion that Philip almost couldn't perform it. Vivienne floated out the famous phrases as if she were inventing them on the spot. When she asked, "At what o'clock tomorrow shall I send to thee" and he answered, "By the hour of nine," she cried " 'Tis twenty years till then!" with such breathless longing that Philip wanted to leap up on her balcony and grab her.

"Now, Philip," Miss Beltane called from the front row, "I feel you aren't giving me enough in either the balcony scene or the one in Juliet's bedroom. You

78

are *in love* with Juliet, you know. Somehow you seem to be just saying the lines."

Miss Beltane was aware that Philip had a crush on Vivienne. He was always looking at her. But Miss Beltane imagined that Vivienne, daughter of the lady-like China Dane, did not let Philip get very far with her. Looking was probably all he got.

"Philip," Miss Beltane suggested, "why don't you come to my apartment this evening for some extra coaching?"

Philip thought a moment and then agreed. Vivienne had been complaining about his acting. She didn't want a wooden Romeo. Philip might be awkward just because he felt so much, but the performance was only a week away and, at the moment, the play was all that mattered to Vivienne.

The same spirit pervaded the rest of the cast. They realized they had a powerful play and wanted to do it well. Even Hellraiser had become so gung-ho that he frothed at the mouth in his death scene, thought it would be a good idea if James really nicked him, and his cry, "A plague on both your houses!" chilled the blood. The swordplay had become fierce, the timing brisk, the prompter no longer needed. The set was minimal but effective, and Miss Beltane had designed dramatic lighting to heighten the sense of fate overtaking the lovers.

Word was out all over Eyreville that *Romeo and Juliet* would be excellent. People heard that Vivienne Dane made an electrifying Juliet. The day the tickets went on sale, they sold out, and there were even reports of scalping going on. It was flattering to Vivienne. But alone she couldn't justify all the excitement. She had to have a Romeo.

After dinner that evening Philip walked the three miles from Crosstree to the outskirts of Eyreville. Miss Beltane lived in the upstairs apartment of an old Victorian house a block from Trinity Academy. Philip climbed the outside stairs and knocked on her screen door hoping she had something in mind to help him.

"Come in, Philip."

Miss Beltane opened the door and Philip looked at her in surprise. She was wearing a green kimono embroidered with golden dragons, and her red hair hung down loose around her shoulders. She gave him a wide-eyed green gaze, repeating, "Come in."

The room he entered was dimly lit and full of a strange smell. He blinked. In one murky corner a white china Buddha sat on a pedestal and the smell, he saw, came from a stick of incense burning before it. Huge, heavy pieces of Victorian furniture filled the living room. There was a long wooden bench with elaborate carving, and a horsehair sofa strewn with swatches of silk in various colors. The walls were full of theatrical posters, including several for *Oklahoma!*, and vases of grass and wildflowers stood on small tables here and there. A grand piano occupied one shadowy corner.

"Sit down." Miss Beltane sank onto the end of the only comfortable-looking sofa and patted the cushion beside her. A small, intricately inlaid table in front of the sofa held a Chinese teapot and tiny tea cups.

"Have some tea," she said, leaning over and pouring out two steaming thimblefuls.

Philip sat down beside her; she had positioned herself so that the only lighted lamp was on the end table behind her, and the light framed her hair becomingly and helped erase the age lines on her face. Philip thought with surprise that she was rather pretty. He took the hot tea and drank it down. It wasn't English tea.

Miss Beltane put down her own cup.

"Now, Philip," she said. "Your swordplay is excellent, and the scene with Mercutio is one of the best in the play. You're doing everything well except the love scenes. Perhaps—is it that you've never been in love yourself?"

Philip blushed. "I guess I'm embarrassed," he said.

"You do like Vivienne, Philip? As a friend, I mean?" Miss Beltane leaned closer.

"Yes, of course."

"But it's hard for you to imagine really making love to her, isn't it? I mean, if you know nothing of love." Miss Beltane's red lips were suddenly within two inches of Philip's face. Philip was too startled to move back; surprise held him immobile. A sweet bath-powdery smell emanated from Miss Beltane.

"I thought maybe," she went on in a whisper, "this would help." Her lips brushed Philip's cheek.

Philip was already warm from his three-mile walk and the tea; now he broke out in sweat. Miss Beltane's lips traveled to his own and she actually kissed him. Philip had no idea what to do. He respected Miss Beltane; she was an excellent director and a person with a lot of brains—if somewhat addled—but in his wildest imaginings he hadn't thought of this. She withdrew her lips, untied the sash of her kimono, and let it fall open. She had a fleshy, freckled, but not unpleasant body.

"Don't be afraid," she said. "Touch me."

"Miss Beltane!" Philip said. His words came out in a croak. "I really will try to be a better Romeo, but—"

As he spoke she pressed her body against him, pushed up his tee shirt and kissed him hard on his right nipple. That did it. Philip could move at last. He slid back across the sofa, but Miss Beltane pursued him and actually put her long-nailed hand between his legs. He felt suddenly aroused—this couldn't be happening! Philip stood up, but Miss Beltane rose with him and dropped her green kimono. In a moment her arms went around his neck in a stranglehold, and Philip gasped, trying to loosen them and retreat. A small table crashed over as he staggered backward. What could he do? He didn't want to hurt Miss Beltane, but she had him in a death-grip. They bumped into the piano, and he sat down onto the keyboard, making a crashing, dissonant chord. Philip wanted to laugh. He was blocked; his

81

back was against the piano and she was literally climbing up him. Her hands found and loosened his belt buckle and she pushed down his trousers. Struggling, Philip crashed down again onto the keyboard as she flung herself against him. The concert was over in one minute. Miss Beltane slid down him and onto the floor and stared up at him through strands of her red hair, panting hard.

She was never without a line, and when she caught her breath she delivered it.

"*That* is what passion is," she said impressively.

Philip wanted to howl with laughter. With trembling hands he fastened himself up. He took a deep breath, but the sandalwood incense almost choked him.

"Yes, well, thank you," he said, wondering if he could edge past her without a second attack.

Miss Beltane stood up and flung her head back in a dramatic I'm-naked-but-dignified pose. Her pubic hair, he saw, was as red as the hair on her head.

"Philip, if it will help your performance, you can come to see me anytime," she said. "Do you understand?"

"Yes, ma'am," he said, determined to bolt for the door.

"*Don't* say ma'am! You're beginning to sound like a southerner."

"Yes, ma'am—Miss Beltane. I have to go now. Good-bye."

She didn't interfere, and Philip reached the door in safety. He pounded down the stairs and ran half the way home to Crosstree; then his legs suddenly went weak under him and he collapsed into a ditch and laughed. God, the world was funny. After a while, he got up and went to Land's End and stood in the woods looking at the light in Vivienne's window.

The next day Philip was worse on stage than ever. It made him as nervous as a cat to know that Miss Beltane was out there in the darkness of the auditorium watching him pretend to make love. When they came off after the wedding scene, Vivienne kicked him in the shins.

"You stink," she said. "Philip, if you ruin this play I'm going to be *mad*."

Romeo was due back onstage to slay Tybalt, and Philip rushed on and threw himself heart and soul into the duel.

"Man, don't really kill me," James muttered before bellowing his line, "wretched boy."

"Oh, I am fortune's fool!" Philip howled with proper conviction.

"Why can't you make love the way you fight?" Deidre demanded when he came off stage again.

Philip went down the hall and into the boys' bathroom for some peace.

Hellraiser joined him.

"Boy, I wouldn't mind makin' love to Viv," he said. "We could have the weddin' night right onstage. What's the matter with you? If you don't do better, she'll put real poison in that bottle. I'm sheddin' real blood, you know." In front of the mirror he pantomimed his death, crumbling to the floor crying, "I am sped." He writhed in agony.

Julian crashed open the door. "Romeo and his prick, wanted onstage in five minutes," he yelled.

Philip leaped on him and wrestled him to the floor, and all of them squirmed over the hard cement, Hellraiser moaning " 'Zounds, a cat, a rat, a mouse, a dog —no, a dog, a rat, a mouse, a cat, to scratch a man to death!" Julian tried to get a torture-hold on Philip.

"What the shit's going on in here?" James asked, pushing open the door. Hellraiser grabbed James's leg and pulled him down on top of the struggling wrestlers, groaning hoarsely, "Ask for me to-morrow, and you shall find me a grave man."

"Viv sent me for Romeo for the wedding night," James gasped, threshing amid the bodies. "Want me to take your place?" He imitated Philip's accent on a rising pitch: "I must be gone and alive, or stay and *stink!*"

Philip tried to kill both Julian and James. The fight broke up when Scat Honeychurch tore in with a cold six-pack of Budweiser he had stolen from the Honeychurch refrigerator. They sat around panting, draining the beer and discussing the high school's football prospects for the coming fall, until Vivienne pounded on the door for Philip.

"Ugh, beer," Vivienne said in his ear after he kissed her in the next scene.

Maybe he could get drunk and do a better job with the role. He proposed the idea to Vivienne.

"You get drunk and I'll kill you," she said. "You're going to do it cold sober and do it right! Honestly, Philip."

He was determined not to let her down, but the harder he tried, the worse he seemed to grow. The dress rehearsal the day before the performance went well in all other respects, but Philip felt he was terrible. Laura Beltane assembled them onstage afterward.

"You did it well," she said. "Today's performance was good by any standards, and excellent by high school standards." She looked around at them. "However, you have a chance here to do something *really* worthwhile. Think about your roles. Become your character. And we'll see what happens. There will be no rehearsal tomorrow afternoon; everyone should rest. Report here at five-thirty for makeup."

Philip walked out beside Vivienne.

"Come to the river tomorrow around one, can you?" she said. "We can rest together."

He nodded and she smiled.

The next day was cloudy and unexpectedly cool for the last week in August. The feel of fall made Philip suddenly remember Vivienne's imminent departure. They had scarcely looked past the play all summer; so far he really hadn't thought about what life next year was going to be like, with Vivienne away at college.

He reached the tree early and sat down on the rock, feeling despondent. What if he were absolutely rotten tonight? He hadn't done it right yet. What were his opening lines? He panicked. He couldn't remember.

He was considering jumping into the river and swimming out to where the current could take him to sea, when Vivienne's hand suddenly touched his shoulder.

He jumped, startled. Vivienne kissed his cheek and sat down close to him.

"What's the matter?" she said.

He couldn't look at her. He stared before him, at his clasped hands. "It's so hard," he said finally.

"What? Acting? No, it isn't. It's easy." She took his hand and stood up, pulling him up too. She looked around. As usual, there was no sound at all. No one but them ever came to that spot. She tugged on Philip's hand and led him to a sheltered flat space bordered by the bushes and the river.

"I'll help you," she whispered. She lay down and looked up at him. In the cloudy light, her pupils seemed enormous, filling her eyes, and her lips were pink and appealing. He knelt beside her and touched her face with his hand.

"Say 'I love you,'" she said.

Philip had never said exactly those three words to her before. He drew a breath. "I love you," he said.

Without a word she pulled his body down against hers.

"Philip, I love you too," she said.

She had always stopped him short of total lovemaking, and he was amazed when she started taking off his clothes.

"Vivienne—"

"It's all right," she said. "It's a safe time for me. We can."

What she was saying took a moment to get through

85

to him. Then he threw off the rest of his clothes and with a cry of joy clasped her to him.

"You darling," he said. She helped him pull off her jeans and her shirt. When she was naked she shivered. He wanted to hold her close and warm her, but desperately he wanted to look at her naked body, and for a minute he let her lie there, cold and covered with gooseflesh, while he stared at the pink round nipples of her pretty breasts and the whiteness of her flat stomach. Her ribs made a frail arch above her waist, and her hips flared in twin crescents; the black shiny hair covering her small arched pelvis looked like ebony on snow.

He pulled her arms up over her head and looked at the sweet hollows of her armpits, and when he could wait no longer, he kissed her right in the armpit where she seemed the most Vivienne of all, her strange musky odor the strongest and most entrancing. She moaned and he kissed her under the other arm, holding her wrists above her head with his hand. She shivered, but it wasn't from cold; her body had turned rosy. His lips traveled to her breasts and he bit her nipples, gently, releasing her hands, and she put them around his neck and caressed him. She began to breathe hard. All the times they had done everything secretly, with clothes on, seemed not to exist in his memory—this was the first time; and he kissed and kissed her nipples and then put his mouth over hers and kissed her lips until he felt dizzy. He wanted to wait, to hold back, to taste every single part of her slowly, in a kind of endless conquest, but he was conquered himself by feelings he couldn't control. In a minute more he had parted her legs and begun to kiss her on the pretty lips between her thighs, knowing he had struck the right place when she gasped and arched her body. He used his tongue and he used his lips. They had done this before, many times, but this time just short of rapture for her he pulled her up against him and she spread her legs wide. He was terrified of hurting her, but she clung to him and said, "Go on!" and he let his tense shaft penetrate her soft body, as carefully as possible. Then he could think of nothing at all, not of being tender or careful or of anything. He cried her name. His sensations of darkness and falling and hot delight seemed to last forever, and yet to be only a second long. He dissolved into Vivienne, into his love, and became a part of her forever.

His emotion and his choked cry gave Vivienne a climax far more powerful than any she had experienced before; why, they were the same person! They were actually joined physically the way they had always been joined in spirit; she felt a happiness that was beyond joy.

Thank God she had found out that there were such things as safe days. She was sure today was safe, and the knowledge gave her a wild joy, a feeling of freedom at last, and beyond that a savage primeval sort of fulfillment. She wanted to encompass Philip, to possess him body and soul, to hold him and release him, to give him everything he wanted.

"I love you so much, Vivienne. I'd die for you. You know that."

"I know. And if you wanted to do it again during the play—"

"During the *play*? Do you think we could?"

"If I'm not too sore. I feel a little—you know, you're big down there? But are we ever both offstage for long enough? There's intermission, but then everyone's around. Could we do it then?"

"I don't know. At least we could kiss."

"I'll meet you every time we're both offstage, down the hall in that classroom where we rehearsed." Vivienne licked Philip's lips. "We will be good tonight," she said.

He nodded, staring into her eyes. He could remember every line from the beginning to the end. His mind was clear.

"In case we don't have time tonight, could we again, right now?" he whispered.

"Yes. But take it easy." Vivienne smiled at him and closed her eyes.

That night Vivienne was serene as she put on her velvet dress in the girls' dressing room, wound her dark hair up with pearls and let Mab apply her makeup. Mab emphasized Vivienne's dark eyes with mascara and eyeliner, and matched the red of her dress with carefully brushed-on lipstick.

"Vivienne, you look *marvelous*." Miss Beltane swept in and paused before Vivienne. A look passed between them, and Miss Beltane smiled. Vivienne was going to be magnificent.

"Down the hall, girls. Join the rest of the cast," Miss Beltane ordered.

The girls hurried along the corridor behind her, to the band room. There the boys were striding about, displaying various states of nervousness. Hellraiser muttered, " 'Tis not so wide as a well nor so—no, *deep* as a well nor so wide as a Churchill" with a look at fat David.

Miss Beltane called them to order.

"The house is packed. People are sitting in the aisles," she said. "We have our audience. Let's give them a show." She looked around at everyone. "Make me proud of you," she said with intensity.

Dressed like a high priestess, in a white robe, Miss Beltane went before the curtain and spoke the prologue about the star-crossed lovers. Then the curtain went up and the play began.

In the classroom Vivienne held Philip's hot dry hands in hers. He had never seen her so beautiful. Her face glowed, and the ruby red dress with its tight bodice and the pearls gleaming in her dark hair made her look like a dazzling princess from some far-off imaginary country. She blew her breath gently into his ear and whispered, "How fast could we make love?"

"Right now?"

"Do you think we could?"

He kissed her hands and looked up at her. The sounds of swords clashing came from the direction of the stage. Someone called "Romeo" out in the hall.

"Go, darling," Vivienne whispered. "I'll be with you."

He rushed on. The moment he spoke his first line, he felt confident. He could sense the expanse of people on the other side of the footlights but could not really see them, and they seemed a friendly presence.

When Juliet appeared and he cried, "What lady's that?" Philip felt more than confidence—the stage was charged with electricity.

In the spotlight Vivienne's beauty was unearthly, and a murmur ran through the audience as the lovers moved downstage, alone together as the dancers at the Capulet ball pantomimed in silhouette. Then Romeo and Juliet spoke to each other for the first time, and for Philip, it *was* the first time. He felt alone with Vivienne in the bright circle of light.

"You were great!" Vivienne cried as she ran around to the other side, behind the stage, tearing the pearls out of her hair.

"You're on again," someone said to Philip.

In a minute Philip came forward out of the darkness to find Vivienne on the balcony in a dim silver light, her hair released and hanging down to touch his face. She looked into his eyes. Vivienne would equal but not surpass that performance even at the height of her powers. After the balcony scene, the audience rose and shouted "Bravo!"

"Keep it up," Miss Beltane commanded them in the wings. She was tremendously excited. Something had happened, and they were giving a startling performance. Hellraiser died so well it stopped the show, and during the dueling scene Philip and James clashed so realistically that a girl screamed. The audience was on the edge of its seats. Philip had no fear. The carefully rehearsed parry-thrust went exactly as planned. James died and Philip was banished, and the first half was over.

"It's fantastic!" people in the audience exclaimed to each other during the intermission. "They are *really* good."

"Vivienne Dane—Philip Alexander—" Their names were on all lips.

In the classroom, Vivienne almost got Philip too aroused to go on again. She had changed to her night-dress for the early morning scene and she pressed herself against Philip so lovingly that he had to beg her to stay away. He was desperate to make love to her. But there wasn't time. They were due back onstage.

When, again, he was alone with her in the spotlight and they had to part, Philip felt truly desolate.

He watched from the wings as Juliet's father ordered her to marry Paris. He was off for a long time, until he had to go back and learn of her death. It really seemed to be happening to him. He struggled with Paris outside the tomb in a frantic mood, and entered the vault to find Vivienne lying dead. The audience, seeing his strained face in the light of the torch he carried, fell completely silent. He deposited the torch in its holder and bent over Vivienne. She didn't seem to be breathing. In her red dress she lay very still. But Vivienne—surely Vivienne couldn't die and leave him? Had it actually happened? He looked at her wonder-ingly, pulling the netting from her face and staring at it. Miss Beltane held her breath. This was nothing they had rehearsed. Philip looked confused. He leaned over Vivienne. "I—will stay with you," he said slowly. He looked around the dim tomb and a tear rolled down his cheek. "Eyes, look your last." His voice was choked, and someone in the darkness sobbed loudly. Philip didn't hear it. "Lips—" he said, bending over Vivienne and kissing her.

Philip hesitated for a silent moment before he drank the brandy in his vial. He managed "With a kiss, I die," and kissed Vivienne for a last time before he fell at the side of the bier.

Lying on the floor, Philip actually felt as if he weren't breathing. Vivienne woke up and found him. Her tears dropped on his face and she pulled the letter opener out of his sash. It glittered in the light as she looked up at it for a moment before she plunged it into her bodice.

Bells pealed out and the curtains closed; the audience was silent. After a moment, wild applause exploded. Vivienne leaped up from her position slumped over Philip and with a glowing face pulled him up. The curtains opened again, and some romantic soul tossed daisies onstage as the audience cheered. During the standing ovation, Scat Honeychurch rushed out and gave a dozen red roses to Vivienne. She kissed a rose and gave it to Philip, and he seized her hand and kissed it, feeling an enormous relief that the whole thing was over. He had almost believed he had lost Vivienne. Acting was scary.

The cast bowed to the applause for what seemed an eternity. People began to flock up onto the stage to offer congratulations. Miss Beltane was presented with the cast gift, a music box that played Brahms, and pictures were taken. Philip's parents struggled through the crowd to declare themselves amazed. He really *had* learned to act. His little brother Champ grabbed a foil and pretended to duel.

Miss Beltane kissed Vivienne on the cheek and then hugged and kissed Philip. "I knew it," she said. "I knew you could do it. Philip, you were *marvelous*."

Moving up the aisle toward the stage, China Dane had a stunned expression on her face, and Bascomb was puzzled by China's look. From all sides came nothing but praise of their daughter. China should have been delighted. Friends crowded up to congratulate them. But as they moved along, in a kind of royal procession, Bascomb detected a strain in China's manner. She almost seemed disoriented. Mab, walking beside her mother, received compliments for Vivienne and said thank you, and no, she didn't act, too, and behaved as her usual well-brought-up self, but China was definitely distracted.

"Are you feeling well?" Bascomb asked her. "Is it too warm in here?" He spoke into China's ear.

China didn't answer for a moment. "What?" she said. "Oh. I'm fine." She gave Bascomb a reassuring smile. "I'm just a bit overcome by Vivienne. She was so"—China lowered her voice—"so excellent, wasn't she?"

It was half of the truth. Vivienne's performance had exceeded anything even China had been prepared to see. Miss Beltane was right; Vivienne was brilliantly talented. She had moved her own mother to tears. But more than that fact caused China's distraction of the moment. It was *Philip's* performance, Philip's emotion, Philip's tears. China was sure that he had not been acting at all.

China knew that for the last two summers Vivienne had seen Philip daily at the Drama Circle, but since Vivienne seldom mentioned Philip at home, and since she regularly let James or Julian take her to movies and dances, China had scarcely thought of Philip Alexander. But now the truth was obvious. That had been real passion she had witnessed.

Chester Honeychurch and Nancy Cunningham intercepted the Danes for a round of mutual congratulations over their children, and China managed to put her thoughts aside and say the right things. She agreed that Miss Beltane was a genius, and just what Trinity needed.

When they reached the stage, Vivienne embraced her mother. "I'm so glad you liked it! I'm so glad," she said.

While Bascomb kissed Vivienne, China turned to Philip, who stood beside Vivienne.

"You did very well indeed, Philip," China said. "Are you interested in acting as a career?"

Philip blushed. "Thank you, Mrs. Dane. No, I don't think I'll be an actor." He avoided looking toward Vivienne, but as clearly as if he had said the words, China heard him think, "I only did it for her."

China made a point of speaking to Philip's parents for a few minutes. She was always gracious to the Alexanders, but tonight she was positively warm. China wondered if she should invite the Alexanders to visit her at Land's End? Or perhaps she should just go over to the store one day and speak with them? She hadn't been inside the Crosstree grocery store twice in her life; either she or Ella always telephoned in the Land's End order. The Alexanders would be surprised by her appearance. Still, one way or the other, China thought, she must have a discussion with Philip's parents. She looked again at Philip, who was trying to get the foil away from his little brother. A handsome boy, Philip, but what were their plans for his future?

China Dane often simply ignored things she couldn't bear. Pain, sorrow, and suffering affected her tender-hearted soul so deeply that in order to function at all, she had to try not to see what she couldn't help. In her own realm, she allowed no unkindness to exist. Her nature created around it what it needed, a peaceful island where no raised voice or hasty action intruded, where each person was given his due and the very best possible construction was put on all actions. She never criticized or complained, and she listened to criticism and complaint with courteous interest and quietly went about putting things right if she could. The world's strictures on race and color and religion and social standing had no real meaning for her, for again she looked the other way, or rather looked as far as she could into the soul of each person she met, seeing that person as a product of his circumstances and treating him gently and pleasantly, whether it was a black child at Land's End or the president of the Garden Club of

93

Eyreville. She was loved by all, not so much for the good she did as for the good she was.

Where Vivienne was concerned, she resolved to be very cautious. Her daughter would be leaving in less than a month, off to college at Radcliffe, where she would meet new people and find new interests. Surely Philip's influence would fade. But if they were attracted to each other as strongly as China suspected, there might be trouble ahead all the same. Philip was very handsome and appealing. After further thought on the subject, China again resolved to speak to the Alexanders.

On the next Friday evening the cast of the play was invited to Miss Beltane's apartment for a good-bye party for Vivienne and the other graduates of the Youth Drama Circle. China was sure that Philip would go. Julian Royal came by to escort Vivienne, and as soon as the two left, China telephoned the Alexanders.

Mary Clermont, who answered the phone, sounded surprised when China asked if she might call on them for a few minutes that evening. Of course, Mary cordially invited her to do so, and went in to put on the kettle.

"I don't know why, but Mrs. Dane is coming over," Mary said to Thomas, who as usual was at his desk writing.

Thomas looked up in surprise; he was about to write a line, but the news knocked it quite out of his head.

Within a few minutes Mary heard a light tap at the door. She and Thomas welcomed China formally, and Mary brought out her best teapot and dishes.

China had never drunk tea after dinner, but she smiled and accepted a cup and settled in a chair beside the open window. It was already dark outside—the days were shortening. From a freshly plowed field across the road a smell of earth came in on the night breeze.

China was carefully dressed as always. Tonight she was wearing a dark blue silk dress and pearls, and her

94

hair was twisted into its usual chignon. Thomas liked looking at her. Years ago, before he went to England, he had been struck with admiration whenever he saw young China Austin driving past in her open automobile. She was the belle of Eyreville. Once, making a delivery to the Country Club—his father was running the Crosstree store then—Thomas had seen China in a tennis dress, playing on one of the courts. She wore her hair in a short bob and moved with unbelievable grace. Tonight, in their living room, she looked more dignified, but scarcely much older.

For a few moments they discussed the weather, Miss Beltane, the evening's party and the performance of last week. Then China took the plunge.

"Bascomb and I," she began, fudging terribly since she had not said a word to her husband, "have been wondering what your plans are for Philip's education. I know college is still a year off for him. Vivienne has a high opinion of Philip. He was certainly excellent the other night."

She paused. Both of the Alexanders looked puzzled.

"Your daughter's going to Radcliffe, I believe," Thomas said.

"Yes." China paused and then forced herself to go on. "Frankly, you see, I think perhaps Philip and Vivienne are rather attracted to each other . . . at the moment. And I wondered if there was any, well, help we could give—"

China spoke very softly, and it took a few minutes for her words to register on the Alexanders. Part of the reason for her hesitant manner was her fear of offending them, and part was the uncomfortable knowledge that Bascomb would have a fit if he knew she was making any such offer. She didn't know herself what she meant by it. Actually she just wanted information, but it was so much a part of her nature to be helpful that she couldn't ask without offering. That charitable heart, Bascomb often said, would ruin them in the end.

Ask China Dane, and ye would receive, as every poor family in Eyreville knew.

At last Mary Clermont took in China's meaning.

"Mrs. Dane, that's extremely kind of you," she said. "But we have had some *very* good news." Mary glanced at Thomas, who was staring rather foolishly at China, she thought. "In fact, wonderful news. We both think so, at least, and I'm sure Philip will come to agree with us. You see"—Mary drew herself up proudly, and her accent became more crisply English—"my brother Charleston, who lives in London, has his own corporation now. A financial holding company. He has done very well for himself. But his wife recently died and Charleston has no children. Just last month we received a magnificent offer from my brother. He wants to educate Philip in England and give him a job afterward at Downforth Enterprises, his company—Philip will be his heir."

"That is marvelous!" China said.

"We were thrilled. Philip is to go to Cambridge. So you see there's no problem at all."

"I'm sure Philip must be delighted," China said.

Thomas spoke up. "Well," he said, "I think Philip will like the idea in time. Right now he's involved at his school . . . football, you know; he didn't seem to think he'd much like going back to England when we told him about Charleston's offer."

"At this age, they scarcely look ahead at all," China said.

After a few more minutes of chat, China rose to leave, feeling profoundly relieved. Philip had a good life ahead of him, in no way tied to the Danes.

"Now what do you make of that?" Mary asked her husband when China had departed.

Thomas pondered. "Mothers with beautiful daughters have a way of taking care, maybe. Philip certainly made an excellent Romeo."

"Nonsense. That was just acting. Philip isn't interested in girls at all. I've never heard him ring one up.

96

And he didn't even take a date to the junior prom last spring."

"But Vivienne Dane—"

"Philip should know better than to think of Vivienne Dane."

"Well"—Thomas sighed and shook his head—"she's a nice lady, China Austin."

Mary tried to think of grounds to disagree with this observation, but could find none. In the back of Mary's mind, she was somewhat worried about Philip's reaction to Charleston's proposal. Philip had said flatly that he wouldn't go back to England. Well, he was going, like it or not. Young people never saw the reality of life's situations.

"Thomas, I think we shouldn't mention Mrs. Dane's visit," Mary said. "No use stirring Philip up all over again about going to England."

Thomas agreed. When Champ appeared at the door to demand a glass of water and ask, "Who came to visit?" Mary glanced at Thomas.

"Mrs. Dane just brought back some groceries that were sent to her by mistake," she said. "Now, you get back to bed, young man, or I'll have the ruler out."

Tall candles lit Miss Beltane's large dark living room, and a stick of incense burned before the china Buddha. The guests arrived to find bowls of pretzels and potato chips and plates of cheese and crackers out on the many small tables scattered through the room. In the dining room stood a large crystal bowl of fruit punch, which Miss Beltane had mixed for the party, and which Hellraiser immediately spiked with a fifth of vodka when she wasn't looking.

As Julian went to get Vivienne a glass of punch, she sat down on the horsehair sofa between Philip and James. Everyone talked about *Romeo and Juliet* and the sensation they had created in Eyreville.

"My great-aunt Martha cried," Vivienne said. "Anyway, her eyes watered at the right time. My sister told me."

"Hellraiser, I heard your little sister Sugar cried all night and wanted to know why Romeo and Juliet couldn't just tell their parents they were married," Deidre said.

Hellraiser grinned. "Sugar cried worse than that when I told her the true story—you know, about how they were tortured to death with straight pins. She really dug you kids." He chuckled, looking at Philip and Vivienne.

"I'll bet she wasn't a bit sorry to see *you* die," James said.

"She knew it was coming. I'd practiced it quite a few times around the house. Ah! I am hurt—"

Hellraiser went into his death scene, crumpling, and Julian poured a bowl of potato chips over him as he thrashed on the carpet.

Miss Beltane thought the punch had really turned out delicious, and she had several glasses before she called the group to order.

She struck a bronze dinner gong. "Listen, everybody," she cried. "I have an announcement. Two announcements. First of all, we all want to wish Vivienne and James and Julian good luck in college. And second of all, I want to say good-bye."

"Good-bye!" A roomful of surprised faces turned to her. Miss Beltane beamed.

"You people did it! I am so grateful. The owner of a workshop-theater in Atlanta came to the play the other night. I didn't know it at the time. My cousin Wallace brought him to the performance. He was so impressed that he offered me a job at the workshop. I'll be able to put on plays and coach in his professional drama school as well. It's *exactly* the opportunity I wanted, and I thank you all."

There were cries and groans of disappointment, but Miss Beltane looked so happy no one could begrudge her a future as a drama coach. Mr. Grayson had promised to find a dynamic substitute for Trinity, she said, and she'd come back for many visits.

Vivienne was startled to hear that Miss Beltane was leaving. For a minute she sat perfectly still, staring at her. Miss Beltane was wearing her hair long, and for the party she had donned a loose lavender robe tied with what looked like a gold snakeskin. As always, her complete disregard of the dress-code of Eyreville was awe-inspiring. Laura Beltane was a messenger from the world of drama, theatricality itself. Since Miss Beltane had told Vivienne she could act, Vivienne had never doubted it. She thought back to that first day in Dramatics class, to their first exchange of glances.

Miss Beltane struck the gong again.

"I have a farewell speech, or I had," she continued. "What was I going to say? Oh yes. A rule. Never have a cannon onstage unless it goes off. Never promise and then not deliver. Vivienne and Philip won't be guilty of that, I know." Miss Beltane looked fondly at her stars, and Vivienne's eyes filled with tears.

Swiftly Miss Beltane crossed to the sofa, kissed Vivienne on the cheek and whispered in her ear, "Someday you'll be famous." She looked at Philip, sitting next to Vivienne, wondering what had happened to turn him into such an excellent Romeo, and rather regretting that it hadn't been *her* influence. She patted Philip on the cheek as he flushed, and then proposed a toast to their faithful backer, Wallace Hastings.

After numerous other toasts, everyone grew jolly again. Scat played ragtime on the piano, and Miss Beltane gave imitations of teachers at Trinity, including Miss French giving the girls' hockey team a pep talk ("You've got to hit! You've got to *hit!*") and Mr. Bonecutter chaperoning a seventh grade dance (he wrongfully fancied himself the master of the Crocodile Rock.)

When Vivienne left the party, she clasped Miss Beltane's hand and looked into her green eyes.

"Miss Beltane, if I can, someday I'll do something

to thank you," she said. "You have meant so much to me."

"We've helped each other," Miss Beltane said, looking happily around at her apartment, which was a shambles. "I want to hear all about your roles in college, don't forget."

The sound of the dinner gong being rung by Hellraiser followed Vivienne out to Julian's car.

Parting hurt. Philip was in no way prepared for how much it hurt. He and Vivienne could spend only two more Sundays together, and only one of those was "safe." He made love to her that last time in silence. Vivienne's face was wet with tears. As he held her she sobbed, and promised a hundred times not to look at the boys in Boston, and to write long letters to him. Christmas wasn't so far off, she said; less than three months. That wasn't much comfort to Philip; Vivienne was going away from him, away from his touch and his reach. He pulled her close and wished that he could hold her like that forever. She alone mattered to him in the entire universe.

Vivienne suffered at the moment of saying goodbye, but inevitably she was soon caught up in the excitement of going north to college, to a place so different from Eyreville. She looked forward to trying out for plays, to roommates and parties and deep discussions about life, and to snow, which she had never seen. Her grandmother Elizabeth Austin had studied at Radcliffe; Grandmother loved to tell Vivienne about a sleigh ride she remembered, racing over the hills with bells jingling and snow falling through the darkness. She described dances where the galoshes piled up behind the doors, and The Game with Yale, and ice skating, and nights when Harvard boys standing in the cold under the stars had serenaded them beneath their windows. Vivienne was sure she would love it all.

Bascomb and China flew to Boston with Vivienne to

see her settled. The campus seemed very strange at first, but Vivienne liked her roommates and soon felt at home in the colonial elegance of her surroundings. When she saw her first professional play downtown, a drama headed for Broadway, she knew the theater was where she belonged. It was wonderful! She tried out for a production of *Much Ado About Nothing* and got the role of Beatrice, a coup for a freshman. Miss Beltane's work to erase her southern accent had been successful, and the director said she had great flair.

Back in Eyreville, there was nothing but the football season to keep Philip's mind off Vivienne. While he was actually playing the game, he didn't think of her, but he thought of her all the rest of the time. He missed her painfully. At first he hoped she had been mistaken about the safe days, and that a letter would come telling him she was pregnant—that they would have to get married. But her letters brought no such news, just accounts of her acting experiences and her classes, and the beautiful colors of the leaves in the fall. She sent him many words of love, but they were little consolation. He read every letter until he knew it by heart. On a calendar he marked off each day until Christmas. He felt more and more lonely.

Vivienne wrote fewer letters in November. Philip was afraid that she had met a boy in Boston. Jealousy ate at him. He read every word she did write over and over, trying to decide if she sounded less ardent. What if she came back at Christmas and wasn't interested in him at all?

When football season ended, he grew more morose. Thomas knew that adolescent boys had their ups and downs, but he was a bit worried. Philip walked around like a zombie. Mary was not pleased to see all the letters arriving from Boston. She wanted nothing to affect the plan to send Philip to her brother. The fewer Philip's entanglements here in America, the better. Mary was proud of Philip. Philip would show her family that she was worth something after all—that in a way, she was as successful as Charleston. He had a business, but she had a son. Philip would do her great credit, and she was resolved that nothing go wrong with her scheme.

China had not mentioned her knowledge about Philip's going to England to anyone at Land's End. Bascomb didn't have the slightest interest in Philip's fate, and Vivienne might wonder how China had come by the information. China did not know that Philip had been so horrified by the plan when he heard it that he had never mentioned it to Vivienne.

The matter had to come up again, however. Philip wanted to apply to the state university for next year.

When his mother heard this, she raised holy hell. Finally Philip had to say he would *consider* the England plan at least, would not "throw his whole future to the wind." At this point Philip was so miserable about Vivienne that he didn't care, anyway. What if she had fallen in love with someone else? In that case it didn't matter what happened to him.

Vivienne hadn't.

The day she came home for Christmas vacation they had an ecstatic reunion in the woods. Philip skipped school and waited by the river the whole day, praying that she could find a way to join him, and when she ran to him he couldn't believe the joy of it. She looked the same, or perhaps prettier. And, she told him at once with shining eyes, she had gone to the doctor at her school and gotten a certain device, so they could make love anytime!

It had to be brief, that day, but they managed more meetings, and he questioned her closely. Did she go out on dates? Well, she had to, sometimes. She'd seem strange, otherwise. She didn't write to him about her dates, she said, because they weren't important enough. Philip couldn't pin down his suspicions, but they weren't allayed.

"Look, I'm not worrying about *you* every minute," Vivienne said. She smiled and her dimple showed.

"But I'm here and you're there. I mean, you *know* there's no one else for me."

"Really? Philip, you've never had a single date?"

He shook his head.

"Maybe—" Vivienne began, but she stopped. Maybe Philip should go out with other girls, she thought to herself; but he had awfully strict notions about faithfulness. It was nice that he was so true to her, but she felt a little uncomfortable under his questioning. She had kissed a few Harvard boys. They had meant nothing to her, but she'd hate for Philip to find out.

Philip was happy during that Christmas vacation, but not deliriously so, the way he could remember being when they were younger. He was too afraid of losing Vivienne. It kept him tense.

IV

Vivienne went away again and the days dragged until spring vacation; February was two thousand years long. Mary said Philip needed a spring tonic, and she actually brewed up some horrible stuff and made him drink it. He didn't care. He wished it were poison. He went around in a dull funk during March.

When Vivienne at last came home in April, she thought Philip looked thinner than she remembered, and she asked if he had been sick.

"Of course not," he said. "I just—missed you."

They were snuggled together in the barn; the rest of the family were away on various missions, and the Kings who farmed the Land's End property had as usual taken Sunday off, so they had the place to themselves.

Vivienne felt guilty. She hadn't lost a pound; in fact, she was very happy at Radcliffe. Her initial homesickness had worn off. She missed Philip, too, but lots of boys admired her and asked her out and she didn't stay home and brood. She wished Philip could get a little more fun out of life. But then, he wouldn't be her Philip if he were different. Whatever he did was done with single-minded intensity.

Even during their lovemaking Philip was suspicious. Every nerve in his body stretched, trying to detect any difference in Vivienne. Had she made love with anyone else? Had she always kissed quite so expertly, or known how to drive him so wild, keeping right on the edge of an orgasm and delaying and delaying it until he was on the point of madness? Had she learned that from someone in Boston? He felt like picking her up and holding her close to him and snarling at everyone in the world to keep them away, so that he might have her to himself alone. Maybe he only imagined there was a change, that she was more avid, less modest. She was more exciting than ever—*that* he knew for sure. But why?

Now there were only two more months to get through, before she would return for the whole summer. Tenderly, Vivienne planned it with Philip. She would stay home. Her grandmother, who was ill, was coming to live at Land's End, so they would probably all stay home that summer, and she would see him frequently. It would be a blissful time, months and months together. She didn't think beyond it. And Philip didn't want to.

Philip knew that matters couldn't simply drift. His mother fully expected him to go to England in the late summer. She would have tried shipping him off as soon as he graduated from Eyreville High, except that Thomas needed his help that summer. Thomas could not afford to pay wages to anyone but his butcher now; the Alexanders had to man the store themselves, thanks to the loss of business caused by the unspeakable new A and P in Eyreville. Philip would have to work full-time in Crosstree. In the fall, Mary was prepared to sacrifice and work full-time in his stead. They would get along without Philip for the sake of his future.

"I could stay here a year and work," Philip said. "I don't have to—"

Mary cut him off. "Nonsense," she said. "Charleston is expecting you."

Philip no longer argued. It made things more comfortable around home to let his mother believe what she wanted to. He had begun at last to realize that the prospect of England was a serious danger. He knew he could not face life over there without Vivienne, with-

106

out even a glimpse of her or a hope of her for four years. A plan began forming in his mind. Suppose— just suppose—what would happen if they ran away and got married?"

The very thought left him breathless. Then Vivienne would be his and the whole world couldn't tear her away. If his uncle still wanted him, he would have to take Vivienne, too. There were wonderful acting schools in England—there was the Royal Academy! She might want to go. If his uncle wouldn't have them, they could go to the state university here in South Carolina. He'd get a job and support them, and they could get loans for their tuition. Or if Vivienne wanted to go back to Boston, he could accompany her and work there and not go to college at all. In any case, their marrying would bring matters to a head, and next year they would be somewhere, together.

The more Philip thought about it, the more it seemed to be a simple and beautiful solution. In the late spring before Vivienne returned he grew more cheerful. Thomas was glad to see adolescence loosening its grip on his son. Philip had an appetite again and sometimes even whistled as he carried groceries.

The days grew longer. As Vivienne's return drew near, Philip resolved to meet her with no questions at all, just to make her happy. He saw her trunk delivered to Land's End, and then the next day she was there in the woods with him. This time he felt they were reunited for life. He was so happy that he could only look at her, warm and alive and with him; he couldn't speak. Vivienne was glad Philip didn't question her or seem so bitterly jealous; he was growing up, she thought with the superiority of a college sophomore.

For a time, they lived an idyll. The June weather was beautiful, long clear days with a faint breeze bringing the salty smell from the sea, and the sun overhead pouring liquid warmth down onto the green fields. Vivienne had not forgotten how lushly lovely Eyreville and Land's End were; Miss Beltane said once that Curzon's

107

Neck reminded her of Eden. Philip was sweeter to her than he had ever been, and more handsome, too, really the handsomest boy Vivienne had ever seen. Since her mother was busy taking care of both her little sister Cypriana and her grandmother, and her father was always in his library, and Mab was usually at the dance studio, no one noticed that Vivienne went for daily afternoon walks along the river, walks that ended at the bridge at two o'clock just as the Alexander grocery store truck rounded the bend and parked behind an unused barn.

Sometimes Philip and she stayed inside the back of the truck, climbing in among the bags full of food, and sometimes they went into the old barn. Philip managed to spend almost an hour with her every day, making the time up by rattling the truck furiously up and down the shoreline drive later and rushing in and out with the deliveries, "as if he were going to a fire," one cook remarked.

Philip used those hours with Vivienne well. Like a butterfly collector going after choice specimens, he concentrated on gathering information about Vivienne's preferences in lovemaking. She was older now, more sophisticated. Having found out that the soles of her feet were sensitive, he would tickle them and kiss them until he had her crying for mercy. After that he'd kiss the backs of her knees and trace her spine all the way up her back with his lips until she turned over and begged him to kiss her on the mouth; then they would be locked in a long, dreamy kiss that teased them both and made their bodies tense. Vivienne loved to feel his tongue in her mouth, and she would relax completely in his arms and let him explore with his tongue; then she would lick his face in turn, using just the tip of her tongue and sticking it into his mouth and withdrawing it until he was in an agony of his own from wanting her. She let him try every sort of intimacy. In the darkness of the vegetable-smelling van, the confinement and the closed-in feeling made their final physical unions more ecstatic than ever, mountains that they climbed together in a dark inward country of their own making, a country of pleasure that they almost could have mapped, although they only felt its features with their senses.

Intense as things were in the dark, they were just as good in another way when the two of them crept into the unused barn through a broken slat and lay on the ground on top of Philip's shirt and had room to tumble around. She didn't mind if he tussled with her and gently pulled her hair to make her do what he wanted her to, and she willingly tried anything he ordered, although she sometimes laughed at the ideas he had. When she laughed, he kissed her until she couldn't breathe. The sound of Vivienne's throaty, breathless chuckle delighted him more than any other sound she made, even more than her soft moans or the occasional loud outcries that she couldn't control.

Her enthusiastic responses made his love for her sharper and yet more painful at every encounter. What was in her heart? He knew Vivienne completely, and yet she sometimes seemed the person in the world most mysterious to him. He couldn't understand the contradiction. He knew how to give Vivienne an orgasm in three minutes, yet he had no idea what she was thinking. The more he wanted to know, the more it got confused with his physical desire for her; or maybe they both *were* the same thing, what was in her head and what was deep inside of her body that he longed to reach and touch physically, so that the passionate arch of her body under his would cause the shattering of his own control and their souls would seem to touch each other.

"Oh, God, I love you, Vivienne," he cried at the height of their encounters, and he would repeat it later, cradling her against him and caressing her while the last delicious sensations faded. "I love you too," she would always whisper. And why did he doubt it?

They still met and made love at their old place at

the river when they could. Usually on Sundays they'd go swimming there first, swinging out on the rope swing and dropping into the water together, kissing while they submerged. One Sunday Mab almost caught them, but fortunately she came down to the rope swing when they were paddling around in the water and not engaged in their other pursuit. Mab preferred swimming at the ocean beach with her girl friends; she thought the river was too muddy. And Vivienne furthered Mab's aversion by describing the blood-suckers that sometimes fastened on Philip and her. "Oh, you can pick them off. You just bleed a little," Vivienne said in a casual tone, but Mab shuddered and went back up to the house, clutching her towel. Philip grinned at Vivienne as they watched Mab's figure disappear through the trees.

Later that afternoon the sun slanted through the pines on the other shore and filtered across the water, making little needles of green dance in the depths. For a while, Philip lay with his head in Vivienne's lap, staring at the river; then she leaned down and kissed him, and her lips were warm and sweet. He sat up and pulled off his swimming trunks and the two pieces of her bathing suit and stretched out naked with her. He closed his eyes, and she closed her eyes too. The scents of the river and the earth were all around them, and their slow-paced embrace seemed just another element of nature; bees buzzed around some clover blossoms close by their heads, and the water of the river lapped softly against the shore just a foot away. Their rhythm seemed like the rhythm of the whole summer world—a slow, then quickening heaving, then a sharp delight and finally a blissful interlude of peace.

"Oh, that was wonderful," Vivienne whispered, opening her eyes and looking at Philip. He was already looking at her. Their bodies were tangled together.

"We belong to each other," Philip whispered.

She repeated it back to him.

"I'd do anything in the world for you," he said, looking into her dark eyes.

"So would I."

"Would you truly? Would you prove it?"

Vivienne smiled. "Sure. What do you want? Blood?"

"Vivienne, will you marry me?"

She lay perfectly still. She didn't know, thinking about it later, why his request caught her so much by surprise. They had belonged to each other for five years and she had never pictured not belonging to Philip. And yet she had never pictured marriage either.

"We can do it, you know. Lila McCracken and Joe Friend did it, went to Stewburg and got a justice of the peace to marry them in the middle of the night."

"But, Philip!" Vivienne stared at him.

"Listen." Philip pulled his swimming trunks on and sat up. They had been lying on his towel, and he picked it up and wrapped it around her. Then, pulling her close to him, he put his arms around her and kissed her cheek. While she sat leaning against him, he told her for the first time about his mother's plan for him to go to England. If he refused, Philip said, she'd throw him out. The best he could do was work his way through school somewhere, or just work. But if Vivienne wanted to go to England with him and study acting! Maybe, if they were married, his uncle would want them both. Or—and he gave her the other alternatives.

Vivienne stared out at the river. She was stunned to learn that Philip was threatened with exile to England. Her mind could not take in all the choices he presented at first. She didn't know what she wanted to do most—go to England, go to the state university, go to Boston—but one thing was clear to her. If Philip wanted to marry her, if he thought it would solve his problem, she would marry him. After that they'd worry about what came next.

Philip drew back from her, so that he could look at her face as she contemplated the question. He was almost too frightened to breathe. Would she say no? After all, he was asking her to give up her freedom,

111

her education, possibly—maybe even her acting—he really doubted she would do it. In fact, he despaired. He swallowed hard. He mustn't let her see how much her refusal would hurt him.

"Vivienne Alexander," she whispered. "I like it."

"You mean you will?" Philip almost shouted with amazement.

"Of course. How could you think—"

But he smothered her answer in frantic kisses. She was his, his darling; why had he ever doubted her?

Mary Clermont Alexander was anything but stupid; at least, she had grown smart. She had been stupid once, when she let a fanciful romantic poet convince her that the anticipated role of wife of a man of letters would bring fame, moderate wealth, and the respect of her bookish family. What marrying him *had* brought was poverty, disrespect and a rotten grocery store. That plan had failed abominably, but it had taught her to take more trouble with her future schemes.

Since last winter, when one day she had found one of Vivienne's letters from Boston in the mailbox and had taken it to her kettle to steam open, she had known all about Vivienne Dane. The little bitch. Mary couldn't tell from the things Vivienne wrote just how far matters had gone with Philip, but she could guess. There were references to meetings they had, reassurances that she didn't love anyone else—all quite a revelation to Mary. She gritted her teeth with fury, but she had to bear the knowledge alone. She couldn't go accusing Philip or telling Thomas, considering the way she had come by the information. Mary sealed the letter again and gave it to Philip with as good grace as she could muster.

Her hope was that if Philip came up with any fancy plans to avoid England, the girl would have none of them. Getting Vivienne pregnant, marrying her—Mary had to face these possibilities, to judge from Vivienne's letter. There was no mistaking the general tone. But surely Vivienne Dane wouldn't consent to these measures. She had everything to lose and only the stupid lout of a lad to gain; Mary saw Philip now in a harsh light. She thought of her son purely as an annoying pawn to be maneuvered.

Mary watched Philip closely after Vivienne came home; she could tell that the girl was back when the Land's End grocery order was increased. Vivienne must be home eating the extra lamb chops, the bloody bitch who'd turned Philip's head around on his shoulders! Philip was obviously happy, but he was quiet. Subdued. It was strange. He didn't quarrel with Mary when she reserved a ticket to London on a Pan-American flight leaving New York August 7. Charleston had sent her the money for the ticket. Philip said nothing when she told him. Mary had decided to speed up the time of Philip's departure. She would have made him leave for England immediately if it wouldn't have looked funny to her brother.

In mid-July Philip suddenly offered one day to take Champ to a carnival in Eyreville. The same week he insisted that his father rest and let him take over the morning delivery route in addition to his own afternoon rounds. He weeded Mary's garden without being asked. He talked more at dinner. Something had been decided, obviously.

Mary played her trump. She called China Dane on the telephone and asked her to drop by the next Sunday evening. That day, she suggested to Thomas that he take Philip somewhere for once. Why didn't he take Philip bowling? Champ could go along with them and watch. Thomas was astounded, but he agreed. He had never bowled, but Philip said he would teach him how.

While the gutters received Thomas's balls at the Eyreville bowling alley, China climbed the stairs to the Alexanders' rooms over the store, feeling apprehensive. What could Mrs. Alexander want?

Mary welcomed her and gave her a cup of tea. She had thought a good deal about how to proceed. Obviously, she couldn't say she had read Vivienne's letters, but she could tell China of their existence.

China was surprised. They had written to each other that often?

"I think they meet each other when we don't know it," Mary said. "I don't want to alarm you, but I think we must talk about it. When you came to see us last summer, frankly I didn't think there was anything to it. But after Philip received so many letters, I changed my opinion. I don't believe he wants to go to England, and I don't believe he plans to. I think instead he is going to try to make your daughter do something rash."

"Oh, surely not." It was very difficult for China to think in negative terms.

"If they were to run away, say, afterward he might think it would be up to you to support them, to educate him. That's my feeling about it. And needless to say, it's the last thing I want to see. Philip is being a stubborn fool about his prospects in England. I am determined to *make* him do the smart thing."

China was thunderstruck. She had been preoccupied with her invalid mother that summer. Between caring for her and keeping up with Cypriana, her lively toddler, she had not spent a lot of time worrying about Vivienne or monitoring her moods.

"I am so glad you told me," she murmured to Mary, and took her leave.

China mulled the matter over very carefully. She watched Vivienne more closely. The child did go somewhere often in the afternoons, but then she had always taken walks. She loved being out of doors. Still . . . could Mary Alexander be right? Were they meeting each other? Was Philip putting Vivienne under pressure?

A host of unacceptable alternatives occurred to China. Suppose they did run away and marry. Then it would be up to the Danes to do something for them. Bascomb often asked her to economize as it was, and she didn't think he would be pleased to have another to support and educate. But more important, what

114

would happen to Vivienne's bright talent if she became a housewife and perhaps a mother? Her professional life would be over before it started. China was sure Philip was a very superior boy, but young people had no idea of the difficulties that beset one in the world.

China was in a dilemma. Vivienne did seem to be up to something. She hummed cheerfully, she did little kind things for her mother, she read to her grandmother—as if, China mused, she wanted them to store up happy memories of her in their minds.

Other mothers might have had no hesitation about speaking out right away, but China had always felt such trust and faith in Vivienne's ability to know what was right that she was in a quandary. It didn't seem right—it seemed a breach of faith to bring up the possibility that Vivienne had been deceiving her. However, she had to do it. She prepared herself. The night she arbitrarily chose for their discussion was, in fact, the last night possible for it. Vivienne was planning to meet Philip later that evening, down by the river. They were going to take the truck from the store and drive to Stewburg to find a justice of the peace. It was all planned, and Vivienne was tremendously excited. She had decided to wear her favorite pink cotton dress and her best strap sandals. They were laid out in her room. She was coming out of her bath when China called her.

"Come to my room for a minute, dear," she said.

Vivienne, who always heeded her mother's gentle requests, went into her mother's bedroom and flopped into the middle of the comfortable king-sized bed. She had washed her hair that afternoon, and it hung straight and shining, a few tendrils curling a little around her face from the steam of the tub.

It was a hot night; Vivienne was wearing a thin white robe embroidered in blue, and she looked especially pretty and vivacious for some reason, China thought.

"Vivienne, have you been seeing Philip Alexander?"

Sitting down in her favorite wicker armchair, China asked the question softly.

Vivienne looked confused. She blushed.

"Well, once in a while," she said, "I see him." What was this, she wondered. China had never in her life questioned either her daughter's motives or her actions.

"Dear, we must talk a little bit. Philip's mother told me you wrote to him last year."

"Well, yes, after *Romeo and Juliet* we were close friends and he—he wanted to know what college was like."

"Do you know his plans for college?"

Vivienne was silent for a moment. She moved uneasily on the soft bed. "Well—Philip wants to go to the state university, I know. And his mother—doesn't she want him to go to England?"

"Yes. Vivienne, I must be frank. The Alexanders think that Philip doesn't want to go to England and that he"—China paused. This was hard for her. She put it as delicately as possible—"may be trying to get you to help him avoid it."

"What do you mean?"

China blushed.

"If anything happened . . . oh, say, you got married or you—had to get married, the Alexanders think we would be forced to take on Philip and educate him, to support you both since they cannot. Vivienne, your father couldn't—I don't know what he would do in that case. It would hurt us so much, if you were to be so rash. I'm probably saying too much. But I love you, dear."

Vivienne was stunned. Her mother had actually guessed what they were planning! And from what she said, the Alexanders had guessed, too.

"You know, you can't always be sure about people," China went on. "Philip might be hanging onto you just so he can avoid going to England. It's easy to say things about love and all. But it's what you do that counts. If Philip really does care for you, Vivienne, he'll want you to have your chance in life, to try acting, to finish your education at Radcliffe. If Philip really cares for you, he'll wait for you, won't he? A few years don't make that much difference. It would be selfish to make you give everything up. You've done so well! You've had parts in four plays already, and your grades are excellent; we are so proud of you. It could be the best time of your life. I don't want you to—ruin it."

Her mother so seldom put a bad construction on anyone's motives that her words had great force with Vivienne. What her mother said made sense in a way. She was giving up a lot, and Philip nothing. But still, if he needed her . . . !

"Mother, *would* Daddy help educate Philip?"

China sighed. "Dear. There's you, and Mab, and your little sister to send to college one day. There's your grandmother and the nurses she needs—your father has a lot of expenses. I don't believe we could afford it. I am so sorry. We'd like to do everything we can for people. But it sounds as if Philip has a fine offer of his own. Why doesn't he want to go to England?"

"Oh, Mother, it's because of me." Vivienne threw away all pretense of not being in the situation China hinted at. To tell the truth, marriage was a big step and she had wished she could talk to someone about it. And her mother was always so sweet to her; she felt really unhappy about deceiving her.

"What do you mean, it's you?" China asked, looking closely at Vivienne.

"Philip thinks I'll find someone else in college. He is very jealous."

China shook her head. "That's not a good reason," she said. "Philip should trust you if he loves you. If he goes to England and you go back to Boston and you *do* meet other people you like better, then it will be a mercy you didn't marry him. And if you don't change your mind, if you find that you love each other best, then you can always get married after Philip is out of college."

Vivienne had to agree that her mother's words made sense. She hadn't thought of matters that way.

China saw Vivienne looking thoughtful and followed up her advantage.

"I can't see any other reason for Philip's urging you to do something right now, except that he doesn't want to go to England. And if that's so, he's just using you. I hate to say it. But it—might be true."

China stood up, went to Vivienne and touched her on the arm.

"Think about it, darling. You have such promise. You know, in our world, we think of women as—well, as wives and mothers. We think that's their best fate. And yet, when a girl has a chance to see what she can do on her own, without a man choosing her life for her—sometimes I wonder what would have happened to me or your grandmother if . . . You know, your grandmother played the piano so beautifully. She had an offer for a concert tour in her youth and your great-grandfather Royal had a fit. He forbade her. Women didn't belong on the stage, he said. Your grandmother never got over it." China had lowered her voice as if her mother in the next room could hear her. "Everything is different now, and women can do these things. I'd think hard before I'd throw away the chance."

Vivienne nodded. Leaving her mother, she went into her room where the pink dress lay spread out on her bed. She stared at it. She was shaken. What if her mother were right? What if Philip were using her?

She had to see him, she thought. She had to see Philip, to ask him, and then she'd know. Quickly she put on some lipstick and pulled on the pink dress. When she left her bedroom, she saw her mother across the hall sitting beside her grandmother, reading a book aloud. Vivienne went to the open bedroom door. Propped up on silk pillows, her grandmother Elizabeth smiled at her. She was still a handsome woman; people thought Vivienne looked like her. Drawn close to the bedside light, China was a picture of quiet calm. Vivienne knew her mother trusted her to make up her own mind. China looked up and smiled, too, pausing at the end of the sentence she was reading.

"I'll be out for a while," Vivienne said.

"Have a good time, dear." Her mother never demanded to know where she was going.

Vivienne hurried out of the back door and started across the field toward the river. Earlier that day she had left her pocketbook at the rowan tree. She hadn't been able to figure out a way to smuggle out a suitcase, and she had ended by deciding simply to spend her wedding night naked and wear the pink dress until they came back. If they came back. If they went away at all. She had left no note with Nancy Browning, Ella's daughter, as she had planned to do; Vivienne was supposed to pay the girl to give the note to her mother first thing in the morning, before she was missed. But Vivienne had not written a note. Her palms felt sweaty and she dried them on her skirt. What would Philip say? She wished she didn't have to find out.

The night was hot and overcast; Vivienne panted as she ran across the end of the field. When she came to the path she stopped and looked back, wishing it were less dark. Heat lightning flickered around the horizon on the other side of the road, and she could just barely make out the white pillars of Land's End and the dark shapes of the barn and the cookhouse.

Vivienne felt her way along the path cautiously. In a moment Philip was beside her.

"Darling," he said, pulling her to him. His arms locked around her and he gave her a long kiss. "I was almost afraid you weren't coming. Let's go get the truck. Did you leave the note?"

"Philip, wait. I want to talk to you. Let's go down to the rock a minute."

"What is it?" Philip was immediately anxious. He followed her down to the river's edge, and she drew him beside her onto the rock. The river smelled dank in the darkness as it moved sluggishly past them.

119

Vivienne took Philip's hands in hers.

"Philip, your parents and my parents both know about us."

"What?"

"I found out tonight. Your parents talked to Mother. They told her they think you are really determined not to go to England, and that you might get me into trouble or we might run away just so you wouldn't have to go."

"My God." Philip struggled to see Vivienne's face in the darkness. "How could my parents possibly say such things to your mother?"

"They told Mother about my letters to you. And Mother thinks that—that if we ran away, you'd just be using me."

Philip seized her shoulders.

"Vivienne, you don't believe that!"

"I don't know what to believe—I mean—"

"My God. How could you think for a second that I would take advantage of you? You know me. You know how much I love you. I thought you *wanted* to marry me."

Suddenly Vivienne wanted to cry. Her throat felt tight.

"Philip, Mother said Daddy couldn't help us financially, if we ran away—she doesn't think he would. So if you were thinking of that, it wouldn't work."

He was still holding her and he shook her.

"Vivienne, this is me, Philip! What are you talking about? I'm not thinking about the Dane money. I'll take care of you. Sweetheart." He pulled her close to him, stroking her hair and trying to see her dark eyes. "It will be all right." Philip felt dazed. Waiting there, he had pictured their wedding and their happiness, he had been full of excitement and hope. Suddenly it seemed as if Vivienne were betraying them.

"You didn't tell your mother anything?" he said.

"Not about tonight. But she wants us . . . she thinks you should be educated at Cambridge and then we

120

could be married." Vivienne touched Philip's face, wishing she could see his expression. "She doesn't see why we couldn't do it that way."

"Your mother! What does she know about anything? Vivienne, I can't live without you. Not one year, not *four*. Let's go now, just as we planned. If they already know, it will be less of a shock."

"Oh, Philip, how could I? I mean, I just talked to Mother." Vivienne began to cry. She was miserable. "I really think we should wait. We can still—"

"You won't go?" Philip spoke in a low, tense voice. He had taken his hands away from her; he wasn't touching her.

"Not tonight. Let's talk, let's—"

"Don't do this, Vivienne. Don't do this to us. Don't let other people run our lives."

"But there are other people in the world! Other considerations. And if you love me—"

"You think I don't?" Philip sounded furious.

"I don't know. You don't seem very loving, if all you can think of is running to Stewburg and getting married." Tears fell down Vivienne's cheeks.

"Listen to me. Vivienne, if you won't go with me, you don't love me."

"Yes I do! Why do you have to be so determined? Why is there only one way—your way? If nothing but marriage contents you, maybe you are using me."

"Don't." He put his face in his hands and his single word came out like a moan.

"Philip, what else can I think?"

He would have prevented it if he could have, but all the resentments, the suspicions and the jealousies of the last year rushed into his mind, and he almost burst with rage. He accused Vivienne of liking someone else, someone in Boston.

"You have somebody there, don't you?" He seized her and his grip hurt.

"No, don't be stupid. Let me go."

"You have someone, admit it." Vivienne couldn't

believe it when she heard him say, "I'm just your summer fuck. You've got someone in Boston! You want to go back to him!"

"No," she screamed. "Let me go!"

But he didn't let her go. There, on the rock, he pushed her back, calling her a bitch, saying that he'd have what he wanted before someone else got her. Vivienne had always wondered what Philip would be like if he got completely carried away some time. He was usually very tender, unless she made him jealous, which she sometimes had in the past, just a little, to add spice to things. But then he was merely sulky. Now she found out to her sorrow what jealousy could do to him. She struggled frantically, scratching his face and his back, but he forced her legs open and pushed himself into her as if he didn't even feel her blows, and it was the most frightening experience she had ever had. If he had been a complete stranger, it couldn't have been worse. He took her savagely and when he was finished, pushed her down contemptuously. She lay humiliated, and he stood over her.

"I hate you," he said, panting hard. "I never want to see you again. I'm nothing to you, nothing beside the Dane name and the Dane money! And your bloody stupid mother, and your stupid career and all the rest. You let me think you'd marry me just to see me suffer, just to amuse yourself this summer. Well, God damn you to hell, Vivienne Dane! Nothing on earth could have torn us apart, but *you* did it, you killed it. I hope you're satisfied."

He turned and ran, sobbing, his heart so full of fury that he thought it would explode. Blind with rage and sorrow, he crashed into a tree and stumbled on, uncaring.

Vivienne lay still and wept. She was in physical pain and she was bewildered. This couldn't happen. You thought you had something unbreakable and then you found out it could break all the same. She would never see Philip again. She never wanted to. He had insulted her and half-killed her and had proved that he just wanted to use her as a way out of going to England. She cried so hard she almost choked on her tears.

When she finally crept back over the field after midnight, heat lightning still flickered on the horizon. The house was dark except for lights left on for her, on the front porch and in the front hall. She pulled herself up the stairs and crawled into her bed. She couldn't sleep and she listened to Mab in the next bed breathing regularly. Vivienne was in terrible pain. It didn't seem possible that it had happened to her. So many people warned you that the world was not a good place; why didn't you ever believe them? Why did you have to find out they were right? Her tears fell into her pillow.

Philip went up the stairs of his house two at a time. His mother and father were just getting up from their chairs to go to bed, and they paused in amazement as Philip came through the door. His cheeks were scratched, his shirt tail hanging out, his forehead bruised, and he had a set, grim look on his face.

"Did you have a fight?" Thomas asked, thinking that Philip looked as if he had gotten the worst of it.

Philip slammed the screen door behind him.

"No. Yes. I want to know one thing. I want to know why you felt you had any right to go to China Dale and tell her that Vivienne wrote to me." He stood with his back to the door and spoke each word with cold intensity. His eyes glittered in his battered face.

"Why, son, we didn't," Thomas said, taken aback.

Philip looked at his mother.

"*She* did, then," he said. "What business was it of yours? How did you dare?"

"You're not to talk to me like that, young man! Not under my roof."

Philip didn't move. He gave his mother a long look of cold hatred. It traveled through the air between them. He spoke very slowly and distinctly.

123

"You meddling idiot. I don't want to live under your roof. I don't ever want to see you again." His tone was low and menacing. "I can't go to England fast enough. You'll get your way, all right. You just don't have a son, that's all. Not after tonight."

"Philip, don't speak that way!" Thomas's face twisted with distress. Philip turned to look at him; oddly, it was a look of sympathy. Philip stood there as if he might say something more, but then he turned and walked into his bedroom and shut the door.

"I knew he'd see the light," Mary said. She didn't sound triumphant, but she sounded satisfied.

"What did you do?" Thomas asked, puzzled. "You talked to China Dane?"

Mary sniffed. "China Dane knows how to look after her daughter without me," she said. "Come to bed. This will all blow over in the morning. And Philip said he'll go to England!"

The victory she had gained really seemed worth any temporary loss of family peace. Like a general striding briskly past his own dying troops to collect the foe's sword and offer the glass of Madeira, Mary had won the day and knew you never won without losing, too.

Thomas was just confused.

The next day, he watched a silent Philip present himself for work, and he shook his head. "What is it?" Thomas asked. "What is it, Philip?"

Philip simply asked him some questions about the route. Well, Thomas thought, if Philip didn't want to talk about his troubles, he couldn't force him to. The silence lasted five more days, and on the sixth, Philip left. At the airport in Columbia, Mary tiptoed up and kissed his cheek, but his expression never changed. He looked like—what? Thomas thought. What did Philip remind him of? Of an Englishman, that was what. Cool, reserved, his thoughts his own, no emotion showing.

Thomas shook his son's hand heartily and wished him good luck with all his heart. Maybe this was the best thing. Unless one was Huntington Hartford, the grocery business would no longer sustain anyone who wanted to do more than write poetry.

Of Philip's good-byes, only his farewell to Champ had warmth in it. Philip had given his little brother his football a few days before, and now he hugged him and promised to return someday to watch him make a touchdown in the Alexander style.

Then he was gone.

At Land's End, Vivienne repaired the damages of that terrible night before she faced anyone the next day. She threw the pink dress away and worked on her face with cold water for half an hour. By the time she came down for breakfast, everyone else had finished, and by lunchtime her swollen eyelids had subsided a bit. No one seemed to notice anything; her grandmother had taken a turn for the worse and her mother was distracted.

As the days went on, China did notice that Vivienne was dragging around Land's End morosely, and she wondered if their talk had fomented some sort of crisis with Philip. When Miss Beltane telephoned one day, China was happy to hear that she was in town visiting Wallace Hastings. She quickly invited Miss Beltane out to dinner.

It disturbed Miss Beltane to find Vivienne so quiet. Philip had gone to England, she'd heard in town. Perhaps Vivienne missed him? Better not ask. Instead, she inquired about Vivienne's acting and was glad to get a complete report.

China excused herself after the three of them had some sherry in the library, waiting for Bascomb to return from town. China said she wanted to check on her mother. Actually, she wanted to leave them alone together. She hoped Miss Beltane could help Vivienne.

As it turned out, Miss Beltane could. The very sight of her tripping up the path wearing an outlandish flowered chiffon dress and a black picture hat had

125

brought a smile to Vivienne's lips. Now Miss Beltane drained her glass and inquired about the methods used in Vivienne's acting classes. They were a hodgepodge, Vivienne said; one teacher was devoted to classical English methods and another espoused the Actors' Studio ideas.

"What I tell *my* actors is simple,". Miss Beltane said. "I tell them how lucky we in the theater are. We can look on life differently from other people. Whatever *we* experience, good or bad, goes into our storehouse. We draw on what's there for our art. Do you know what I mean? *All* experiences are good for us, because all are useful. If we suffer, then we can portray suffering the better on the stage." Miss Beltane's pinktipped fingers swept through the air. "What poet said, 'All experience is an arch, wherethrough we pass'? I don't remember—I was *never* a very good English teacher—but I love the thought. We should go through life as if we are passing under crossed swords at some grand affair. *Laughing*, you know?"

"Will that really work?" Vivienne asked. "Thinking of everything as just usable material?"

"Of course," Miss Beltane said. "Otherwise you'd go mad in this world, darling—so would any sensitive person."

Miss Beltane paused and then changed the subject. She described how a trapdoor had accidentally opened one night in Atlanta, underneath a young actor playing Stanley Kowalski, just as he prepared to rape Blanche in *A Streetcar Named Desire*. In mid-attack, Kowalski had disappeared into a hole in the floor.

"The audience was hysterical. *Fortunately* there was matting below, but the poor boy was ruined for a week. After that night, whenever he was supposed to rush around the stage, he'd step about so gingerly it looked as if there were tacks on the floor—he was Stanley Kowalski in a field of land mines! I cured him at last by telling him if he kept it up, the only role he could qualify for would be Peter Pan."

126

Vivienne laughed heartily. "And what did that experience give him?" she asked.

"Oh, my dear, a respect for the unexpected. We may all fall into holes before we're done, even sometimes in the midst of our best scenes—ah, Mr. Dane!" Miss Beltane rose and greeted Bascomb with theatrical aplomb, and their tête-à-tête ended as they joined the others in the dining room.

Vivienne felt better at the end of the evening; just to hear all the theater talk was bracing. She began to be eager to go back to Boston, and she promised Miss Beltane to write her all about her roles.

In the months and years that followed, in her meditations, Vivienne managed to split Philip into two people. There was the boy who was her lover. And there was the one who went to England. Whenever she had to play a scene of passion, she thought of the first, her Philip. She never thought of the actual Philip at all, unless she was forced to. Sometimes when she was back in Eyreville, people told her news about Philip Alexander, supposing that since he had been Romeo to her Juliet, she would be interested in hearing that he had done well at Cambridge, that he was in his uncle's firm now, that he had bought a house near Crosstree for his parents, that he this or that he that. Vivienne wasn't interested in that Philip. No, but the other one, the Philip in her soul, how often she had called on him to supply her passion onstage. Miss Beltane was right. He was her material; out of him she made Cleopatra and Antigone and Ophelia, Sarah Nassau and Eustacia Vye, and the doctor's wife at the train station in *Turn of River*, for which she won the Academy Award.

V

Twenty years.

She should be able to look back, Vivienne thought, with a different perspective. They said time did that for you. Was their fight perhaps merely that common thing, a lovers' quarrel? Would it have blown over in a week or two if Philip hadn't left before his anger cooled? She thought not. If he gambled now, certainly that fit in with the obsessiveness Philip often had demonstrated as a youth . . . and his anger—perhaps that had never cooled. Had he wanted the real Vivienne at all, with her imperfections? Or was there a real Vivienne?

Her thoughts seemed to spin without direction. She could summon up *her* Philip at will; she had almost never, until today, let herself remember what happened when they parted, or think of the Philip who lived in England. It was all so—useless.

She didn't know how long she had been lying motionless in the steam room chair. Twice someone had tiptoed past; probably the attendant checking on her. Vivienne stirred under the wrappings, and in a moment the girl was beside her.

"Oh, Miss Dane, I'm sorry," the girl whispered as Vivienne sat up. "Your cotton pads were too wet." Water had run in rivulets all over Vivienne's temples and down the sides of her cheeks.

"That's all right," Vivienne said.

The girl unwrapped her, and Vivienne dabbed her face dry with one end of a sheet. She did not feel very rested. The attendant led her into the scrub room, and she lay on a long marble bench while a heavyset woman wetted her down, massaged her body with castile soap and then went over her using a hand spray attachment. Vivienne felt every muscle relax under the warm water.

"Would you like to be gunned?" In the usual finale of the ritual, you stood naked at the end of a long narrow room while streams of cold water were shot over you. Vivienne decided to skip it. She'd had enough shocks for one day. She let them shampoo her and dry her hair with heat lamps and give her a minimum makeup. Several women who heard she was in the salon approached her to sign autographs for them as she waited in the reception room for her car.

At her apartment, the doorman told her a basket of roses had just been delivered. They were waiting by her door. The note with them was from Tom Clancy, asking if she'd have dinner with him at nine.

Vivienne let herself in and looked at the clock. It was eight-thirty already; well, why not eat with Clance? She could throw on something quickly and be ready when he arrived. She would call Mab first and tell her Cypriana's plan for a house party at Land's End. She went into her bedroom and dialed Mab's apartment in Chicago, but Mab didn't answer. Her service picked up on the call. Vivienne left word for Mab to call her back, no matter how late it was, that night. Mab hadn't told the service where she'd be or when she'd be back in. But Mab never stayed out late.

Vivienne pulled on a black satin shirtwaist dress and added a rope of tiny diamonds. Well, there she was, she thought, looking not half-bad. Keep the old chin up, you there in the mirror; I'll bet Philip looks worse than you do.

Suddenly, insanely, Vivienne giggled. What *would* Philip look like? And what would he do when he had to say hello to his hostess at Land's End?

Clancy was delighted to find Vivienne smiling when she opened the door to him. It wasn't a really joyful smile, but it was sweet; she was making an effort. God, he loved her.

VI

A monstrous red squirrel confronted Mab Dane.

Seven feet high, it was spread across the entire far wall of the middle gallery at Bendeli's showrooms. Its beady eyes watchfully observed her as she approached. The waving plumy tail, curving ears, delicate paws and enormous body were all perfectly lifelike. Painted on a green background, it almost seemed to breathe.

On the opposite wall behind Mab, a giant six-foot-long black ant was frozen in mid-crawl against a fire-red background. Each jointed round section of its body gleamed like jet.

Mab glanced over her shoulder at the ant, and then back at the squirrel. Her face betrayed nothing of what she was thinking.

Carson Koppit, the painter whose squirrel and ant Mab was viewing, lounged in the gallery door holding a glass of champagne tightly in his hand, watching her. Carson was wearing tight blue jeans and a black tee shirt; his thin body was taut, in contrast to his casual pose. A curl of black hair had fallen over his forehead, and underneath it his brow was sweating despite the air-conditioned cool of the rooms. His palms felt damp.

It was Carson's first showing. He had no practice in the art of seeming unmoved when people looked at his work, especially those persons who could change his entire world with one word. His head cocked on his rigid neck, he clutched the glass to his chest, spilling some champagne on his shirt without noticing it. He was busy cursing the fact that his success or failure was

131

currently dependent on a woman he had loved. *Had* loved? Still loved. Mab Dane had stopped seeing him six months ago. Was it because she had known that the moment was coming when she would have to judge him as an artist?

The art critic of the Chicago *Tribune,* the gallery owner Mr. Bendeli, and Carson's friends and relatives respectfully waited in the room behind him; they moved about, talking in low voices, drinking champagne and looking at the enormous mosquitoes and the large purple finch that occupied the walls there. None of them would venture past Carson into the room with Mab or cross to the third room beyond, where Arthur Windsor stood alone, observing an eight-foot-long timber wolf. In the room with the wolf was Carson's first animal work, a raccoon made of various-colored jelly beans put together to form a mosaic.

When Mab Dane and Arthur Windsor turned up at a gallery or studio, there was inevitably a magic circle of silence and respect around them. Windsor was the director of the Concordia Museum of Modern Art in Chicago. A word of praise from him would be highly encouraging to any young artist. But the real power to make reputations lay with Mab Dane. She was senior curator of painting and sculpture for the Concordia, and she alone decided what the public would see there as the current height of modern art.

For someone so young and beautiful as Mab to wield such influence seemed incredible to Carson. When he'd come to Chicago the year before, a friend at the Art Institute had pointed Mab out to him, telling him how important she was. Mab had been walking around a Matisse exhibit, and Carson and his friend had surreptitiously followed her for half an hour. Carson was stunned. He had never seen such a beautiful woman. The proportions of Mab's body were perfect. She had a small head, a long neck, long perfect arms and legs, and a small-waisted torso. The balance with which she

132

stood, like the grace with which she moved, made her body seem an art work in itself.

His friend enjoyed Carson's reaction to Mab. "She's a legend around here," he said.

Mab Dane and Arthur Windsor had come to Chicago together, after leaving the prestigious Lauvray Museum of Contemporary Art in New York, founded by Mrs. Remington Lauvray. The Lauvray Museum was elegant but tiny. The Concordia was large, with plenty of exhibition space, but its reputation at that time was small. It was known for its boring shows. Its board of trustees felt certain that the renowned Arthur Windsor could change the Concordia's image, but when he arrived with a beautiful young lady and announced she would be senior curator, great speculation arose. Mab's advent was initially greeted with skepticism, even by people who knew the simple truth, that the gift of taste is given to a rare few without regard to their sex or appearance, creed or nationality, and a beautiful girl might very well possess that unique ability. It just seemed unlikely that such a talent should be matched by such physical loveliness.

But the two did match. Arthur Windsor always knew what he was doing. Thanks to Mab's eye, within a few years the Concordia had launched the careers of five artists currently internationally recognized. Except for the museums in New York, the Concordia was now considered to have the finest modern art collection in the country. Large crowds thronged daily through the special exhibitions and permanent displays. The public was always amused and intrigued by what Mab selected to show.

Carson, scarcely able to breathe, tried to take his mind off the decision she was making and studied Mab instead. She was wearing a long flesh-colored chiffon dress, which was wrapped in a way that left one lovely shoulder bare. Her chestnut-brown hair was twisted into a simple knot at the back of her head. Mab never wore jewelry. Her slender neck was bare, her ears unadorned; the lack of distraction let one notice all the more her tilted-up brown eyes and the way all her features and parts fit together. Carson had begged Mab to pose naked for him, but she had laughed and refused. Secretly he had made some sketches of her while she was sleeping. Looking at her now, he thought, I don't care what you say about my work, Mab. Just say yes to me again.

Arthur Windsor appeared in the opposite doorway. His white hair was carefully groomed, and he was meticulously dressed in an immaculate tuxedo. His face was impassive. He paced into the room, his footsteps sounding loud in the silence. He looked at the ant. Mab still peered at the squirrel. After a few minutes they traded places without a word or look at one another. She looked at the ant and he looked at the squirrel.

Mab knew what Arthur was thinking. They almost always thought alike. Years ago in New York they would converge on the same works, at museums and galleries and artists' studios. They'd look up and see each other, struck by the same painting or sculpture. At first it was a joke. Arthur Windsor enjoyed finding pretty Mab Dane standing beside the very piece he had previously decided was the best in the place. Looking at her was an esthetic experience in itself. But deeper than that, Arthur was thrilled to find another person whose standards so closely conformed to his own. Mab was just an assistant's assistant at the Whitney Museum then. Arthur inquired about her. Eventually he gave her a position assisting him at the Lauvray, which he had single-handedly built up to its present eminence. With him tutoring her, Mab developed sound values. He had no hesitation about bringing her with him to the Concordia. And he certainly had been justified in placing his faith in her.

As Arthur pondered the squirrel, Mab glanced at Carson Koppit. He was staring at her with his gray eyes wide, and she scolded herself. When would she

134

learn? She had been stupid to get involved with him. She sighed.

Arthur cleared his throat and turned around. Carson straightened up with the expression of the accused about to hear the verdict. Mab felt sorry for him. If Arthur and she indicated approval, asked Carson to send a painting to the Concordia for further inspection, the word would be out in twenty-four hours, and he would become a rising young artist. If they simply thanked him and walked out, he would feel rejected, feel he had lost. Yet he was so young that it was nonsense to think this was a serious crisis in his life. Her judgment was made. His work was good, but it lacked the certain quality that made work special, made it something for the Concordia.

Arthur took her arm.

"Are you ready to go?" he asked softly.

She nodded and they walked together up to Carson, who stood rigid as if expecting a bullet from a firing squad.

"Thank you for letting us see your work. We'll keep our eye on you," Arthur said graciously. He shook Carson's hand. Mab hoped this was a sufficient good-bye for both of them. She would have walked away with only a smile, but Carson seized her hand. They had to move from the door; people were starting to go into the next room. A distinguished-looking dowager bore down on Arthur for a word, and Carson took the opportunity to speak alone to Mab.

"I have to see you," he said into her ear. "Not to try to influence you. I wish you'd understand." He looked around for Arthur.

"Please, Carson," she said.

"I'll be over tonight," he said in a low voice.

"Don't. I won't be home."

"I'll wait for you."

Mab was exasperated. Arthur moved back and took her arm. They made their way out, their stately progress observed by most of the people in the room. Mab

135

wished their exit could be faster. Finally, they reached the front door and the street. The warm June air outside was a pleasant contrast to the chilled galleries.

A limousine waited at the curb to take them to a dinner party at the home of one of the museum's trustees, Mrs. Cooper Truesdale. They had stopped to see Carson's opening on the way to Mrs. Truesdale's North Shore mansion.

"The best piece was the raccoon," Arthur said as their car joined traffic on The Loop.

Mab frowned slightly, looking out the window and away from Arthur. She could remember the day Carson showed her the bags of jelly beans he had just bought. She remembered laughing at him. The very moment he started gluing the beans onto the canvas, she had been kissing his neck. Mab was glad that Arthur for once had no idea of what was in her mind.

"In a few more years he might—" She let the words trail off.

Arthur turned to her with a fond expression on his face. "You're looking radiant tonight, my dear." Then he sighed. "I do hope Mrs. Truesdale's nephew who paints won't be among the dinner guests. Didn't you have a hard time fending him off last time?"

Mab smiled. "Yes. I remember. He told me, 'I only paint the sky!' Just like that—very dramatic. I told him to send me some slides. He paints the sky all right, but only on totally overcast or totally clear days. All the paintings were squares of either blue or gray. Rather nice, perhaps, hung all together, like a chessboard. But not for us."

Arthur chuckled. They chatted together comfortably. They shared so many passions that they were never without a topic. The excitement of being part of the world of current art, as it was being produced, keenly affected both of them. As for older works, they were jointly addicts of seventeenth century Dutch paintings, of Michelangelo's drawings, of anything at all painted by Turner, of Flemish tapestry and eighteenth century

English furniture, and dozens of other irresistible eras and areas. Arthur was unmarried; he lived alone; his beautiful personal art collection kept him company and provided all the love-objects he needed. He adored Mab Dane as he adored the finest of his acquisitions; he guided her and was awed by her simultaneously. They had spent ten years together happily in search of visual thrills. It was an ideal relationship.

The limousine turned in through iron gates and took them up the drive to the Stanford White-style Truesdale mansion. When they joined Mrs. Truesdale's guests they did not find the sky-painting nephew, but instead a Truesdale son-in-law who was a Zen Buddhist and who wanted to discuss "the eternal moment in art" with Mab. He cut her out from the dozen or so other people in the living room and kept her listening to his theories all during cocktails.

"The impressionists recognized the truth, that reality is a crutch," he said, fixing Mab with his intense protruding blue eyes. "Now, we have photorealism, superrealism, the ultimate expression of fantasy, don't you agree? America itself is Lewis Carroll's Wonderland—an abstraction by Picasso viewed from above, a painting by Hopper at eye level, and from below, the perfect Jackson Pollock—the underside of a kitchen floor painted by a madman."

He paused to draw breath, but Mab could think of nothing to say. Experts at dinner parties frequently tried to impress her and usually only baffled her. In this instance she was spared by the company's being called in to their hostess's Queen Anne dining room, where Mab was not seated next to the son-in-law, although he kept trying to catch her eye and say something from his place down the table.

Six excellent courses were served. The man on Mab's right, a banker, simply ate steadily through them. The man on her left lectured her on the Fauvist school of painting and tried to press his knee against hers.

137

Fortunately, because Arthur wanted to leave early, Mab was spared any further talk after dinner. Arthur told Mrs. Truesdale some tale to cover their early departure, and their car was brought to the door.

"An excellent mousse," Arthur said as they passed the gates. "Mrs. Truesdale's son-in-law, the one who spoke to you so long, came up to me afterward and offered us a gift of fifty thousand dollars. Whatever did you say to him?"

"Good heavens. Nothing. He must be a rich Zen Buddhist."

"Something has turned him into an art lover." Arthur smiled at her. "He muttered about an exhibition of art as the eternal moment. I leave you to cope with that, my dear."

"For fifty thousand, I can think of something."

They discussed a jeweled Maltese cross that Arthur was trying to obtain for his collection. Both had fallen quiet by the time the car drew up to The Towers, the apartment building overlooking Lake Michigan where Mab lived. Arthur escorted her to the door of the modern, glass-sided lobby, and said good night. Mab was relieved when she reached the tenth floor and her apartment door with no glimpse of Carson. She had worried, on the way home, that he might actually be waiting there.

Mischa, her poodle, heard her footsteps coming down the hall and barked joyfully as she unlocked the door.

Her apartment was small. The excellent view of the lake from double windows in both the living room and the bedroom made it seem larger than it was. Mab had furnished it with great care. There were landscape paintings on the wall; the living room held authentic Hepplewhite cabinets and chairs, and under the window was an excellent copy of the peacock-feather Hepplewhite sofa on display at the Metropolitan Museum. The parquet floor was covered by an elegant Oriental rug, one corner of which Mischa had sampled. Curled on the green and yellow striped satin of the sofa's cushion, Mab's Himalayan cat Rudi looked up, a defiant gleam in his round blue eyes. Mab swooped him up and hugged him.

"You rascal," she said, putting the cat in his basket, which had a satin cushion of its own.

Mischa whined by the door, waiting to be walked, so Mab snapped on his lead and took him downstairs in the elevator. At night she never ventured out of the circle of light cast by the lobby; she walked Mischa up and down at the curb until he was ready to go upstairs again. As she turned to walk inside, Carson Koppit suddenly stepped under the awning.

"Mab?"

"Carson, I asked you not to come."

Carson appeared to have drunk too much champagne to care what she said.

"I've got to talk to you, Mab," he said. "Don't you see? Your decision is made, now. You don't have to feel that I'm trying to influence you any longer. Won't you let me come up?"

Mab flushed in embarrassment. The doorman could overhear Carson. She might as well have it out with him in private.

"Come on up then," she said. "But just for a minute."

As they rode up in the elevator, Carson slumped against one wall, his eyes on her face. He followed her down the hall as she opened the apartment door and unsnapped Mischa's leash. The poodle ran off to his water dish. Closing the door slowly, Mab turned to face Carson.

"What do—"

Before she could get out a sentence, Carson pulled her into his arms. "Let me hold you, Mab. Please."

She tried to withdraw from the embrace. She didn't want to hurt Carson's feelings, but she was determined not to start anything with him again.

Carson didn't seem to feel her reluctance, her stiffness. He kissed her for a long time, turning his mouth

139

against hers, parting her lips. Finally she was less stiff. Sometimes, especially on balmy June nights, she did get an ache in her throat, a wish that she had someone to make love to.

But she remembered her resolve and pulled her head back.

"I thought you wanted to *talk* to me," she said. "How—how did your show go?"

"The people who count didn't like it."

He kissed her hair and her temple, and his lips slid down to her earlobe.

"You don't think that I care about the show?" he murmured into her ear. "I tried to tell you before, Mab. I love you. I'd never try to use you. I know I couldn't. I know what you are, Mab."

He put his mouth over the pulse at the base of her throat. Over his shoulder Mab could see Rudi, again installed on the sofa. The cat's round blue eyes stared unblinkingly at them.

"Please, Mab," Carson said against her skin. He slid the chiffon off her left shoulder and kissed the hollow of her collarbone. "I would have begged you before now. But I waited until after the show, so you'd believe I wasn't trying to use you." He shook her slightly. "Dammit, it's true."

She began to tremble, and he pressed his body closer to hers. He managed to pull the top of her dress completely down, and he kissed her breasts.

"Let me stay," he whispered.

She stroked his dark hair with her hand.

"Carson, I will, if you'll promise me something," she said softly.

"Anything."

"Will you leave afterward? Right away?"

With his lips still pressed to her right breast he bent down, put one arm under her legs and lifted her up.

"Carson?"

"I'll do whatever you like," he said, as he carried her into the bedroom.

140

He began unzipping her dress immediately. After that she couldn't get any further commitment out of him. He made violent love to her and she almost had an orgasm. She pretended she had.

Carson lay beside her, gasping; a few minutes later, he got his breath back and turned his head to kiss her, but she got up and walked over to the closet. Taking out a negligee, she wrapped it around herself, then she picked up his pants and shirt from the floor and handed them to him. He looked at her with surprise.

"You want me to go now?"

She nodded.

Carson frowned, but he got up and pulled on his clothes. When he was dressed, he turned to her with an anxious expression on his face and said, "Will you call me, Mab?"

She smiled but started for the door; he followed her.

"Hey." Catching her by the arm in the living room, he asked, "You're not mad?"

"No, of course not. But let's go easy, okay? Not push it?" She led him to the front door.

"I don't understand you." Carson caught her hand as she reached up to undo the chain lock. He looked at her hand for a moment, turned it over and kissed the inside of her wrist. When he let go, she opened the door.

"Good night," she said.

Carson said nothing. He turned and walked to the elevator.

When she closed the door, she felt relieved. It was stupid to get involved with Carson, she repeated to herself. She should live like a nun, live the way Arthur did, a life devoted solely to art. Why did she let talk about sexual freedom touch her, make her go in for these experiments that were always disastrous?

The thought made Mab want a drink. She locked the door and walked into the kitchen. Rudi's Friskies bowl on the counter was empty and she filled it. She tried opening the refrigerator door softly, but Mischa

141

heard it anyway and capered into the kitchen. As she took out a bottle of white Burgundy, Mischa nosed her, and she decided to give him a treat. She opened a can of sardines for him and, watching him gobble them down, pulled the cork from the wine bottle.

Mab selected a goblet from the cabinet, carried it and the bottle back into the living room and sat down next to Rudi. Feeling rather strung out, she poured a glass of wine and drank it quickly. She would sit up until she felt sleepy—maybe some music would help . . . if she had enough energy to walk over and turn on the stereo. She sighed. Postcoital depression. Wasn't it men who were supposed to suffer from that?

Carson had pulled her hair down. She removed the last pins and shook it out over her shoulders. Rudi climbed into her lap and curled up, purring. In a flash, Mischa jumped onto the sofa and took the spot beside Mab, laying his head on her thigh. She`petted them both a minute and drank another glass of wine, staring at the objects in the room, the Chinese enameled vase on its pedestal, the crystal bowl of delphiniums on the Pembroke table . . .

People often asked Mab how she first got involved with art. If one were a sculptor or painter, it was obvious; you did what you had the talent to do. But Mab had always known she couldn't mold or draw or paint more than superficially well. She was not a frustrated artist. Her love for art had a different source.

She closed her eyes. She could still clearly picture every detail of the large library at Land's End. It was there that she had begun to love art. The library—she always felt like smiling when she thought of it. Her father's castle, his refuge. Her father, having made a distinguished marriage to China Austin, was given a wedding present of enough Dane money to allow him financial independence; by the time Mab was born he had inherited the rest of the Dane fortune. Bascomb Dane could thus live exactly the life he chose, a regular and unvarying daily routine centering around the high-ceilinged library with its window seat and rows upon rows of books, its fine editions of all the classics, its representative volumes on almost every subject, and its particularly handsome collection of books on art.

VII

Bascomb Dane's day at Land's End began promptly at seven in the morning. He would rise and dress, go downstairs and directly into his library, where he pulled back the green draperies at the tall windows to let in the daylight. As soon as his footsteps were heard on the stairs, George Browning, the cook's husband, who served as a combination butler and chauffeur, would bring Bascomb a tray with a cup of coffee and the *Eyreville Times*.

Bascomb read the newspaper until breakfast time, when he joined his family for coffee and toast. Then he went back to his library and closed the door. In solitude he fussed about, cataloguing, ordering new books, reading reviews, and writing scholarly papers for obscure journals. For the *Greentree Magazine* he unearthed details of ancient Roman festivals. For the *Classic Digest* he conjectured on the true nature of Akhenaton's religious beliefs. These articles took him a long time to compose.

The morning ended with a half-hour walk around his property, from eleven-thirty until twelve, unless it was raining heavily. After luncheon, Bascomb took a nap upstairs. At two-thirty he came down and called his broker in New York. When the call was finished, he devoted a few minutes to his accounts and bills. Then he read until five o'clock, at which time he went upstairs to bathe and change. At six-thirty, promptly, he drank a cocktail, a Manhattan in the winter and an old-fashioned in the summer, with his wife, who told him news of her day. At seven-thirty he dined, sitting at the head of the long table in the dining room. Often they entertained guests, but even when they didn't, the meal was a formal one.

At eight-thirty every night Bascomb opened his library to his daughters. The lamps would be lit, and coffee and cambric tea and brandy served, as Bascomb devoted himself to the education of his girls. He was delighted when Mab showed an interest in the art books. With her, he pored over reproductions of great paintings and pictures of great sculpture. He ordered many more art books for her.

Eventually Mab began to see even the objects around her in terms of their shapes and colors and relationships. She stared at the yellow-green of the willow trees in February, outlined against the soft rose color of the side of the barn. She observed the dark pines in the woods silhouetted against the gray winter sky, the flowers that bloomed in the summer. She studied people's faces, the fascinating contours of Vivienne's cheeks, the sweet beauty of her mother's expression, Nancy Browning's coffee-with-cream complexion, the baby's dark blue eyes.

But while Mab was developing her own way of looking at the world around her, she was also looking at herself. It wasn't that she was particularly fond of her own face or body—they pleased her well enough, but she did not look at herself out of vanity. Mab danced in a room whose walls were mirrors. She had danced since she was five, at first for an hour a week, then an hour a day, then two hours daily, then four. By the time Mab was fifteen she had been excused from all sports at Trinity, and went straight from lunch at school to the mirrored room, where she worked in classes until seven o'clock, when George picked her up. Vivienne also took several classes a week, but they were just to keep in shape and to train her in movement. Vivienne was not a serious ballet student like Mab.

Miss Colene Phipps ran the Dance Academy in

146

Eyreville. Over the years Miss Phipps had watched Mab and her development closely. Miss Phipps did not possess an effusive nature. She directed the school with rigid discipline; the highest compliment she had ever been heard to utter was "good." She said it very few times, never to Mab Dane. But when Mab was sixteen, Miss Phipps telephoned China Dane and suggested they get together for a discussion.

China promptly asked Miss Phipps to tea, and dispatched George with the car to bring the teacher to Land's End. China was waiting by the front door as Miss Phipps walked up the path with a light step. Miss Phipps's carriage was perfectly erect and her toes pointed outward; she covered the ground in a graceful manner. Though she was in her forties, Miss Phipps still had the body of a young girl. Her working day was spent sitting on a stool dressed in black stockings and a black tunic, her brown hair netted sternly back from her face. When she dressed for the street she wore gray, either a gray skirt and white blouse or a formal-looking gray suit. The day Miss Phipps came to visit China she was wearing the suit.

China could not help contrasting Miss Phipps with effervescent Laura Beltane. Miss Beltane had rushed into the door of Land's End bursting with the news of her discovery of Vivienne's acting talent, instantly predicting a future of nothing but triumphs and hit shows. Mab's teacher did not rush. She walked in with aplomb, sat down with composure, took a cup of tea from China and spoke of the weather. She refused any food. When she finished her cup, she placed it on the tea table and came to the point.

"I am glad you could see me, Mrs. Dane. As you know, Mab has studied with me for over ten years now. She is a fine student. If she works very hard—"

Here Miss Phipps paused. When she spoke again, it was a little more warmly. "You know, in ballet we must wait. We must always wait. We cannot judge a child's chances until we see how her body develops.

147

I don't have to tell you that Mab has exhibited extraordinary physical abilities. Her sister Vivienne is beautiful—I understand she is acting in college, now?—she too has a talent for movement, but it does not compare with Mab's. My old teacher, Mr. Van Domm from Charleston, recently watched Mab in class and he confirmed my own opinion. Mab can be"— Miss Phipps paused; then she seemed to throw caution to the winds—"a supreme dancer."

That from Miss Phipps! China was dazzled.

"Mab must work as she never has before," Miss Phipps went on quickly. "Eight hours a day, for seven or eight more years. But in her case, the work will never be thrown away. She will dance."

"I'm really overwhelmed to hear this," China said. "Thank you for—"

"I want to make a further arrangement with Trinity. Mab must be released earlier in the day. She must take no long vacations in the summer. And on Saturdays she should spend from nine to five at the studio."

"I know Mab will be thrilled to do it," China said. "She loves dancing. Though I don't think she really expected this. . . ."

"She will go far. We will be proud of her. You'll tell her about the extra hours, then?" Miss Phipps rose to leave.

Miss Phipps's solemn presentation certainly differed from Miss Beltane's predictions, but China was equally pleased. She couldn't wait to tell Mab—Mab was going to be a famous dancer!

The news of Miss Phipps's praise thrilled Mab. She ran to the telephone and called Beebee Cunningham, her best friend and Miss Phipps's other leading dancer. Beebee sweated beside Mab every day; together they groaned over their stretched muscles and aching toes.

"So the old cat finally admitted you're good," Beebee said. "I could have told you that for the last ten years. Anyone who can do a développé as high as yours . . . !" Beebee wasn't jealous. She had once wanted to be a

148

ballet dancer, but since she had proved better at tap and jazz, she now dreamed of starring in Broadway musicals.

In the next year Mab's pointe work grew stronger, her line excellent. She led the ballet classes for Miss Phipps and in addition took a long private lesson daily. In the spring recital that year Mab created a sensation. She danced a variation from *Swan Lake,* wearing a white tutu and tiny orange blossoms in her hair. She drifted around the stage like a leaf in a breeze. Her elevations were breathtaking, her turns polished; and, best of all, she had an indefinable something that linked all the steps into a smooth flow of motion, a perfect episode. Every gesture was beautiful, every movement completed.

There was tumultuous applause at the end of her dance, and people crowded around China Dane, complaining that it was unfair she should have *two* such talented daughters.

Looking back, Mab couldn't believe she had done what she did, that year and the following one. Her world was a mirror and the girl inside it, legs in pink tights, body in black leotard, arms bare and hair back. Mab took a purely professional interest in the movements of that body. *Glissade, pas de chat, coupé, piqué, chassé, assemblée, échappé.* Miss Phipps called out combinations and Mab performed them. "Up! Up! Elevation! Don't let me see the effort. Only give me your beauty. Now *dance* it."

Mab remembered those days the way a veteran remembers a war—the ballet war, fought in her youth, the constant striving and exhaustion, the struggle to hide the stress. "If you make a mistake, don't let it show in your face," Miss Phipps said. "Be serene. Now *look* at yourself. No one else can make you do it right."

Mab danced on and on in the room full of mirrors. She practiced longer and longer hours at the barre. She was stretched out, turned out, perfected. She danced.

Like the ballerina in "The Red Shoes," she couldn't stop, but she grew pale. Her mother saw it.

Mab was the daughter most like China herself. Mab had a tender heart. China knew from experience how tenderhearted people could get into things in life and sometimes not be able to get out of them. One Sunday morning China walked into Mab's room and asked her what was troubling her.

It took Mab quite a long time, and some coaxing, to admit that anything was wrong. There were actually two things bothering her, but only one was something she could discuss with her mother. Finally, Mab admitted to China that she wasn't sure she wanted to become a dancer.

"I thought that might be what was the matter," China said.

"Mother, I feel like there's a part of life I'm not living. I don't know how else to explain it." Mab looked earnestly at her mother, who needed no further explanation. After China had left the room, with a promise of "We'll see about it," Mab went over to the window and stared at the way some clouds looked hanging low on the horizon.

China consulted with Bascomb, and the upshot was a trip for the three of them. They went to Boston, visited Vivienne, saw Radcliffe, and then flew to New York City and checked into the Plaza Hotel. Their first night there China took Mab to watch the New York City Ballet at Lincoln Center. The performance thrilled Mab. The dancers were so good! Still, she was very familiar with all the movements she watched.

The next day Mab walked up the stone steps of the Metropolitan Museum and what she saw inside amazed her. She stared at her first Turner, at an Ingres and a Dali, at Renoir and Van Gogh. The originals transcended all her expectations. She wanted to spend all day there. Then she discovered the Frick Museum and the Modern. She lived in a dream.

When they went back to Land's End, China helped

150

Mab break the news to Miss Phipps. Mab wanted to continue dancing during her senior year at Trinity and would be glad to lead the ballet classes, but she was applying to Radcliffe and hoped to go there to study art history.

The unemotional Miss Phipps came close to tears at this development. Her best student! Miss Phipps comforted herself, however, with the thought that there was a little Parker girl in her six-year-old class who reminded her of young Mab, and who perhaps would prove less flighty.

The other problem bothering Mab, the unmentionable one, was sex. China helped her win the ballet war, but Mab knew that her mother could never bring herself to mention such a thing as sex to any of her daughters. Vivienne gave Mab a few bits of information, about menstruating and so on. Mab knew that Vivienne had met Philip Alexander secretly, knew that Philip had a crush on Viv. But Vivienne did not supply any details. Mab was three years younger and not entirely in her older sister's confidence. Whatever went on with Philip seemed to be very private, just between the two of them, and certainly a permanent part of Vivienne's life until Philip went away to England. Vivienne drooped around after that for a while, but she went back to college soon after. Philip seemed to have left for good, and Vivienne never mentioned him again except once, the first Christmas after he left. No gift or card had come from England for Vivienne, though Philip had always given Vivienne something at Christmas, on Valentine's Day and her birthday, secret presents that sometimes Mab had to pretend *she* had given Vivienne, to explain their appearance. When Mab asked Vivienne what had happened with Philip, Vivienne told her quietly that they had quarreled before Philip left and that everything was over for good. Vivienne said she didn't ever want to hear Philip's name again, if Mab didn't mind.

Mab was curious. She was curious about a lot of things to do with boys. Basic things she knew now, of course. In grammar school, she had heard hints about the existence of a body of knowledge on the subject of the difference between boys and girls, facts which were nasty indeed, to judge from what she gathered in bits and pieces. When Mab was eleven, she got some firsthand information. She was over at the Cunninghams' big house in Eyreville playing with Beebee. Beebee's twin brother Buckshot made them a treasure hunt, with clues that had them running from place to place around the house. One clue led them downstairs to the fruit room in the basement, a windowless cubicle whose shelves really held canned goods, not fruit. The fruit room door locked from the inside. Mab rushed into the fruit room first, with Buckshot behind her, and before she realized it he had locked the door and flipped off the light.

Mab screamed. The darkness was total. Outside, Beebee beat on the door and hollered as Buckshot grabbed Mab. His hands felt her body thoroughly. Mab struggled, backing up against the shelves. Beebee yelled that she was going to call their mother. Buckshot, panting, felt his way back to the door, flipped on the light and opened the bolt. He shoved Beebee to one side as he walked out.

"Stinker! It was just a trick—you didn't *have* any treasure for us!" Beebee shouted after him. Buckshot did not deign to turn around. He held up his middle finger.

Beebee and Mab went upstairs and short-sheeted Buckshot's bed to get even; Mab heard later that Buckshot stuck his feet right through the sheet that night. He always went headlong into things, like his older brother Hellraiser.

When Buckshot's hands had touched her, Mab had felt very strange. For years Mab could recall those sensations in her shocked body. But Buckshot had gone off without a look at her. Afterward, there was no bond between them. At dancing school Buckshot never asked her to dance. He was awfully thin and suffered from acne and Mab told herself she didn't care; she didn't want to dance with him. But in a vague way she felt she had failed some test.

It was Beebee who explained to Mab why China had the new baby. Her father stuck his thing into her mother at night, stuck it in guess where? and babies came out if you did it right. Beebee was sure about it; Mab had doubts. Later Beebee got much more information out of Hellraiser, who not only had stolen two sex manuals out of the Eyreville Bookstore and rented them out to friends, but who also trafficked in stolen *Playboy* magazines. Every month Hellraiser sneaked several *Playboys* out from under the counter where Mrs. Peabody stacked them in the drugstore. He sold them for two dollars a copy. One article on French kissing spread cold sores throughout the entire upper school at Trinity. Mr. Grayson feared the water fountains were unsanitary. He installed containers of Dixie cups for the children to use, a boon to the water fights in the halls.

Up to that point Mab had never kissed anybody and didn't want to. She had no opportunity to get cold sores; her long hours of dancing removed her from after-school gatherings in recreation rooms. When she went to evening parties that included both boys and girls, she hung around with Beebee and the other girls.

When Mab got to Radcliffe, Vivienne casually asked her if she wanted some protection, in case she "got into something with a boy." Mab hid her lack of sophistication and agreed. Vivienne took her to see a doctor. The inspection that ensued was horrible. Mab walked out of the office very weak in the knees, carrying a rubber disc in a little case with the firm resolution never to use it if she could help it.

But she knew she was just fighting a delaying action. Her resolutions and reservations and modesty would crumble someday; someday someone would make clear

153

to her the joy of physical love. Vivienne told Mab she bet her a dollar she would meet someone she liked within a month. The Harvard boys always looked over the Radcliffe freshman class.

Within a month Mab had met somebody. His name was Cary Parrish and he sat next to her in Mythology of Greece and Rome. He stared at Mab in class. She didn't pay much attention to him until the first assignment was due. They had been asked to write a paper discussing the judgment of Paris, the famous decision Paris had to make when the goddess of discord dropped a golden apple marked "For the Fairest" into a feast of the gods on Olympus. Hera, Athene and Aphrodite all claimed the apple and the young mortal boy had to make the choice. Hera offered him power and Athene offered him wisdom, but Aphrodite promised him the most beautiful woman in the world for a wife and he gave Aphrodite the apple. The story was ridiculous, Mab had written. If Paris became the most powerful man on earth, he could get any wife he wanted; if he became the wisest, he might not want the world's most beautiful woman for a wife.

"Did anyone defend Paris's choice?" the instructor asked.

Cary Parrish raised his hand.

"Why, Mr. Parrish?"

"Being wise doesn't make you happy, and neither does having power, not necessarily. But any man would be happy to have the most beautiful girl in the world as his wife." Cary looked straight at Mab as he spoke. "Paris's choice is Parrish's too," he said softly to her.

Mab blushed.

"What is your opinion, Miss Dane?"

"It was just a way to start the Trojan War," Mab said.

"Exactly. That was a war in heaven, remember, as well as on earth, and every side felt justified—"

The instructor went on talking but Mab stopped listening and looked through her lashes at Cary Parrish. Although he had an almost pretty face, he also had broad shoulders, and he was tall and thoroughly masculine.

When class ended, Cary asked Mab to have a cup of coffee with him. They went to a student hangout and talked for an hour. Cary was from California, and he swam on the Harvard swimming team.

He asked her to the movies the following Friday. They went with his roommate and another girl, and drank beer afterward. Then he asked her to go to the football game; again it was a foursome. The next time he asked her to the movies and they went alone.

They saw Cary Grant—"I was named for him," Cary said—and after the movies he took Mab back to his rooms. His tiny sitting room had a sofa littered with books, papers and clothes. The only possible place to sit down was in the adjoining bedroom, on the bed. Cary led her into the room, and then he pulled her down onto the bed beside him and kissed her. Mab was tense. Cary kissed her a lot more, and finally she relaxed a little.

Cary wound a strand of her hair around his finger and looked into her eyes.

"How much experience have you had, Mab?" he asked softly.

Mab laughed.

"Well, there was the time in the fruit room," she said.

"What happened in the fruit room? What's a fruit room anyway?" Cary chuckled.

Mab made up her mind. She had brought along her diaphram—in case. She was frightened but determined. This was it. She'd stay the night if he wanted her to. She felt like kissing him again; he had a nice mouth. She kissed his cheek.

Cary got up, warned off his roommate with some sort of prearranged signal, came back to bed and proceeded to initiate her. When he found she was an innocent virgin, he was amazed. He couldn't remember meeting one in bed before.

155

"Your beauty is like a protection around you," he said. "I think you scare men a little, Mab. I'm glad you feel close to me."

Mab thought it was strange to lie naked with him in bed. She didn't mind the things he did to her, but she didn't particularly like them, either. It was better than she expected, less painful, but she was glad when it was over. They fell asleep together.

The next morning Cary rushed around dressing for an early class as if nothing had happened at all. Mab felt that she might as well have been his roommate. He saw she was awake, asked her to lock the door behind her when she left, and was off, without even a kiss. Mab was stunned.

Two weeks later, she was terrified as well. She thought she was pregnant, despite the diaphram which she had left in place for two whole days afterward just to make sure. After another week she was driven to confide in Vivienne. Vivienne laughed at her and said changing drinking water had thrown her off schedule. Thank God, Vivienne proved to be right.

Next Mab thought she had VD. She came down with all the symptoms detailed in the sex education pamphlet that she had picked up in the doctor's office. Finally she went back to the doctor for a test. The doctor chuckled. She didn't have VD, she had monilia, a mucusy condition that proved hard to cure.

While all this was going on, Cary was cutting Mythology class. When she saw him again, he was walking around Harvard Yard with a redhead.

There were other boys and Mab tried again. There was still no rapture, and lots of red tape. She didn't spend the whole night with someone again until her senior year. Buckshot Cunningham, who went to Yale, came up to Boston for the game between the two schools and looked her up.

Buckshot had improved in looks. He was still thin and wiry, but now he was tall, and his sandy hair was longish. His skin was pitted from the acne he'd had as a boy, but it wasn't too noticeable, and he had burning dark eyes. Mab went out drinking with him after the game. Crowds of kids were all over Boston, running into each other at street corners and in campus hangouts. It was a gala night. Mab drank a lot. At one point she was alone in a booth with Buckshot and he leaned close to her.

"Mab, remember the fruit room?" he asked.

Mab was amazed that he did. It turned out that he remembered many details of their childhood, the dance recitals he had been dragged to, the time Beebee fell out when she lost her balance in a *fouetté* turn, the time he and Hellraiser put on pink tights and black leotards stolen from Beebee's drawer and pranced onstage at a dress rehearsal doing high kicks to win a twenty dollar bet from James Hastings.

"If we'd done it at the recital, he would've given us fifty dollars," Buckshot said. "That kid was loaded. Hellraiser was for it; in fact, he planned to collect for both the rehearsal and the recital, but he pulled a muscle in the high kick. Of course, when Mother found out about it she locked us in our rooms during the recital. She made us apologize formally to Miss Phipps. You've heard the expression 'stony look.' Hellraiser said later that he shrank an inch when Miss Phipps looked at him. Mab knew exactly what Buckshot meant. Man, that lady took ballet straight."

It was five in the morning before they sneaked back into Mab's room. As a senior she had one of the single rooms in her dormitory that year; Buckshot was the first boy she had invited to stay the night.

There should have been something really satisfying about having sex with Buckshot, after she had thought about him for so long, but he was not. He had drunk almost too much to enjoy the event. Before Mab fell asleep, she worried about the time it took Buckshot to have a climax. Mab was beginning to feel a certain fear.

She woke up the next morning apprehensive, almost

frightened to see what would happen. Buckshot was still sleeping, his head pillowed on his arm. She studied his pitted face. Oh, Buckshot, she prayed, please. What she wanted was tenderness. She wanted someone to wake up beside her and seem thrilled to be there—well, happy; thrilled was too much to ask. After Cary's matter-of-factness Mab had gotten a complex about next-mornings.

"Hi, Buckshot," she whispered, kissing his ear.

His dark eyes opened.

"Hi," he said. He groaned. "Remind me not to drink Black Russians, will you? Man. I need some coffee."

This can't be happening again, Mab thought. Without a kiss or a word of kindness, Buckshot got out of bed and asked if it were safe to go to the bathroom down the hall. Pulling on a bathrobe, Mab went to check. The bathroom was deserted. It was two o'clock on Sunday afternoon. She gestured that the coast was clear.

Buckshot washed up and came back to her room. He glanced out the window to check the weather and decided that it looked like rain.

"I gotta catch a train. I'll see you, Mab," he said. With a kiss on her cheek, he left.

Mab lay back on the bed and cried. There was something wrong with her. Maybe it was her breasts. She didn't have really big breasts. Perhaps all men expected you to have big breasts. Because of her dance training, she had excellent posture and a well-developed rib cage which made her look bustier in clothes than she really was. Probably men were disappointed when they saw her naked. Or maybe she was too large inside. She had read something about that—women had vaginas of different shapes.

Tears drying on her cheeks, Mab sat up. She was suddenly struck with that possibility. Maybe that was why Cary and Buckshot seemed to take forever to have orgasms. Maybe that was why they pulled her legs up

158

around their bodies and positioned her in awkward poses.

Mab stood up and walked to the full-length mirror on her closet door. She took off her bathrobe and looked at herself naked. There she was, all perfect proportion on the outside. But inside, she was all wrong. Men would prefer someone like the redhead Cary was still dating, someone with fat buttocks and heavy breasts and even a sagging stomach, so long as she was tiny inside. Mab knew that her diaphram size was seventy-five. Was that huge? Was it normal? Whom could she possibly ask?

In the end she decided that if that were fate's joke on her, if she were all right outside and all wrong inside, at least she could stop setting herself up to be hurt, stop courting disaster. She didn't have to bear that particular pain. When men chased her, she'd sometimes let them catch her, but only for as long as the sex act itself took. Then she'd get away.

She tried this plan for a while. Gradually her interest in the rushed encounters faded. Men never seemed to do the right things with her. Maybe it was because they thought they were going to bed with Helen of Troy and then she just turned out to be a thinnish dancer with a —well, she knew the slang words for it but they hurt too much to say, even to herself. With a large interior.

As if to compensate for the lack she imagined in her inner shape, Mab took more and more care of her hair and skin and appearance. She shopped around for elegant, interesting clothes to wear. She looked better and better while she felt worse and worse.

Graduation day finally came, and afterward Mab moved into Vivienne's apartment in New York. For a while she worked at a Madison avenue art gallery. Then she got the job with the Whitney Museum. A banker with a large sculpture collection wooed her while she was at the gallery; she had a brief affair with him, but he had a wife. She didn't know what he thought of her in bed; she didn't stick around long enough afterward to get a clue. At the museum she found that most of the people she met were primarily interested in art and she was swept into this world. At the Whitney, in studios, and at galleries and shows, there was another language, a visual language that absorbed them all, the language of the subjects of art and the form and proportion of their presentations.

Eventually, Mab met Arthur Windsor, who fulfilled her in a non-sexual way. Ultimately he gave her a position which would be envied by anybody. She made a handsome salary and could live as elegantly as she chose. When her parents died, Arthur had helped her through her grief. Her father's death had been more or less expected; she had felt great sorrow but not shock. China's fast departure, without a word, without a good-bye look, devastated Mab. Her mother had always turned to her for understanding. They both hated ugliness and wanted life to be a series of pretty pictures. Mab felt supported by the fact of her mother's similar reactions to the world. But suddenly her mother was gone and Land's End was gone. At the Concordia, Mab plunged into work to heal her feelings of desolation. She was lucky that she could depend on her work; the thrill was always there.

And Arthur was always there. They had a box at the symphony and season tickets for the ballet; they went everywhere together. Certain things, however, could make her long for sex chords struck on the notes around middle C, oddly . . . and any tender pas de deux, a man and a woman dancing together as if they existed alone in the world and lived only to touch each other. But Mab would be sitting next to Arthur when these twinges came, and looking over at his fine-boned profile, she would remind herself that her world was art. She was a beautiful woman on the outside who carried too much emptiness inside.

Her sex life held nothing more than an occasional affair for a long time. Then Carson Koppit began pursuing her. She gave in one Christmas night and stayed with him in his studio. In the morning he woke up ready to start painting, with no particular further thought of her; she was ready for his reaction. She knew she was nothing special. She stayed around for a week. Then she realized how dumb she was being. Carson was working toward a one-man show in the spring, and he was obviously trying to use her. She broke it off, And she was positive that the only reason Carson had shown up tonight was that he still hoped to influence her. He probably gritted his teeth when he made love to her. She believed nothing Carson said. She was finished lying to herself. In the sex wars, she had lost.

VIII

Rudi was still curled up next to her purring contentedly, and the wine bottle was almost empty. Mab looked at it in surprise. Sitting there, thinking about her past, she had almost finished the whole bottle! She didn't usually drink heavily at all.

She picked up Rudi, put him carefully into his basket, and took what was left of the wine back to the refrigerator. She still didn't feel sleepy, but she decided to go to bed anyway. Maybe she'd read. Looking at the clock in the kitchen she saw that it was ten minutes after midnight.

She turned off the lights in the living room and went in to the bathroom. It didn't take her long to wash her face and brush her teeth. Mischa had already hopped onto the bed when she climbed in. After she set the alarm clock, she picked up the telephone, remembering suddenly to check her calls. There would be a message from a painter whose work she was currently hanging at the Concordia, she was sure. He had been coming to the museum every afternoon arguing that special lights should be installed over his paintings, and he called her at home in the evenings to plead his case.

The service answered. "Miss Dane? Let's see," the girl said. "Howard Carteret called at six-thirty and wants you to call him anytime up to ten o'clock. And your sister Vivienne called from her New York apartment and asked you to call her tonight, no matter how late you come in. That's all."

Thanking the operator, Mab broke the connection

and looked at the clock. Twelve-thirty—it would be one-thirty in New York. What could Viv want? And what was she doing in New York? Since Vivienne had bought back Land's End, she'd been calling Mab regularly from down there, to ask advice on restoring their old home and report on her progress. Land's End had needed quite a bit of renovation. But the book collection in Bascomb's library, which had been sold along with the house, had been bought back intact. Mab was happy about that.

She punched out the telephone number of Vivienne's apartment. After two rings, Vivienne answered.

"Hi, what's up? It's Mab. You said to call—I hope I'm not waking you. What are you doing in New York?"

"You didn't wake me; I wasn't asleep. I'm here on some business. How's life in Chicago?"

"Fine. How's the house?"

"Almost finished. Mab, can you come down to Land's End on the weekend of June eighteenth? That's a week from this Saturday. Cypriana wants us all to get together. A house party, and even a ball upstairs on Saturday night. It sounds like fun, doesn't it?"

Mab checked the appointment book she kept beside the telephone. There was nothing important going on June eighteenth, just a concert she could skip.

"I'd adore to," she said. "You know I'm dying to see the house. How is Cypri? I don't think she knows how to write."

"She's just been to England. That's the thing—that's why she wants us to get together. You won't believe who is also coming—Philip Alexander."

Vivienne paused. Mab heard Viv swallow. Mab didn't breathe. *Philip?*

Mab thought fast. If Philip were going to show up, she'd better mention to Vivienne now that she had seen Philip in London last February. He was bound to say something about it. Mab had not mentioned seeing Philip to Vivienne. Whenever anyone mentioned Philip to Vivienne, Viv seemed pained. Because Mab feared that the feeling might be mutual, she hadn't mentioned Vivienne to Philip or said a word about Vivienne having bought back Land's End. Besides, it hadn't seemed important; Philip was so remote from Eyreville. Mab didn't think he'd ever been back except once two years ago, for his brother Champ's wedding, which Vivienne had not been able to attend.

But if he were coming back to Eyreville now—

"Viv, you know, I saw Philip last February," Mab said.

"You did? You didn't mention it." Vivienne sounded very surprised.

"Well, I just didn't think . . ." Mab let her words trail off.

"What's he like now?" Vivienne said.

"Oh. Older, of course, but still very handsome. He really looks about the same—I mean, he hasn't gotten fat or anything. I've been to London several times, you know, but I didn't see Philip until this last trip. At Champ and Cypriana's wedding—you knew that Philip came from England to be best man, didn't you? —anyway, he said he'd like to see me if I ever came to England." Mab tried to make their encounter sound as if it had been very casual. "So I called him and we went to dinner one night."

"Did you go gambling?"

"Gambling? No. We went to the theater."

"You didn't see this gambling firsthand, then. Cypri has some tale that Philip is destroying himself. She says he has endangered his company. It seems that for about two years he's gambled almost every night. Mostly roulette, she said."

"Good God. That's shocking. He certainly didn't seem like—" Mab felt the blood come to her cheeks. Fortunately, Vivienne interrupted her.

"And here's the first act curtain. Are you ready for this? Cypri has got up some sort of engagement between Philip and Daisy."

"Philip and *Daisy!*"

165

"Isn't it unbelievable? I felt the same way. You know, our little sister has a wild imagination. I don't know what's true and what isn't. But she said that marrying Daisy is going to save Philip from ruin or some such nonsense. Sometimes Cypri is just too much. Anyway, we'll find out all about it in a week and a half." Vivienne sounded as if she were smiling. "I scarcely give the engagement story much credence."

Mab was stunned. She couldn't think of any words to express her amazement, and she made a surprised sound like "Uh."

"So look, I'm flying home tomorrow. You know I've turned the old cookhouse into a guest house. Philip can stay there, and the rest of us in the house. Bring something dashing to wear to the ball; Cypri will probably invite everyone in Eyreville. And let's make it fun. You know, dress for dinner and so on. I've been wanting to show everyone Land's End in style. It will be exciting." Vivienne paused a moment. "Mab, did Philip really seem all right when you saw him? All right in the head, I mean?" Vivienne gave a short laugh. She sounded nervous.

"He seemed like a perfectly proper Englishman," Mab said, not quite telling the truth. "He didn't bet so much as a tuppence on anything that night."

Vivienne was silent for a moment. Then she spoke again. "Call me when you get your plane reservations. Can you come down on Friday?"

Mab looked again at her appointment book, turning the page with a finger that suddenly trembled.

"There's a trustee's meeting that morning. If I can catch an afternoon flight I will. Otherwise I'll come Saturday morning."

"I hope you can get here Friday night. Let me know and I'll meet your plane—or send someone, if I get too involved with the last-minute preparations."

"Fine. Viv, I'll be so happy to see you and Land's End again."

"And Philip. Won't it be strange? All of us there,

166

I mean." Mab wished she could see the expression on Vivienne's face. Vivienne's voice had a peculiar inflection; it seemed a little hard for her to get her words out, as if she had a lump in her throat.

"Really strange," Mab said.

"Well, good night. Sleep well. Pleasant dreams."

Mab slowly hung up the telephone. She was shaken. Mischa, who was always sensitive to her feelings, crept closer to her and licked her hand. Mab stared straight ahead of her. She played the entire telephone conversation back again in her mind. She was glad she had decided to tell Vivienne about seeing Philip in London, so that if it came up during the weekend—but what was this about gambling and Daisy?

After a while Mab sank back onto her lace-trimmed pillow and let herself relive her past trip to England, her day and night with Philip. Even though it was painful, there were parts of it she liked remembering.

IX

Mab had flown to London to see the work of a young English sculptor and to negotiate setting up an exhibit at the Concordia. Arthur suggested that she take a week for the trip and have some fun, tour all the galleries. He thought perhaps she needed a winter break. She had been looking pale.

Her first day in London, Mab didn't do much but recover from the flight. But the next, a Saturday, she woke up feeling marvelous. After a big English breakfast, she dressed quickly and went straight off to the Tate gallery to look at the Turners, like a thirsty man rushing to a refreshing spring. She lingered in front of each painting, finally reaching her favorite, *Interior at Petworth*, a mad orange, white and gold swirl of paint that celebrated the effect of sunlight upon a dull cavernous English music room.

Mab was all alone in the room that contained the painting for some time; then, she became aware that someone else had come into the room and looking at her, instead of at the painting. He had stopped a short distance away. She paid no further attention, absorbed as always in trying to figure out what Turner meant by the mystical picture. It resembled a double or triple exposure, as if he had wanted to portray all the rooms in all great houses in one painting. The tone of it seemed darker than she remembered it; the Tate ought to clean it, she thought.

"Pardon me, madam, but can you tell me the way to the men's water closet?"

The man who spoke stood right at her elbow. Mab jumped. She turned to face him, surprised at the cheeky request, and then she recognized Philip Alexander.

"Philip! What are you doing here?"

Philip laughed, looking very pleased with himself.

"Guessing right, is what I'm doing. I thought you'd be here. I couldn't resist shocking you; sorry. You looked so abstracted. I was afraid you were about to vanish out of this world and into Turner's, right before my eyes. And you're much, much too pretty for me to stand by and let that happen."

He smiled at Mab warmly and seized her hands as he spoke, holding her arms wide apart, taking in her shining chestnut hair, her tipped-up hazelnut eyes, her high cheekbones. His words were not an exaggeration— Mab looked marvelous. She was wearing a brown turtleneck sweater and a jumper made of lightweight brown suede. The graceful skirt brushed the tops of her brown boots.

"You know, Mab, you were wearing all brown the first day I met-you, a little brown creature like a fairy," Philip said.

"Philip, I was going to call you this afternoon. But how could you possibly know I was here?"

"Don't forget we have mutual relations now. My brother Champ wrote me that you were coming over February fourth. I must say I was glad to hear it. But you hadn't told Champ and Cypriana where you were going to stay. So, rather than calling all the hotels in London, I thought, where would Mab go first? And the answer was simple. Remember, you told me at the wedding that you always went to the Tate gallery first? Well—I just popped round this morning, and here you are."

"That's amazing." Mab was charmed to have been tracked down so cleverly, and flattered that Philip had remembered her words for two years.

"I hope you have today free, because I do, and I

want to spend it all with you." He gave her another wide smile. He had dropped her hands, but he still looked at her with open admiration. "Wherever you are going, you have a companion, if you like."

"Are you sure you want to do that?" Mab smiled back at him.

"I entrust myself to you. What is our itinerary?"

"Well, first we stand here for an hour—no, I'm only kidding. I was just finished with the Turners. Maybe we could have a cup of coffee and then go to the British Museum?"

Philip looked at his wristwatch. "It's after eleven. I'd suggest we walk by the river a bit, up to St. Stephen's Tavern. That's where Parliament drinks, when it's in session. Cocktails there. Then for a further touch of Old England, we could go on to the White Horse tavern for a chump chop—or to a new restaurant that serves nothing but caviar, if you'd prefer. *Then*, the British museum."

"That's a much better plan. Marvelous, in fact."

Reclaiming her cream-colored wool coat for her, Philip gallantly helped her put it on. The morning was fresh and not too cool. Mab enjoyed walking by the Thames in the sunshine, watching the traffic on the river. Philip asked questions about her work, confessing he knew very little about modern art in America, but that he had read strange things about what was considered art now. Was there really a fence in California that ran over the dunes for miles? And why was it considered art? They chatted about the current art scene. Philip seemed in a very good humor and made droll comments on what she told him. Since the people she usually talked to took modern art very seriously, she found his comments both amusing and fresh.

"The sculptor I'm going to see on Monday is very much avant-garde," she said. "He saws up trees."

"Saws up trees?"

"Yes. Into different lengths—the trunks of only

171

certain trees, however. That's his current phase. He places the lengths in various ways on black floors. We are going to exhibit him, if we can."

"You mean stumps? Sections of trees? Just put about on a floor?"

"I'm afraid so." Mab looked up at Philip mischievously. "Our trouble is, there are insects in the trees. When they are put into galleries for display, sometimes the bugs warm up and come out and swarm through the museum. I'm worried that we're going to have trouble importing the tree sections into America, because English bugs are—"

"Stop!" Philip took her arm as they crossed the street. "I can't believe it. What a job you have, Mab."

Inside the picturesque pub, they sat at a small table and ordered Bloody Marys. Philip obtained a London *Observer* from the bartender, turned to the theater section and asked if she would like to go to a play with him that evening.

"I'd love to," Mab said.

"Let's see what would tempt you. London seems full of plays about beds." Philip chuckled. "Here's *A Bed Full of Foreigners*, *The Bed Before Yesterday*, and oh, one about tables, a revival of *Separate Tables*. And Robert Morley's in *Banana Ridge*; I've heard that's funny. Or if you don't care for a comedy, there's *Otherwise Engaged*. Though it's rather funny too, I believe."

"Philip, haven't you seen some of these already?"

"No. I haven't been to the theater much, recently. I was waiting for you."

Philip smiled, and Mab was afraid she blushed. Philip was certainly being charming. Mab had been very much attracted to him at Cypriana's wedding. That night they'd danced together, and Philip had stayed with her most of the evening. He had driven her back to Aunt Martha's, but since her cousin Daisy had been along, the evening hadn't ended romantically. Now, she wondered about this evening. As Philip sat reading the theater listings, she looked at him closely. He seemed a trifle thinner than she remembered him being, but equally dashing. He wore a beautifully-tailored gray suit, obviously custom-cut to fit his handsome body. She liked his dark eyes. When he smiled, they lighted up, and the tiny wrinkles at the sides gave him a friendly look.

"Why don't you decide, Philip," she said. "But is it possible to get tickets at the last minute?"

"If one has a good ticket broker. However, I should ring up now, if we pick a hit. Have you seen *A Chorus Line*?"

"Yes, it's been in Chicago. But I wouldn't mind going again, if you'd like to."

"That's right. *A Chorus Line* is about dancing, isn't it? I haven't forgotten watching you dance."

"You watched me dance?" Mab was surprised.

"Yes, I did. I went to one of Miss Phipps's recitals. A friend of mine had a girl friend who danced at the school, and I went with him. You did a solo. I remembered being very impressed. Do you still dance, Mab? You look like a dancer."

Mab came close to blushing again. "I take a ballet class during my lunch hour almost every day. That's all. Just classroom work."

"It certainly keeps you looking fit. You do prefer the art world to the dance world still, don't you? My mother once wrote something to the effect that you had to make a choice. Are you glad—I mean, have you been happy with it?"

He looked genuinely interested as she answered.

"If I had gone on with ballet, I wouldn't have many years left now. But as a curator, I can look forward to many more years of coping with artists and their temperaments."

"And their termites," Philip said. "To speak of your current problems."

Mab smiled. She wanted to ask Philip if he were happy that he had made the decision to come to

England so long ago, since they were talking of past choices. She opened her mouth, but closed it again. There had been some sort of climactic breakup with Vivienne beforehand. He might have left Eyreville in anger. She noticed that Philip never mentioned Vivienne. He had never asked about her during the time he was home for Cypri's wedding, and he didn't mention her today. So she said nothing about Vivienne, either; not even to mention that she had bought back Land's End. Mab did not want to bring up a possibly painful topic. They were having too good a time.

"I'm supposed to explore a method for spraying the tree segments with plastic," Mab said. "You'd be amazed at our technical problems. A degree in engineering is a better preparation for curating these days than art history."

Philip finished his drink. "Please tell me what play you'd like to see."

"I refuse to pick, but I will make one suggestion. Let's see something funny."

"Done. How about *Banana Ridge*."

"It sounds perfect; I love Robert Morley."

Philip made a quick telephone call and came back to ask where she'd like to lunch. She agreed that the place he'd mentioned, the White Horse, sounded appealing. It turned out to be a typical Old English tavern with elegant service. Mab ordered a shrimp salad, leaving Philip to eat the chump chop. When it arrived, he insisted she take a taste. "I must work you up to mutton," he said. "A little at a time."

She nibbled the morsel off his fork and pronounced it delicious. Philip was feeding her in public as if they were lovers; Mab was pleased that Philip didn't seem to care what others might think. At the beginning of the meal, he had ordered a bottle of champagne, and now he lifted his champagne glass to touch hers in a toast.

"On to the British Museum. I haven't been there in an age. What are we going to see?"

"Aphrodite," Mab said. "At least, she may be Aphrodite. An archeologist named Iris Love discovered a head in the lower storerooms of the museum several years ago. She maintains it is the head of a famous lost statue by Praxiteles—the first completely naked statue of Aphrodite."

Philip smiled into her eyes. "I'm for seeing nude goddesses."

"This is only her head. And there's a controversy over that."

The champagne seemed to be making her giddy, and Mab was glad when the coffee arrived. She drank hers black and restored herself to sobriety. She mustn't lose her head over Philip. Perhaps he was just being kind to her because he felt he owed it to their family connections.

When Philip took her hand as they walked up the worn stone steps leading to the vast museum, however, she began to hope that it was more than just a friendly gesture. It made Mab feel young and gay.

They found the Greek and Roman antiquities department and Mab filled out a request to see the sculpture. The request was quickly approved and a thin young man in a white lab coat joined them at the information booth.

He announced himself as "Hatte, curator of the Greek statues downstairs." They introduced themselves and Mr. Hatte herded them into a large elevator to take them to the basement. There he led them into a cluttered room, disappeared around a stack of shelves full of pieces of statuary and in a moment staggered out holding the head in his arms.

"The head of Persephone, we call it," he said, and deposited the head without ceremony in front of them on a large table full of marble bits and pieces. "There she is."

The nose and the entire jaw of the woman's head was missing.

"Praxiteles finished his statues so carefully that the

175

marble was said to feel like skin," Mab said softly. She ran her fingers over the head before her, feeling the cool surface of the cheeks. "This really feels right. Touch it, Philip, and tell me what you think."

Philip moved close to Mab and did as she asked, gently running his fingers over the statue's brow and then her cheeks and neck. There was something very sensuous about watching Philip's long square-tipped fingers glide over the white marble. Mab repressed a shiver. She felt warm all over.

"She does feel lifelike," Philip said in a low voice, ... "I think. Could I compare?"

Before Mab realized what Philip meant, he touched her right cheek in a caressing manner and his fingers traveled slowly across and touched her lips for an instant. Then he turned back to the head and touched it again.

"Exactly like a woman's skin," he said solemnly.

Mab was a bit breathless. Mr. Hatte watched these proceedings with interest, but did not so much as clear his throat. Embarrassed to look up, Mab pretended to study the would-be goddess of love with close attention until she was sure she wasn't blushing.

"Praxiteles ground the—the surface of his statues in a certain distinctive way," she said, trying to sound professional again. "I wonder if we are really touching a piece of his work. He's my favorite sculptor."

Philip was quiet, absorbed in watching her run her fingers over the head. He stood very close to Mab, and she was conscious of every part of his body. What was happening to her? Aphrodite must be putting her into an erotic mood, she thought. She wouldn't have minded going back behind the shelves with Philip that very minute.

"Uh. Thank you, I'm finished now," she said to Mr. Hatte. He replaced the head. They were standing in a wonderland of marble and stone; Mab looked around curiously. Heads large and small were stashed everywhere, and there were full-sized statues, as well as arms, legs, and torsos overflowing the shelves and resting on the floor and the table.

Philip looked around, too.

"Mr. Hatte, who is this little girl?" he asked when the curator reappeared. Philip indicated the marble head of a small, pretty child.

"Ah. Well. *That's* a bit of a mystery," Mr. Hatte said. "Many of these items unfortunately are minus their acquisition papers. We don't know where they came from."

Philip was surprised, but Mab explained: in the heyday of Empire, English archeologists raided all parts of the world for treasures and sent them back to England, where they were shoved into the basement of the museum, often getting separated from any accompanying papers.

"That's why all countries have antiquities laws now," Mab added.

"There's even a move afoot to give the Elgin marbles back to Greece," Mr. Hatte said.

One statue led them to another, and they passed an hour with Mr. Hatte, going through the articles stored there and conjecturing about their origins. Mr. Hatte and Mab exchanged stories of curators' problems. She promised to send him some brochures from the Concordia. Philip seemed content to listen to them, and genuinely interested in the objects they examined, stones and statues dating back to Celtic and Norman times. Several statues of Mithras fascinated Philip, and Mr. Hatte discoursed on the Mithraic religion in England.

Finally, Mr. Hatte was paged. He was needed upstairs, and they had to leave.

"Are you ready for tea now?" Philip asked as they left the museum.

"You know, it's a mystery to me, but whenever I'm in England there seems to be an extra hour that folds out of the day. Though I love tea, somehow I never have time for it in Chicago."

"Let's go to Brown's hotel. They put on a substantial tea. If we eat a good amount, perhaps we can wait to dine until after the theater," Philip said.

Mab agreed. She loved to have dinner late in the evening. They took a taxi and soon were chatting in the old-fashioined lobby while tea was served to them in elegant style. Mab tasted several of the little sandwiches and tarts and declared them excellent.

When Philip dropped her at the Savoy, he promised to return promptly at seven. As she entered her room, she felt happier than she had in years. She looked at herself in the mirror over the vanity table. Her eyes were shining and she was smiling. Arthur was right. She had needed a rest, a change.

While she soaked in a hot tub, she considered the possibilities for the coming evening. Philip was— ardent. That was the only word she could find to describe his manner. He wanted her, Mab was sure. That was nothing new; most men did want her when they saw her. She was usually the one who drew back. But Philip was so appealing. He was a bachelor, and nothing stood in her way if she wanted to go home with him tonight. Nothing except the fact that she had promised herself not to do this again.

Nervously, she licked her lips. What if they did go to bed? Wouldn't it be like all the other times? He would probably be secretly disgusted. He would be too much of a gentleman to let her guess it, of course, but then there would be the next morning. She'd have to face it. Philip might just say a cold good-bye the way the others had.

She could delay giving in, and keep him dangling. After all, she was staying in England for a week. She could sleep with him only on the last night, and then she'd be the one to rush off—to catch her plane.

She picked up the soap. It was lavender-scented. Lathering the washcloth, she soaped herself slowly, thinking. The trouble was, she wanted Philip. She closed her eyes and pictured his fingers touching the

178

head of Aphrodite. Philip was sexy. But he was far more elegant than any of the men with whom she was usually involved. He was like Arthur, intelligent and sensitive, but unlike Arthur, Philip was nearly her age and desirable and handsome. And he wanted her. Maybe this time . . .

Well, if it did turn out badly, she wouldn't have lost so much. After all, she wouldn't have to see Philip again. Maybe she should try it. She was not going into the affair with any unrealistic notions. Why not try and see?

Her decision was made by the time she had finished her bath. She was happy that she had a new outfit to wear, one she had just bought at Saks in Chicago. It was a long cream-colored satin skirt topped by a white batiste camisole. The low-cut bodice was edged with cream-embroidered scallops. Mab twisted her hair up into a knot high on her head, and fastened a cream-colored ribbon around her neck. She made up her eyes very carefully, using white underneath the outer edges to emphasize their tilt. She shaded the lids and brows with mauve and silver. When she had finished outlining them and applying mascara, she was pleased with the effects. Her skin looked luminous tonight, blooming—it must be England's damp climate. She painted her lips coral and added some L'Air du Temps.

As she was taking her evening coat of brown velvet and gold satin out of the closet, she heard a rap on the door. Her heart beat a little harder as she opened it. Philip, looking unbelievably handsome in a black tuxedo, stood there holding out a small nosegay of white and purple violets.

"Good evening," he said. "I brought you—good heavens, Mab, you look smashing! You take my breath away." He stepped in. He seemed truly struck with her appearance, and he stared earnestly at her for a few seconds.

She thanked him.

"I'd reform and go to the theater every night if I could take you," he said finally, offering her the bouquet.

"What lovely flowers," Mab said, putting the flowers to her nose and sniffing. A little stiffened lace surrounded the delicate violets. "I'll take them with me."

Philip helped her into the evening coat and escorted her downstairs. A Rolls Royce with a driver was waiting for them. It was chilly outside, but the night was clear. As they sped through the streets to the theater district, Philip sat close to Mab.

"What is that scent? Your perfume?" he asked.

She told him the name of it.

"I like it. And your hair up like that is beautiful. You know, you look exactly the way you did dancing in Miss Phipps's recital. I can't believe you look so young—sixteen, maybe."

"Philip, please."

"I mean it." He studied Mab's face in the lights from the marquees they passed now on either side of the street. "It's phenomenal."

Banana Ridge was a zany comedy and Mab loved every minute of it. They drank champagne during intermission, and the second half seemed even funnier. When they left the theater, Mab was hungry.

"After our tea, I thought I'd never eat again," she said. "But my appetite is back."

"I made a reservation for us at Rules. I hope you'll like the place; it's a favorite of mine, not as fancy as Etoile, but open late, at least. Many places aren't."

Rules was another old-fashioned resturant. Mab liked it. The walls were covered with landscape paintings, and it was dark; small lamps with pretty shades provided the only light. The booths and tables were filled with well-dressed people having late dinners. She and Philip were escorted to a large, dark booth, almost a small room to themselves. They sat down across from each other.

180

"The salmon here is famous, if you care for salmon," Philip said.

Mab ordered the salmon, with soup to start, and Philip asked for the same.

"You have such good taste, I should follow your lead in everything," Philip said.

Mab was pleased. Philip reached across the table and put his hand over hers. He looked into her eyes, searching.

"You have a strange quality, Mab. You seem rather wistful."

"Wistful?" she said.

"When you were looking at the Turner painting this morning, you looked—as if you were longing to unlock some secret. The way you approach art is so interesting. It's as if you were a child on a treasure hunt."

"How odd that you should say that," Mab said, feeling rather warm again from the pressure of his hand over hers. "I loved treasure hunts when I was young. We were always sending each other around looking for clues."

Philip smiled. "You're just like that now. You go from piece to piece with that excited breathless manner that youngsters have when they're rushing about hunting for something. But you're wistful, too. As if you knew you could never get what you really wanted. Never find a treasure really worth finding."

Mab's lips parted in surprise and she stared at Philip, intrigued by his words. The waiter brought them glasses of sherry, but Philip didn't take his hand away from hers. What sort of person was he, anyway? He had changed from the boy she remembered. She didn't recall his ever being either as jolly as he had been today, or as thoughtful and deep as he seemed to-night. She sipped her sherry and looked at his face. He seemed younger in the dim light, almost as young as she could remember him being back in Eyreville.

"I never thought of it until this minute," she said, "but my life is a sort of giant treasure hunt, isn't it?"

"And do you find the treasures you dig up rewarding enough?"

"Of course."

"That wistful look says no."

The continued contact with his hand was making Mab feel positively hot. Philip didn't drink his sherry; he just looked quietly at her. The subdued buzz of conversation and the clink of dishes beyond their booth did not intrude on their quiet contemplation of one another.

"Sorry," Philip said, lifting his hand off hers. "Amateur psychiatry. One should never indulge in it."

Mab had liked having him touch her and she was sorry when he took his hand away.

The waiter arrived with their soup in a silver tureen and served it with a flourish. Mab cast about for something to say.

"Years ago," she said, "I got trapped into going into a dark room by a false clue in a treasure hunt—you just made me remember it. It was my very first experience with a boy."

"What happened?"

"Oh, nothing at all, really." Mab smiled. "The boy's sister—do you remember Beebee Cunningham?—hammered on the door threatening to tell their mother. We didn't even kiss."

"Hellraiser?"

"No, Buckshot. Did you know he went to college at Yale? That surprised me. But then later he became a hippie. I understand he came back to Eyreville once, in a sky-blue satin suit with a full beard and long hair, and he sat in the gutter in front of the drugstore and played the guitar all day long. Mrs. Cunningham washed her hands of him. Now I think he builds roads up in Canada."

"Really? I did hear something about Hellraiser," Philip said. "I find it hard to believe, but Champ says that he went in for politics and became a state senator."

"They say he's going to run for governor soon. *He* says he'll run for president after that. Cypriana told me. She's quite interested in his campaigns. He makes dramatic speeches, she says."

The salmon arrived. After drinking the white wine that accompanied it, and sharing a split of champagne with dessert, Mab felt in a blissful mood. Coffee arrived.

Philip suddenly asked a question in a serious voice: "Mab, do you think that Cypriana and Champ are happy?"

"Yes," Mab said. "I'm not in Eyreville often, of course, but I visited them at Christmas a year and a half ago. And occasionally Cypri calls me—she never writes letters. Everything seems to be fine with them."

"Champ certainly seemed happy at the wedding."

As Philip spoke, Mab thought he looked a trifle wistful himself. Her hand lay in front of her on the table, and he reached over and gently ran his index finger across the back of it, tracing her delicate veins.

"Mab, would you like to come back to my flat?" he asked, looking down at her hand.

Mab let her hand turn over and grasp his. Philip looked up and she met his dark eyes.

"I would," she said.

Philip smiled. "Thank you," he said softly; then, "let's go."

The Rolls took them through the dark streets and drew up to an exclusive-looking old apartment building. Mab was only able to get a fleeting impression of the lobby, since they were through it and into the elevator in a moment. Philip quickly opened his door, turned on the lights and led her into the living room.

"Oh, this is charming," she said looking around. "I like the colors especially."

The room was basically blue and white with touches of red. Red velvet sofas faced each other at one end of the room, and dark oil paintings covered the walls. The woodwork, fireplace and high carved ceilings were white.

"I must confess I deserve no credit," Philip said. "A decorator did it. I'm not really artistic, myself."

"I think it is elegant. The carved ceilings are beautiful."

Philip removed her coat and hung it up.

"How about some champagne? There's always some in the fridge. Or I'll fix you a drink if you would like."

"Philip, you are ruining me. How much champagne have we drunk today? I feel giggly as it is."

"I'll be right back," he said.

Drinking so much had done one thing for her. She didn't feel at all nervous. She curled up in the corner of Philip's velvet sofa and smiled at the walls.

Philip came back with a cold bottle of champagne and two wine glasses. After he poured a glass for her and for himself, he sat down on the floor just in front of her.

"Let me look at you there, Mab," he said. "You are a picture, sitting on that sofa. This room needs a beautiful woman to complete it. Mab, do you know what I'd like? I'd like you to stay here, stay with me tonight."

He leaned over. Her hand was resting on the arm of the sofa and he pressed his lips against her fingers. Mab ran her other hand over Philip's head, through his thick hair.

"I'd love to stay," she whispered.

Oh, Philip, Mab thought, I'd love to give everything to you, everything you think you want, my body, my thoughts. Those things are easy to give. The voice inside her head warned, *Even though Philip wants me, he's going to be disappointed*. Letting him make love to her was simple, but the possibility of having to face his indifference tomorrow, of having to face her inadequacy once again, oppressed her. Her hand on his

184

dark hair shook a little. Maybe she should just go to the Savoy.

"You're sad, Mab. What is it?" Philip spoke so tenderly that when he reached for her, Mab gave up and sighed and let herself slide down onto the floor, into the circle of his arms.

"What's the matter?" he whispered. He held her as if she were very fragile, looking into her face. His lips were close to hers and she wanted to kiss him. Suddenly, the desire to touch Philip, to kiss him, was stronger than all her other feelings. She drew a sharp breath and moved her lips toward his cheek, but Philip immediately put his lips over hers. Mab began to tremble. She closed her eyes and just let herself kiss him. She wanted to hold onto that beautiful moment forever. Her body was responding to Philip's kiss in a way she'd never responded before. Philip was trying to kiss her very carefully, but when her arms went around his neck she felt him tremble as well, and their lips seemed unable to part. His arms tightened and he made a little sound in his throat. Opening her eyes, she saw that his eyes were closed, the dark lashes curling close to her cheek. It touched her that Philip had closed his eyes. The kiss became very passionate. Mab was overwhelmed with her feelings. The flesh on her bones seemed almost to belong to someone else, someone abandoned to sensation alone, as she gripped Philip harder. Finally, Philip lifted his head slightly, so that when he said her name his lips still lightly touched hers. She whispered his name in answer.

When Philip stood up, his arms carried her up with him and her body felt as light as air. Swiftly, Philip walked with her into the bedroom, and putting her carefully down on the bed, he kissed her again, bending over her and pulling her up against him. After a while he caught her lower lip gently between his lips. Then his mouth traveled across her face to her ear and he whispered, "Shall I help you take off your clothes?"

Mab made a sound of assent, and watched as Philip carefully unhooked the front of her camisole. She slid out of her satin skirt and her underthings and looked up at Philip. He was staring at her body. In the light from the lamp there were little pools of shadow in the hollows of her stomach and her hips.

"My God, you are beautiful," Philip said. He had an awed look on his face. "I don't think I've ever seen such a beautiful body on any human being."

Mab squeezed her eyes shut. Please, God, she prayed briefly. Just this once, let it happen—let it be perfect. Let it be the way it's supposed to be.

Philip took his own clothes off rapidly, and she looked at his hard, strong body. When he stretched out beside her and she could touch him, she whispered, "I love your body, too," and caressed his back and his buttocks as he kissed her on the insides of her ears and her throat and shoulders. No one had ever kissed Mab the way Philip did, or touched her with such sure hands. He seemed to know exactly what to do. He must be very experienced, she thought, because he was bringing her close to fulfillment before they even actually made love. Her body was hot and quivering, and she gasped, finding it hard to breathe, and harder to believe she could get so close to bliss. "Oh, Philip," she cried, parting her legs and moving against him. He murmured to her, something she couldn't hear, and kissing her nipples, he held back for a few more agonizing moments, and then she felt him inside of her, and she cried out when the release came. It was as if she were going over the top of a waterfall and hurtling down and down far below into a wide dark lake of pure pleasure.

Hours seemed to pass, and gradually Mab's heart slowed its mad pounding. She felt sweat break out on her brow, as if she had been dancing. Her skin glowed all over, and she felt as if she weren't really there at all, on the bed or even inside her own skin, but instead was in some timeless, nameless place, discovering at last what it was like to be completely happy.

She drew a long breath and blinked. Philip was pressed full-length against her and his body was hot as fire. She could feel his heart beating fast, right under her ear. In a minute he put his hands under her arms and pulled her up so that their faces touched again, and he gave her light little kisses, covering her hair and her temples and her cheekbones. Mab closed her eyes and sighed.

In a few minutes Philip kissed her passionately again. She kissed him back with all the fervor in her; he was a darling, an angel; she loved him. This time their union seemed an even deeper experience. Tears came to Mab's eyes and she blinked them away. If only this night could last forever, this night when everything happened the way it should. It was miraculous.

For a while, they rested clasped together. Then they made love again. Mab began to feel thirsty sometime in the early morning. Gently she pulled herself from Philip's arms, intending to find his bathroom and get a drink.

"Where are you going?" he asked, immediately opening his eyes.

"I thought you were asleep. I just want some water."

"I'll bring you some water. Here, darling. Wait." He spoke to her the way one speaks to a beloved child. In a moment he brought her a glass of water, and she drank it and smiled at him. When she put the glass down, he took her in his arms again, and held her tightly. From the light faintly showing through the draperies, she could tell it was morning. She didn't feel at all tired, although she hadn't slept.

Philip had taken the pins out of her hair and it hung down over her shoulders. He played with it and kissed it, and then he wanted to make love again. It seemed to take him rather a long time to reach a climax this time. A warning bell went off in the back of Mab's mind. Was it her old problem? Maybe it was.

187

When he began trying again, she used her mouth instead, which seemed to surprise him. But Mab had read that all men liked that. And it was easy to make him have an orgasm that way. Surely Philip would keep on liking her, if she showed him she'd do anything to satisfy him.

He lay still for a while, and lying close to him, Mab wondered what would happen now. The night was over. What she passionately wanted was for Philip to continue to be tender, to be so intensely interested in her. She wished he would bring her breakfast in bed, and feed her, and she would do the same for him, and they could laugh together the way they had yesterday. She would tell him she loved him, if he asked her. She loved him and she loved his naked body, the back of his neck with its covering of fine hairs, and his spine and his long, muscular legs. Turning her head, she softly kissed the back of his neck. She hoped he wouldn't mind. She really loved the back of his neck.

Philip blinked his eyes open. Just as he looked over at the clock on the table beside the bed, the telephone rang. He pulled himself up to a sitting position and picked up the receiver.

"Hello. Alexander here."

Mab was struck by the sudden businesslike tone Philip assumed as he spoke. She moved a little away from him. She looked around the room. Her skirt and top lay on the floor beside the bed, and her shoes were in the middle of the rug.

"Yes, Arnold, right. What? Are you sure?" Philip sounded surprised by something. "Wait a minute. Let me change telephones."

Philip put the receiver down on the bed. Mab thought he would say something to her, but he gave her a blank look, got up and went to his closet for a bathrobe. Wrapping the robe around him, he walked out of the room without a word.

"This is a complete surprise—" she heard him say a minute later, from the living room.

My God, Mab thought. Did Philip want to get rid of her this very minute? It was Sunday morning. Surely he didn't discuss business on Sundays. And yet it sounded like business. From the living room she could hear his voice, asking questions rather abruptly, then pausing while he listened to long answers.

The rudeness of it stunned her. Her body was still feeling so involved with his, and he had just walked off. Drearily, she thought, I should know the script. There was a pain in her throat; she couldn't swallow. He must want her to go. Just to get out quickly. Philip had stuck himself with her for the night and, he had behaved like a gentleman, but now he wanted her out of there.

Mab jumped out of bed. The mirror over his dresser reflected a big-eyed girl with hair amazingly mussed. She picked up Philip's hairbrush and brushed her hair. It took several minutes to tame it properly. Then she went into Philip's bathroom and washed her face without even a glance at the rest of herself. She hated her body.

Back in the bedroom, she could hear Philip's voice from the living room; he was still talking on the phone. Well, she certainly wouldn't stick around to be insulted. Her hands trembled as she dressed. She was going to look pretty funny walking into the Savoy in evening clothes. At least she had her long coat.

When she walked into the living room, Philip's back was toward her. He was standing by a small desk, still listening to the voice on the telephone. Mab picked up her evening purse. It lay on the coffee table beside the bouquet of violets. She left the bouquet, went back into the bedroom and put on some lipstick, and then crossed the living room to the closet by the door where her coat was hanging. This time Philip noticed her.

"Arnold, wait a minute. There's someone here." Philip put the telephone receiver down on the desk. "Mab. I'm sorry—this is business I can't delay. I'm afraid—"

"It's all right," she said. "I'm leaving."

She dragged her coat out of the closet and pulled it around her.

Philip looked bewildered. "Leaving?" he repeated. He seemed to have his mind on something else.

Mab looked at him, and the pain in her throat was intense. It hurt so much to admit the truth to yourself.

"Thanks, Philip, for yesterday. Good-bye," she said, opening his front door as she did so.

"Wait. Do you want my car?"

"Don't bother," she said. Her tone was cold. "I'll take a taxi."

Quickly she closed the door behind her and rushed down the hall to the elevator. Downstairs, the doorman found her a taxi. She wondered what the doorman thought. No doubt he was used to women leaving Philip's place in the mornings.

She jumped into the taxi and directed it to the Savoy. When it started moving, she felt slightly better. A fast getaway was the only satisfaction her pride could have, but it was something. Philip had humiliated her. He could get up in the morning and discuss business, in spite of all the desperate cuddling and holding of the night. She wondered if that was Philip's technique with all his women. Probably he had millions of girls and she was just another one, pretty perhaps but a dud in bed. She wanted to cry. Oh, you bomb out every time, she said to herself. You never learn, and I'm sorry I have to live inside you.

Mab was crying by the time they reached the Savoy. Blindly she handed the driver a fistful of English bills and coins, and turned and fled into the hotel. She thought the driver called something to her but she didn't hear what it was. The elevator she took upstairs was empty. She managed to control herself until she was alone in her room, and then she sobbed aloud. While she cried, lying on the bed, part of her was saying, You asked for this. I tried to warn you. You set yourself up again, didn't you? Dope.

X

Dope. Mab repeated the word to herself. She sighed, sat up in bed and reached for her appointment book. She flipped it open to Friday, June seventeenth, and wrote, "Mischa to kennels." She added, "Get Joe to feed Rudi." At the bottom of Friday's page she wrote, "to Eyreville?"

She'd check the airline schedule in the morning. She turned the page. The thought at the top of the page for Saturday, June eighteenth was "Wise men learn more from fools than fools from the wise." It was too late at night to ponder the import of that message. Mab stared at the blank page. So, after only four months, she was going to see Philip again. She was amazed to hear that he was in trouble—gambling. She couldn't have guessed that from the day and night they had spent together. Just briefly, Mab let herself recall the rapturous part again. She had been over it all in her mind a thousand times. Just remember the good things that happened to you, and look away from the bad—her mother had taught her that. *Remember the good.*

Her mother had been good, too good to them all, probably. Perhaps they were all doomed, China's girls from Land's End, doomed to go through life looking for the same blind tenderness, kindness, sweetness she had given them. It didn't seem to exist in men, or to coexist with sexuality, anyway. Arthur was kind, but he certainly wasn't sexy.

At least her little sister Cypriana had found a man

to marry. But then, from what Mab heard, Cypri had never gone around wistfully looking for love; she always demanded it and got it. Mab wondered how Cypri managed.

Thinking of Cypri reminded her of Daisy. What on earth was this about Philip's being engaged to Daisy? The child was only twenty-one years old. Philip must be thirty-seven or thirty-eight. Of course, men liked to marry young girls—but *Philip*? He had not seemed that type. Besides, Daisy was a nervous creature, shy and quiet.

At any rate, she would see Philip again. Mab looked at the small calendar in the front of her appointment book and counted. In nine days. She'd see Philip in just nine days. She'd have to buy some great clothes to wear. Something new and daring for the ball. She'd go shopping tomorrow. She'd buy something to make Philip—well, make him what? Sorry?

Mab sighed. Carefully, across the page for June eighteenth, she printed the words "Land's End." Then she turned out her light and settled back on her pillow, but she didn't go to sleep for a long time.

Book Two:

Cypriana and Daisy

XI

On Friday, June seventeenth, the day before the Land's End house party, Cypriana Dane Alexander and Daisy Sykes both had four o'clock appointments at the Eyreville Beauty Parlor.

They were late, a not unexpected occurrence. The young doctor's wife never bothered to be exactly on time anywhere, and her cousin Daisy, who was two years younger, had no say. Daisy lived with Cypriana and her husband.

There was a fuss when the two did arrive. Cypriana was a generous tipper. The three operators of the Eyreville Beauty Parlor gathered to greet her, even though Thelma Baker, the beauty parlor's best operator, always did her hair.

"Who's doing Daisy?" Cypriana asked, slinging her white pocketbook down on the magazine table. "Betty Lou? Betty Lou, Daisy has to look great. She's getting married."

"What?" The girls all exclaimed. "That's wonderful." "Who is it? Do we know him?"

Daisy's face turned red.

"I'm not really—not right away—"

"Tomorrow Daisy's fiancé is coming from London to go to Land's End with us for the weekend. And that reminds me"—Cypriana flopped down into the chair beside the sink and tossed her hair back, ready for her shampoo—"we need you to come out there tomorrow afternoon to fix our hair. We have to look ravishing. Daisy's having an engagement ball. If I send Chooky with our car, can you come out around five-thirty?"

Cypriana barely troubled to raise her voice in question; she expected Thelma to agree. And, though Thelma would have to change a late appointment and would probably lose the goodwill of the steady customer involved, she didn't dream of saying no. No one said no to Cypri Dane.

Thelma fitted the plastic cape carefully around her client's neck and ran the water to a perfect lukewarm before wetting the thick dark hair.

"Conditioner, too?"

"Yes, I liked your new herbal thing." Cypriana closed her eyes and sighed with pleasure as Thelma's fingers massaged and soaped her scalp. Shampoos made her feel sexy.

"I've never been inside of Land's End. I'd like to see it," Thelma said, rubbing vigorously.

"Vivienne has been working on it, restoring it, all spring. My sister Mab is coming for the house party, too."

"And your cousin is engaged! When did that happen?"

"While we were in England. She's going to marry Champ's older brother." Cypriana spoke with her eyes closed. "Philip. Do you remember him?"

"No. My goodness, I've heard of him, though. Isn't he"—Thelma lowered her voice, looking over at the sink next door where Daisy was under the ministrations of Betty Lou—"very—"

"Rich," Cypriana finished for her. "Yes." She laughed. "Daisy hit the jackpot. He's handsome, too. You'd be surprised. Nothing like Champ. He's dark."

"I think Dr. Alexander is very handsome," Thelma said, rinsing her hair carefully.

Cypriana did not reply.

The rich sweet smell of hair spray mingled in the humid air with the scent of the pseudo-natural herb shampoo and rinse. At the next sink, Daisy did not seem to want to discuss her good fortune. She replied minimally to Betty Lou's questions. Betty Lou noticed that Daisy was not wearing an engagement ring. Perhaps her fiancé was bringing a diamond with him for the engagement party weekend—if that was what it was to be. Betty Lou longed to ask. But Daisy seemed tense; her body was stiff and she looked uncomfortable.

Betty Lou massaged Daisy's scalp longer than usual, trying to get her to relax.

"Beautiful weather," she said. "Not really hot. Unusual for South Carolina in June." Betty Lou used the rubber shower head to rinse Daisy's hair. "Shall I put on conditioner? Make your hair shiny."

"Give her the works, Betty Lou," Cypriana replied for her cousin. Thelma was already twisting Cypri's hair up in a white linen towel.

Betty Lou smiled. Daisy remained grave.

The cousins sat at adjoining mirrors for the blowdry. The noise of the machines limited their ability to hear, and everyone fell silent. Betty Lou and Thelma in concert pulled out the long hair, twisting it around the circular brushes, maneuvering their hand blowers expertly as the dark strands of Cypriana's straight hair and the long fair strands of Daisy's were blown back in the breeze.

The girls' faces were reflected in the oval mirrors in front of them. Denise, who had no customer until five, stood watching from the doorway. People could not say enough, ever—could not get over the beauty of the Dane family, the three sisters and Daisy Sykes, who was considered to equal them in beauty. Daisy's hair was long, straight, and light gold—she was the only fair one—and her eyes were a clear blue. Her face was small and her features delicate. Her habitual expression, the look of being a little bothered, was oddly at variance with her soft young skin and youthful, awkward movements.

Nothing was at variance in Cypriana Dane's look, or ever had been. From head to toe, she was tightly strung up to dominate the world; early a tomboy, later

197

imperious, she had always stood with her elegant head up and her weight equally distributed on both feet, the way a fighter stands. Indisputably, she owned the air around her. All her life she had driven boys crazy. Her long and heavy silky dark hair swung close around her sensual, perfect facial features, framing them in ebony; from this dark shelter her blue eyes stared out boldly, eyes of such intense blue they tended to shock the observer at first.

"She looks like pussy," Champ had whispered to his best friend when Cypriana was twelve years old and had passed him on the street with a dark glance and no greeting. Cypriana would scarcely have spoken to an *Alexander* then. That was eleven years ago. Now she was married to Champ. He got a full share of the bargain; she was as sexy as she looked.

With the gentle tugging on her head as Thelma brushed out her hair to dry it, Cypriana again felt the tingle she had experienced during her shampoo. She glanced in the mirror at sharp-featured Thelma's face and then over to the next oval mirror, at Daisy's face reflected there. Daisy's eyes were closed. Cypriana smiled.

. . . Running naked together over Land's End lawn in the moonlight . . .

The image came into Cypriana's mind again an hour later as she lay with Daisy in the king-sized bed she usually shared with Champ. The minute they got home from the beauty parlor, she had rushed Daisy upstairs. There wasn't much time before Champ was due home. Cypriana had torn off Daisy's clothes and her own, flung the clothes to the floor, pushed her cousin onto the bed and pasted her lips to Daisy's pink nipple, the left one, the fuller one.

"Oh, God," Daisy moaned as she writhed against her cousin.

"The beauty parlor makes me feel so sexy," Cypriana said, biting Daisy as she spoke. "I want to rape. Rape

Thelma. Only she's so dour. Don't you think so? Would you like me to rape her?"

"Oh, God. Keep on. No, please." Daisy was moaning. "Don't stop. Please love me. Not Thelma. No."

"Did you think of me while Betty Lou shampooed you?"

"*Yes*, honestly I did. *Please*."

"You're a liar." Cypriana transferred her attentions to Daisy's thighs, licking them thoroughly.

"Please."

"You whine like a dog, did you know? Like Aunt Martha's chow."

Daisy began to cry, tears rolling down her cheeks. "Cypri, I love you. I don't care what you do to me. Please, please—"

"We have to hurry. I'll give you one minute more. Then you're on your own. You have to get under the bed."

"*No*." Daisy's voice was raised in a wail. "Oh, Cypri, don't stop, please don't stop, don't make me—"

"Yes." Cypriana stood up abruptly, clambering off the big bed onto the white shag carpeting. "On second thought, until you show a little more appreciation for everything that's done for you—"

"*No*." Daisy was sobbing, curled into a fetal position on the bed.

"Get under the bed." Cypri stood naked and supreme, her white body tense. Daisy looked at her and shuddered.

"You have before. You *like* it." Cypriana smiled. "Oh no. God, no."

Downstairs, the front door slammed.

"Cypri?"

It was Champ. Cypri went to the sliding doors of the closet, opened her side, and took out a white chiffon negligee trimmed with ostrich feathers. She pulled it on.

"Up here," she called.

The sound of feet climbing the carpeted staircase

199

galvanized Daisy. With a despairing look at Cypri, sl..
uncurled. Cypri grinned at her. Daisy started for the
closet. Cypri forestalled her.

"No you don't," she said softly. "You get under the
bed or I'll tell Champ you—"

Cypri didn't finish the threat, but began kicking
Daisy's clothes and shoes under the bed.

Champ had reached the second floor. Panic on her
face, Daisy looked at Cypri, who squeezed her arm
so tightly that the pressure was bound to leave a bruise.

As Champ opened the bedroom door, Daisy threw
herself on the floor and wriggled face-up underneath
the king-sized bed.

"Hi, sweetie."

Champ came in. He was a broad-shouldered, square-
shaped young man, with sandy hair and gray eyes.
Cypri turned to look at him, licked her upper lip and
let her chiffon robe fall open.

"Ummm, that's nice," Champ said. He sat down on
the bed and pulled Cypriana onto his lap. "Well, tomorrow's the big day. Are you ready?" He ran his
blunt-tipped fingers through the silky dark hair of
Cypriana's pelvis.

Cypriana put her arms around Champ's neck and
gave him a long kiss. "A party at Land's End without
Mother there—it will be different," she murmured. "I
was just thinking about that."

"God, I had a hell of a day, but I should be off
duty now for the weekend," Champ said. "Let me get
out of these clothes."

Champ stripped off his gray and white striped seer-
sucker jacket and pulled off his gray pants. Cypri
unbuttoned his shirt, and pulled his shorts off and threw
them down on the floor. When Champ was naked
they rolled together over the bed and Cypri giggled
when Champ licked the inside of her ear.

"Stop it! That tickles me," she said.

Champ pulled her chiffon negligee down her back
so that it imprisoned her arms; when she struggled,

200

he tied the chiffon into a knot. The bed heaved under Cypri's gyrations as she tried to get free.

"Stop it, Champ!" Cypri giggled, but Champ held her down. When he ducked his head to kiss her breast, Cypri suddenly heaved herself over onto her stomach and Champ got a mouthful of ostrich feathers instead. Cypri squirmed around to watch him spit feathers out of his mouth.

"I'm buying a new negligee tomorrow for that," she said. "You're tearing it apart—"

"How would you like some feathers in *your* mouth?" Champ took the last feather from his mouth and ran it across Cypri's stomach. She gasped.

"You bastard. Stop it."

Champ pulled a handful of feathers out of the robe and tried to force them into Cypri's mouth and she spat them out. She was breathless and laughing. In a minute he began kissing her again, his arms around her. They turned over, and when she was on top of him, he gently loosened the chiffon that held her. Once her arms were free, Cypri locked them around Champ's shoulders and refused to touch him where he wanted until he made a handsome apology. The physical method he chose for this concession made Cypriana gasp and then cry his name loudly, her fingers clutching his hair; after her violent climax she twisted down and began to kiss him avidly. In a moment Champ cried out sharply and pulled Cypriana's body between his knees, and the up and down motion of the bed increased rapidly. They both moaned.

Under the bed, Daisy lay rigid. It was not the first time she had been there. Cypriana often made her lie there and experience, secondhand, heterosexual love.

Salty tears ran sideways down Daisy's face, wetting the shiny blond hair over her temples. The bed creaked on, above her, and the carpet she was lying on smelled faintly dusty. An old bedroom slipper of Champ's was lying on its side near her head and it reeked of foot powder.

How she, Daisy Sykes, had come to such a pass, was perfectly logical to her. She deserved no better.

XII

June seventeenth was the date in 1937 on which China Royal Austin had married Bascomb Dane. "The union of two of the leading families of the South," the *Eyreville Times* put it. Only the Austins, in Eyreville, equalled the Danes in family prominence. China's father had been Ambassador to China, and she had been born in Peking and named for the country of her birth. When her father returned from government service, he moved back to his birthplace, Eyreville, where the piece of land named Austin's Neck testified to the family's original land grant from King George. In terms of family, China was definitely Bascomb Dane's peer. In income, the two families were evenly matched; the heads of both households were wealthy landowners. Only in the eventual distribution of that wealth to the heirs was there a difference. China came from a large family; she had two sisters and four stepbrothers. Bascomb was the only child of his parents. At the time of his marriage to China Austin, the elder Danes happily gave Bascomb enough stocks and bonds to ensure that he could live the life of a gentleman and buy the house on Curzon's Neck called Land's End for his wife.

The wedding was splendid. Many people said dark-haired China Austin was the most beautiful bride they had ever seen. The ceremony took place at Gardens, the Austins' estate overlooking the river just outside Eyreville. Gardens was justly named; it was surrounded by gardens, and it was in the rose garden at the height of its flowering in June that the wedding ceremony was read by the minister of Eyreville's Episcopal church.

China's twelve-year-old sister, Catherine Allison Austin, was the youngest bridesmaid, thrilled with the decolletage of her rose chiffon bridesmaid's dress. Catherine Allison vowed a vow to herself. Her own wedding when the time came would be even more splendid. But there was not a Bascomb Dane in her future.

Nineteen years later Daisy Sykes was born in a hospital in Galveston, Texas, and so complete was Catherine Allison's break with her family that she did not even send a birth announcement to anyone in Eyreville. Let them find out for themselves! It was a year before China Dane heard about her niece's birth. Daisy's father was Catherine Allison's second husband, and neither of her weddings had been in a rose garden. Her first marriage had been to a soldier who was killed in Korea. Her young husband's last post, before he shipped overseas, was Galveston; they had lived there together in a trailer. Catherine Allison stayed on in Galveston, assuaging her sorrow with drink. She hated her family. None of them had suffered in the war. It was such a strange war, hurting only a few and yet hurting those few so deeply. Her father had not approved of her marriage to her darling Tony, just because he was a little younger than she and his brother had been convicted for burglary. Her father had never understood her anyway. Catherine Allison nursed her pride; she was, after all, an Austin and you were what you were born; nothing could alter that.

She dated oil-field workers. She didn't care if they were crude and loud; at least it was a change. She had never been a good Austin anyway; China and dopey Gwendolyn, now a voice teacher in Columbia, were miles ahead of her. The family was proud of them. She supposed they wanted *her* to come home and sit around so they could feel sorry for her and never approve of anything she did—well, the hell with that. She worked in a jewelry store so she could buy costume jewelry at half-price and she loved to see those roughnecks' eyes bug out when she sashayed into the Derrick Bar and Grill in her new long skirt with her low-cut blouse glittering. Her bust was full. It always had been, not flat like ladylike old China's or dopey Gwendolyn's. She gave the men an eyeful.

Barry Sykes had once played fullback for Texas A and M, and he certainly hadn't been hurting for notice since. He was famous; at least at the Derrick Bar and Grill. Men bought him beer every night to hear about some famous big game in Dallas and the one at the Sugar Bowl. He'd gotten through the Korean War just fine, in Special Services the whole time. Catherine Allison fell headlong in love with him when she first saw him. When Barry learned that Catherine Allison owned a trailer and got payments from the government, he became interested in her as well. They loved to drink together. They loved to dance together. They loved to sleep together. Sex with Barry was strange and exciting, sometimes with an element of violence. Catherine Allison didn't try very hard to be careful, and pretty soon she was pregnant. It got Barry to the altar, or rather, to the county registrar's office.

While she was pregnant, she was often sick. The baby began to seem like a high price to pay for a wedding ring. Barry was an oil-field worker who brought home a good wage, but a good deal of it went for liquor. He lost a lot playing poker, too. She adored him, she never said an angry word to him, but sometimes, sitting alone while he was out with his cronies, Catherine Allison cursed the stupid teachings that had made her want to nail herself down in marriage. Why was nothing else any good?

In a bad mood she went to the hospital. The baby was a girl. Funny. All the time she had thought it would be a boy, who would play football like his daddy. Now there was never going to be a Sykes for

Texas A and M because she was determined never to have another baby. She was staggered by the demands of the infant on her time and patience. In the low-ceilinged trailer, the baby's crying sounded like the howling of a pack of wolves. Sometimes Catherine Allison screamed, too. She was exhausted, getting up at night for the feedings, boiling bottles, washing diapers. Somehow the little girl didn't get to her at all, even when other women cooed over her blue eyes and wisps of light blond hair.

So far everything in her life had turned out strangely. Catherine Allison wondered what would happen if she just ran off, maybe to New Orleans, and changed her name. What was almost as good as a new life, though, and less trouble, was starting out the morning with a little nip of bourbon after Barry had left. It got you along. A martini or two before lunch, cold, ice-cold, and beer with the afternoon soap operas . . . and then Barry'd be home for his pick-me-ups and she'd join him. They had lots of friends, too. The Bar and Grill wasn't far and Mrs. Royal next door would listen for the baby.

Around the trailer court, most people were an odd lot, but Catherine Allison liked Mrs. Royal. Royal had been Catherine Allison's mother's maiden name. She told Mrs. Royal that. They weren't related, though. The older woman was from Oregon, a middle-aged widow who lived in Galveston to be near her son and his family. Mrs. Royal went to visit her son every Sunday and the rest of the time she was available to look after Daisy. She liked Daisy.

Things got a little easier when Daisy finally was toilet-trained, and easier still when she was old enough to be sent to kindergarten. The school was just two blocks down the road, so Daisy could walk there and back with the other kids. Daisy turned out to be a good little girl, mostly because Catherine Allison was far too nervous to put up with bad behavior. Daisy knew what the back of the hair brush was for, all right. Catherine Allison kept the kid up to snuff. Not that Barry agreed; he said she spoiled Daisy. Sometimes when Barry was drinking he'd show Daisy what sort of discipline *he* had gotten as a kid. It didn't take much to set him off. Daisy would sob for hours afterward. Catherine Allison came in for a few blows here and there, herself, but that was just—well, you expected it.

She didn't tell Barry that she had had her tubes tied while she was in the hospital. Sometimes he wondered why she never got pregnant again, but he didn't honestly care. He didn't really like kids. Or so Catherine Allison thought, until Barry took up with a sixteen-year-old bitch who was the daughter of the man who owned the Bar and Grill. When Catherine Allison found out about it she was hysterical. She told Barry to get out and he went. He left Galveston altogether eventually, but he sent back a little money every month. If Catherine Allison skimped on food—she could make a can of Spam last two days, for just Daisy and herself—there was money enough left to get a bottle of Thunderbird or something cheap, something just to keep a buzz on and not have to face everything all at once.

Daisy was much happier with her father away. She cleaned the trailer, shopped and cooked, even though she was only in second grade. Her great friend was Mrs. Royal. Mrs. Royal sometimes made Daisy dresses to wear to school. Once in a while Catherine Allison would take Daisy shopping, and in a burst of generosity buy her anything she liked. She *wanted* Daisy to have a happy childhood; it was just that sometimes it seemed to her that Daisy's childhood wasn't really taking place at all. In South Carolina, that's where you had a childhood, the cool fields to run over and the servants to wait on you and huge rooms to explore. Catherine Allison occasionally wondered what her brothers were doing, her sisters—it was an odd lot she had put in with here. But after a vodka or two they didn't seem too bad.

207

XIII

By the time Daisy was in third grade, her mother's drinking had gotten to the point of making her physically ill. She stopped for three months. Daisy was really happy then. Daisy's teacher Mrs. Murray said that Daisy was smart, the smartest pupil in her class and always well-behaved. Catherine Allison was pleased. She took Daisy shopping and bought her a new bathing suit. They would go to the beach more; a bus went right out there.

However, Dusty Devon rolled into the Bar and Grill one night while Catherine Allison was sitting there just sipping an orange juice. One of her friends knew him. He was fat. He was also huge in other ways. He was six feet four, and he couldn't stand up in her trailer. He bumped his head on everything. Still, he moved in. He was a truck driver, there all the time for a while and then gone for a week or so. Daisy was grieved. Dusty was dirty and smelled bad, and after a few Scotches with her mother he would send Daisy to bed and she could hear funny things happening. Sometimes the whole trailer rocked and her mother cried out. Once a neighbor—maybe Mrs. Royal— called the police and they came. But her mother said nothing was going on, and why didn't people mind their own business?

Once, Dusty was there and her mother wasn't, and Daisy was trying to do her arithmetic problems and he —when she wouldn't do what he asked her to, he hit her so hard she passed out or something. Daisy woke up in bed and her head hurt. She couldn't go to school and then she caught the flu. She was ill for a week and her mother was testy because she had to wait on her. Dusty had gone on a trip but he came back. Someone at the Bar and Grill had told Dusty something about Catherine Allison and another man, and all of a sudden the trailer was shaking again and Daisy could hear pounding. Daisy knew why Dusty was beating her mother, because he kept shouting all the time that she had been up to something while he was gone and he'd teach her.

Catherine Allison thought the world was odd. It was slanting now, slanting away from her all the time. She went to put down a glass and it would slide off the table because the table was slanting. The whole trailer was sliding somewhere these days, sliding in and out of reality. She scarcely bothered with anything. She was drinking, sure. Dusty was there to see that she stayed in line; or he wasn't there—she could hardly tell whether he was there and had just gone to the men's room or if she was alone at the Bar and Grill and another man was buying her drinks. She knew men. Christ, didn't she. All the same guy. Big shots. Heavy-handed. Tony'd never hit her. But he wasn't so good in the hay, she remembered now. Not like Dusty; he was fantastic. Mrs. Royal had noticed Catherine Allison's bruises. What of it? Most of them were from falling down on the slanting floor. Things—happened, but Catherine Allison couldn't sort them out any longer. She could only remember part of any conversation with anyone. Mrs. Royal wanted to help her. It was strange. She didn't need help. Just a drink.

Then came a night when Daisy got out of bed, terrified by the silence that had fallen. The trailer had been reverberating, shaking, until there was a particularly loud crash and then nothing at all. Nothing for a long time.

Quietly, Daisy opened the door of her small bedroom and looked out. The door of the trailer was open to the dark night. She crept down the short hall, feeling the hot air pouring in. They had air conditioning and her mother always said to keep the door shut.

Her mother was lying on the kitchen floor. She'd been there before. But this time she didn't breathe. Dusty had hit her and killed her. Or she'd fallen. No one knew; there were no witnesses. When Dusty was picked up by the police, he said she had fallen. Still, he hadn't tried to help her. He was charged with manslaughter.

Mrs. Royal took Daisy in and helped the police find her relatives. She remembered that Catherine Allison had said her family came from South Carolina; she even remembered the town—Eyreville.

A day later, the police located old Miss Martha Austin in Eyreville. Miss Martha was the only Austin who still lived there. Gardens belonged to a distant cousin now. Miss Martha Austin was Catherine Allison's aunt; she had heard from her, yes, not regularly, but the child always said she was happy, she liked Texas, her little girl, Daisy, was smart and pretty . . . It amazed Miss Martha to find out the truth.

She drove straight out to Land's End and told China.

China Dane arrived at the Galveston trailer camp two days later.

Her sister's body was already on its way home. China had made those arrangements by telephone. It had taken her two days to get things organized at Land's End so that she could fly to Galveston. Bascomb was unable to leave his bedroom; a stroke three years before had left him partially paralyzed and he needed constant nursing. He had actually frowned on her going; couldn't someone else make the trip? he had asked. But China had taken counsel with her three surviving brothers and with Gwendolyn. Gwendolyn was a spinster with arthritis and could not leave Columbia to take such a long jaunt. And all of China's stepbrothers were in their sixties now. Their families

211

were long ago grown up. Not one had wound up particularly well-fixed in life, though all were comfortably retired. Her eldest brother lived in Florida, the youngest one in Raleigh, and the third was in a nursing home in Charleston. It was obviously China's duty to go sort things in Galveston out. If the child's father couldn't be found, China must settle the little girl's future.

China wondered, now, could her life at Land's End have really been so busy as to have kept her from going to visit Catherine Allison or even, for years at a time, from thinking about her. Still, the two of them had never been close. There were eight years between their ages. And the family row that preceded her younger sister's runaway marriage had been a wounding one. Not long afterward, their father had died, and Catherine Allison had not come home for his funeral. The family was shocked. It was said that Catherine Allison was in Texas with her husband and that because he was about to go to fight in Korea, she wouldn't leave him. Aunt Martha wrote to Catherine Allison describing her father's funeral. She also wrote her five years later when Gardens was sold to a relative of her mother's, and Catherine Allison's mother herself came to live with China at Land's End.

In China's house Elizabeth Austin contented herself with getting news of her sons' families, which were large and flourishing, and with the concerns of her beautiful Dane granddaughters Vivienne and Mab and the darling baby, Cypriana. Elizabeth's daughter Gwendolyn wrote to her faithfully. But not Catherine Allison, who had been a troublesome child, coming along unexpectedly after Elizabeth's childbearing days seemed over, clattering noisily around Gardens. Boy-crazy as a girl, and never as smart as the others, Catherine Allison wouldn't listen to anyone, especially not her mother. When Elizabeth died three years after she'd come to Land's End, Aunt Martha, who was Elizabeth's sister-in-law, managed to locate Catherine Allison again down in Texas, but Catherine Allison

212

didn't come home for her mother's funeral, either. She sent flowers.

China felt guilty now. Even if Catherine Allison hadn't come home when she should, how could she have neglected her little sister for so long? China had scarcely even *thought* of Catherine Allison. It was her sister's choice to be out of the family; still, was that an excuse?

Daisy had been staying in Mrs. Royal's trailer since the night of her mother's death. The woman was worried about the child. Daisy hadn't said much, and as far as anyone knew, she hadn't cried yet. The police had questioned her about Dusty and about her real father. They were tracking him down.

"Your aunt is coming to see you," Mrs. Royal told her, but the words did not mean much to Daisy. She had barely heard of an Aunt China. What came to mind was a porcelain figure, a china doll—Aunt China? Daisy sat very still on a chair all day. That way, she wouldn't do the wrong thing. Something she had done before was really wrong, because now her mother was dead.

Daisy heard footsteps coming up to the trailer and a knock on the door. She sat still while Mrs. Royal answered it.

"I'm China Dane."

The woman who came into the trailer was not like anybody Daisy had ever seen before. At least, anywhere except maybe on a downtown street or on television. Mrs. Royal was old and wore long print dresses; her eyes were hooded with heavy lids and were wrinkled at the corners. Two of her teeth were missing. And Mother—Mother had worn slacks or shorts most of the time except at night when she went out, and then she put on a silky dress and lots of jewelry, and fluffed out her fair hair, but she was so thin, and somehow she always looked put together all wrong, as if she hadn't really had her mind on dressing. So Daisy stared in wonder at her aunt, who had on a light cream

213

linen suit and black high-heeled shoes, and a frilly white blouse. Her hair was carefully coiled, and over its glossy darkness China wore a small white straw hat with white net which came down over her face. She was wearing wrist-length white gloves. She swept the veil back off her face.

"Mrs. Royal, I cannot thank you enough." Her aunt's voice was amazing—modulated, low and soft and strangely accented. "This is my niece? Daisy?"

"This is—"

Daisy was swept up in a hug. Her Aunt China smelled amazingly good, like a flower but like soap, too, and powder. She kissed Daisy on the cheek.

Mrs. Royal told Aunt China the particulars of Catherine Allison's death, in very polite terms. At first the two women suggested that Daisy go outside and play, but when Daisy looked distressed, Aunt China drew her to her side and said she could stay right there. It was a hot day and Daisy was grateful. The air conditioner whirred in the window. Aunt China hid her amazement over what Mrs. Royal told her.

The three were still sitting there when a police officer arrived. He was very polite. He sat down and accepted a glass of iced tea. Aunt China had one too, taking off her white gloves. The tea was reviving and it was sorely needed. The news the officer brought was not good. Barry Sykes had been found. He was in a hospital in Oklahoma City and was expected to die of lung cancer within a few months. He was sorry to hear of his wife's death, but his own parents had been killed years ago in a highway accident, and he had no idea what should be done with Daisy. His wife's family should take her, he supposed. He had not mentioned wanting to see Daisy again.

China glanced at the child. A sadder sight, China thought, she had never seen. Daisy was small for her age, to begin with. Her hair had not been washed recently, and it hung limply around her ears, a kind of dirty yellow in color. Her blue eyes were a pretty,

214

light shade, wide open and appealing. But she wore such a worried expression on her face that her other features were too twisted to be judged for beauty.

When the police officer took his leave, China put her arm around the child.

"I am your Aunt China. Do you understand? I am going to take care of you." Her dark eyes looked calmly into Daisy's frightened blue ones.

It was as if she were entering a dream world. Daisy had no adequate words to describe her feelings. The airplane flight was exciting, and being met by a big white car at the airport took her breath away. A black man named George drove them a long distance, out of the town and for miles and miles through green fields and lanes full of trees and bushes. They were going to somewhere called Land's End, but where that was Daisy had no idea. It had a vaguely threatening sound. Still, it was where Aunt China lived, and Daisy clung to her aunt now with all her strength. She was frightened that something would happen and she would be separated from this soft-voiced, gentle lady whom everyone was so polite to. She wanted to stay with her forever.

They drove down narrower and narrower roads. There was a little settlement and a grocery store at one crossroads. Aunt China said that was Crosstree and that Daisy easily could walk to the Alexander Grocery store from Land's End; they were almost home.

"I know how to shop and I can cook too," Daisy said. "I can help you."

But it seemed that there was someone named Ella who did the cooking at Land's End. However, Aunt China said Daisy could make brownies anytime she wanted to.

The land was flat, and from far away Daisy could see the gleam of six huge white columns. In the slanting sunshine of late afternoon George drove them up to the enormous house, and Aunt China helped Daisy out. The air was soft and sweet-smelling, country air. Birds were singing. No other houses were anywhere around, just a long lawn and then fields. Nine cool blue stone steps led up to the front porch, between delicate wrought-iron railings. Aunt China held Daisy's hand tightly as they mounted the stairs.

"You'll be happy here," Aunt China said. Daisy held fast to her.

The porch was enormous, the largest porch she had ever seen, with four tall windows divided into many squares and framed with green shutters set against the red brick of the house. The large front door was open, and when they entered, they could see straight through to the back of the house, where there was another door exactly like the front one. A staircase swept up and across the hall, and double doors led off the hall on either side. It was cool inside and the sunshine coming through the back door made the walls glimmer. From behind one set of double doors, several people came hurrying out to meet them, and someone came from the back at the same time. It was too much for Daisy. She hid her face against her aunt's side and burst into tears.

"She's tired." "Poor child." "This is Great-aunt Martha, Daisy—"

She heard the words through her sobs. Then the very large woman called Ella took charge, and before Daisy could take in any more of the place that was to be her new home, she was being carried up many stairs and tucked into a large four-poster bed in a big room and promised a bowl of vegetable-beef soup.

Across the hall on the second floor her Uncle Bascomb in his bed was astounded to hear of her arrival. China had gone at once to his room.

"No, nothing else. There is nothing else to be done with Daisy," China said firmly. "I *never* saw such a shocking place as she was in, Bascomb, and we have no excuse not to take her to live here."

Bascomb thought there was a great deal of excuse;

he could not get China to realize that times had changed on the market and with his illness costing so much and Cypriana yet to be educated—now, to take on another child, apparently a penniless orphan!—but he knew from the start that his arguments would fail. He knew the Austin pride. China would make up for all the wrong she now felt had been done to her little sister. Daisy Sykes would have the moon, and Dane money would pay for it. Their quarrel was bitter, but it was short, and China, ignoring his remarks as the peevishness of an invalid, won all the way.

Bascomb refused his dinner that night and had two double whiskies that no one but George knew about.

Bascomb was of course excused from the funeral the next day, but everyone that remained of the Austin and Royal families, any mobile cases, turned up in force. The Royals at Gardens and their second cousins at Southwind invited all visiting Austins to stay with them. Repentantly, they would all see Catherine Allison to her grave.

Daisy woke up after hours of sleep feeling disoriented and afraid. She discovered in a minute that she had had an accident in her sleep, and she was terrified. In the big bed! However, Ella came in presently to open the draperies at the huge windows, and she was very cheerful. Daisy started to cry. Ella laughed when she understood why Daisy was crying and told her not to worry about it. She'd change the bed and never tell a soul. Breakfast was ready and Daisy should go on down, Ella insisted.

While Daisy dressed in the new white dress Aunt China had bought her just before they left Galveston, she heard the noises and bustles of a southern household readying for funeral guests. Feet hurried everywhere, above and below her. When Daisy timidly opened the door of the bedroom, she was overcome with fear. Ella, coming out of the opposite bedroom, found her just standing there.

"Good heavens, come on, child," she said. "You have to hurry."

Ella led Daisy downstairs and through the large hall into a great kitchen where coffee steamed and bacon crackled on one of two vast black stoves. Daisy had nothing in her experience to compare that kitchen to. The ceilings were so high! Ella sat her down and fed her the biggest plate of eggs Daisy had ever seen, scrambled in butter too, and there was a tall glass of milk, and toast, and a dish of four different jellies, each in a compartment. Daisy examined the jelly dish as if it were an artifact from a puzzling new continent.

All around her she heard soft voices. Sometimes Daisy couldn't understand what they were saying to her. Aunt China took her off to church in Eyreville right after breakfast. It was a morning funeral, as was the custom in the hot summer months. The Church of the Good Shepherd was not air-conditioned.

Daisy's legs stuck to the pew. She had no idea what to do. Aunt China helped her to stand up and sit down, to kneel and rise, when everyone else did. Only toward the end of the service did Daisy suddenly realize that it was her *mother* inside the long box at the front of the church. It must be. The coffin was closed and there were flowers on it. China had considered asking Daisy if she wanted to see her mother for the last time, but she had decided against it. Daisy had memories enough of her mother.

Everyone knew the circumstances of Catherine Allison's end, and Daisy was eyed with pity.

They left the church at last and walked next door to the cemetery in the churchyard. It had rained briefly during the service and then cleared, and now the odors of damp grass and wet ground rose into the air. Some men carried the coffin, and Aunt China and Daisy walked close behind it together. Aunt China, who was wearing a black veil over her face, held Daisy's hand tightly. The men stopped beside a freshly-dug grave and the coffin was lowered in on straps.

One of the Royals from Gardens had picked all the roses in the garden that morning and brought them to the church. Some of the red ones were used to decorate the altar. Great-aunt Martha brought the rest out from the vestry, a mixture of whites and pinks and yellows. After the minister finished speaking, he scattered just a little earth over the top of the coffin, and Aunt Martha came forward slowly with the roses, giving some to China and some to Daisy. Daisy watched as Aunt China leaned over, her veil dropping down, and gently placed the roses in the grave. She motioned for Daisy to do the same with hers. The scent of roses filled the air. Aunt Martha wiped tears away from her face.

Then it was over, and everyone headed back to Land's End. A flock of people followed them for an afternoon of eating. Long before the relatives began to leave, Daisy had been taken back upstairs. She was exhausted, almost stuporous. Ella brought her some ham biscuits and Aunt China came in twice to check on her. Out the big window, Daisy watched the sun set through the huge weeping willow trees at the back of the house.

The last thing Aunt China did when she tucked Daisy in for the night was to remind her that her cousin Cypriana would be coming home from camp in just two weeks. Then Daisy would have a playmate.

"Daisy Sykes!"

Cypriana Dane stood on the back steps of Land's End and pronounced the words in tones of deep scorn.

"What kind of name is that? Sykes!" Cypriana spat the word out as if it polluted her mouth.

Daisy stared up at her, her heart pounding. She was as astonished as she was dismayed. She hadn't dreamed that her cousin Cypriana would be so tall and so— Daisy didn't know the word for what she was; she looked dangerous. Her cousin had the arms and torso

219

of an athlete, and long tanned muscular legs with skinned marks on both knees. She wore short, business-like tan shorts and a boy's blue shirt hanging over them, the cuffs flapping open at the wrists. The faded blue of the shirt did not match her eyes. Those eyes were a bright, blazing blue, the darkest blue eyes Daisy had ever seen. As Cypriana spoke, they glittered from beneath the thick dark lashes that fringed them. Her long dark hair hung straight down on either side of her face from a widow's peak at the top of her brow. Her mouth, curled now in a grimace, was insolent in shape, the lips rather full.

Cypriana had been back at Land's End only an hour; the first order of business was to get this matter of her cousin coming to live there straightened out. When Cypriana had gotten word at camp of the development, her imagination had actually supplied a rather superior little girl, something like her second cousins, the Royals, with their noses in the air. A girl two years younger than herself and contemptible, of course, but still someone to reckon with.

She almost laughed aloud when her mother presented this creature. She had never seen such a scrawny scaredy-cat in her life. Glancing back over her shoulder to make sure that Ella was in the kitchen and her mother was out of earshot, Cypriana drove in for the kill.

"How old are you?"

"Nine." Daisy's voice was faint.

"You look *seven*." Cypriana's eyes took in all of Daisy. "You'll get murdered on the hockey field. Wait and see."

With this promise, she angled off down the steps, hollering at a boy she had just spotted coming out of the barn. "Hey, Frank, I'm back."

Daisy had not expected even this much of her cousin's time. No one could rank her claims lower than she ranked them herself. Two weeks of the minis-trations of Aunt China and Ella had not been enough to erase a lifetime habit of wishing she weren't there. Wherever she was, she was always in the way—this much was clear to Daisy.

It had nearly broken China's heart to see the way the child crept around Land's End the first few days, as if she were fearful she would break anything she touched. The vastness of the house frightened Daisy, who was used only to a trailer. She would have been afraid of getting lost except for the absolutely regular plan of the house, understandable even to a child. Aunt China had taken her on a tour. The house was a huge square, divided by main halls on both the first and second stories. The downstairs consisted simply of four drawing rooms, all opening off the oyster-green hall by means of large double doors. Four chimneys, spaced regularly around the outside walls, supplied a large fireplace to each room. In the old days when the house was first built, Aunt China explained, the rear left drawing room had been used for dining. It connected by way of an outside door with a walkway, fenced with white railings, and the walkway led to a large white two-story house in back that had once been the cookhouse, where all the meals were prepared; processions of servants had brought the food, in covered silver dishes, from the cookhouse into the dining room. The rear left drawing room was still the dining room, but for many years the drawing room across the hall from it had been used for the kitchen. The cookhouse out back was now the home of Ella and George. The front room on the left was *the* drawing room, and the front room on the right was Bascomb's library. There, books lined the walls from the fifteen-foot ceiling to the floor.

Upstairs, the second story was divided into four huge bedrooms; because of the four bathrooms that had been installed, the bedrooms were not quite the regular squares they had been originally, in the days of outdoor plumbing. The bedrooms also had fireplaces, and their large front or back windows overlooked twin balconies front and back. Tall doors led out onto the long balconies from the center hall.

The staircase swept on up to the third story. There —to Daisy, the greatest wonder of all—was a ballroom extending the entire length of the house, with a large window and fanlight at either end. The ballroom was empty; its walls were lined with deep closets no taller than a man—the ceiling of the ballroom slanted down to the closet doors. Aunt China, describing the balls once held there, showed Daisy where the musicians had sat and pointed out dusty chandeliers on the ceiling. She had to hold Daisy's hand to encourage her to look out of the ballroom windows; they were dizzingly high, and from them the flat green world spread to the blue water of the ocean. You could see the river which ran along in back of the property and down to the sea.

On her second day at Land's End, Daisy had scarcely had time to feel easier with her new home, when Aunt China announced that she must meet Uncle Bascomb.

Daisy had already heard Uncle Bascomb issuing commands and complaints from the right front bedroom. She jumped at the sound of any male voice, and her imagination painted him with a dark angry face and scowling brow. Terror went through her at the thought of facing him. The fact that he stayed in bed and everyone waited on him made him seem even more powerful and frightening. She could not speak her fear.

China looked Daisy over. Ella had scrubbed the child and washed her hair until it glistened. Daisy was really quite pretty, China thought; when she was interested in something, her face relaxed its worried expression and you could tell that she had regular and pleasing features. Even a nice smile, when it could be coaxed from her. Daisy was dressed in an outgrown skirt and blouse of Cypriana's, a peach-colored outfit that cast a little color onto her pale skin.

"Yes, this afternoon, right after lunch before he has

his nap," China said. "Your uncle is anxious to meet you."

Daisy could not eat her creamed tuna on toast in spite of Ella's fussing. Even the dread she had felt of her own father and of Dusty Devon had not choked Daisy so badly. When Aunt China led her upstairs, only a heroic act of her will kept her from grabbing hold of the banister and never letting go. Each step she took seemed to jar her entire body. She forgot to breathe.

Aunt China opened the door.

"Here's Daisy, Bascomb."

"That was *not* fresh asparagus," he said, indicating the green stalks on a plate sitting on a tray beside him. "Well, come in, child. I don't bite," he added, as Daisy hung back.

Aunt China advanced her into the room.

Propped up against pillows, Uncle Bascomb lay and stared at her. For a moment, Daisy returned his scrutiny. He was a very handsome and not really old-looking man; although his hair was silver-white, his face was not lined. He was wearing black-rimmed eyeglasses. He did not scowl at her, although he did not smile, either.

"Come and let me see you."

Timidly, Daisy stood beside his bed, her eyes on the floor.

"She looks like an Austin," Uncle Bascomb said. "See? Around the eyes. A little like her mother, maybe." He did not make "looking like an Austin" sound as if it were a very desirable thing.

"I don't know," China said. "I don't see it. No, not like Catherine Allison. Maybe a little like Daddy."

"Nonsense. Your father had dark eyes. That brow, though. That's pure Benjamin."

"He means your Uncle Benjamin who lives in Florida," China said to Daisy. "He wasn't at the funeral. Maybe someday you can meet him."

"Maybe *someday*," Bascomb said, echoing her. His

223

words had an upleasant sound. China shot him a look.

"I think Daisy's very pretty, whomever she takes after," China said ."She's a very good girl, too."

"Can you read?" Bascomb shot the words out abruptly.

Daisy was surprised at the question. She was going into fourth grade. "Yes, sir," she whispered.

Bascomb regarded her. "You can come and read to me sometime, then," he said. "But if you read any of the books in my library, please be careful with them."

He sighed. The interview seemed to be over with. "Daisy is very careful," Aunt China said. "And she is going to make you some brownies soon. Ella is ordering the chocolate drops."

Uncle Bascomb grunted. "I like brownies," he said. He closed his eyes. "Wake me up in time for *The Guiding Light*, will you, China?"

Aunt China picked up the luncheon tray, and soon they were safely back in the hall. Daisy's heart beat again.

"He's rather cross because he's sick," Aunt China said. She smiled at Daisy. "That wasn't so bad, was it? And maybe you can read to him and amuse him. He gets tired of bed."

Daisy's heart was not touched by her uncle's plight. Even though she could see that he was ill, and he had not been unkind to her, she felt the same way toward him as before. He was a man, one of the race who controlled things, who ran the world, and Daisy feared him and hated him. Her legs shook for half an hour after the visit was over.

Bascomb lay back on his pillows after Daisy left and did not go immediately to sleep. He wondered what Cypriana would make of the little thing when she got home from camp. Perhaps they would be good for each other. The child looked like she needed livening up, and certainly Cypriana could benefit from a quiet example around the house. Bascomb's youngest child disturbed him, both literally with her noise and also somehow physically and even psychically. She always had. Baker could almost be blamed on her.

Baker! Bascomb frowned. Baker was the mistake of his life. Trying to cope with the whole thing had brought on his stroke, he felt sure. And somehow it seemed as if it had been Cypriana's fault. It *had* begun with his attempts to discipline her. He had spanked Cypriana, though he had never dreamed of touching her older sisters when they were children. But Cypriana exasperated him. Bascomb had spent hours in his library with Vivienne and Mab, training their minds, teaching them to love the classics, introducing Vivienne to Shakespeare and Mab to the world of art, with spectacular results. Vivienne was now playing Shakespeare on the stage, while Mab worked in one of the world's best art galleries. But when Bascomb took Cypriana into his library, it was to spank her. She got on his nerves and she talked back. She wasn't particularly studious, but Bascomb realized that not every child in a family could turn out a scholar. He didn't mind that Cypriana wasn't interested in studies. There was something else about her, something that he couldn't put his finger on. Cypriana never complained to China, for instance, about his punishing her, though he would have expected her to. He always chose times when China was gone to spank her; he knew China wouldn't approve.

Many things about Cypriana bothered Bascomb. She seemed rather—earthy. Bascomb was not inclined to take physical life too seriously. He knew he had a treasure beyond compare in his wife China, and he had been faithful to her, even when China's ailing mother came to live with them, and China became so preoccupied in caring for her that their minimal love life shrank to nothing. Bascomb had always been a gentleman of fussy habits, who spent most of each day in his library; the calls of the flesh were foreign to him. But in his later years he began to think more about sex. Certainly he *read* more about it; you couldn't pick up a novel these days without getting the full details of what had been a mystery in his boyhood.

One day Cypriana broke the top of a footed jelly dish which had been his mother's pride. The silly girl tripped over the leg of the table the dish was sitting upon, causing the glass top to fall off and shatter. Cypriana always ran pell-mell through the house. Bascomb was incensed. He spanked her in such a rage that he twisted his back, reactivating an old injury he had suffered in school.

The next day Bascomb felt terrible. The pain in his back was so intense that he stayed in bed. Nancy, Ella's girl, came up and gave him a rubdown. He was dressed in his pajamas and decently wrapped in a sheet for the occasion, but he wondered what it would have felt like if he hadn't been.

Nancy Browning was a senior in Eyreville High School and hoping to get married in spite of Ella's insistence that she go to college. She wasn't interested in college. Nancy enjoyed giving Mr. Bascomb what became his daily massage. He said she was good. Maybe she could get a job doing it, she thought. People loved to have their backs rubbed.

Bascomb's back trouble persisted; the only relief he got was from Nancy's rubdowns. He paid her very well. In the warm afternoons of early spring, Bascomb would watch out of the windows of the library for Nancy to come up the walk after school. Nancy was a pretty girl, with creamy brown skin and wide dark eyes, and the best figure at Eyreville High. When she walked, she swung her hips.

In the late spring, Bascomb gave Nancy a raise and they became lovers. He was amazed at how much good it did him. He felt like a new man. Cypriana bothered him no more. She could run wild for all he cared.

Nancy liked her secret about Mr. Bascomb. Wouldn't her mother have a fit, though? Nancy had grown up thinking Mr. Bascomb such a fine man, handsome, almost princely. And now here he was, so grateful for what she provided. She thought it was funny.

When she got pregnant, Nancy stopped thinking it was a joke. The diaphragm that her friend had given her, promising it would protect her, had not helped. Nancy had forgotten to use it once too often.

Bascomb was horrified. He offered Nancy a lot of money so that she could get an abortion. Nancy was horrified in turn. She knew of two girls who had died trying to get rid of babies. She wanted nothing to do with that. She'd rather tell her mother the truth and be done with it.

Mention of the truth threw Bascomb into a panic. He offered even more money, a handsome settlement, if Nancy would say the baby was someone else's. He'd give her five thousand dollars in cash; he took it out of a cash box and showed it to her.

Nancy agreed. Ella and George were told that she was pregnant. They were scandalized, but no one could get Nancy to name the father. Late in the winter, Nancy gave birth to a girl, who was named Baker for her aunt in Dentspur. Ella ended up rearing the child there at Land's End while Nancy went off to Columbia and into a physical therapy training program, with the money she got from the baby's mystery father.

Bascomb had a stroke.

Now when the breeze was right he could sometimes hear, faintly, Baker playing in the back yard or calling to her grandmother. It all seemed like just too much.

China had taken Cypriana aside after dinner on her first day home from camp.

"You know, Cypriana, I want you to be really sweet to your little cousin Daisy," China said, leading the way to the window seat in the library; the red light of evening falling on the fields could be seen out of the tall side window. "Sit down and let me tell you why."

227

Cypriana sank onto the leather cushion beside her mother.

"Are you going to let Daisy stay in the guest room?" she asked. "You're not going to make me have her in *my* room?"

"Well, not right away, of course, dear. We'll see how things go. If Vivienne or Mab comes home—but let's not worry about that. What I want to tell you is that Daisy has had some bad experiences. We must be kind."

"Bad experiences?"

"You'll hear about it anyway from someone, I'm sure, so I'll tell you. Your aunt—you never met her, but your Aunt Catherine Allison lived down in Texas in a trailer camp. Daisy's real father left them—he's dying, now—and my poor sister was"—China paused for a moment—"thinking about marrying another man. But she was in bad health, and she fell and hit her head, and the man—didn't help her. He was a cruel man. Daisy was afraid of him. She's been through some bad times and now both her parents are lost to her. We have to help make up for that. Will you be nice to her?"

Cypriana pondered this information. Only part of it interested her. She grinned at her mother.

"Sure."

"In time she'll be more comfortable here; she'll get used to us. I hope Daisy will be happy. She will be like a sister to you."

"Is she going to school with me at Trinity?"

"Of course."

Cypriana cast her eyes up. "I don't know," she said, though she didn't say what she didn't know about. China ignored this.

"I'm sure I can count on you," she said. China was very fond of her high-spirited youngest. Cypriana was her darling. She was glad to see that Cypri went immediately to look up Daisy, who was in the kitchen talking to Ella.

228

Cypriana had been planning to kick around a soccer ball, as she usually did in the long summer evenings. However, her curiosity was aroused.

"Come outside," she ordered Daisy.

Daisy followed her without a word. Ella looked at them as they left the kitchen, curious about what Cypriana was up to. Ella had been wondering for two weeks how Cypri was going to like this addition to the family. Cypri Dane was strong-willed and used to getting her own way.

Outside, Cypri looked toward the smooth piece of ground beside the barn where soccer was played. Frank and Bob King were there as usual. The King family, who lived three-quarters of a mile away, farmed the land belonging to Land's End. Frank, who was Cypri's age, and Bob, a year younger, usually came back after dinner to see to the final chores in the barn and kick the ball around with her. As Cypri watched, Frank rushed down the field, the ball between his splayed-out legs, expertly keeping control of it despite Bob's attempts to get it away. Cypri glanced back at Daisy.

"Come here," she said, leading Daisy under the walkway to the back house. There was a comfortable niche between the brick pillars, just the place for an exchange of confidences. Cypriana hunkered down, and Daisy did the same. In the twilight, Daisy's face looked pinched and anxious.

"Tell me about the man who was cruel," Cypriana said, her blue eyes blinking as she looked intently at her cousin.

Daisy looked back so blankly that Cypriana had to explain further.

"The one who wouldn't help your mother when she fell and hit her head! Were you there?"

Her gaze gave Daisy a funny feeling. It was odd to have someone look at you with such interest. Daisy nodded her head.

"Well, tell about it!"

"He—I just came out of the bedroom, and Mother was on the floor and he was gone."

"Oh." Cypriana sounded disappointed. "What was his name?"

"Dusty." Daisy whispered the word. "He was so big; he was huge, fat and tall both."

"Was he mean to you?"

Daisy nodded.

"But what would he *do*?"

"Well—" Daisy thought, trying to please her cousin. "Once he—Mother was gone and he told me to come and sit on his lap, and I didn't want to." She involuntarily shuddered at the memory. "And he hit me in the head so hard everything just went black."

"*Really*?" Cypriana looked impressed. "What else?"

"He'd always tell me to go to bed. Even at five o'clock or six o'clock at night, he'd make me go to bed."

"Did he hit your mother?"

Daisy looked at the ground. "Yes," she said. She didn't want to cry; Cypriana would think she was a baby. She was afraid tears were going to come into her eyes.

Cypriana drew a deep, pleased breath. This was exciting.

"What happened to him?"

"I think the police—they were looking for him."

"The *police*?" Cypriana was delighted. "Listen, did they find him?"

"I don't know."

"Maybe he went to jail for what he did. Then he would hate you; maybe he wants to kill you."

Daisy stared at Cypriana in surprise.

"Kill me? Why?"

"Because he had to go to jail," Cypriana answered, in tones of impatience. "He might be coming to Land's End to get you."

Daisy looked so alarmed at this that Cypriana

230

changed the subject quickly, before the kid started crying or something.

"Did Dusty ever spank you?"

"No. But my real father—" Daisy paused. "He would."

"Hard?"

"Yes."

"My father—" Cypriana glanced toward the house. Her face wore a contemptuous look. "He spanked me a couple of times, but it didn't even hurt. Not at all." She sounded sorry that she had so little to contribute to the pool of bad experiences.

For several minutes more, Cypriana pressed Daisy for details, until she was the mistress of all the violent episodes her cousin could remember. Wait until she told everybody! Nothing as interesting had happened in Cypriana's circle for a long time, since Celia Honeychurch's concussion, at least.

Cypriana got up to leave. Daisy looked forlorn, scrunched down into a corner with her arms wrapped around her legs. In gratitude for the information she had provided, Cypriana asked Daisy if she wanted to play soccer. There was still time to kick the ball around for a while before dark. Daisy said she'd rather watch. She had never played soccer, or even heard of it. When her cousin started in the direction of the big boys by the barn, Daisy hung back.

"Oh, come on, the boys won't hurt you," Cypriana said impatiently. "And I'll tell you what," she added on the way to the field. "Tomorrow we'll fix you a place to hide when Dusty comes to kill you."

Cypriana quickened her pace, loping over the ground, and Daisy in a terror hurried after her. Behind them, the six white columns of the back porch glimmered in the darkening air. Daisy looked back. Could Dusty really find her? Her whole body turned cold at the prospect. And the two boys in the field, kicking the ball back and forth, seemed scarcely less menacing. They ran over to Cypriana, who said, "This is my

231

cousin Daisy. She hasn't any mother or father."

The boys were as tall as Cypriana, and strong-looking. The one with red hair and freckles grinned at Daisy; the other, who was blond, simply stared. Cypriana grabbed the ball from the redhead and raced off, kicking it along the ground with the insides of her feet. Both boys chased after her. Daisy stood deserted. An owl hooted from the willow trees, and a flock of birds swooped low around the eaves of the barn, crying.

"Shut up, Charles Honeychurch. Don't forget your aunt hung herself. And your great-uncle Samuel saw an angel in his garden. In the carrot patch. An *angel.*"

Cypriana delivered this reminder to the small brown-haired boy standing in front of her and tossed her dark hair back over her shoulders with a loud snort.

Charles Honeychurch took a step backwards, somewhat abashed. Cypriana had caught him asking Daisy what it was like to have your mother murdered. Daisy had been backed against the brick wall of the academy, and Charles, her questioner, had been standing aggressively only a foot away, while a ring of fourth-graders blocked any escape route. It was the first day of the fall term at Trinity Episcopal.

Cypriana had warned China that Daisy would have a hard time.

"Daisy sounds so funny when she talks," she said. "They'll laugh at her."

"People in Texas have a different accent. You know that."

"Yes, but it sounds so low-class. She doesn't say her *g's. Comin'* and *goin'.* The kids will make fun of her."

"I'm sure she'll soon talk just the way they do."

Her mother didn't understand at all about Trinity. Cypriana had position at the academy. She ran everything worth running. She was the star center on the hockey team and team captain of the Blues, who com-

232

peted with the Reds in all athletic events and usually won. And she would probably get the lead in the Christmas play. She was the most popular girl in dancing class. She did the best cartwheels in gymnastics. And her lineage was impeccable, Royal, Austin and Dane blood. Since Royals, Austins, Danes, Hastingses and Rushes made up the bulk of the private school's claim to class, the uniting of three of these families in Cypriana made her standing unassailable. And her older sister Vivienne was an actress in New York. Cypriana had position.

It was about to be strained, Cypriana feared, by the advent of a cousin with a crass name, a crass accent, and a cringing manner. Cypriana knew how to fix the situation with her sixth-grade friends—thrilling tales of the beatings Daisy had endured would fascinate them—but she was certain that the sixteen dumb fourth-graders at Trinity were going to find Daisy a low-class customer even if she had been *tortured*. And Daisy belonged to Land's End now and therefore to her, Cypriana. She felt toward her cousin the way she felt toward the King boys. They were farm boys and attended public school, but they belonged to Land's End and therefore could be admitted to acquaintance with her. She would defend them if she had to, though of course no one ever had to defend the King boys— they were the biggest and strongest kids around. In the same way, Daisy was hers, like it or not. Though Daisy would not bring any credit to Cypriana, if possible she must be kept from actually disgracing her.

"There are some bullies at school," Cypriana said to Daisy in a preliminary talk. "The Honeychurches are the worst. They think they are everything. Their father's our doctor. You'd think he was God. Those kids. Any boy Honeychurch is bad news. I think one is in fourth grade—Charles, a nasty kid. You tell me if he bothers you."

As Cypriana told Daisy this, she was getting her shin guards and hockey stick out of the ballroom storage

233

closets. She showed these items to an awed Daisy. The shin guards were beaten-up looking.

"Mother is getting you some new guards. These are too big; you wouldn't be able to bend your knees. Otherwise I'd give you these. I guess I need some new ones. These are limp.". Cypriana smiled. "I get lots of bruises."

Daisy looked at the equipment with respect. She still didn't believe she was going to play hockey, although Cypriana had informed her that she would have to.

Cypriana closed the closet and looked toward the last closet door, the one beside the far window. Daisy followed her gaze. Underneath the shelves of old feather beds and army blankets was a large bottle of water and two boxes of Saltines, placed there two weeks ago by Cypriana. If Dusty ever showed up, Cypri had sworn to tell him that Daisy was dead, while Daisy ran upstairs and hid in the closet. If he stayed around for days, they were prepared. Daisy had assured Cypriana that she could live for a long while on soda crackers.

"Don't forget," Cypri said softly to her. "Don't hide in the wrong closet."

Daisy nodded.

Cypriana proceeded to stuff Daisy full of further school information which might be useful: the fourth-grade teacher was a Mr. Bonecutter who was dumb and liked the War Between the States, so if Daisy knew anything about the Battle of Atlanta, be sure to say so; Mr. Bonecutter was particularly fond of what had gone wrong there. Cypri thought the prettiest girl was someone called Miffy, though she hadn't heretofore paid much attention to the fourth grade. The smartest kid was Barbara Rush, probably—all the Rushes were smart. All the boys in the class were dumb. And Daisy should not try to be an inner or a wing at hockey— they got more beat up.

Aunt China presented Daisy with a sky-blue tunic,

Trinity's uniform, and three white blouses with Peter Pan collars, and Daisy was ready for school.

It did not take Daisy long to find out the value of what Cypriana had told her. That first day Daisy was prepared for Charles Honeychurch, who actually turned out to be rather shorter than she had pictured him, although more venomous. What Daisy hadn't been prepared for was Cypriana's vigorous defense of her. Daisy knew Cypri considered her a kind of amoebic form of life, and yet, when Daisy was set upon in the schoolyard, Cypri sprang to her defense. Daisy was speechless with gratitude. The ring of persecutors broke up, and Barbara Rush actually offered to walk out to the hockey field with Daisy.

"Cypri is a really good player," Barbara said, looking ahead to where the older girls were walking together, hitting their shoes with their hockey sticks. "Can you play hockey?"

Daisy shook her head.

"Well, you'll learn here. Trinity has the best teams anywhere around." Barbara sounded gloomy.

In a few minutes Daisy was introduced to the sport. She was put on a scrub team, told to try to knock the ball down the field and into the goal, and left on her own in her new shin guards. Daisy had been dreading the moment, but to her amazement, she liked hockey. She was short, but she was fast, and she could control the ball fairly well even at first. Miss French praised her at the end of the session. Daisy took after her cousin, Miss French said.

After that, every afternoon after classes they went down to the hockey field, and Daisy quickly surpassed Barbara, who hated hockey, and even Miffy, who didn't like having blue ankles. By Halloween, Cypri was gratified to hear that Daisy had made the lower school second team. Even though she was small, she was scrappy, Miss French had said.

"Good," Cypri said to her cousin. The word thrilled

235

Daisy; over and over in her mind she heard Cypriana saying "Good," with a look of approval.

.When report cards were issued at midterm, Mr. Bonecutter gave Daisy straight A's. This did nothing for her with Cypri, but it made Aunt China happy. Aunt China said she was sure Uncle Bascomb would be proud.

Daisy had gained ten pounds and grown an inch by December.

"Cypri, when the girls come home for Christmas, I have to have somewhere to put them."

China looked questioningly at Cypriana. Since his stroke, Bascomb had had one front bedroom for himself; China had moved across the hall into the other front bedroom. The rear left bedroom had always been Cypriana's; the right rear was the guest room, occupied since July by Daisy.

"You do have twin beds in your room, Cypri. Is it all right if Daisy moves in?"

"Well, I guess." Cypriana wasn't gracious. Still, the arrangement made sense. Vivienne and Mab were coming home for Christmas and had to be put somewhere.

Daisy was honored to be allowed to move in with Cypri, whose room featured colored photographs of sports stars torn from magazines and pasted on the walls with scotch tape. Jimmy Clark regarded them from over the vanity, Wilt Chamberlain and Jim Ryun from over the bureau.

Uncle Bascomb managed to come downstairs for the Christmas gatherings. They were the most festive occasions Daisy had ever witnessed. The house was decorated with holly; its bright green leaves and red berries trimmed every painting and were twined around the banister in a rope. Greens stood in every receptacle throughout the rooms, and the Christmas tree in the drawing room with Italian creche figures beneath and angels flying from its boughs was the most beautiful thing Daisy had even seen. Fires burned in the library and drawing room and even in the dining room, where the table was laid with a white cloth that had a silver garland pinned around it in scallops; tall red candles stood in the large silver candlelabra at either end of the table, and beneath the red candles dangled silver balls that reflected the scene in curving perspective.

Amid the bustle of preparations, Vivienne and Mab arrived, the elder sisters of whom Daisy had already heard so much.

"Oh, she's so *pretty*," Mab exclaimed upon being introduced to Daisy. "I love fair hair."

Staring up at Mab's nut-brown hair and oval face, Daisy wanted to return the compliment a hundred-fold. And when Vivienne, with her enchanting eyes and thrilling voice, took Daisy's hand and said, "I'm so glad you're here, Daisy," Daisy was overcome with the honor and hid her face by turning away to put a log on the fire.

Having Mab and Vivienne in the house seemed to make it a different place; Uncle Bascomb, when he came downstairs, was very civil, almost jolly. Aunt China rushed around seeing to meals and schedules. A group of carolers from Eyreville came by, were asked in for eggnog, and right there in the hall sang a thrilling version of "O Come, O Come, Emanuel." Neighbors dropped by with gifts. Everyone but Uncle Bascomb went to midnight mass at the Church of the Good Shepherd, where the bells in the tower marked the birth of Jesus. The congregation knelt in silence as the bells rang.

Christmas morning, Daisy's stocking held a gold ring with a pearl, and candy and fruit and pecans. Vivienne and Mab gave her beautiful dresses, and Aunt China gave her a sweater and a Madame Alexander doll too pretty ever to be played with. Cypri gave her a washcloth which she had knit herself. It had started out to be a sweater, but it was really better in its present incarnation. "But you better wash your face easy," Cypriana warned.

The Christmas dinner was something to behold, ham and turkey and roast beef—all three—with so many accompaniments that Daisy grew dizzy counting them. Everyone, even the children, drank elderberry wine, and Daisy actually felt a bit jolly by evening. It seemed as if she had always lived at Land's End, with the silver gleaming and Ella waiting on her and fussing over her appetite, and George driving her and Cypriana to school in the mornings—and she didn't even have to make her own bed! Galveston began to seem far away. Daisy didn't even worry about Dusty very often anymore.

XIV

It was warm in bed. Daisy first was conscious of her relaxed body. It was comfortable. For a moment she resisted any further awareness. Then her eyes opened. She drew a sudden, surprised breath. Two inches away, Cypriana's deep blue eyes stared fixedly into hers. Daisy started awake.

"They say you can wake someone up just by staring at them," Cypriana said. "Just by staring at their eyes."

"Oh, that makes me feel so *funny*. Like the way I felt when you tried to hypnotize me." Daisy couldn't analyze her strange sensations. Cypri was lying full length beside her, outside the coverlet. Her head was propped up on her arm as she hung over Daisy's face.

"It took five minutes of staring to wake you up." Cypri didn't move away; she still looked deep into Daisy's eyes. It was bright in the bedroom; there was sunshine on the drawn shade of the side window. Cypri's pupils were tiny black circles inside the whorls of her blue irises. The whites of her eyes seemed very white; only a faint red tracing was in the corner of the right one, a tiny red river. Daisy could feel Cypri's breath on her face. A strand of dark hair tickled her cheek.

Cypri shivered. "It's chilly out here. Let me under." Cypri wore only her white cotton nightgown. As she spoke, she lifted the covers and slid in beside Daisy, shoving her over to get into her warm spot. Daisy complained, almost falling out the other side of the single bed. Sliding back against Cypri, she felt the hardness of her body. Cypri didn't push her away, and their legs tangled together.

"I'll close my eyes and you stare at them," Cypri said. "I want to see if it makes me feel funny."

Daisy looked hard at the double crescents formed by the dark eyelashes which curled up from Cypri's closed lids. She could see Cypri's eyes move underneath the smooth white skin covering her eyeballs.

"I guess you have to be alseep," Cypri said, disappointed. She opened her eyes. "I didn't feel anything."

For a moment, she regarded her cousin closely. Daisy was still hanging over her; after a minute Daisy lay back on the pillow beside her.

It was a Saturday morning in March, and they didn't have to get up early.

"Daisy?"

"What?"

Cypriana turned her head and whispered into Daisy's ear. "Have you ever—?" Her warm breath tickled Daisy.

Under the covers, Daisy could feel Cypri's hand pulling up her nightgown. Suddenly Daisy's body felt prickly all over; her head felt hot. Cypri's hands were on her buttocks. She lay completely still, in a combination of horror and delight. Cypri's hands slid over her skin.

"Does that make you feel funny?"

"Yes," Daisy whispered.

"Do you like it?"

"Yes."

"Do the same to me."

For a moment, Daisy couldn't move. Then she obeyed, finding Cypri's hard flesh and feeling it with her fingers. Cypri had long smooth muscles in her legs and back. As Daisy stroked her, Cypriana sighed.

"I like that." Cypri worked her own hands around to Daisy's stomach and suddenly Daisy felt wildly excited. Her entire body seemed alive, every skin cell

240

and nerve end screaming for something—but what? She twisted against her cousin.

"Oh, Cypri." She breathed the words softly. She could sense that Cypri was excited, too. It was as if they were journeying into a beautiful and forbidden country together, but how beautiful and how forbidden, Daisy was not certain.

Cypri's fingers found secret places, and Daisy hung suspended, not even breathing, until she felt an ecstatic release. Her entire body broke out in sweat and she stared at the white ceiling above her without a single thought in her head.

"Now me," Cypri whispered. "You do it to me."

When Daisy probed her cousin, Cypri had to bite the pillow to keep from yelling. She was giggling with delight the whole time until she bit down hard on the pillow; then Daisy could feel her cousin's entire hard body convulse. The bed shook. Cypri gasped for air.

Afterward they lay together with their heads on the pillow looking at the ceiling while their breathing slowed. A long time seemed to pass. Finally Cypri stirred. She hopped up, throwing back the covers.

"Get up, sleepyhead," she yelled, grabbing the pillow from under Daisy's head and battering her with it.

"Hey, wait." Daisy was knocked half out of bed by repeated attacks. Cypri slung the pillow into the corner, grinning.

"Get dressed. I told Frank we'd help him clean the barn."

Cypri pulled on her jeans as if this were just any Saturday morning, and after another minute Daisy got up. She still felt funny and rather dizzy, but she was hungry for breakfast.

Just before Daisy's eleventh birthday, Bascomb Dane died.

It wasn't unexpected. Dr. Honeychurch and two specialists had prepared the family for the possibility after Bascomb had suffered several more small strokes. Early on the morning it happened, China knocked on the girls' door and went in to tell them. China had tears in her eyes.

Daisy tried to feel sad, but she could number on her hands the times she had spoken to Uncle Bascomb in the years she had been at Land's End. No devotion between them had ever developed, although once he had called her into his room to say that he was proud of her high grades. Daisy knew that it was ungrateful of her not to weep; she was living on Dane money, after all, as Cypri sometimes pointed out. But her fears of her father and of Dusty were still with her. Though her father was long dead, and she didn't think Dusty was coming to kill her any longer, her once active fears had become simply a continual running unease with all men. She didn't trust them. However, for Aunt China's sake she pretended to be sorry Uncle Bascomb had died.

Vivienne and Mab both came home for the funeral at the Church of the Good Shepherd. They both wept at Bascomb's grave. Daisy observed Cypri narrowly; she didn't cry, but she acted properly subdued. Aunt China looked beautiful and dignified in her black suit and veil. The church and graveyard were packed with Danes from everywhere, a sprinkling of Austins and Royals, and half the town of Eyreville.

Actually, Daisy thought, Aunt China seemed to be relieved when it was all over with. At first Aunt China had long sessions in the library with Bascomb's lawyers. There were regular meetings for a while; then they stopped, and life at Land's End went on as usual except that Aunt China had more free time now and could join the Garden Club again. She even laughed more, usually at some observation of Cypri's on the Eyreville social scene.

Aunt China mentioned once that the girls could each have a bedroom now if they would like.

Daisy drew a breath, looked at Cypri, and said

242

nothing. Cypri, who eyed Daisy casually, said, "Oh, I've gotten used to Daisy."

Their sexual explorations together were practically nightly occurrences, taking place in silence, although the walls of Land's End were a foot thick and the privacy of the rooms was absolute. The thought of Aunt China's ever learning about what they did chilled Daisy to the bone. But Aunt China never would. The idea would never even cross her mind. And Daisy's guilt and fear made her relationship with Cypri even more thrilling.

Daisy had grown; she was only half a head shorter than Cypri now and not so thin. Cypri at thirteen had developed a large bosom in the last year, the last straw to the girls at the academy since Cypri already had the slimmest legs and flattest stomach and prettiest face. All the boys were in a state over her.

At first, Cypri took the male adulation cynically.

"Oh, *yeah*," she said, "I *bet*," when Celia Honeychurch told her that Roland Parker was in love with her. When Roland came through with a large box of chocolates on Valentine's Day, she grew less skeptical, however. Daisy was sorry to see Cypri's change of attitude. Daisy thought boys were hideous pests; they interested her not at all, but suddenly the walls of their bedroom held pictures of handsome young male television and movie actors instead of sports stars. Cypriana spent hours talking on the telephone. Daisy could tell when it was a boy on the other end because Cypri dropped her voice very low and tried to sound sexy.

Next, Cypri began to have dates. None of the boys could drive as yet, but their fathers or mothers would bring them out in cars to pick up Cypri and take her to the movies or dances.

Cypri went out only with boys from Trinity, but Daisy knew that Frank King had the biggest crush of all on her. He would ask Daisy whom Cypri had a date with, and say, "Oh. That rich bastard." Frank

243

finally got Cypri and Daisy to come and watch him play in a freshman game at the high school. Cypri had to admit that Frank was the fastest boy on the team. Eyreville High's varsity had been undefeated for three years. Their star quarterback was Champ Alexander, a boy who lived only half a mile from Land's End. Champ was Frank's idol. Frank was always telling Cypri and Daisy about how much yardage Champ had gained or how many passes he had completed. Cypri was unmoved by the account of Champ's exploits. Champ lived over the Crosstree grocery store and was nobody to her, in spite of his athletic fame. Sometimes when Daisy and Cypri went to Crosstree to buy candy bars, Champ would be behind the counter waiting on people. Although he acted very businesslike, Daisy saw Champ sneak long looks at Cypriana.

Watching boys watch Cypri made Daisy feel queer inside. She didn't want Cypri to like it. But Daisy did not dream of complaining. Cypri would do what she wanted. And with her mad appetites and avid curiosity, that was plenty. She made Daisy listen to whispered accounts of what boys did, and what boys wanted, and Daisy would writhe to hear them. "Oh, don't, Cypri, don't," she pleaded sometimes, but Cypri went right on hurting her, whispering to her and making love to her, all at once.

The worst was to come, however. Cypri came home one day to announce that she'd heard from Celia Honeychurch that Charles, her brother, liked Daisy. Charles wanted to take Daisy to the seventh grade dance.

"And I'll bet Mother will let you get a new dress," Cypri said.

"I don't want to go!"

Daisy meant it. Charles was now taller, although not so tall as she, and had fat haunches. Daisy couldn't bear the idea of going anywhere with him. But Cypri looked on Charles as a conquest.

"You have to go," she said. "I said you would."

Daisy cried for an hour, to no avail. She was decked out, on the appointed night, and sent forth with Charles Honeychurch and his father, Dr. Honeychurch, who had driven Charles out to Land's End to pick her up. Charles was extremely polite and sat nowhere near Daisy in the car; as he didn't dance himself, they sat in chairs on the side of the dance floor the whole night. When two other boys asked Daisy to dance, she refused, and then Dr. Honeychurch picked them up and drove Daisy back to Land's End. Charles had not touched her even once.

If all dates had been like that one, Daisy would have known less misery, but summer came, and Frank King made his move. He invited both girls to a party at his house, and China said they could go. Cypriana said they *had* to, or else Frank would tell everyone in the world that they were rotten snobs. Daisy was puzzled; Cypri had never minded being thought a snob before.

The King boys' parents were out for the evening, and Beatles music was blasting out the doors and windows when the girls arrived. Except for Daisy and Cypri, all the kids there were from Eyreville High. To show them her sophistication, Cypri drank four boilermakers, a concoction, mixed by Frank, of beer and rye whiskey that freed her from reality. She danced wildly with Frank, tossing her heavy dark hair and swinging her hips. "Look at those boobs," Daisy heard one boy say. Every boy in the room was watching Cypri.

"Your cousin can really dance," Bob said to Daisy. He often spoke to Daisy when he saw her around Land's End, though Daisy never made any effort to be friendly back.

"Would you like to dance?" Bob asked.

Daisy shook her head. What she wanted was to get out of there. But a few minutes later Cypri and Frank disappeared out the door into the summer darkness.

245

An hour passed. Bob tried to interest Daisy in drinking a boilermaker. She declined.

When Cypri reappeared, she was laughing wildly, and Frank pulled her across the dance floor and into the kitchen, where he tried to get some coffee into her. A crowd gathered to watch, while Cypriana giggled and carried on, trying to find where Frank had hidden the rye. She found some graham crackers in one cabinet and ate the whole box.

"Will her mother be waiting up?" Frank asked Daisy.

Daisy looked at the clock. It was one in the morning.

"I don't know, but we'd better go," she said.

The boys walked them home over the fields, Frank with his arm around Cypri to steady her. She was talking a blue streak to him, and he hushed her as they reached the willow trees.

"The porch lights are on. But I don't see any other lights. Your mother must have gone to bed. I hope," Frank said.

Cypri flung her arms around Frank and he hugged her back and kissed her for what seemed like ten minutes.

"Come on, Cypri," Daisy said.

As they tiptoed onto the porch, Cypri was still giggling, but the house was still. Daisy managed to get Cypri upstairs and into bed. Cypri fell asleep right away.

She felt terrible the next morning. But she called Daisy to her bedside.

"Guess what we did? I'm not a virgin any longer. Out in the shed. It was terrific! Listen—"

"I'll get you some aspirin," Daisy said, and quickly left the room. Eventually, however, she had to hear all of it.

At the end of the summer Frank got his driver's license. Since Cypriana was only fifteen, China would not let her go out alone with Frank.

"Would you say okay if Daisy went too?" Cypriana

246

asked. "Frank just wants to take me to the drive-in movie. Please?"

The drive-in movie, with Daisy and Bob going along, sounded respectable, China thought. Actually China was making rules for Cypriana simply because all the mothers in China's circle made rules for their daughters —when to come home, where they could go, with whom, and so on. China herself trusted Cypriana completely. It was not in China's nature to be suspicious. She had brought all her daughters up to be ladies, and she couldn't believe that they weren't, even if she saw evidence to the contrary, which Cypriana was careful to make sure that she didn't. China was positive that Cypri knew right from wrong.

China agreed to the drive-in movie.

Cypriana announced to Daisy that she was to be a chaperone and come along with Bob. When Daisy refused, they quarreled. Daisy cried and gave in.

The movie was *The Monster at Terror Island*. After Frank drove them there and parked the car at a speaker in the back row, he and Cypri traded places with Daisy and Bob. Daisy sat as far over as possible on the front seat of the old Dodge sedan and stared at the screen as if she were totally absorbed. By slow degrees, Bob seemed to be inching her way, even as the monster inched its way up to a lighted window, where it peered in at a girls' slumber party.

Daisy could hear beer cans being opened in the back seat. She could tell without turning around that Cypri and Frank were lying full-length across the seat. She could hear them whisper from time to time. She wondered if they could even see the screen.

"Are you scared?" Bob whispered to her. She looked at him in the dim light from the movie screen.

"Are you kidding? I think the monster looks like a big rubber duck," Daisy said.

Bob put his arm over the back of the seat. He did it casually. Trying to be just as unobtrusive, Daisy shrank further over until the door handle dug painfully into her side. Bob seemed not to notice her retreat. He was staring ahead again at the screen, but he didn't take his arm down.

Suddenly Cypri giggled loudly. Daisy could hear a scuffle taking place in the back seat. She stared at the screen for all she was worth. The girls in the film were screaming and fleeing in all directions as the monster floundered through the woods after them. One girl tripped and fell on a tree root. The monster pounced.

The Dodge began to rock back and forth and the back seat springs creaked. Daisy sat frozen, looking at the screen so fixedly that tears almost came into her eyes. The creaking in the back of the car went on. Bob reached over and turned up the speaker, so that the screams of the girl being mauled by the monster drowned out any sound from the back seat. At least two more victims were devoured before there was a subsiding back there. Beer cans popped again.

"Daisy." Bob moved his head close to hers and spoke her name softly. "You know, I'm not like—I wouldn't—"

He stopped. Daisy sat rigid. She didn't turn her head, but she could sense that Bob's face was red. He sounded embarrassed.

"Hey, kids, want a beer?" Frank's head suddenly came up behind them. Daisy shook her head. Frank handed Bob an open can over the seat.

"Oh. Yeah, okay." Bob took the can, but he just held it. He didn't take a drink. Frank sank from view, and the back seat resumed activity. The car rocked slightly for a few minutes and then grew still. Daisy heard Cypri giggle.

"I mean, I think you're a nice girl," Bob whispered as the monster was hunted down by the entire police force of the seacoast town. Daisy pretended to be absorbed in the movie. After a while Bob took his arm down and moved back behind the wheel, clutching the full can of beer in both hands.

The movie seemed endless. Finally, dynamite routed the monster and he flapped, wounded, into the sea.

"Boy, grade Z," Cypriana said, sitting up as the outdoor lights came on.

As they exchanged seats, Daisy could see Cypri's dishevelment; her hair was rumpled and her skirt twisted, the zipper in the wrong place; her cheeks were flushed and her eyes bright.

In the darkness of the back seat on the way home to Land's End Bob put his hand over Daisy's hand for just a moment, as if it had been an accident. Daisy jerked her hand away. She felt like jumping out of the car. But Bob didn't touch her again.

"Honestly, Daisy, the way you treat Bob," Cypriana said when they reached their bedroom. "Frank says Bob is crazy about you."

"Oh, Cypri, how could you?" Daisy threw herself face down on her bed. "How could you do it with him like that, right in front of—how could you? I can't stand it."

"Well, that's just too bad." Cypri sounded annoyed. When Daisy said nothing more, she began to undress, taking off her skirt and then her blouse. She kicked off her sandals and shed her underclothes.

"You just don't know what's fun," Cypri said.

Daisy didn't move; her head remained buried in the pillow.

Cypri turned the overhead light off and came over to Daisy's bed.

"Look at me," she said.

For a moment Daisy kept her eyes tightly shut.

"Daisy."

Daisy turned over onto her back and opened her eyes.

In the soft light from the bedside lamp, Cypriana stood naked, the pink nipples erect in the center of her full white breasts. The round globes stood out whiter than the tanned skin surrounding them. Cypri's lower hips and pelvis were also white—the part sheltered by the smallest bikini bottom China would allow Cypri to wear to the beach. The white skin emphasized Cypri's silky black pubic hair. Her smooth brown thighs rounded inward; everything seemed to lead the eye to the point between her legs.

Daisy moaned. Cypri jumped on top of her. "Put your hands on me," she whispered.

"I want you to love me," Daisy said, almost sobbing. She caressed Cypri frantically. "I love you so much."

"Hey, be careful," Cypri said. "I'm a little sore."

Daisy tried to think of things that Frank would never have thought of. Her avidity surprised her. It was as if she were fighting a battle for Cypri's body, a battle she knew she would lose. Cypri would never be all hers.

Sometimes, when Daisy would look at Cypri, just the sight of her—the curve of her upper lip or a flash of her blue eyes—would make Daisy feel so sexy she would have to excuse herself hastily from whatever she was doing and go up to their room and pray that Cypri would be in a mood to follow her. Daisy would wait in the room until Cypri could find an excuse to join her and they would fall together, breathless, on the bed.

"It's your age, almost sixteen," Cypri said one evening. "I remember when I went through it. You feel sexy all day long."

Daisy giggled. "*You* are one to sound superior," she said.

Cypri had been nice to her all that day, and Daisy was in a good mood. Recently, their relationship had seemed more stable. By now, Cypri was old enough to go out alone with boys, and she could stay out as late as she pleased this summer; because Cypri was going away to Chapel Hill in the fall, China had loosened all strictures. Cypri had stopped forcing Daisy to go along on double dates, or to go out at all, telling her to stay home and be a stick-in-the-mud if she wanted to. Cypri still made Daisy listen to the account of everything she did with her dates. At least, Cypri always came back to her. Once, Cypri had even told Daisy she thought she was pretty.

Cypriana was currently busy buying college clothes and writing letters to her roommates-to-be. Daisy had accepted the inevitability of the coming separation. Her plan was to double up on her own school work. By taking extra courses, she could finish at Trinity in the spring, and next year join Cypri at college.

In the coming year, Daisy wanted to study hard and to spend a lot of time with her aunt. Aunt China had said many times how glad she was that she would still have a girl left at home. With all her heart, Daisy wanted to please Aunt China and show her how much she loved her. Daisy had hesitated to do everything she would like to have done for her aunt, because she didn't want it to seem as if she were competing with Cypriana, who was affectionate with her mother but didn't go out of her way to be loving. Next year, Daisy thought, she could be close to Aunt China without feeling guilty. There wouldn't be the terrible secret to worry about either. Aunt China with her gentle ways and kind words made Daisy feel ashamed of what she did with Cypriana. Sometimes Daisy almost looked forward to the quiet and peace of life without Cypri.

However, Daisy wasn't thinking of quiet and peace that evening. It was one of her last nights with Cypriana and she devoted herself to finding every possible variation of delicious sensation.

The next morning as Daisy and Cypriana were walking downstairs together, they saw China standing in the hall with a strange look on her face. China was looking up at them, and her expression was so peculiar that Daisy's first thought was a horrified "She knows." Her foot suspended in air, Daisy stopped; Cypri was suddenly motionless, too.

China looked pained, as if she had just heard or seen something devastating. Her lips parted slightly, but she made no sound. Her dark eyes stared at them. She laid her right hand on her heart.

"Mother?"

Cypriana sprang down the stairs.

"Mother. What is it?" She reached China's side in time to catch her. China folded against her. "Mother!" Cypri screamed.

Ella appeared at the library door and rushed to China's side. She grabbed her, and together she and Cypriana dragged China to the hall bench. Daisy couldn't believe what she was seeing. China's face was drained of color. Daisy ran down the stairs.

The doctor was called. The ambulance arrived inside of ten minutes. Cypriana, weeping, never stopped administering mouth to mouth resuscitation until they placed China on the stretcher. Everyone in the house had run for remedies, for blankets, for brandy, for ice. But China never moved. She was dead.

Cypriana shoved Daisy into their bedroom, closed the door firmly, and pulled her by the arm over to her bed. Violently, she pushed her down. As Daisy, red-eyed, her face twisted and pale, stared vacantly at her, Cypriana drew back her hand and slapped Daisy across the face as hard as she could. Daisy's head snapped to the side. She cried out. Cypriana hit her again, across the same cheek. The red print of Cypri's hand was so distinct it looked raised on Daisy's pale skin.

"How dare you!" Cypriana spit out the words. She grasped Daisy by the shoulders and shook her. Daisy's head bobbed back and forth. Feebly, she tried to ward off Cypri's hands.

"Please. I'm sorry."

"Screaming like that—you sounded like an idiot!" Cypriana's blue eyes blazed with anger as she regarded Daisy, crumpled before her in her white dress.

"Poor Mother. You disgraced us all. Thank God, Mother wasn't here to see you. I thought you were going to jump into that grave after her. Yelling that you'd killed her! Now everyone thinks you're insane. Keep this up and that's where you'll land, in an insane asylum!"

Cypri drew back her hand to administer another slap. Daisy stared up at her with a dull look in her red-rimmed eyes and made no move to defend herself. Cypri dropped her hand.

"What did you mean by it, anyway?" she said. Her eyes seemed to bore into Daisy's head.

Daisy said nothing.

"Answer me, Daisy, or you're going to be sorry." Cypriana's tone was full of so much menace that it got through to Daisy even in her befuddled state. Daisy looked up and tried to make an effort to answer, but when she opened her mouth nothing came out.

"You were hysterical, sobbing out all sorts of things. You said you'd killed Mother. Now what exactly did you mean by that?" Cypriana stood over Daisy; her body was taut with fury.

Daisy tried to think. "I was hysterical?" she whispered.

"Don't pretend you can't remember. You disgraced the family. If I hadn't gotten you away, they would have taken you to the booby hatch, you stupid girl."

"Oh, Cypri." Daisy put her face down in her hands and burst into tears. She couldn't remember the events of the last hour, only that when she had looked at Aunt China's coffin, she had felt separated from all the good in the world.

Cypriana watched Daisy sob. They said it was good for people to cry. God knows *she* had cried. She and Mab and Vivienne had wept together at various times in the last three days. Daisy had seemed to be too stunned to cry; she had been walking around like a robot, no help to anyone. Then, at the funeral that afternoon, Daisy had cried more than anyone in the church; in the graveyard she had literally had to be restrained from throwing herself into the grave after China, yelling all sorts of incomprehensible things.

253

Cypriana had dragged her away by the arm and gotten her into one of the limousines and home. Daisy had really gone over the edge.

It was a hot August afternoon and the sun streaming into the back windows made it uncomfortably warm. Cypriana wiped beads of sweat from her brow. Her anger diminished a little and she put her hand on Daisy's shoulder.

"Come on, Daisy. God knows, it's terrible for all of us."

The pain in Daisy's throat eased slightly. Cypri roughly wiped the tears off Daisy's cheeks with her hand, and Daisy leaned against Cypri and tried to catch her breath, making hiccuping sounds. Her left cheek stung like fury* and her eyes hurt almost as much; her arm ached where Cypri had grasped it to pull her out of the churchyard. Daisy's mind was dim, full of shadowy pictures. In the church during the service she had remembered her own mother's funeral; it had been suddenly clear that she had killed her mother, and now Aunt China was dead, and Daisy must have killed her, too. She had done something wrong—

Between that point and Cypriana's slapping her, Daisy could summon no memories at all.

"Come on, Daisy." The familiar voice repeated the words. Cypri patted her shoulder. Cypri! Cypri would never understand.

"I killed my mother," Daisy said.

Cypri pulled Daisy's face up and looked her in the eyes.

"No, you didn't," she said firmly. "Your mother either had an accident or that man killed her." Her voice was very positive.

"But Cypri—you and I—what we do together, it's wrong, and Aunt China—"

"Listen to me, Daisy. If you had never come to Land's End, Mother would still have died just the same. Even if you'd never lived. You know what the autopsy showed. It was a heart attack." Cypri spoke slowly and distinctly, emphasizing each word.

"But it seems I—I keep losing everyone—"

"Look at me, Daisy. You've got me. You won't lose me. I'm perfectly healthy. Now cut all this out and pull yourself together. Mab and Vivienne will be back in a moment. We should go downstairs and receive people. If you wash your face and put on some makeup and act like a human being, maybe people will forget what happened. You were just temporarily overcome. All right?"

Somehow Daisy seemed to be back in the real world again. She did feel better, if weak all over.

"Cypri, I'm sorry; thank you."

"Let's see you behave yourself now. I guess you needed that, but now you're over it. Just forget it and come downstairs."

The gathering below was extremely quiet. Ella had cried as much as Daisy, to judge from her eyes. Ella's granddaughter Baker also had swollen, red lids. What seemed like the entire population of Eyreville filed past and pressed Daisy's hand. After a while George brought Daisy a glass of brandy and suggested she take it, as the crowd cleared out. No one stayed very long. There was no party atmosphere at this funeral. Everyone had loved China Dane. Everyone had been shocked at her early death. She had been only fifty-five.

That night Vivienne chose a line from *Romeo and Juliet* to be carved on China's tombstone. Everyone agreed it was the perfect inscription: *China Royal Austin Dane. 1916–1971. Beauty too rich for use, for earth too dear.*

Relatives vied with each other in kind offers of help. It turned out to be needed. When Vivienne and Mab finished going over the accounts, they called the girls and Ella and George into the library. Vivienne made the painful announcement.

"Land's End must be sold."

All of them were stunned at the words. Vivienne didn't believe them even as she said them.

"We must sell," Vivienne went on. "Neither Mab nor I can leave what we're doing to move down here. Cypri and Daisy have to go to college. And there isn't that much extra money. I don't know how Mother managed, but after the bills are paid, we're going to need the money from the sale of the house to pay college expenses."

Cypri and Daisy stared at Vivienne in silence as she went on to explain that part of the Dane estate was entailed. Only the income on that part could go to the sisters during their lifetimes. Their father had spent the unentailed capital, and Mother had let everything slide for the last five years.

Daisy immediately offered to work her way through college, but Vivienne would not hear of it. It wouldn't make that much difference, she explained. The real trouble was more than college fees.

Ultimately, a distant cousin who had always wanted to own Land's End was permitted his wish. The house was sold. Great-aunt Martha Austin's invitation to the two younger girls to come live with her was accepted. The day came when Daisy packed her clothes and George drove her into Eyreville, to the big white Victorian house on Fillmore street, a house smelling of lavender and potpourri and clove oranges. Daisy could not bear to look behind her as the pillars of Land's End disappeared.

Cypri had already gone to Chapel Hill. She didn't write letters, but when she came home at Thanksgiving she was enthusiastic. College was great. Cypri looked excited, full of vitality, as she perched in Great-aunt Martha's parlor amid the bric-a-brac and lace pillows. Daisy was thrilled to see her. They had a lovers' reunion after Aunt Martha retired, and things between them were better than ever. Cypri's sex life at school was active, but she had actually missed Daisy, she said. Daisy couldn't put into words how much she had missed Cypri.

In the spring when Daisy was graduated from Trinity she was the valedictorian of the class.

"Good job you got out of there early," Cypri said. "God, another year at Aunt Martha's and you'd dry up. I break out in hives in that place. Only thing I can stand is the sherry hour."

Every afternoon at five, in the blue sitting room, Aunt Martha was served sherry by her ancient cook Susan, and she drank enough to make her animated at dinner and, shortly afterward, ready for bed. Wars might be fought, leaders be assassinated, administrations change, scandals erupt, blacks get their rights and women be liberated; Aunt Martha heard vaguely of these things, but they all passed and the verities remained; in seventy years she had never missed her afternoon sherry. She was in remarkable good health and spry as a cricket. Her black chow dog Chang went everywhere with her. Chang did not care for anyone but Aunt Martha. Sometimes he growled at the two girls.

"Rowrrr, yourself," Cypriana growled back. At least you could get a rise out of Chang. Aunt Martha calmly regarded the presence of the Dane girls as something that would also pass; beyond civil inquiries as to their health each morning, she left them to come or go as they pleased. On their birthdays she served them champagne, and Susan, the cook, baked them chocolate cakes.

"I don't know how you've stood this year," Cypri repeated. "Wait'll you see Chapel Hill." Daisy's application had been accepted, and .Cypri was busy planning Daisy's college wardrobe with an eye to borrowing the clothes whenever she needed them. Daisy was actually the same size as Cypri now. Daisy had turned out very well, Cypri thought. .If she weren't so quiet, people would notice her more, but when you did look, her figure and features and hair were lovely.

257

"Daisy! Wait a minute."

One afternoon at the end of summer, just before she was to leave for college, Daisy heard a boy call her. She was outside the Eyreville drugstore and she turned around to find Bob King running across the street toward her; he was panting.

"Hey. How are you, Daisy?" he said. "I haven't seen you in so long."

"I'm fine," Daisy said.

"Look, can I talk to you a minute?"

Bob seemed a little nervous. His freckled face was flushed.

"Sure," she said.

"I'm going into the army next month."

"You are?"

"Yeah. You know Frank's been in for a year. He's in Vietnam now. I heard you were going to college."

Daisy nodded.

Bob drew a deep breath and plunged. "I was wondering, Daisy. If I wrote to you, would you write back and tell me the news sometimes?" He looked at her face closely.

"Okay."

"You'll have to give me your address."

"Just write in care of the university. I haven't got an address yet."

"Okay, I will. And would you like to go to the movies tonight? If you're not busy, I mean."

"I'm sorry. I've already seen both movies."

"How about the one at the drive-in?"

"I've got something to do tonight. I'm sorry." Daisy felt as if she were being mean, but she definitely didn't want to have anything to do with Bob King, even if he was going into the army.

Bob looked embarrassed and said he'd ask her again sometime.

Well, maybe Daisy did have something to do tonight, Bob told himself as he watched her walk on down the street. Probably she did.

Less than two months later, Daisy received a letter from Bob. It was full of details about his training and signed, "Very truly yours, Bob." Daisy wrote back, a short letter with all the local news she knew, signing it, "Very truly, Daisy." The next week she got another letter. The tone was the same except at the end. There he wrote, "I wish we had gotten to know each other better, Daisy. Sometimes I sit and just think about you for a while. I hope you don't mind." It was signed, "Love, Bob."

Daisy did mind. She didn't answer the letter. Her life was all worked out now, and she led it with a considerable amount of poise. She left boys alone, and for the most part they left her alone, although Cypri sometimes forced her to go on dates "so she wouldn't look like a queer." Her aloof attitude intrigued some boys, but eventually they all grew discouraged and left her in peace. Daisy knew the truth about herself. She was afraid of boys and she really didn't like other girls, either, not *that* way; all she wanted was Cypri. When they could manage a few minutes alone together, Daisy was in heaven. The rest of the time she simply existed and studied. Her grades were terrific.

"They say she'll do it with a dining room chair." Champ laughed.

Cypriana Dane had a racy reputation, no doubt about that. But Champ happened to know that Pete Parker, who offered this observation in the spirit of friendship, had been trying, unsuccessfully, to date Cypri Dane for two years. She'd have nothing to do with Pete; he was too short. However, she once had allowed his younger and taller brother, Roland Parker, to take her to a country club dance. Champ wouldn't expect Pete to find in her favor after that.

"You two are *really* getting married, Champ, no kidding?"

"Next June."

Pete let his breath out in a long stream between his front teeth and shook his head. He was astonished to think of Cypriana Dane as a bride. She didn't seem the type. And he was doubly astonished at a Dane's marrying an Alexander.

For such a wedding to be possible, Champ could thank in equal measure his brother Philip and Damn the Torpedoes.

Damn the Torpedoes was the Honeychurch family rock band. The three oldest Honeychurch boys had formed it during the mid-sixties, Junior on bass, Walker on drums, and Scat on lead guitar. They actually began to make money playing at dances, and the effort grew serious.

Their father, Dr. Chester Honeychurch, was not musical. The boys' bent toward music came from his wife, who for years had conducted the choir at the Church of the Good Shepherd. Dr. Honeychurch was not only not musical, he hated rock music. Medicine was his life. When his last child, Charles, gave no indication of growing up to be more than back-up guitar, Dr. Honeychurch sadly relinquished his dream. Not one of his children would carry on for him.

Hard on this realization, Champ Alexander had consulted Dr. Honeychurch about medical schools. Dr. Honeychurch knew the boy by reputation, as the finest quarterback Eyreville High had ever had. The doctor had treated the boy's father, Thomas, for shingles. Aware that the Alexanders were far from a rich family, Dr. Honeychurch asked Champ how he planned to finance his education. Champ explained that his brother Philip, who'd been in England for many years, had become his uncle's second-in-command in the conglomerate empire Downforth Enterprises. Philip had offered to pay for Champ's medical education.

"Of course I want to pay Philip back," Champ said. "It will just be a loan."

Dr. Honeychurch had been on the point of offering

Champ help himself. He had no one to educate except his two youngest girls, who wanted to go to the state university and later become models. Dr. Honeychurch sighed at the thought and asked Champ more about his medical plans. Champ wanted to attend a three-year medical school, readying himself for family practice, which required only a two-year rolling internship to complete. Champ was eager to start in actual practice; by going to summer school he had already made up a year of college.

Dr. Honeychurch was sure the Lord had provided. He was feeling his age, and here was a smart young fellow on his doorstep. They had a long talk. Ultimately Dr. Honeychurch arranged for Champ to come to Eyreville Hospital for his internship, and offered him a full partnership upon its completion.

With this prospect before him, Champ came back to Eyreville in high spirits. Although his schedule at the hospital was arduous, he had time on his days off for tennis and golf, and he joined the Eyreville Country Club. There he saw Cypriana Dane for the first time in years. He knew her at once. He had remembered her all through college and medical school. She was his idea of a sexy babe; she always had been, even when she was only a kid coming into the grocery store for Milky Ways. He knew that the Danes had sold Land's End and that Cypri lived with her aunt in town when she came home from college. His mother kept him up on Eyreville gossip.

There she was, whacking a tennis ball over the net with so much force that it was a wonder the ball didn't explode. Champ watched with pleasure as Cypriana leaped about the court, her silky hair swinging and the tiny skirt of her white tennis dress flying up. She was playing Celia Honeychurch, and she beat her six-love, six-love.

The match had been the women's semi-final in the club's championship series. Cypriana drank some water out of her tennis ball can. Barely breathing hard, she was putting the cover on her racket when Champ approached her.

"Say, that was good."

Cypri's blue eyes narrowed to regard him.

"I'm Champ Alexander," he said when she seemed not to recognize him. "From Crosstree. Remember?"

Celia came running up to join them. "*You* know Champ, Cypri," she said. "He's going to become Daddy's partner."

"Oh, yeah. Hi."

Celia turned on the charm and asked Champ how he thought she could improve her backhand. As Champ answered, Cypriana looked him over. He was cute. He wasn't extra tall, but he walked like an athlete. He had a square, very muscular build and broad shoulders. She remembered that he had been a football hero; Frank King had talked about him endlessly. His face was a little freckled; he had pleasant features and lots of light brown hair.

"—like Cypriana does," he said, demonstrating for Celia. "You notice she is never off balance. Her weight is always evenly divided on both feet." He took Celia's racket and made a couple of passes. "How about a drink, girls?"

They agreed to meet him after they took showers. Champ waited at the bar. When Cypriana walked in— her dark hair still slightly damp at the edges, her expression haughty—wearing a pair of tiny cut-off jeans and a tight yellow halter, Champ got an erection. He could feel it, but he hoped she couldn't see it. He couldn't imagine how Cypriana got through life without being raped every day.

He had a nice smile, Cypriana thought as she ordered a Tequila Sunrise. Celia, who had stopped for a full makeup, found them laughing together. Cypriana was describing life at Great-aunt Martha's.

"So the postman just throws the mail down on the lawn if Chang is outside. And her Siamese cat drinks sherry—I swear it. I've seen him. He waits until Aunt

Martha's looking away and then he laps it out of her glass. Living there drives even a cat to drink."

Celia looked at Champ and then Cypri. Both of them were animated. Cypriana didn't bother to be amusing unless she liked someone. Oh, no, Celia thought, there goes *that* cute boy. Damn.

"And the food—God. The other day I asked Susan what she'd put on that veal roast. It had a really different taste. And she said she just sprinkled it with a can of nutmeg—the way she usually does. And she heats vinegar in a skillet and throws in fresh oysters, and then takes them out and adds chopped dill pickles, and that's oyster salad! I couldn't believe it."

"Your aunt's got the secret of long life, all right. Maybe it's vinegar and dill pickles."

"Try it. I don't think you'll live long at all. My cousin Daisy lost ten pounds living there. If it weren't for the sherry and the wine at dinner and the brandy after, we'd both be dead. It must be the alcohol that nourishes us. Yesterday we had a geranium-leaf omelette."

"Cypri, you made that up," Celia said. Sitting down beside them, Celia ordered a Tequila Sunrise, too. Might as well drown her sorrows. Champ was *gone*; she could see that. She felt like saying, "Well, when's the wedding?" That would have made Cypri furious, but as it turned out, it wouldn't have been a bad question, at that.

XV

Great-aunt Martha was distantly related to the Alexander family on her mother's side. She approved of the match and offered to underwrite the wedding.

Cypri was delighted. She wanted a big affair. It took six months to plan it. When the night of June seventh arrived, every detail had been considered. Fortunately, almost all of the relatives would be there. All except Vivienne, who was out of the country on location making a movie. Vivienne sent her little sister a handsome check, a set of exquisite Venetian glass wine goblets, a few other small mementoes and many apologies. Cypri didn't mind. People always paid a lot of attention to Vivienne when she was around, and Cypri didn't want anyone to upstage her at her own wedding.

As the time grew near, Cypriana actually couldn't wait for it to hurry up and be over. She grew sick of telling everyone why she had decided to get married. She *liked* Champ, he would soon be making lots of money, and meanwhile, thanks to his rich brother Philip, she could have a house of her own and servants and a base for whatever she decided to do with her life . . . without Aunt Martha. Champ was really a sweet guy who wouldn't get in her way, and he was madly sexy, too. So why not? She had no patience with such discussions.

The wedding march finally sounded.

Frank and Bob King, who were Baptists, had never been inside of the Church of the Good Shepherd before.

They looked around in amazement. It was nine o'clock at night, and the interior of the white-walled building glowed with the light of hundreds of candles, burning in two hanging chandeliers and in candelabra on the altar and on all the window ledges. The end of each long white pew was decorated with American Beauty roses, ivy, and cherry-colored ribbons, forming a path up to the white-draped altar, which was surrounded by American Beauty roses spilling out of dozens of white baskets. The whole place was a bower of roses; their perfume was in the air, and the hundreds and hundreds of burgundy petals were radiant in the candlelight.

Outside, the moon high in the sky made a silver twilight through which the girls in their gleaming gowns walked solemnly up the steps of the church. Everyone was waiting inside; the yellow glow of the candles turned the church an unearthly golden.

Celia Honeychurch went first. As the organist sent the march booming forth, the congregation inside the packed church stood and turned to look at the door; a murmur swept through them as Celia appeared. She looked spectacular, like a bride herself, in a white satin gown with a short train. Her blond hair was bound up with a circlet of cherry ribbons and ivy, and she carried an armful of long-stemmed American Beauty roses. She started down the aisle.

At the same moment, two men in formal white tie and tails entered from the side of the altar and stood by the railing; Champ, looking rather pale, and his brother Philip. Celia's face was solemn as she paced toward them.

Behind Celia appeared a second girl in white, Betsy Churchill, Cypri's college roommate. She was a slender girl with big gray eyes that looked smoky in the golden light; her dark hair was also bound with ivy and cherry ribbons, and she carried roses.

Bob caught his breath sharply; as the music continued, Daisy took her place in the door. No bride, Bob thought, could possibly be more beautfiul. He felt an ache in his throat. The white satin of Daisy's dress was no more lustrous than her skin; they seemed to blend together, and Daisy's hair was a halo around her face. Its tawny strands were twisted up with the ribbons and ivy, and as she moved under the chandeliers, her head collected a nimbus of light about it that almost hurt the eye. The expression on Daisy's face was indescribable. She looked as if this were the last thing she was going to do on earth—Bob didn't know why that thought came to him. Slowly, Daisy marched forward with her lips slightly parted and her blue eyes fixed on the altar as if she saw nothing but the large gold cross upon it. Bob did not take his eyes off Daisy. Everyone else looked back once more. A stir went through the gathering. Mab entered the door, and as she glided forward, she smiled. Mab's chestnut hair was also twined with the ivy and ribbons, and she carried roses as the others did, but somehow on her the white dress looked different. The other girls were lovely and Daisy was beautiful, but Mab was exquisite. Her bare shoulders emerged dramatically from the low neckline of the gown, and her superb long neck gave her a regal look; her oval face and small, perfectly-formed head were those of a fairy queen. She seemed to float as she walked, and a faint aura of perfume clung about her. Some in the church, following Mab's progress to the altar with awed expressions, forgot to look back again. But then someone actually cried "Oh!" aloud, and all eyes, even Bob's, swung back to the door as the bride appeared. Every candle flame in the church wavered and the light flickered as the air was disturbed by a hundred gasps. Cypriana was literally breathtaking.

Bob saw his brother's hand shoot out to the pew ahead of him. Frank grasped the top of the pew's back and clamped his hand down so hard it turned white. Bob felt Frank's body go rigid.

All his life Frank had loved Cypri. When he got back from Vietnam she would rarely go out with him, but he still considered her his girl. Only the fact that she was marrying Champ Alexander saved her now. Frank still worshiped Champ—enough, at least, to keep him from rushing down the aisle and snatching Cypri up and tearing off with her into the night. Frank stared at her in pain.

Cypriana was a shocking vision. After all the white, which the candlelight had turned to ivory, Cypriana stood in the doorway in a long full gown of pale ice-blue satin, low cut, with a tightly-fitting bodice. Its startling color made her white skin gleam in contrast. Her silky dark hair, piled on top of her head, was held by a diamond tiara, and from this coronet, gauzy blue illusion fell to the floor, stirring with every movement and outlining her with blue radiance. The lipstick on her mouth glistened in the light and her incomparable blue eyes blazed with excitement. The vitality that was Cypriana's essence seemed almost to leap out from her and grip everyone in the church. The misty blue veil, the ebony hair, the burgundy roses in her arms, the shimmering dress that turned her eyes to glittering sapphire made the beauty that had preceded her seem pale in contrast.

Cypriana started down the aisle alone, enjoying the sensation she was creating. Uncle Benjamin had been suggested to her as an escort, or Thomas Alexander, or even Dr. Honeychurch, but she had declined all offers. She had no intention of being given away. A slight smile on her lips, Cypriana walked alone down the aisle of roses.

Frank King gripped the pew so hard he almost sprained his hand when Cypri came abreast of him. She did not look to the right or to the left. When she reached the point halfway to the altar where Champ could see her for the first time, she looked directly at him. With a small cry, Champ left his post beside Philip and rushed to her. Cypriana smiled radiantly. She turned and handed her roses to a startled little girl on the aisle, and when Champ reached her she held out both hands to him. He grasped them, said something no one could hear, and pulled her to the altar. Cypri laughed; the minister, Reverend Pedicord, standing ready with the prayer book in his hand, grinned broadly; and everyone in the church, except Daisy and Frank King, smiled at Champ's impetuous gesture.

The organ music stopped. In a glimmering array of whiteness, the four bridesmaids stood at the side of the altar, Celia and Betsy behind and Mab and Daisy in front. Daisy stared fixedly at the cross. She had rehearsed the wedding a thousand times in her mind, trying to prepare herself, but now every familiar phrase of the service struck her as though she had never heard it before. "Dearly beloved," Reverend Pedicord began, ". . . the sight of God . . . the face of this company . . . in the fear of God." He turned to Champ. "Beauchamp Lewis, wilt thou . . ." and then, "Cypriana Anne, wilt thou have this man . . ."

After Cypri responded, Reverend Pedicord said, "Who giveth this woman to be married to this man?"

Cypriana had refused at the wedding rehearsal to tell them what she intended to do at this moment, when traditionally the bride's escort gives her hand to the bridegroom. Reverend Pedicord paused. Cypri turned. She crossed to Mab in a flutter of blue, embraced her and kissed her on the cheek. As everyone strained to see, Cypri turned to Daisy and did the same, giving her a hug and a kiss on the side of her face. Then she stepped back to the first pew on the right, where Great-aunt Martha sat in state, dressed in rose silk. Cypri gave Aunt Martha a kiss, too, on her papery cheek.

The realization struck many in the church that, except for Vivienne, this was Cypriana's entire family now, and tears came to some eyes. China and Bascomb should have lived to see this day.

Cypri quietly resumed her place beside Champ and gave him her hand. The minister cleared his throat and intoned the words of the troth, which were repeated

269

first by Champ and then by Cypriana in steady, clear tones. The rings were exchanged. Finally everyone in the church knelt as Baker Browning sang "The Lord's Prayer," her clear young soprano voice building surely to the climax: ". . . for ever and ever. Amen."

"Chester, that was the most wonderful wedding I've ever seen. It wins hands down," Mrs. Honeychurch said to her husband as the wedding party retreated up the aisle, resplendent. "Even if she didn't wear white," Mrs. Honeychurch added. She wiped her eyes.

Frank relaxed his grip on the pew. His hand was numb. The second before, on her way out, Cypri had looked straight at him, and something about a mischievous quirk of her mouth seemed to say that maybe everything wasn't all over between them. He didn't know why he interpreted her expression that way, but he felt comforted.

Though Bob had not taken his eyes off Daisy for the entire service, she hadn't smiled or looked at him, even going out of the church.

After the ceremony, everyone drank vintage French champagne, courtesy of Aunt Martha, at the Eyreville Country Club. In fact, the liquor consumption hit an all-time high mark for wedding receptions in Eyreville. It was such a great party that Cypri didn't want to leave. On the dance floor friends from her childhood and college were all bopping together, in their dinner jackets and long dresses, to Damn the Torpedoes' acid rock. As a concession to the rest of her guests, she had another band for alternate sets, so that those who knew how to waltz and fox-trot would have their chance.

At midnight she and Champ cut the cake, a three-tiered concoction of formally-scalloped white frosting over white cake, topped with ice-blue sugar swans. A magnificent supper was served at long buffet tables covered with the lace tablecloths that Aunt Martha had bought in Belgium as a girl.

Celia found Cypriana in the ladies' room fishing something out of her silver shoe.

"The darn thing is giving me a blister," Cypri said.

"What?"

"The sixpence Vivienne sent me to wear at my wedding. You know, for luck: 'And a sixpence in her shoe.' The dress is new and blue, and the tiara is Emily Royal's—I knew she had it stuffed away in a bank vault. You know, it once belonged to my great-grandmother. So that was borrowed."

"What was old?"

"Oh." Cypriana thought for a moment. "I've forgotten. Oh, the tiara I guess." She put the sixpence down on the vanity top.

"Cypri, this wedding is just—it's fantastic."

Cypriana grinned.

"And your new brother-in-law is a dream! Why does he have to live in England?"

"To make a fortune, dope. I hope he stays there and gets richer and richer. Did you know Champ's uncle left Philip all his money? He died last year. Philip is running Downforth now. Philip told Champ he doesn't have to pay him back for college and medical school; Champ wants to, but before I'd marry him I made him promise not to pay it back right away. What does Philip care? I mean, he has millions. And he's been really sweet. He advised Champ to go ahead and get married."

"Really?" Celia's eyes were wide. "And Philip's not married? He's never been married?"

"Probably why he's rich."

"When he waltzed with your sister Mab, everybody in the place was watching. They'd make a great pair."

"Mab and Philip? That's interesting. I hadn't thought of that." Cypri put another coat of lipstick on her lips and then zipped the lipstick case back into her silver bag. "Romance is in the air. I saw you dancing with Pete Parker."

"He's okay, but he's so short that even if you're wearing flats—"

"Shave the soles of your shoes down with a razor blade. That's what Betsy did once."

They went out together. Later the maid found the sixpence and thought it was an odd tip to leave. It might work in a dime vending machine, but then, there were no dime vending machines any more.

The wedding reception seemed to Daisy to be lasting forever. She wandered out onto the deserted country club veranda thinking about Cypriana's pre-wedding lecture, which had been echoing in her ears all night:

Honestly, Daisy, you're going to have to shape up. You've been going around like a walking nervous breakdown lately. Why don't you get a little fun out of life?

It was cool and dark on the shadowy porch, and Daisy could smell night-blooming jasmine. She watched the fireflies flickering low over the ground. Fireflies communicated in a code, like Morse code, trying to find their mates. She had done a biology paper on fireflies. There were dozens, maybe thousands, of varieties, and each species would mate only with its own—

She ought to go inside, to see if she could help Cypri change, if indeed Cypri ever decided to leave. Aunt Martha had abandoned the scene long ago, but most people were still drinking and eating and dancing. Since Damn the Torpedoes had just started a new set and Cypri was dancing with Champ, her blue skirts swaying wildly, Daisy presumed that meant that it would be some time before Cypri was ready to leave. The newlyweds were not catching their plane to Bermuda until the next afternoon in Charleston.

Bob King had been watching for a chance to speak to Daisy. He wanted to dance with her, but she seemed to be avoiding him. All evening, whenever he started toward her, Daisy melted away, or began a conversation, or headed quickly for the buffet table. Finally,

Bob wandered downstairs to the billiards room for a while and shot some pool with Frank. When he came back upstairs, Daisy wasn't around, but he didn't think she'd go before Cypri did. On a hunch, he checked the verandas. Daisy was standing all alone at the end of one. He had her trapped.

She looked around, startled by his approach. Bob had drunk enough champagne to give him courage, and without saying a single word, he grabbed her.

"Bob. Don't."

They struggled together briefly, but she didn't yield to his kiss. He succeeded in getting his lips over hers, but it was only for a moment, and he had to hold her so tightly that he was afraid he would hurt her. Her body was stiff under the satin. He dropped his arms.

"I'm sorry." He leaned back against a trellis.

Damn the Torpedoes blasted into a new piece, and Dr. Honey_____ walked by below the porch, heading _____urse. When he was out of earshot _____ please tell me what's wrong. You _____ If you'd just give me a chance— _____ not good enough for you, but to _____ he only girl I'll ever love."

_____y's face in the dim light, trying _____xpression. He wanted so badly _____ them. He knew Daisy didn't have _____ e had checked on that. If she _____ him a chance . . .

mp had hanging up with hospital He had a wed what d it was tin dress. floor

What if she told Bob the truth? Daisy thought. What if she finally told someone the damned truth, that she loved Cypriana?

Daisy barely let the thought form before she scratched it. God, life was so painful. It wasn't worth it. You couldn't tell the truth. She was insane even to have the momentary impulse. And to tell Bob King, of all people! She peered at him; he looked so sad, staring at her with a woeful expression on his face. His freckles gave him a comical appearance in spite of his look, like a sad-faced clown.

"I hear you're going to college," Daisy said finally.
Bob nodded.

"You'll meet someone there, Bob. Really. It isn't
that I don't like you as a friend. I just never could—
I mean, there wouldn't be any use in it . . . in our
trying. Do you understand?"

"No."

Daisy sighed.

"You know, life sucks," she said.

Bob peered at her in startled amazement.

All right, Daisy thought, suddenly savagely pleased
with herself. She could say words like that—Cypri did.
In a way, it did make her feel better. Maybe someday
she could stop being such a—such a victim.

"Come on, let's dance," she said.

Bob thought either he'd drunk more than he thought
or he was dreaming, but Daisy led the way to the dance
floor. About a dozen couples were still at it, Cypriana
in their midst dancing with abandon. Cha
turned his tails jacket inside out, his hair
in his face, and he was hard at work keeping
Cypri. Bob wondered what the nurses at the
would think if they could see Champ now. H
huge grin on his face.

Daisy had a cute style, Bob found; she follo
he was doing, but she added a bounce, an
weird to see the gyrations of her white sa
Damn the Torpedoes was really into it. As the floor
vibrated, everybody loosened up even more, throwing
their arms up, turning, dancing with each other, trad-
ing partners, as if they were bound in some sort of
fellowship.

Daisy had her eyes closed; it seemed as if nothing
could stop her from repeating the step over and over
to the insistent beat; they could pull the floor out from
under her and she would still be there dancing, suspended in space. She was dizzy. She opened her eyes.
Cypriana was dancing toward her. Cypri had doffed
her veil long ago, but she was wearing the tiara, and

citing person he had ever met. And she was his now! He couldn't believe his luck.

Back in their room, Cypri insisted Champ wait and watch her take a bath. She was maddeningly slow, soaping herself all over while he sat on the bath mat in agony. She adored teasing him.

After a week of honeymooning, Cypri felt that straight sex was beginning to seem a little one-dimensional. Cypri had been sure Champ would agree to let Daisy live with them. There would be plenty of room. They had bought a new ranch-style house in the chicest outskirts of Eyreville, and Cypri had hired Chooky Browning, Ella's son, as a combination cook, valet and gardener. Baker Browning was to do part-time cleaning after school. When they got back, Cypri planned to carpet the entire house in white, and buy some striking modern furniture in Charleston. Decorating would take a lot of time, but there would be spare moments, and having Daisy around would be grand. The games that could be invented! Cypriana laughed just thinking about it. Then, tumbling over the side of the tub, she fell onto Champ's swollen shaft with little cries of joy. Life was fun.

The newly-returned honeymooners called on Great-aunt Martha at the sherry hour, and were duly served the finest Bristol cream. After a description of their idyllic trip, Cypri turned to Daisy.

"Daisy, Champ and I want you to come and live with us. Aunt Martha has had you for years, and now it's my turn."

"Cypri!" Daisy was astonished. For a moment, astonishment was her only emotion.

"You won't have much but a bed at first, but you can help me furnish the house." Cypri's face wore a bland expression; only a tiny impish glimmer came into her eye as she looked at Daisy.

Aunt Martha was not surprised. The girls had come

277

and now they would go. But first, they all had another round of sherry.

When they were alone at last, Daisy asked Cypriana if she had intended all along to have her come live with them.

"Of course," Cypri said. Her tone was offhand. "You know you've always got me, babe."

"I really suffered during the wedding, Cypri. I didn't know what you meant to do."

They were lying naked together on Daisy's new bed; the bedroom was otherwise a vast expanse of white carpet. Nothing else had been delivered yet.

Actually, Cypriana had enjoyed watching Daisy struggle with her emotions while she married Champ. It gave a different twist to the event. Cypri liked life to be unusual and exciting. Think how dull it would be around Eyreville if she didn't work at stirring things up! She stroked Daisy's breast, running her finger around Daisy's right nipple.

"I love you, Daisy," she said. "It's too bad Champ's so square. The three of us could have a beautiful time."

"Cypri, you wouldn't!"

"Done in the best of families these days. But you're scared of Champ, aren't you? I can tell, just from the way you act when he's around—like you wish you were invisible. Maybe you were better off at Aunt Martha's?"

They had just enjoyed an hour of orgasms together, and Daisy gasped at this idea. Maybe it was wrong, maybe it was terribly warped, to be living like this, but she hadn't been happier since they were little girls together. At least she got *some* of Cypriana this way. She laughed at Cypri's last remark and kissed her. Life was bliss, if only she could hang on to Cypri. Cypri could have her own way in everything. Daisy would die for her.

Her last year at Chapel Hill inevitably parted them, and Daisy was less happy, but at least there were

Christmas and spring vacations. Cypri came to watch Daisy's graduation, and to celebrate the two of them took a trip to New York to see Vivienne in *Rivers to the Sky*, her new hit play. Vivienne couldn't resist telling them that she was negotiating to buy back Land's End.

"You don't mean it!" Cypri cried. Both Cypri and Daisy were thrilled. "I have never driven past once," Cypri told Vivienne. "Not once. I couldn't bear to see it."

Vivienne smiled.

"Don't tell Mab yet," she said. "I want to surprise her. The deal could fall through. But I think the Bosworths are willing. They know how we feel about the house. If I do buy it, I'll take some time off when the show closes and restore it—make it a real showplace."

Cypriana was so delighted she could hardly speak. Daisy rarely said much anyway in the presence of Vivienne. Despite Vivienne's kindly manner, Vivienne had so much glamor in Daisy's eyes that she was always shy around her.

They heard no more about the house until the next winter. Then the sale went through as planned, and Land's End again belonged to a Dane. Daisy and Cypri could drive down the road again—and they did, frequently, just to look at the place. Vivienne herself did not come down until spring.

XVI

At the end of May, Champ came to Cypriana with a worried look on his face.

"I got some news from Crosstree that isn't so good," he said. "Mother called me this morning and asked me to drop by."

Cypri, who was dressing to go out to dinner at the club, put down her lipstick brush, and looked at her husband.

"Tell me quick," she said. "You have to shower and change."

When Champ sat down on the edge of the bed, she turned around on the vanity stool to face him.

"It's about Philip," Champ said. "Mother heard it from a relative of hers, not from Philip himself. It seems Philip has gotten into some trouble on the exchange. Apparently he did something illegal—or unethical or something—to pay off some gambling debts."

Cypriana stared at Champ. "My God," she said. The first thought that came into Cypri's mind was about the thirty-five thousand dollars Champ owed Philip for his education and so conveniently didn't have to repay.

Champ frowned. "I won't bore you with details. It's apparently been in the newspapers over there. But it may not be as bad as it looks. Things usually aren't. Mother and Dad don't know what to do. Philip hasn't written them anything about it—but then he seldom writes anyway. The folks want me to go to England and find out what's up."

"Really? It's that serious?"

"Apparently it could be. But you know I can't go. I'm handling half the practice now and I can't just take off. How about you?"

"What do you mean?"

"Well, suppose you took Daisy or someone and went over to see the sights of London? Hasn't the nursery school gotten out? Daisy's been around the house—"

"The teacher Daisy was filling in for came back. But—well, that's great. Go to London." Cypriana blinked a couple of times. A trip was just what she needed. Then she frowned, remembering the cause.

Champ continued. "It would be pointless for the folks to go. Philip wouldn't like it if they came prying around. But if you could just casually be on the lookout, look up this cousin who wrote to Mother—you know, find out what's wrong."

Cypriana nodded. "Philip has never been married, has he?" she asked.

" 'One of London's handsome young millionaire bachelors—' that's how one newspaper described him. Mother showed me the clip."

Cypri's expression was abstracted. She stared straight ahead of her, deep in thought. Then she looked up.

"Champ, you know, the loan for college and medical school—"

"That's not all, I'm afraid. Philip gave us the money for the down payment on the house and made the first two years' mortgage payments. We can afford Chooky and Baker only because we aren't repaying the money yet. But if Philip should need it—"

"Oh, God!" Cypriana's dismayed expression reflected Champ's own rueful look. "What would we have to do? Move?"

"Let's hope it won't come to that, honey. Maybe his troubles have been exaggerated just to make good copy. But why don't you go over there and find out?"

"I certainly will. And I'll figure out a way to straighten him out if it's the last—he's normal, isn't he?"

"Normal?" Champ chuckled.

"Not a fag like so many Englishmen?"

"Absolutely not! I think he's had lots of girl friends. He's just not a marrying type."

"We'll see about that. What Philip *needs* is a wife. Someone to settle him down."

"It's what I needed." Champ stood up and chucked off his clothes. "Look, let's have a little fun first, and then we can plan your trip on the way to the club."

"God, I've done my hair already." Obligingly, Cypri let her wrapper slide off and hopped onto the bed. "We'll have to hurry—not that that's any worry of yours. You're always fast—Champ, stop it." She giggled as he tickled her.

"Take that remark back or I'll lick the soles of your feet."

Cypriana, who was tremendously ticklish all over, writhed in agony under Champ's fingers.

"All right, you're slow."

"That's better." Champ kissed her mouth and began to slide back and forth inside of her to demonstrate. Cypri's mind wasn't on it. She sighed. Something *definitely* had to be done about Philip.

Cypriana started packing the next day. Champ attended to the airline reservations and arranged for a suite at the Ritz. Daisy was delighted but puzzled. Cypri flatly stated that the trip's purpose was to bring salvation to Philip.

"If your brother-in-law *is* in difficulties, Cypri, what can you possibly do about it?" Daisy asked.

"Don't ask what I can do, ask what you can do," Cypri said. She was sitting at her dressing table looking at Daisy in the mirror. There was a strange expression on her face, and Daisy couldn't tell if she were kidding or not.

"What?"

Cypri said nothing. She examined her skin in the small magnifying makeup mirror. There was a tiny spot by one eye; she wondered if it were a mole or a blackhead, and debated whether to squeeze it. She let Daisy's question hang in the air.

Piles of clothes were all over the bed, and tissue paper had fallen in drifts to the floor of the bedroom. Three suitcases were waiting, open, for Baker to pack when she came from school. Baker knew how to pack clothes nicely. Also, there were a number of things that needed ironing. Baker did the ironing.

Daisy still looked at Cypriana with an inquiring expression.

"First you were my battered child. Now you'll be my bartered bride," Cypri said, squeezing the spot. It was a blackhead. It popped out.

Daisy collapsed onto the edge of the bed and laughed.

"Cypri, you are the craziest person alive! Someone ought to write a book about you. I'm serious."

"So am I." Cypri swung around on the stool. "Actually, I'm thinking of divorcing Champ and marrying Philip myself. A conglomerate empire, whatever the hell that is, sounds like just what I should be running. Downforth. Maybe Philip will be knighted after I reform him, and I'll sit around in diamonds with a butler like Hudson saying 'Yes, my lady,' and 'No, my lady.' I think I'll like England."

"Have you told Champ this delightful plan?"

"He'll probably kill himself or something when I leave him. Blood on my second marriage from the start. 'Ah, but my darling, what man would not prefer death to life without you?' " Cypri tried to imitate James Mason's English accent. Daisy laughed and shook her head.

"I'm going to England with a loon," she said.

Cypri giggled. "We're going to have fun! I wouldn't mind a spot of gambling myself. I love roulette. You know, I kept winning on number seventeen last time the club had a Vegas night."

Baker came running up the stairs as Cypri spoke.

"Hello, Mrs. Alexander. How are—" Baker stopped, looking around the room in surprise.

"Baker, we're packing to go to England tomorrow. We just decided last night. Isn't it exciting?"

Baker smiled into Cypriana's sparkling blue eyes. Mrs. Alexander was fun to work for. Baker liked her much better than Uncle Chooky did. Chooky was a thin-faced, bookish type; he had been a short-order cook at the local Hotte Shoppe before he came to work for the Alexanders. Cypriana had tried to get Ella Browning to abandon the Parkers—Ella had worked for them since Land's End was sold—and come to work for her. Ella suggested that instead, Cypriana could hire her son Chooky and pay Baker for part-time cleaning and the combination worked out fine. Uncle Chooky was very respectful around the Alexanders' house, and he never criticized Mrs. Alexander to his mother, who loved all Danes; but to Baker he said privately that Mrs. Alexander's husband spoiled her rotten because she was so gorgeous. She didn't do a lick of work around the house, and he couldn't see that she did anything for humanity outside of it, either. Baker's own ambition was to be exactly like Cypri.

Cypriana's eyes lingered on the child. At fifteen, Baker was a beauty. She wore her hair in two braids wrapped around her head, giving her a close-cropped, classical look, like an ancient Egyptian princess. Her skin was light brown in color and creamy in texture, and her features—really, Baker reminded Cypri of somebody in her own family. Even of herself—a version of a Dane in brown tones. Cypri knew that Nancy wouldn't say who Baker's father was; it was thought to have been some man from town who got her into trouble. Even in Cypri's wildest imaginings she couldn't believe it had been her father. That fussy old man! Still, you couldn't tell about people. Hidden depths. Often Cypri looked musingly at Baker.

"You look nice in red, Baker," she said. "I like that sweater on you. I just saw a red dress in the closet that you might like. It never fit me right." Cypri went over to the mirrored closet doors and pushed them back, burrowing through the wall of clothes hanging there. "Here," she said, emerging with the dress. "Try it on."

Baker was delighted. "Oh, thank you," she said, taking the dress. All Mrs. Alexander's clothes were darling. She had perfect taste.

"Try it on right now."

Baker stripped off her red sweater and shed her skirt as Cypriana watched. Cypri's eyes went directly to Baker's tightly filled brassiere and the brown skin of her tiny waist, encircled by the elastic of her short pink half-slip.

Daisy looked at Cypri. There was something about Cypri's expression . . . Her eyes swung to Baker. Baker pulled the dress over her head and wiggled it down.

"It's loose on you, too, in the waist," Cypri said. "Our figures are alike. But maybe Ella can take it in for you."

"Oh, I can take it in myself. I can sew. But would you like me to fix it so you could wear it, Mrs. Alexander?" Baker said.

"No, no, it's yours. It looks good on you. Well, let's get busy here. Is my blue blouse in the wash, the one with the long sleeves?"

Daisy walked across the hall to her bedroom, where she had almost finished packing her own suitcases. Baker. Cypri surely couldn't have designs on Baker! Daisy dismissed the thought. She had more to worry about than that. Cypri often said things in jest that she meant in earnest. When Cypri was in a good humor, everything was a big joke. What did she mean by "bartered bride"?

Vaguely uneasy, Daisy sat down at her dressing table and began to collect the makeup she intended to take to London. From across the hall she could hear Baker laughing at something Cypri said.

Silver eye shadow. Should she take the silver eye shadow? Daisy couldn't keep her mind on what she was doing. Suddenly, instead of appearing just a gay jaunt, the trip had another aspect. Something in the air around her was gathering power, like a summer storm brewing, like Cypri's sullenness growing and growing until her rage broke in a tantrum. Daisy's palms were sweaty. What was going on? Why did she have such thoughts? Cypri was laughing, in a blissful mood; she wasn't angry. Outside it was a lovely June day. Flowers were blooming, and she could hear Chooky below working in the garden. The scent of the freshly turned earth rose in the air and came in at the open windows. Birds were singing. Why did she think of a storm? Why did she feel so—alarmed?

Daisy looked closely at herself in the mirror. Perhaps she should be prepared for—just anything at all to happen in England.

She packed the silver eye shadow. After a moment she packed all her eye shadows, raining them into the white leather makeup kit like somebody filling his cartridge belt with bullets before going downstairs to the shadowy street.

Philip Alexander drove out to Heathrow Airport picturing his soon-to-arrive beautiful sister-in-law and her beautiful cousin. He had not been back to Eyreville often, and before Champ's wedding he had been only vaguely aware of the two girls' existence. At the wedding, however, they left marked impressions: he remembered Daisy's hair etched in light and her grave, soulful expression in the church, and like everyone else he had experienced an electric shock at the sight

count, Daisy would not have be—
had a courtly manner. But he was not en—
he young Englishman on the airplane who ha—
hroughout the trip at Cypri and her. That one
oked like a china figurine from a drawing-room
antel. Although Philip wore the same type of splen-
ily cut suit, he did not give the impression of over-
nement. Quite the opposite, Daisy thought. She
a familiar prickle of fear—shyness, she preferred
all it. She gave Philip a sidelong, measuring glance.
was handsome, even more handsome than she
mbered—his face was slightly drawn now, giving

of Cypriana, her icy gown, her vivid lips, her blue-violet eyes. Certainly Philip had understood why Champ ran down the aisle to meet Cypriana. South Carolina produced gorgeous women. At least, the Danes—he skirted that thought carefully. Philip did not like to dwell on Cypriana's relationship to Vivienne.

Strange that Crosstree still seemed like home to him, despite the fact that he had spent only five years there, and thirty years and more in England. Of course, his parents still lived in Crosstree; perhaps that accounted for his feeling that his roots were there. They had been impressionable years, those years spent over the grocery store. After his brother's candlelit wedding, Philip had returned to England with the feeling that the event had been a dream—the little town of Eyreville on a southern June night, the people with their soft voices and ready laughter, their slow and graceful movement through life. Each person seemed to have a place and a part to play. Even his mother had finally capitulated. She liked the South now, she said, though she would never become accustomed to the way the women in the big houses lazed around; why if a southern woman did something in the morning, chances were she'd take the afternoon off to lie down.

Certainly a contrast to England. After he returned from the wedding, the contrast seemed almost too sharp. Philip thought about it and realized that his present feelings about the emptiness of his existence began *then*—as if he had seen something in that dream world that was missing in his own brisk life. When he heard that Mab Dane was coming to London last February, he had been eager to see her, to perhaps recapture the feel of that world.

Philip frowned, staring out of the windows of his Rolls Royce without seeing the passing streets. Thinking about Mab's visit brought back the moment when he had been rudely interrupted by the telephone call from his lawyer, Arnold Coy. Arnold had called to

by hand like a surprise
Perhaps h... was not an inspired
He curs... had sounded so cool
she le... ...n't wait to be gone. He th...
perh... ...er not call her. If she ca...
...k hi... see her again. He ... evening out, then he coul...
weeks of his life coming up, but if Mab...
resolved, he'd drop everything to see her...
hoped she would call.

He had waited in vain. Once he wal...
Savoy. Once he broke down and called...
room didn't answer. He decided not t...
sage. Surely Mab would call him if sh...

a romantic cast to his features. Taller than Champ and somewhat smaller-boned, he looked lean and fit.

"I have a car waiting outside," Philip said. He escorted them out of the terminal and over to a Rolls Royce, handed them both in and saw to the storage of the six pieces of luggage that accompanied them.

"Isn't this great?" Cypri said to Daisy. "What a car!" Leaning closer to Daisy, Cypri lowered her voice so that the driver couldn't hear. "And what a brother-in-law!"

"All right, ladies, off to the Ritz," Philip said, jumping in and taking the folding seat opposite Daisy. "You've missed a night's sleep, I believe."

"I feel fine," Cypri said. "Just a little chilly." She shivered. "Everyone told us to bring warm clothes."

"Indeed, yes. I can remember that when I was a child in Cambridge, my father suffered terribly in the cold and damp here. 'It's summer at home,' he'd say. 'My blood's too thin for England—southerners have summer blood.'" Philip smiled at them. "It's hot in South Carolina now, isn't it?"

While Cypri discussed the weather with him, Daisy looked out of the car window. She was fascinated by the streets and houses and people they were passing. Men on bicycles pedaling away with brimmed caps pulled over their eyes seemed like characters dressed for roles in a film. As the limousine neared the Ritz Hotel, the streets looked like a stage set for an English play. When Daisy caught sight of Big Ben, she was awed. She really was in England.

Cypri chatted all the way, telling Philip the latest gossip from Eyreville. Did he know *their* big news, she asked suddenly—that Vivienne had bought back Land's End?

"Land's End?"

The inflection in Philip's voice as he repeated the words made Daisy turn her head to look at him. Philip seemed very struck by what Cypri had just said. Almost jolted, Daisy thought. For a moment his lips parted; his urbane manner vanished. Something kindled for a second in his dark eyes; then it was gone.

"I'm sure you're pleased," he said flatly, sounding almost indifferent. He didn't seem to want to pursue the subject. Anyway, they had arrived at the Ritz.

A few minutes later Philip left, promising to return for the evening. They took possession of their suite, settling in quickly. Daisy unpacked Cypri's bags into the spacious bureau drawers while Cypri sat on the bed and talked.

"Isn't this great? A living room and two bedrooms— I love it, and look at our view! Daisy, tell me this minute what you think of Philip." Cypri didn't give her time. "He is divine. I love to hear him talk. That accent! Which reminds me—what time is it?"

Daisy yawned as she looked at her watch. "It's almost eleven, by their time. I set my watch on the plane."

"Then I can call Mrs. Alexander's cousin. She gave me his number." Cypri burrowed in her pocketbook. "The one who wrote the letter about Philip's troubles. I wish it would turn out that it's all just imaginary. Here it is—Henry Burnet. He lives here in London."

Cypri piled the bed pillows against the headboard, sat back and picked up the telephone. The first call got Mrs. Burnet. After a brief explanation of who she was, Cypri was given the number of Henry Burnet's law office.

Daisy sorted out a pile of clothing that would have to be pressed, and listened as Cypri made another call.

"Yes, I want to speak to Mr. Burdet. I mean Burnet. This is Cypriana Alexander." She tapped the telephone impatiently. "Hello, Mr. Burdet—Burnet. Yes, this is Beauchamp's wife. Yes. My mother-in-law got your letter about Philip, and she wants me to thank you; she'll write to you. Yes. Anyway, I've come over to get a little more information, if possible. My husband is concerned about his brother. Could we meet, or—I see. Yes, later on, the beginning of next week, would be fine. But can you tell me more right now?"

Daisy watched as Cypri listened intently for what seemed a long time. Cypri's blue eyes narrowed, staring into the space before her. At first she tapped her fingers absently on the red satin bedspread; then all motion stopped. It grew so quiet in the room that Daisy could almost make out the words being said, in a very proper-sounding English, on the other end of the line.

"I see," Cypri said slowly, at last. Her expression had changed during the conversation; now she looked like a patient who has just been told of terminal disease. "Yes, thank you. I'll call. Certainly. We're at the Ritz. Tea would be nice. Till next week, then."

She hung up and looked at Daisy.

"Worse," she said. "Worse than I thought."

"What did he say?"

"Well, he went through all the stuff about the report to the stock exchange that was made in February. Philip was selling Downforth stock to pay his gambling debts. The report didn't mean Philip was ruined—just warned. Humiliating but not fatal to Downforth, Mr. Burnet said. Anyway, the reason he wrote the letter is that Philip just can't stop gambling. Apparently everyone knows that Philip has been to a shrink, and a million friends are giving him advice and trying to keep him away from the tables, but he is—Burnet said this—apparently obsessed. He just keeps going to clubs and gambling all night. I mean, he doesn't stop when he's ahead. Oh, damn. And he's so fabulous-looking and so sexy! Why can't he have some other kind of fun? Know what Burnet said? He said for us to keep Philip busy this week! But that's only temporary. What we want is a permanent cure." Cypri said the last words with emphasis, and looked at Daisy.

Daisy yawned again. "I might be able to think about it after I've had some sleep," she said. "I'm knocked out. Is it okay if we crash for a while? Maybe sleep till time to dress for dinner?"

"Are you sleeping in here or in the other bedroom?" Cypri grinned as she asked the question.

"What do you think?" Daisy pulled off her jacket and pants.

"You'll have to undress me, too," Cypri said, lying back on the bed. "I'm dead, all of a sudden."

That evening Philip took them out to the elegant restaurant L'Etoile, and across the snowy white table-cloth Cypriana carefully observed Philip's reaction to Daisy. Cypri had come to England determined to bring all her powers to bear on the situation, but measures such as forcing Daisy to wear her very low-cut yellow dress were not going to turn the trick. Cypri sighed. She needed more troops. Daisy was too wishy-washy to fascinate a man of the world like Philip.

While Daisy and Philip discussed plans for the coming days of sight-seeing, Cypri looked at them bleakly. Her plan to give Daisy to Philip as a warden would need revision. In truth, she had been wondering about it all along. The idea would meet with some pretty stiff opposition from Daisy, the silly little les. Daisy was definitely more ward than warden. Unless Philip were just swept away by mad passion for her, Daisy hadn't enough strength of character on her own to reform a nun.

However, Cypri cautioned herself against forming too hasty an opinion about anything. There was time to work something out. She knew one thing: she wasn't going to quit until she was ahead.

She snapped out of her reverie and listened as Philip explained his scheme for getting Daisy and her down into the basement of the British Museum—the most interesting part of the museum by far, Philip said, where statues had been piled for centuries, many of them total mysteries as to place or origin. Daisy's eyes shone with interest. Trust her to want to go poking in a cellar. Cypri herself wanted to see the crown jewels, Biba boutique, and Elizabeth Arden's, and you could have your abbeys, your Towers and your Thames. However, when her opinion was solicited as to where to begin, Cypri said for the sake of class, "The Tate gallery"; Mab, Cypri remembered from the dim past, was always going on about somebody-or-other's work "at the Tate."

"I have tickets for *A Chorus Line* for us tomorrow night, and I can get whatever you like for the next evenings," Philip said.

"Oh, I'd love to go to a play every night!" Cypriana said, with a glance at Philip. "If you can take us." Philip looked so handsome in his black tuxedo; why did he have to be a gambler? Well, if Plan A failed, on to Plan B. *She* would wear a very low-cut gown tomorrow, and have the works at Elizabeth Arden's into the bargain.

Daisy was thrilled by London; whirling through the streets in the square black taxis and seeing something historic every moment put her into a state of enchantment. Philip left them on their own during the days, but each evening he faithfully took them to dinner and the theater.

"Do you suppose Philip goes gambling after he takes us home?" Cypri asked Daisy. Cypri had a dark expression on her face. It was Day Four, and Plan B was stalled. Philip seemed conscious of Cypri's charms, but he was relentlessly preserving the correct attitude toward her, his sister-in-law. You'd almost think he was sort of religious; wasn't there something in the Bible about your brother's wife?

Philip invited them to meet him on Friday noon at Downforth, to go to lunch at a quaint spot nearby, a fish restaurant with sawdust on the floor, open bottles of wine on the tables, and an honor system for the bill. They had not yet seen the Downforth Enterprises building, which was in the City, the financial district of London. Their taxi drove them past Threadneedle Street—Daisy liked the name—and drew up in front of an impressive black-sided building with a modern glass front; over the glass doors a discreet gold sign with silver letters read *Downforth*.

Philip had instructed them to take an elevator to the top floor. When they stepped out of the elevator they were both impressed by the lavishness of the glass-surrounded reception hall. A pretty young receptionist rose from a white desk and led them into Philip's office. The room stretched almost the length of the building; the outside walls of glass presented a breathtaking view of London. It seemed to be more a living room than an office; there were comfortable modern leather sofas scattered about, as well as handsome end tables and coffee tables, a long walnut table in the middle of the room, and a large heavy walnut desk surrounded by dark red leather chairs. The thick carpet was dark red. Except for the telephones and machines spewing paper, and the clocks on one wall showing the time all over the world, they might have been in the lobby of an exclusive club.

Philip rose from the head of the conference table as they entered. A half dozen well-dressed men rose as he did. Philip smiled at Cypriana and Daisy.

"That is all, then, gentlemen. Thank you. I would like you to meet my sister-in-law and her cousin."

Philip introduced them to the men around the table. Some of the men were young, some old; all were extremely deferential to Cypriana and Daisy. As Cypri looked around, she could almost smell the power in the air. She didn't know how many industries and newspapers and publishing firms Downforth controlled, but she felt a sharp envy. How nice to run meetings and order people around; how could Philip *think* of throwing all this away? Somehow, his peril had not seemed real, before. Now that Cypri saw his magnificent building, his glamorous office, his polite underlings, it struck her with sudden force—Philip really did con-

296

trol a fortune. Her blue eyes flashed around the table. The men she had been introduced to were now talking quietly among themselves. They must be in turmoil, she thought. No doubt some were plotting among themselves to replace Philip. If she were one of his associates, *she* would certainly be scheming. In fact, she was scheming. She *would* seduce Philip, that very night! She had just bought the outfit to do it in. Cypri gave Philip a long look from under her lashes as he explained the purpose of some machine that Daisy had asked about. Cypri fairly ached to be in bed with Philip. She'd show him some things. Even more than the power he represented, the wild streak in him attracted her. Philip kept it carefully hidden, but it must exist; she pictured him making obsessive plunges with piles of chips at high-stakes casinos, risking all on the turn of a card—there was quite a bit of that sort of recklessness in Cypri's own nature. They would suit each other, she thought.

Philip escorted them downstairs and into his limousine for the short ride to Queen Victoria Street and the cheerful, bustling fish restaurant. Fresh white linen-cloths were on the tables and bar, sawdust was on the floor, and dozens of well-dressed Englishmen stood about or sat together at tables, drinking and chatting.

They found seats with some friends of Philip's. The two men seemed quite dazzled by the sight of Cypriana and Daisy—who, except for the waitresses, were the only women in the place. The fish, as Philip had promised, was delicious, straight out of a nearby fish market. Cypri drank several glasses of Sancerre wine from the open bottle on the table. The thread of her earlier thoughts persisted; what was Philip like when he gambled? Perhaps that was the key, the ploy that would turn the trick: she would seem to be interested in the same thing he was! Gambling together might warm him up. Now that she thought about it, it was time to meet the enemy.

"Philip," she said, as winsomely and innocently as she could, "I've heard there are wonderful places to gamble in London. Do you think you could show us one? Could we go gambling after the theater tonight?"

Beside her, Daisy almost choked on her prawns. While she coughed into a white linen napkin, Philip hesitated for only a moment.

"Why of course. I should be delighted. Do you like to gamble?"

"I always win on number seventeen. Roulette's the only game I really understand."

The two men with whom they were sitting suddenly fell silent, their eyes sliding from Cypriana's face to Philip's. The moment passed; and with British aplomb, one of the men changed the subject. The entire financial district must seethe with curiosity about the head of Downforth—Cypri could sense it.

"Into the lion's den," Cypri said to Daisy as they dressed for the evening. "I think we have to see what we are up against."

"I hope you're right about that," Daisy said. "It's hard to picture Philip gambling—so far he seems so reasonable, doesn't he?"

"I want to see him gamble," Cypri said. "Then we'll really know what's what. Could you lace me up now?"

Cypriana was wearing an outfit by a Dutch designer that she had seen that morning at Piero de Monzi's boutique and had allowed herself to buy as a business expense. Its long black skirt was topped by a black satin corset trimmed with black satin ribbon. It laced up the back.

"Pull it tight," Cypri said. "Tighter."

"Yes, Miss Scarlett," Daisy said. She pulled the laces in hard and then tied them. Cypri turned around to face her.

"You look fabulous! I love it," Daisy said. The

corset exposed a good amount of Cypri's white breast and the effect, they both agreed, was stunning.

"And look." From the box the corset had come in, Cypri took out a black satin ribbon with a single red silk rose attached to it. She fastened this around her neck with the rose to one side. She had spent most of the afternoon since the luncheon perfecting her hair and makeup. The hotel hairdresser had come up to help. She had swept Cypriana's hair up in a simple topknot, which looked perfect with the ribbon around her neck.

"You've never looked prettier in your life," Daisy told her.

Daisy had taken no extraordinary pains herself. She was wearing a plain white silk pants and tunic outfit. Her blond hair hung loose, and a rope of rhinestones and jet beads were her only adornment.

"Yeah, well, I could *feel* better, though," Cypriana said. She put her hand on her tiny waistline.

"Is it too tight?"

"No, that isn't what hurts. I think it's—I had pains in my stomach this afternoon. Where's the stuff Champ gave us?"

"The paregoric? Here."

Daisy found the bottle in Cypri's makeup kit and handed it to her. Champ had insisted they bring it along in case they had digestive problems. "London water has different organisms in it," he said. "It could affect you." And he had added with a laugh, "You know, I owe my life to change of water, according to my mother." When they asked what he meant, Champ reminded them that Philip had been thirteen years old when the Alexanders moved from England to Crosstree; nine and a half months later Champ had made his appearance, and his mother thought his unexpected conception could have been due to the change of water. "But all results of changing water are not so happy," Champ said. He had given them the bottle, explained the dosage and warned them not to take too much, since the paregoric could make them groggy.

Cypri took a teaspoon now, making a face at the taste, and put the bottle into her black evening bag. Philip arrived at their door exactly on time, came in and gallantly bowed as he saw them.

"I will be the envy of all England," he said. He looked from one of them to the other. "Two women as beautiful as you are not to be found on this island."

Philip put their wraps about their shoulders; as he performed this service for Cypriana, she turned her head so that her cheek brushed against his hand. Opening the door for them, Philip thought of how much Cypriana sometimes reminded him of Vivienne. Two years ago, when she walked down the aisle at her wedding—tonight, in the dramatic black outfit—it was almost painful to look at her. Their faces really were not that similar; the resemblance lay in the silky dark hair and certain turns of expression, and the way they carried themselves so proudly.

On the way downstairs, Philip said he wanted them to have an "all-English" day, and to top the luncheon they'd had at Sweetings, he was taking them to dinner at Simpson's-in-the-Strand. This turned out to be a very English restaurant, where roast beef was wheeled up to their table on shining silver carts, carved and served with all the traditional accompaniments. Cypriana did not eat very much. Her stomach still hurt, and the tight lacing made it feel worse. What a relief it would be to get to Philip's flat and let him unlace her! She had decided to get rid of Daisy on some pretext as they gambled, and to accompany Philip home. To this end, she gave him smoky looks over the Yorkshire pudding, and sweetly offered him her slice of the horrible Stilton cheese that ended the meal.

During the farce *Funny Peculiar*, Cypri felt somewhat worse. She cursed to herself. She had been so careful, too, drinking only bottled water, so far as she knew. She looked enviously at Daisy. Daisy seemed to feel fine.

Press on, regardless, Cypri told herself. She did not complain, and laughed at the jokes in as low and throaty a way as she could manage. She often leaned close to Philip for an explanation of this or that, parting her lips and opening her eyes wide and whispering gently into his ear.

When the curtain fell, they stepped out of the theater into the car and in a few minutes were entering the Hartford Club's door. The doorman enthusiastically welcomed Philip, and they were ushered into a world of red plush, sparkling chandeliers, sweeping staircases and grand vistas of gaming tables. A handsome young manager came to their side at once—he too knew Philip by name—and escorted them into a salon off the entrance hall.

The large room was crowded. Elegant men and women surrounded the tables. Everyone spoke in low tones and maintained carefully uninformative faces. It reminded Cypri of the waiting room of a morgue, everyone wearing the self-contained expression of someone wondering if the body under the sheet would turn out to be next-of-kin. If a man who had lost his last halfpence keeled over and died, he would, Cypri thought, have his body discreetly walked out between two attendants. The heavy layer of good breeding present would without doubt be preserved although life, fortune and empire were lost.

Daisy was awed by the lavish decor and the expensive clothes of the crowd. Even the men croupiers wore tuxedos and the women croupiers had on slinky, revealing evening dresses.

As the three of them toured the room, Philip pointed out the games available: chemin de fer, craps, twenty-one, roulette.

"Which is your favorite, Philip?" Cypri asked.

"The spinning wheel. Shall we have a spot of roulette?"

Philip settled the two young women in chairs and gave them each a large stack of chips. Daisy's were blue and Cypri's red. Philip chose purple for himself. Soon they were all busy putting the chips on numbers and losing them.

Number seventeen did not come up except once, but by that time Cypri had given up and put her chip on another number. It was amazing how fast the red pile melted away. The little marble flew around the wheel with such speed, fell in the pocket, and then you were poorer. This game would never win *her* allegiance, Cypri thought.

Daisy had a winner, and her stack of chips was augmented. Cypriana had only three red chips left. She looked back at Philip. He was standing behind them, and as she watched he put chips on several numbers on their table and stepped to the next table, where the wheel was also spinning, and covered at least five numbers there.

"No more bets," the croupier said.

He was echoed at the next table.

In a moment the rake swept all the chips away on both tables. No one had won. Philip gestured for more purple chips and they were produced. The wheels spun. Again he bet both tables. Daisy had another winner. Philip lost. Cypriana stared at him. In the soft light of the room his eyes glittered as he looked at the numbered squares on their table and stepped over to play the other table as well. She was distracted from the game, watching him. His face had the impassive expression of a dancer, as if he were concentrating inwardly on something, struggling to remember the exact steps of a dance. He saw Cypri looking at him, noticed that she was out of chips, and motioned for more red ones to be placed before her. She smiled to thank him, but he had already turned back to the other table. He had a hit on her table; his face did not change as the chips were handed to him, he simply

302

doubled the number of bets he made on the next turn of the wheel.

Cypri began losing her new pile. Her mind was not on the game. She was having pains in her stomach again. She cursed to herself. Perhaps she should go take some more paregoric. She wanted to be in good shape for later tonight. She looked again at Philip. Suddenly she knew what he reminded her of—someone who was hypnotized. The game itself was hypnotic, the clatter of the ball, the monotonous "no more bets!" of the croupier, the sweep of the rake. Philip, fully caught up in it, neither smiled when he won nor frowned when he lost. There were not many occasions for smiles, anyway. He usually lost.

Cypriana looked around the table. The two men sitting next to them were both dressed in expensive evening clothes, and beyond them was a middle-aged blond wearing a gold dress, a feather-trimmed chiffon stole floating across her shoulders.

Cypri leaned across Daisy and spoke to one of the men. "Excuse me," she said in a low voice. "I'm a beginner. What are the denominations of the chips? Are they pounds?"

The man smiled at her.

"They are whatever you agree to, with the croupier," he said. He glanced at Philip, who was placing bets at the second table. "If Philip Alexander brought you here, I'd say they were probably more than pounds. He plays for high stakes."

Cypri thanked the man. Philip stepped back to their table and placed his bets. Again he lost. Cypri's stomach really began to hurt. She put a chip down once in a while for the sake of doing something, but her attention was on Philip. He was quietly going wild. The more he lost, the more he bet. He gestured often for his dwindling pile of purple to be replenished.

How much was he losing? Cypri's hands felt cold. She had truly been stupid to bring Philip here. She had met the enemy all right, and the enemy was winning. Philip gave no indication of wanting to quit. He didn't even look at them, but stepped back and forth, back and forth, the purple chips on more and more losers. My God! she thought. For the first time she began to understand what people meant when they said "compulsion" and "obsession" about Philip's gambling. He was mad. He was going to gamble away her house and her servants right there before her eyes!

Her gastric problem became acute. She put her remaining chips on number seventeen, which didn't come up, and muttered to Daisy that she was going to the ladies' room. Daisy left her own modest pile of blue chips and accompanied her. Philip didn't even seem aware that they were leaving the table, but Cypri couldn't wait— she rushed out and up the stairs. She was in trouble.

Ten minutes later she came weakly out of the toilet booth and washed her hands in the marble washbasin. Daisy was full of sympathy.

"Get me the paregoric," Cypri said. Daisy found it in her evening bag, and Capri swigged it from the bottle. Her plans for tonight were canceled. She had to go home to bed.

"God, I'm so thirsty," she said. "And I can't drink the damned water."

"I'll go get you some bottled water," Daisy said.

"Don't bother." Cypri's tone was short. "Daisy, did you *see* Philip? He's gone crazy."

"The man next to me just whispered that he thought Philip must have lost one hundred thousand pounds by now. He can't *mean* that, can he? Not really—I can't believe it. But those chips—they're fifty pounds apiece, I think."

"Philip is insane! At least my being ill will get him out of here. He'll have to take us home."

Cypri drew a deep breath and they descended the stairs like a pair of countesses, the one in black rather pale, as she could see in the many gilt-edged mirrors lining the staircase. Looking at her image in the splendid black outfit, Cypri cursed again—it was wasted on Philip. Her plans for the evening were in ruins.

Back at the tables, Philip apparently hadn't moved except from wheel to wheel. They found him still playing the two boards back-to-back. Cypri seized him by the arm to get his attention long enough to describe her condition.

"Oh, you're feeling ill?" Philip gave her a surprised look. "I'm so sorry." He gestured toward the manager, who was standing nearby. In a moment the young man was in front of them.

"Martin, can you get my car for Mrs. Alexander? She will be going home. The car's parked just down the street, I think. My driver's waiting." He looked back at Cypriana. "I do hope you feel better," he added to her.

Cypri was thunderstruck. Philip wasn't leaving! She felt like stamping her foot, but the general atmosphere was not conducive to any show of emotion. Curbing her impulse to kick Philip in the shins, she simply swept off. Daisy followed her into the entrance hall.

"Did you *ever*," Cypri whispered to Daisy in a fury. "I have never heard of such rudeness in my life!"

She had fumed for only a moment when the manager reappeared, her wrap over his arm. "Your car is at the door, Mrs. Alexander," he said with a half-bow, holding out her black cape.

Cypri turned to Daisy, who was starting toward the checkroom for her own wrap.

"Listen, *you* stay here," Cypri murmured. She put her hand on Daisy's arm and said in a low, but very firm voice, right into Daisy's ear, "Try to get Philip to stop. If you can. And at least, see how much he loses."

Daisy was distressed. "Cypri, don't you want me to go home with you? You need someone to take care of you."

"No, I don't want you to come. I want to be alone, if you don't mind. I feel lousy and I'm going home to bed. Now do as I say." Cypri took her wrap from the manager, pulled it close around her, and hurried out the front door with as much dignity as she could muster.

As the Rolls hummed through the London streets she bent double in the back seat. Her stomach was killing her! And worse than her cramps was the realization that Philip was probably beyond the reach of all help. She cursed him roundly. She couldn't understand him. All her schemes to keep Baker and Chooky and the house looked like the plans of a child, a child who had no idea about the real world. How silly she had been. Defeat and diarrhea, that was reality. "Hurry up!" she said rudely through the speaking tube to the chauffeur.

It was a strange night, Daisy thought. Everything seemed to have taken a spin into the wrong pocket, like the little marble on the roulette wheel.

Slowly, Daisy walked back through the crowd, which was denser now. What did Cypri mean, get Philip to stop gambling? If Cypri hadn't been able to, Daisy couldn't imagine how she would.

Her pile of blue chips was waiting for her. Daisy sat back down in her chair. Philip was still hopping back and forth between the tables as the mesmerizing wheels spun. He didn't seem conscious of her presence. Daisy felt she couldn't take up a chair without gambling and she ventured a chip on twenty-one, then thirteen, then twenty. Twenty came up, and she was back in business with a good number of chips.

The evening seemed to go on and on. Just as Daisy was about to lose everything, she would win a little, and she didn't have to ask Philip for chips—if indeed she could have gotten his attention. His eyes were glazed. For a while, he bet just at her table. After a win, he returned to commuting. The croupiers changed frequently; they got to go away and rest, but the gamblers seemed never to stop. The woman in gold was winning, and the two men beside Daisy were losing. Several newcomers joined the table. No one spoke. They just gambled. Daisy was tired. She began to yawn. Didn't the place ever close?

Finally she asked someone what closing time was. Four o'clock she was told. Daisy glanced at Philip. No doubt he would stay until then. It was already three-thirty. She had been tempted to run out into the street and take a taxi to the Ritz. But it was only half an hour to wait, and Cypri would want to know the total damage tomorrow, if there were any way Daisy could find out. She supposed Philip would write a check. She wondered if she could get a look at it. It would be for plenty, she was sure. Philip had been having momentary turns in his luck, but the general trend was down, down, down.

Daisy was accustomed to sitting around with nobody paying much attention to her. Still, it was depressing. She lost for several spins in a row. She had a long spell of losing. As the croupier consulted his watch and announced the last spin, she put several chips on number seventeen, thinking of Cypri, and seventeen came up.

Her winnings made a respectable pile. Daisy watched Philip consulting with the croupier. After a discussion, he pulled out a checkbook and wrote out a check. Daisy moved to Philip's side as unobtrusively as possible, but she could not politely manage to glimpse the amount. She could only tell that the check took rather a long while to write.

"Oh. Daisy!" Philip seemed startled when he noticed her. "I didn't realize you were still here. Sorry." Philip passed a hand over his brow. A certain rigid, controlled look, a sort of stiffness in his cheek muscles, relaxed. He attempted a smile. Daisy thought he must be exhausted. She showed him her pile of blue chips.

"Very good—someone won. I'll cash it for you." Philip took her chips. In a moment he came back with a sheaf of English notes.

"You must keep that," she said in haste. "It was your money I was playing with."

"Nonsense. You won it."

"Oh, no. I couldn't."

Daisy sounded genuinely distressed, and Philip evidently decided not to press her in their present sedate surroundings. "We'll thrash it out later," he said, thrusting the bills into the side pocket of his jacket.

As they left the club, Daisy saw that a faint predawn light already glowed in the sky. The Rolls was waiting. The driver had probably had a nice nap. Daisy wished that she had had one. Philip sat silent as they rolled through the deserted streets; Daisy wondered what his thoughts were.

Every night Philip had punctiliously seen the two of them up to their suite, and apparently, now that he had recovered himself, he did not intend to make tonight an exception. He told his chauffeur to park the car, and he walked with Daisy through the deserted lobby, past the solarium, and into the elevator. He still didn't speak, and Daisy did not venture any comments.

The elevator stopped at their floor. Philip walked with Daisy down the hall to her door. As she hunted for the room key in her pocketbook, Philip suddenly said, "I wonder if you would do me a favor?"

His low voice startled Daisy, coming after his long and total silence. She looked up at him in surprise.

"Of course," she said, wondering what he would ask.

Philip attempted another smile.

"It's been a long time since the last drink was served at eleven. Might I come in for a nightcap? I'll order some champagne sent up."

Daisy was more than surprised. It was closer to time for breakfast. However, she said, "Certainly," and opened the door. Philip followed her in.

He went directly to the telephone. The living room

of the suite was dark and shadowy; draperies were drawn over the windows, and only one lamp was burning. Daisy noticed Cypri's black corset flung over a chair beside the door to her bedroom. The ribbon with the red rose lay on the floor. As Philip ordered champagne, Daisy opened the bedroom door and tiptoed softly across the carpet to the bed. Cypri was sleeping soundly, her makeup smudged on her face. Part of her mascara and lipstick had come off on the pillow. For a few minutes Daisy watched Cypri breathing, looking at her face by the dim light from the open door. Then she went back into the living room and closed the heavy door between them.

"She's sleeping," she said.

Philip was sitting slumped at one end of the sofa. He looked up at Daisy, and his eyes were bloodshot.

"So. Now you know, don't you," he said.

Daisy didn't know what answer to make. She stood silent, looking at him.

"You're bloody good to do this, you know," Philip went on. He spoke in a low voice. "After I gamble, I always experience a severe depression. Even if I win. In fact, especially if I win. These are hours I dread, coming down from the high—sometimes I walk the streets."

He gave a heavy sigh and switched his glance to the floor. Daisy began to feel sorry for him. He really seemed to be in despair. She sat down on the other end of the sofa and looked at his bent head.

When Philip spoke again, his tone was flat. "Sometimes I think of killing myself."

His words barely had time to register on Daisy before a knock sounded at the door. For a moment she was startled, and then she remembered the champagne he had ordered. Room service was certainly fast at this hour. Daisy opened the door and a sleepy-looking boy wheeled in a bucket of ice containing a bottle of champagne. He produced two wine glasses, and Philip paid

309

him. When the waiter left, Philip opened the bottle and poured them each a glass.

"I believe this will prove reviving," he said to Daisy, with a return of his urbane manner. They sat down again on either end of the sofa. Daisy emptied the first glass rapidly and Philip refilled it for her.

"I'm glad you stayed at the club, Daisy," he said at last. He smiled faintly, looking at her over the rim of his glass. "You're a good soul. I know this is impossible for you to understand. I try to stop gambling. I know it is destroying me. But I just—can't stop. I don't see how anyone on earth could understand it. I don't myself."

"Oh, but I do understand," Daisy heard herself say.

She drained her second glass of champagne and stared at Philip's drawn, fatigued face with a surprising emotion. Instead of a nervous flutter at being alone with Philip, instead of feeling a bit frightened of him as she would have expected, she looked at him with understanding. His last words were so true. You wanted to stop—but you couldn't. She, too, was doing something that was going to destroy her in the end, and she knew it, and she couldn't stop, either. Involuntarily her eyes went to the closed door of Cypriana's bedroom.

"I completely understand," Daisy said, looking back at Philip's wan face. In a moment it dissolved as she felt her eyes fill with tears. She looked away, so Philip wouldn't see her cry. But it seemed important that she tell him she understood how he felt. She wanted to be a kind person, like Aunt China. She wanted to share other people's problems, to help them if she could. But she always felt her own problem kept her locked away from the rest of the world. "I understand, Philip," she said for the third time. She blinked the tears out of her eyes and sighed. "It's—just there, like a final fact of existence. You can't walk around it or get out from under it, and all the talk in the world, all the rational thought, all the good resolutions, are completely powerless."

Philip stared at Daisy; her face was turned away, and her light hair hung down and covered her cheek. She breathed rather heavily, as if each breath she drew were an effort.

"I didn't think anyone else on earth would understand," she added. She glanced up at him, and fresh tears in her blue eyes brimmed over and rolled down her cheeks; she let them fall into her lap. It was so late. She was so tired; her resistance seemed to be at an all-time low. God, life was painful. She felt sorry for everyone.

"You are the first person I've ever found who's known what I was talking about," Philip said to her in tones of wonder.

They were both speaking in very low voices—the edge of the pool of light cast by the lamp beside Philip seemed like the edge of the world, with just the two of them there inside it, and darkness all around. "I don't see how you can know," Philip added. Suddenly, he felt intensely close to Daisy, as if their souls were communicating.

"How I can know!"

As Daisy repeated Philip's words, she wanted to laugh; at the same time tears rolled down her face. "I know better than anyone in the world. It's the one thing I'm an expert in, not being able to stop. It's—"

For a moment Daisy paused. What on earth was she saying? The impulse that had first come to her after Cypri's wedding, on the country club veranda, the impulse to tell Bob King the truth, came back again, and this time it was much stronger. If she told someone it might ease the strangling pain in her throat, might get rid of the terrible feelings of worthlessness and stupidity and hopelessness that gripped her. Daisy stared at Philip's dark eyes, not really seeing them. For the space of a heartbeat longer she hesitated, like someone poised on the lip of a steep descent. Then she plunged over the edge. Her words spilled out as the tears kept running down her cheeks.

"I love Cypriana! We've been together since we were children. I can't live apart from her. I mean love—physical love. What happens between us is everything to me, my whole world, but she—she likes having sex with anybody. And she makes me hide in the closet while she makes love with Champ, or sometimes under their bed, and she'll kiss him in front of me and torment me any way she can, and it's so painful and she doesn't care and—I've thought, many times, of killing myself . . . just to put an end to the whole mess. Cypri can make me do anything. Wrong things—anything." Daisy stopped for a moment and gasped for breath. "Oh, believe me. If *you* had wanted me, Cypri would have made me—she was hinting that I could guard you and keep you from gambling; how does she have this power over me? How could such things be true? But they are. Just like you, I keep on playing and losing, and God himself couldn't make me stop." Daisy's voice rose and then stopped. She put her head into her hands and sobbed passionately.

Philip made absolutely no movement at all. He stared at Daisy. He was staggered. The revelation that had just come from this fair-haired little girl's lips was the last thing he had expected on earth. He sat immobile with surprise.

Daisy lifted her head. "You don't believe me? Champ will—Champ will be sitting there at night, and behind his back she'll put her hands on me and she'll—and then she'll go sit in his lap and tease him, and later when he's sleeping she'll come to my room and tease me until I want to die. Then she'll make us go back into the bedroom with Champ and right there while—while he's sleeping she—"

Daisy stopped again. Her wet blue eyes were blank and staring. Philip wondered if she knew where she was. She blinked and looked around, puzzled.

A coherent thought at last formed in Philip's mind:

312

My God, here was another Dane victim. Vivienne had given him an almost mortal wound once. Who knew but that it still festered and caused his present difficulties? And Mab was scarcely more kind. Now the third one, Cypriana Dane, had this poor child in an impossible situation. The details of Daisy's sordid existence at Cypriana's mercy confounded Philip. Right under his brother Champ's nose! But could he blame Champ for not catching on? Would he himself ever for a second have suspected such a thing if Daisy hadn't told him? It practically transcended belief.

After a minute more spent reflecting, Philip could move again. He pulled his handkerchief out and offered it to Daisy. He didn't know what to say— "there, there" didn't seem adequate. She took the handkerchief and tried to stanch her tears. Philip looked with sympathy at the poor little thing. She was intelligent, he knew, a beautiful girl whose sweet nature showed through her frightened, timid manner. She sniffed into his handkerchief, slowly growing quieter.

Philip poured another glass of champagne. He slid across the sofa and held it to Daisy's lips. "Here," he said, trying to sound soothing. "This will make you feel better."

Obediently Daisy took a sip, looking up at Philip and then hastily away.

"My God, I never breathed a word of this to a living soul before," she said, taking a shaky breath. She put her hand up to her throat. "What was I thinking of? I must have gone crazy for a minute."

"Daisy, look at me. Can you listen to me a minute?"

Daisy was staring at the floor. She swallowed hard and forced herself to raise her eyes to Philip's face.

He smiled at her. "I'm not shocked. Sexual orientations are very individual matters. But they can be changed. Did you know that? If you are unhappy, Daisy, you may not even be what you think you are. You must go and see a psychiatrist."

Daisy said nothing, but took her hand from her

throat and began twisting the handkerchief in her lap, threading it between her fingers. Suddenly, hunting for some clue to her predicament, Philip remembered his mother's gossip about Daisy's advent into the Dane family.

"Daisy, people's feelings go back to their childhoods," he said. "I believe I once heard that your early circumstances weren't happy. Isn't that right?"

He urged the champagne to her lips again as he spoke, and Daisy swallowed a little of it. Philip wasn't sure she was listening to what he was saying, but he went on.

"Something in your past could have caused your problem. I have an idea that the first part of your cure is to get away from Cypriana, and the second part is to see a doctor. Then I'm sure you will quickly feel like another person. Surely, giving it a try is better than talking about killing yourself."

Daisy looked down at her hands, thinking that it was always easy for someone else to tell you how to remedy your situation.

"I can't leave Cypri," she said. And if Philip says one more word, she thought, I'll ask him why can't he give up gambling.

Even as she thought that, the same idea came into Philip's head. The parallel between their problems was striking. Of course, he *had* tried a psychiatrist, and it had proved of no avail. His doctor had advised him to get married, to find a solid relationship, an interest in life to counteract the feelings of emptiness that drove him to gamble. He couldn't say psychiatry hadn't worked in his case, since he had been unable to bring himself to follow his doctor's advice. Philip gave a short sigh. Their problems were definitely similar; they both seemed powerless to adopt a remedy.

Suddenly a thought darted through Philip's mind so quickly that it was gone before he could grasp it. *What* was it that he had just thought? He looked down at the golden top of Daisy's head. The thought came looping back into his head. Maybe he had been waiting for Daisy. Maybe she was his solution. Could they both rebuild their lives—together? Could they help each other struggle free of unnatural bondage?

Philip's eyes widened. What a fantastic idea that was! And yet—he did wish he could help Daisy. She was pathetic. She was appealing. She was suffering—a Dane victim, like himself. And what did his life matter anymore, anyway? It seemed centuries since he had believed any romantic notions about happiness. God knows it was a wildly romantic notion that he and Daisy might cure each other's ills. But why not try? There was a chance. Again he recalled that his gambling had become an obsession after Champ's wedding.

Daisy's last words still hung in the air. "I can't leave Cypri."

"Daisy, look at me."

Philip spoke compellingly, and Daisy slowly raised her eyes again to look into his. Her cheeks were still damp, but she had regained control of herself. She looked at Philip without any expression on her face.

"Would you leave Cypriana for me?"

Philip spoke the question very simply, and Daisy actually took in his meaning instantly. There was still somehow total communication between them. It was Daisy's turn to be stunned. She said nothing.

Philip went on, slowly, speaking with growing conviction.

"Daisy, suppose we marry? I won't urge sexual relations on you. You can see an excellent psychiatrist for as long as you like. I—it could be a marriage to save us both. We could give it a try. I promise to pull myself up short, to stop gambling completely, if you'll help me. Up until now, I really just haven't cared. I haven't tried. But perhaps together—and if things don't work out, you can leave . . . Only—it is possible that we could help each other."

The idea appealed more and more to Philip. It was strange to feel that after all his life might have a mission, a purpose. He actually felt enthusiastic, alive.

"Oh, my God." Daisy was appalled. For a moment, she couldn't say a word more; she stared at Philip in horror. "*Wait.* Philip, I didn't mean—I'm so sorry I told you anything. Just forget it, please. You don't have to do anything for me. I'm perfectly all right. I'm fine. I'm happy."

She jumped up, but Philip remained sitting. He studied her pale face and red eyes. She looked anything but happy.

"You're tired," he said quietly. "I've kept you up far too late. But you will think about it? Think about marrying me—promise?"

"I couldn't," Daisy whispered. She looked at Philip in distress. "Please—"

Philip stood up.

"Daisy, we must both be strong. This might work. I feel better just thinking about it. You think about it, too. And remember, tomorrow you and Cypriana are coming to take tea at my flat. I'll see you then."

Daisy simply shook her head. What on earth was Philip talking about? Nothing he said made any sense. She was too tired to think about anything at all. She was almost too tired to undress. When the door closed behind Philip, she dragged the tunic off over her head and let it fall to the floor. She made her way into the extra bedroom, pulled the rest of her clothes off and fell asleep as soon as she had crawled into the bed.

Philip woke up at noon feeling splendid. Instead of remembering his gambling losses of the night before, he thought of Daisy.

Clear thinking and direct action were Philip's habits of behavior. His decision had been made. He would marry Daisy Sykes. He would rescue her from her emotional dilemma. She had said no, but that was meaningless. He would force her to leave Cypriana, as a kindness to her.

Poor child, he thought; she had evoked a tender response in him, and he was not accustomed to feeling tender toward anyone. Since his eighteenth year, not much tenderness had been shown to Philip; it wasn't part of the English method of educating an English gentleman. But Philip wasn't completely English, and this fact had helped him at Downforth Enterprises. When he entered the empire, he had watched the action going on close to his uncle. The intricate traffic pattern of class structure left men and projects stalled at crossroads, schemes and plans at cross-purposes. Philip had gone for his objectives without getting caught at the corners, and his uncle had been delighted. Charleston had died happy, certain that Downforth was in safe hands. But Philip had tired of the battlefield. Once the chairmanship was his, the game had lost all interest for him.

Now, once again life held zest for him. He jumped out of bed. He would be very kind to Daisy; he would be tender. He would reassure her; he would heap her with good things. Her lesbian attachment to her cousin did not strike Philip as very important; still he would be patient until she turned to him. He thought she probably would. He was usually very successful with women. And now he had a sweet little fiancée. He felt better than he had felt for years. For Daisy's sake, he would stop gambling. Last night was the last time. Now he would pull Downforth together. After all, he had to have something to pass on to his heirs.

At two o'clock that afternoon, Daisy woke up; far different thoughts rushed into her mind as she remembered the night before. Had she really told the truth to Philip? Surely she had only dreamed it! Daisy squeezed her eyes tightly shut and prayed that it had only been a dream. Please, please God. But she could remember it all too clearly. It had *happened*. She, who fanatically had guarded this secret from all the world for more than ten years, last night had let it all pour

317

out to Philip Alexander! Oh, Jesus. Daisy groaned and cursed the effect of champagne and sleeplessness.

Of *all* people to tell! Well, she forced herself to assess the damage. Maybe—maybe there would be no actual damage in it. Daisy opened her eyes and stared up at the ceiling, thinking hard. Perhaps Philip understood; he had a problem, too. Daisy suddenly remembered Philip's strange words at the end, about helping each other . . . about *marriage*! What in God's name? Philip must have gone as crazy as she. He had actually proposed.

A chill coursed through Daisy's body, and she shivered. Cypri must never find out that Philip had asked her to marry him! She had told him no. She hoped Philip was enough of a gentleman to accept her refusal and ask her no more. A weird idea! Philip had undoubtedly been drunk and exhausted, to come up with that one. Very possibly he would not remember anything about it. In fact, Daisy was certain he wouldn't want to remember a single thing to do with the entire evening. Hastily, she prayed that that would prove to be the case.

The door of the bedroom was violently flung open.

"God, it's already two and I'm starving!"

Cypriana, wearing a bathrobe, jumped into the middle of Daisy's bed.

"You're better, then?"

"Much better in the stomach—the paregoric worked —but tell me quick. What happened last night?"

The blood rushed to Daisy's face; then she remembered what Cypri meant, her report on Philip's gambling.

"I couldn't see the amount on the check Philip wrote out," she answered. "But he lost a lot. An awful lot."

"*Damn* him to the underworld! Honestly, I was thinking this morning that when Champ finds out about this, he ought to come over here and hammer Philip. Or have him committed—I wonder if we

318

could?" Cypri looked thoughtful. "A nuthouse for Philip."

Daisy couldn't help laughing. Cypriana was so mad, so determined to find a way to control Philip, and so thwarted; she looked about to explode.

"Did he just send you home, too?" Cypri asked.

Daisy thought of the empty champagne bottle in the other room and realized that she had to be truthful. Partly truthful, anyway.

"No, he came back, came in and ordered champagne. You know, the casino didn't serve drinks after eleven. He wanted a drink."

"A *drink*! He's got a nerve. What are we running, a pub? Oh!" Cypri beat her fists on the bed. Her dark hair was hanging in strands across her eyes, which sparkled with fury, and Daisy wanted to laugh again. "I've never been so rudely treated in all my *life* as last night. 'Get my car. Mrs. Alexander is leaving.' The bastard!"

A new hope stirred in Daisy. Maybe Cypri would get so mad they could leave England without seeing Philip again.

"Philip didn't seem sorry that you were sick," she offered.

Cypri's eyes flashed around the room. She wanted to pick something up and throw it. She had put herself out to seduce Philip, and he didn't even care if she lived or died. It was too much.

Well, what next? She might as well calm down. She had to think. She had no idea how to proceed but she was determined to keep trying. At least her stomach felt better.

"You know, we're supposed to go to Philip's for tea today," she said to Daisy. "It would serve him right if we didn't show up. Maybe we won't go. Except that I'm dying to see this 'Mayfair flat' that he has. When we come to England again, he'll probably be living in a room over a garage in Bayswater."

"I think it would be a good idea not to go," Daisy

319

said. "We could shop. You wanted to go to that boutique in Kensington near Biba's, remember? The one that has the red dress in the window?"

Cypri considered. "No," she said. "We've got to see how bad things really are. Let's go to tea."

She ordered lunch sent up. They ate chicken salad and were in the process of dressing when Philip telephoned. He spoke to Cypriana. Butter wouldn't melt in his mouth, she reported. He wanted to be certain they remembered about tea. He offered to send his car; in fact, he'd come himself to fetch them if she'd prefer. Cypri coldly replied that the car would be sufficient.

For once the sun was shining outside, and the afternoon air was warm and summerlike. Cypriana assessed the weather from the window and decided to wear a sleeveless dark blue silk dress with a cowl neckline. It looked dignified. The hotel hairdresser came up again and combed her hair into loose curls around her face.

Daisy wore her hair down, too. She put on a yellow linen sleeveless dress; she hadn't worn it yet, and it looked suitable for a Mayfair tea party, an event which she devoutly hoped would be stiffly formal and include no discussion of any part of last night.

Things started well. Philip's apartment building lobby was staid and elegant, full of white marble and mirrors. They were escorted inside by several doormen and taken up in an elevator and deposited opposite a white door that had a shining brass doorknob. Before they could knock on the door, Philip opened it.

"Welcome," he said, smiling at them. His eyes lingered on Daisy. She looked like a Nordic goddess, he thought; he loved her shining fair hair and light blue eyes. He ushered them inside.

Cypriana looked around with an interest that quickly turned to gloom. Such a wonderful apartment that

Philip was going to throw away! It had obviously been professionally decorated. Everything in the living room —furniture, draperies and rug—was in perfect harmony with the lovely proportions of the room and its delicate white carved-wood ceiling. The woodwork and the handsome fireplace were all white; the rug was blue and the twin sofas facing each other beside the fireplace were light red velvet. Across the room, raised by four carpeted steps, a circular dining alcove was framed by windows with small, diamond-shaped panes, making the view of the outside look like a medieval scene. In the center of the alcove, a round table stood covered with a floor-length white cloth and topped with plates of cakes and sandwiches.

As Cypriana took inventory, Philip watched her. Little Miss Fun and Games, he thought, as her dark blue eyes surveyed the scene. The idea of the sexual choreography Cypriana indulged in around her house was rather titillating, to tell the truth. Philip repressed a smile and turned to Daisy.

"I have something for you, Daisy," he said, closing the door. "And if you won't take it, perhaps your cousin will do it for you."

Daisy flushed. She didn't like the solicitous way Philip spoke to her. But she was probably just imagining that there was more gentleness and kindness in his manner toward her than before.

Cypri gave Philip a look of inquiry, thinking at the same time that he didn't seem to have suffered much from last night's debauch. He looked rested and fit, even relaxed; for the first time he wasn't wearing a suit but had on flannel pants and a handsome soft gray sweater. He looked even better in casual clothes than in dinner wear.

"Please sit down," he said. "I believe Mrs. Randall is bringing tea in a minute. She's been busy getting ready." He glanced at the laden table. "Mrs. Randall is the housekeeper," he added, speaking to Daisy.

Daisy and Cypriana sat down together on one of

the sofas. Philip crossed to a small desk, pulled an envelope from one drawer and brought it over to them. When he sat down on the opposite sofa, his close proximity disturbed Cypriana. She was determined to hate Philip, but he was so sexy! Somehow, he seemed even more so than usual, today. Perhaps it was because she was seeing him relaxed and at home. She wondered how many women he had seduced on that velvet sofa. Her eyes darted about the room, but there was no trace of any feminine presence.

Philip waved the envelope.

"Daisy's winnings from last night," he said. "I completely forgot about them until I got home and found the money in my jacket pocket." He leaned forward and offered the envelope to Daisy.

Daisy shook her head. "I don't think it's right," she said. "I played with your money."

"I appeal to your cousin," Philip said, looking at Cypriana. "Daisy won it fair and square."

"Of course you should take it, Daisy," Cypri said. Philip handed Cypriana the envelope.

"You'll keep it for Daisy?"

"I'll see that she spends it."

Something in the shortness of Cypriana's reply reminded Philip that she was miffed at him.

"And how are you feeling today?" he asked quickly.

"Fine," Cypri said. She did not smile at him. She planned to relent soon and flirt with Philip again, but he did owe her an apology. To tell the truth, Cypri didn't think any longer that she could catch Philip or do anything with him if she caught him. She couldn't shake off her gloomy conviction that her plans were doomed. She put the envelope into her blue pocketbook, resisting the impulse to look to see how much money was inside. It was *something* out of Philip, anyway.

Philip began to say something more, but a side door opened, and a large, red-cheeked woman entered. She carried a silver service that sparkled so brightly it sent flashes of light around the room, the silver tray and teapots and cream and sugar containers on it having been polished to jewelry store perfection.

The woman trotted up the steps of the alcove and placed the tray with a flourish in front of one of the three elegant small chairs that were drawn up to the table. Her eyes darted over the dishes already there, checking each one. Then she turned and said, "Tea is served, sir."

"Thank you, Mrs. Randall," Philip said. He rose and offered his hand to Daisy. Hastily, Daisy stood up, touching his fingers only lightly in the process, and Philip repeated the courtesy for Cypriana. They mounted the steps to the alcove.

"Will you pour out, Cypriana?" Philip asked, pulling out the chair in front of the tea service. Cypri sat down, and Philip solicitously saw to Daisy's being seated beside her. When he took his own chair, Mrs. Randall handed Cypri delicate white teacups in saucers trimmed with a gold band, and Cypri poured the tea with as practiced a manner as she could manage, remembering to dilute each cup with a little boiling water from the other pot. Mrs. Randall handed round the cups. Afterward she moved the silver service to a sideboard and retired, not quite dropping a curtsy, but almost, Cypri thought with envy. You could certainly get respectful servants in England!

Spread before them were thin china dishes full of tiny sandwiches—some made of lettuce, some of tomatoes, some of smoked salmon—and a covered platter of hot toast dripping with butter and sprinkled with chopped herbs. Three raised cake dishes held a yellow cake, a pound cake, and a golden fruitcake, all already sliced. There were silver bowls full of cashew nuts, a three-tiered silver stand covered with petit fours, and a compote of what appeared to be Bavarian cream.

"Mrs. Randall must be a treasure," Cypri said as Philip asked what she would like to try. For a few minutes they simply passed dishes around. When her plate was heaped, Cypri took a sip of the steaming tea.

Philip did not answer Cypri's remark about Mrs. Randall. He was busy pointing out things Daisy might like. Daisy felt her alarm grow. Philip was certainly making a point of being nice to her. Hastily she took some of whatever he advised, and sat with a full plate, unable to eat any of it. She wished she were safely out of there.

At last Philip turned to Cypriana. His expression became earnest, and his dark eyes looked directly into her blue ones.

"Cypriana, I believe I owe you a large apology for what happened last night," he said.

Well, that was better, Cypri thought. Make him say it all, she told herself. She gave Philip an inquiring look.

"It was unpardonable of me not to escort you home. I really can hardly believe you will forgive me, unless it's because . . ." He paused. His eyes traveled over to Daisy and then back to Cypri's face. "You know, I'm sure, that gambling can be a disease. For me it is. It's led me to do more than one unpardonable thing. As I'm sure you know, I've even endangered the company. I've been a bloody fool. But last night was the last time. I intend never to gamble again. That's easy to say, I know. Perhaps you'll believe I mean it, however, when you hear my reason. I have fallen in love with Daisy, and last night I asked her to marry me."

Daisy uttered a strangled sound. As his words settled over the alcove, Philip pretended to cough to keep himself from bursting out with laughter at the look on Cypriana's face. Slowly, Cypri digested his words. Her eyes snapped from Philip to Daisy. The expression on Daisy's face was horrified. Cypri's eyes snapped back to Philip. In that space of time Cypri shot from despair to ecstasy. The day was saved! By some god's miracle, Plan A had worked! Cypri's expression of amazement turning slowly to joy kept Philip coughing for several minutes.

"Why—that's wonderful!" Cypri said when she could at last manage words. "Daisy! and you never said a word!"

Both of them looked at Daisy, who was staring at Philip, her expression full of reproach.

"You know I told you I can't—" Daisy began. Her voice was faint.

"Nonsense," Cypriana said. She looked at Philip. "You know my cousin's rather shy and never does herself justice. She'll make a perfect wife."

"I agree," Philip said. "I can count on your support, then, Cypriana? You'll help me persuade her?"

"It's a perfect match," Cypri said firmly.

"And I hope we can be married soon. When are you planning to leave England?"

We can leave anytime, now, Cypri thought. She felt happy enough to dance a jig. Her plan had worked! Her plan had brought all this about, though heaven knew how—it was a mystery to her why men fell in love, though she thanked God they did. Now Downforth was saved and she could continue her good life back in Eyreville.

"You want to get married before we—before I return?" Cypri asked.

"Oh, Cypri!" Daisy finally managed to make her tongue move. "You know I can't—" She didn't finish, but she looked so miserable that Cypri exchanged a glance with Philip.

"Maybe Daisy needs a little time to get ready," Philip said smoothly. "I don't mean to rush her."

"We can fly home and announce the engagement to everyone," Cypri said. She was thinking hard. She'd need some time with Daisy to bring this off. "Could you come over there, Philip? Visit us soon?"

"It would take a few days to arrange it, but I'm sure it can be done."

"Viv has been saying she wants us all to get together for a house party at Land's End," Cypri said. Her mind was working at top speed. She really doubted she could force Daisy to marry Philip right on the spot, here in England, but at home, surrounded by tradition, by reminders of what she owed the Danes, Daisy would surely submit to her fate. "Mab could come too. We can have a big party—maybe a ball in the ballroom—and announce your engagement in grand style, and you can set the wedding date then." Cypri smiled at the thought, struck with her brilliant plan: a gathering of the clan, so to speak; a gathering of all of Eyreville—just the thing to cow conventional Daisy, whom she carefully refrained from looking at.

The plan startled Philip. In his turn, he sat thoughtful. His first impulse was to reject the proposal. He had never seen Vivienne since—but wait. This was the time, he told himself. This was the time to make new beginnings, to tie up old loose ends. Confronting Vivienne might be the best thing he could do. After all, she meant nothing to him now. They had been nothing to each other for over twenty years. Would Vivienne even care that he was marrying her young cousin? If that hurt, he would be pleased. But how could you hurt anyone who had fame and beauty and success in such measure as Vivienne had them?

And Cypriana had mentioned Mab as well. Well, why not? It would perhaps be difficult for him to see Mab again, but Mab cared nothing for him. She had amply demonstrated that in February. Seeing him again wouldn't matter to her; it shouldn't matter to him. After all, he had Daisy now.

"A house party at Land's End sounds like an excellent idea," Philip said.

"And a ball," Cypri added. She kept her voice light and gay, and let her eyes shine with anticipation.

Please, dear God, just let me out of here, Daisy thought. She dug her nails into the palms of her hands to keep from screaming. How could Philip do this to her? How could he trap her so ruthlessly? She knew what Cypri was going to say to her and she could never tell Cypri that Philip knew the truth about them. Philip was counting on her helplessness, counting on Cypri to force her into whatever it was that he had in mind. Daisy looked at Philip and shuddered. Philip didn't look like a monster, but he was one. She felt like a rabbit caught in a trap, powerless to make a sound.

Philip summoned Mrs. Randall and asked for champagne to toast his engagement. The news put the housekeeper into a great bustle; she produced chilled glasses and ice buckets amid declarations of joy and wishes for her employer's happiness. With well-bred restraint, she glanced only in passing at the silent recipient of these attentions, Daisy.

Daisy went through the farce without a word, just touching the glass to her lips. She had decided never to drink champagne again, for the rest of her life.

After the girls left, Philip noticed Daisy's still-full champagne glass on the table beside the couch. He picked up the glass. Poor Daisy, he did feel sorry for her. He was sure Cypriana would bludgeon her to get her to go through with the marriage. Cypriana would win, too; his money was on her. He was sorry that it would be rough on Daisy. But it was for her own good. Philip was perfectly convinced of that, and smiling, he raised the glass toward the portrait of Charleston Clermont hanging over the fireplace.

"I'm finally and at last going to get married, Uncle," Philip said softly, and drained the glass.

"You lucky girl!" The words burst from Cypri's lips as the elevator door closed at the Ritz. She had held her peace in the car, so that the chauffeur would overhear nothing he might report back to Philip, but now she could contain herself no longer. "Think of it! Married to Philip Alexander!"

Daisy said nothing and looked down at the floor

of the elevator, which they were sharing with a fat man. Daisy had to struggle; it took all her strength to keep herself from screaming.

When they reached their suite and Cypri closed the door, Daisy sank down on the sofa and put her head into her hands.

"Come on, now. Listen." Cypriana sat down beside Daisy and patted her knee. "You're so narrow-minded about sex, you dope. You've never even tried with a man."

Daisy looked up at her through tears.

"You made me what I am and now—" Daisy's voice choked.

"Don't be silly. You'll like sex both ways! *I* do. You're so lucky Philip wants you, wants to *give up gambling* for you." Cypri spoke with great emphasis. "I envy you. Really. Think of the life you can lead over here. Rich as Croesus. And you can come and see me all the time, and tell me how right I was."

"Cypri, don't break my heart! Don't you care anything—anything about us and our being together? Oh, Cypri!" Daisy was in almost too much pain to speak.

"I just said, we can visit each other all the time!"

"It's Baker, isn't it? You want me out of the way so you can have Baker! I've seen you look at her."

"You're talking like a mad person."

"I won't marry Philip, and that's final."

"You will marry him, and that's final. Daisy, think. How could you be so ungrateful to us? You've lived on the Danes since you were nine years old. I mean, that's a crass way to put it, but it's true. Don't you think you should pay us back? Do something for us when you can?"

"I'll work all my life and give you all the money I make! I'll do anything you say to pay you back, but I just *can't*—"

"You'll work and pay us back, will you? Get this straight. The only way you can pay us back is to marry Philip and keep him from gambling, and if you won't do that, you can go back to Texas and live in a trailer for all I care! I'm through with you!"

Daisy had known that those were the words Cypriana would say. She knew the way Cypriana's mind worked. The quarrel ended there. Daisy burst into a passion of crying and cried until she had no tears left. Even Cypriana could not sit through such weeping. She went into her own room and closed the door.

It was a very pale fiancée whom Philip put on the plane to America. Daisy gave him her cheek to kiss as they parted, but she did not look directly at him.

"I'll call you as soon as everything is definitely arranged," Cypriana repeated for the third time to Philip. "Champ is going to be thrilled. I can't wait to see him."

Champ, when he met their plane in Columbia and heard their news, was more astounded than thrilled. Philip to marry Daisy! How had Cypri pulled that off? he wondered. Daisy was certainly very pretty, and he liked her himself, so there was really no reason to be terribly surprised, when he thought about it. Still, he was.

"And Philip promised to give up gambling if Daisy will marry him," Cypriana said, her words coming fast. Her eyes were shining in triumph. "Champ, I'm sure Philip means it. And in two weeks—less, ten days—he's coming over here. We'll announce the engagement. I want a big party—we'll invite everyone in Eyreville."

When Cypri paused for breath, Champ looked at Daisy. He thought she seemed terribly subdued for one who had come back with a scalp tucked in her belt. She seemed to have to make an effort just to be present. Mostly, she was still and tense. As they drove home she sat hunched in the back seat of the car; occasionally Champ glanced in the rear vision mirror at her, puzzled. Something about Daisy reminded him of—what? He thought for a while; then he remembered what it was. He was a bird-watcher; he sat every morning in his breakfast room and watched the birds come and go from a feeding station on the back porch. Recently he had noticed a nuthatch who was caught pecking at a sunflower seed as a hawk silently swept into the yard. The hawk lighted on a tree limb. The nuthatch either saw or sensed it, and as he watched, the little bird pulled its head into its body, shrinking into itself to hide. It crouched motionless until the hawk took wing. Then it slid under the porch railing and cowered there for a while before it flew away. Something in Daisy's pose reminded Champ of the frightened nuthatch.

"Wedding nerves," Cypri said when Champ privately asked her about Daisy's mood. "She's delighted to be marrying Philip. Who wouldn't be?"

They had just finished a very satisfying and vigorous reunion up in their bedroom and, as Cypri spoke, she was dialing Vivienne at Land's End. She got hold of Johnny Mae Jones. Johnny Mae told her Vivienne had gone to New York. After an hour on the telephone, talking to agents, hairdressers, and various other stupid people, Cypri finally got through to Viv at the Omega Salon. She told her news and made her request.

It seemed to take Vivienne a few minutes to comprehend it all but then she readily said fine; of course a house party at Land's End would be fun. And it would be great fun to hold a ball in the ballroom. Cypri should do the guest list, invite anyone she wanted. Vivienne said she'd be home soon—in fact, she'd probably fly home the next day. And Vivienne would call Mab herself to invite her.

"Great," Cypri said, hanging up. She went over and kissed Champ. "It's all set." She was in high good spirits, and ruffled Champ's hair as she thought of the sensational dress she intended to buy for the ball.

As the days passed, Daisy drooped even more visibly. The engagement announcement at Land's End was destined to be strictly a formality, since Cypri

330

told everyone about Daisy's amazing luck. Some people appeared almost to doubt it. Philip seemed awfully remote over there in England. Cypri had no doubt, however, that he would show up for the weekend. He had already called twice from London to check on details.

On the Thursday before Philip was due, Champ approached Daisy. She was sitting alone in the living room when he came in from the hospital, and he joined her. He asked a few questions about whether she was looking forward to living in England. Her replies struck him as unenthusiastic.

"You know, my mother didn't like the South at first—" Champ began, but Cypri came in and caught them in their low-voiced conversation. Joining them, she immediately changed the subject, and later peremptorily told Champ to lay off Daisy.

"I have somehow the distinct feeling that Daisy is getting pushed around here," Champ said. "It's in the air in this house. What *are* you pulling off, Cypri? Are you being fair to Daisy?"

Champ's taking *Daisy's* part so incensed Cypriana that she longed to slap his face. She said darkly that if Champ knew his own best interest he would shut up.

"But Daisy—" he began.

"Daisy, Daisy!" Cypriana said in an exasperated tone. "I tell you, mind your own business. Daisy is perfectly happy; she's thrilled to death. You just don't understand her, and you couldn't if you tried."

Cypri tossed her head, glared at Champ for a moment and then went over to her writing desk and sent invitations to the ball out to Frank and Bob King, just to get even with him.

Champ supposed it was true that he didn't understand women too well; certainly he often didn't understand Cypriana. Matters seemed to be under her control, for better or worse, and he held his peace for the rest of the evening.

331

On the eve of the weekend, the afternoon before the house party, Daisy Skyes lying underneath the Alexanders' creaking bed knew exactly why she was there and why she deserved to be. Through the tears in her eyes she caught sight of a white ostrich feather drifting to the floor beside the dust ruffle which hid her. The box springs shook over her head. No humiliation could be great enough for her, Daisy. She knew her fate. You always paid for your sins, didn't you?

Book Three:

Land's End

XVII

Mab had doubted that the seventeenth of June would ever arrive, but the day came at last, and she boarded her flight at O'Hare airport exactly as planned. At eight-thirty that evening the airplane touched the runway of Charleston airport. Walking down the ramp into the terminal, Mab thought the very air seemed different, seemed somehow familiar. She took a deep breath and stepped inside.

Vivienne was waiting. Without a word, the two hugged each other.

"I can't believe that I'm going home," Mab said when Vivienne released her.

"Oh, Mab, I hope you'll think Land's End looks just right." Vivienne was flushed, her dark eyes shining, and Mab immediately noticed that Vivienne's husky voice sounded slightly more southern in its cadence. A departing flight was announced on the loudspeaker in an unmistakably South Carolinian voice. Mab grinned. She felt like saying *y'all* herself. She *was* home.

The crowd around the moving luggage belt looked familiar, too—women with soft expressions and soft voices, men who snapped fingers and organized things. At last her two Vuitton suitcases appeared; she and Vivienne each took one and walked outside. The balmy air smelled of scrub pine and gardenia blossoms. After they loaded her luggage into the station wagon, Mab climbed into the front seat, leaned back and sighed.

With a glance at her sister, Vivienne started the engine and headed the car out of the airport toward the coast road to Eyreville.

"Glad to be back, Mab?"

"I can't tell you how glad."

Vivienne was silent for a moment, negotiating the station wagon through traffic, and then she reported on the purchase of some furniture Mab had suggested she buy. They were trying to obtain close approximations of the original furnishings that had been in the house. The Bosworths had sold a good deal of it to antique dealers. In some cases Vivienne had been able to find the actual pieces and buy them back.

"The new beds are much more comfortable than the old ones, at least," Vivienne said with a laugh.

"It's so wonderful that they hadn't touched the library!"

"That was next. The Bosworths were about to have it assessed when I offered to buy the house. I just found that out."

"My God. Perfect timing." Mab turned her head and looked at Vivienne's profile; Vivienne's high brow and elegant nose and chin were outlined by the light from passing cars.

"Is anyone else at Land's End yet?" Mab asked, trying to sound casual.

"No," Vivienne answered. Vivienne did not look over as she spoke; she was watching the road. "Philip was to fly from London to Washington, I understand, and then on to Columbia. He's already in Columbia, I imagine. He's spending tonight in a hotel there and then driving to Eyreville first thing tomorrow. They'll all be at Land's End in time for lunch."

"Imagine us all sitting in the dining room again," Mab said.

"And the weather is beautiful—should be all weekend. We're lucky."

"Did you get plenty of help?"

"Yes. Johnny Mae is cooking and her sister Estelle

is helping. Cypri is bringing Chooky along to serve, and Baker—remember Baker? She works for Cypri now. She's coming to help out, too."

"I remember Baker." Mab looked out across the flat land to where, from time to time, the ocean was visible. An almost-full moon was rising. They were both silent for a few minutes.

Again, Mab tried to make her next question sound offhand. "Have you heard more about this engagement between Philip and Daisy, Viv?"

Vivienne drew her breath in and expelled it with a short laugh.

"I don't know what to make of it," she said. "There's something going on, all right. Cypri has told everybody in Eyreville that Philip is going to marry Daisy. She's invited more than fifty people out to the ball tomorrow night. We're having Damn the Torpedoes and another band, too—did I tell you? Anyway, Cypri told me she wants to make a formal announcement of the engagement at the ball. Weird, because Daisy goes around quiet as a mouse and says nothing about any of it. I've only seen her twice—Cypri runs out to the house every day and chatters on about it. But both times that I saw Daisy, she didn't mention Philip at all. I didn't ask her why. I didn't want to press her."

"I've been thinking about this gambling report. It doesn't make any sense."

"Apparently that's true. Champ came by the house one day last week and stopped for a drink. He said Philip's gambling has been going on for two years. Last winter a public report accused Philip of bad management because he had sold some private stock in his company to pay his gambling debts. He's been in deep water ever since, but Champ says he just keeps on gambling. Or he did. Night after night—he couldn't stay away. But now Philip has promised to give it up for Daisy." Vivienne delivered the last sentence evenly, with scarcely any irony in her voice.

337

"I just can't imagine—" Mab stopped.

"I know." Vivienne sounded amused.

"How are Daisy and Cypri?" Mab asked after a pause.

"Oh, Cypri is flourishing as usual. She's always at the country club practicing her tennis or golf. Every year she's the club's tennis champion. And Daisy's been teaching in a nursery school. She's very quiet, more so than ever, lately. When did you see them last?"

"I was here for Christmas a year and a half ago."

"Oh, that's right. Well, Daisy's a bit more grown up. I think she's very pretty." Vivienne paused. "Did you bring along a dress for the ball? Half the town's coming."

"I hope to dazzle them with Chicago chic. Tell me some local news. You must know all the gossip."

"Um. Oh, yes, James Hastings married Sugar Cunningham—Hellraiser's little sister, remember? James divorced his first wife and has custody of all six of their kids. Sugar has four kids by her first husband. They're all the same ages or something, and natural enemies, so Sugar spends all day at the club playing bridge, according to Cypri, and being interrupted by telephone calls from home like battle reports from the front. Cypri said it's destroyed Sugar's bridge game. Even Cypri beat her in a rubber the other day."

Vivienne related all the items of local gossip that she could recall as they drove along the highway skirting the edge of Eyreville. The downtown lights glowed in the sky, until they reached the turnoff to Curzon's Neck. Once they left the main road, the countryside grew dark, flat fields and farmhouses appearing on either side. They turned again and the road narrowed. It was bordered now with trees and bushes.

"Oh, smell the honeysuckle," Mab cried. Outside, the air was milky with moonlight and the yellow-white honeysuckle blossoms gleamed on the dark bushes. "There's a way this road smells—"

"I know. I cried the first time I drove down it last spring."

Mab stuck her head out of the open car window and breathed deeply for a minute.

"I've been trying to get the garden back in shape," Vivienne said when Mab pulled her head back in. "I've had two men working all spring. Everything's in bloom right now. I've got roses and daisies and baby's breath in all the rooms."

They drove through Crosstree in silence. The grocery store, Mab noticed, was dark; the Alexanders lived in a nearby house now. The road narrowed even more and they passed the turnoff to the Kings' farmhouse. In another minute Land's End rose before them, its large windows blazing with light.

"Oh, look!" Mab exclaimed at the sight.

In a minute they were in the driveway. As Vivienne pulled the car up near the back porch, Johnny Mae Jones hurried out of the kitchen and down the stairs to greet them.

"Welcome home, Miss Mab," she said. "I guess this is going to be some party. We're still at it." Through the kitchen windows two women waved, and Johnny Mae said, "Estelle's daughter Sue is helping, too."

Johnny Mae carried the suitcases inside. Mab followed and stopped at the door of the kitchen.

"Look at this," Mab exclaimed. Every countertop and table held food in various states of preparation. Estelle looked up and grinned. She introduced her daughter, who was helping to make tiny sandwiches.

"It smells wonderful."

"Are you hungry? Want a sample?" Vivienne asked from behind her.

Mab shook her head. "Thanks, I ate dinner on the plane."

"I thought we'd drink brandy in the library and go to bed early, since tomorrow——"

Mab didn't hear Vivienne. She had crossed the hall and was looking at the dining room. The long table was covered with a heavily-embroidered white linen tablecloth. Six places were set with the Limoges dishes and China's lovely heirloom silverware, which had come with China from Gardens to Land's End. The large white napkins were folded to stand erect, and a small straw basket holding roses and baby's breath stood at each place.

"Those are the Chippendale chairs I told you about. What do you think?" Vivienne was looking into the dining room over Mab's shoulder.

"I love them. Viv, the room looks gorgeous. I want to see everything else."

Mab's light steps made scarcely any noise crossing the polished floor of the hall. At the double doors of the drawing room she paused.

"Oh, it's lovely. It's so much like it used to be. Oh, there's Mother's desk."

Tears came into Mab's eyes. She blinked them away and crossed the hall.

"The library is absolutely the same. That's wonderful."

"Want to tour the upstairs?" Vivienne asked. "The bedrooms are quite changed. Each one's a different color. You're in the blue one on the front."

Vivienne had been about to say *Mother's old room*, but she caught herself. She didn't want them remembering whose bedrooms they had been in the past, whose sickrooms. She had made them all look like dream rooms from *Architectural Digest*.

Mab quickly ran up the stairs, toured the second story, took a look at the ballroom and came down. Vivienne waited by the library doors.

"Everything looks fabulous," Mab said, smiling. "You've worked so hard."

"Let's have a drink. Tomorrow I'll show you the guest house in back. Johnny Mae's staying in one of the downstairs rooms out there, and I'm putting Philip on the top floor."

Mab followed Vivienne into the library and flung

herself down on the leather-covered sofa between the green-shaded lamps. She looked at the book shelves covering the walls, and then at the door. She felt as if her father might appear at any minute.

Vivienne walked over to the silver tray on the table beside the window seat.

"Like some brandy? Or something else? I think I'll have a Jack Daniels, myself."

"Brandy's perfect."

Vivienne brought a glass of brandy to Mab, and settled with her own drink on the other end of the sofa. In the soft light of the lamps, Mab's skin glowed.

"You look great, Mab."

"I was just thinking that you look wonderful, and very rested."

Vivienne sighed. "Clance calls me practically every day. He made me bring down a suitcase full of scripts to read. But I'm enjoying life down here."

Vivienne paused and took a drink. When she spoke again, her voice was lower. "Mab, when I was in New York I saw Alec."

"You did? You mean, you went to the sanitarium?"

"Yes. Havenfield. There has been no progress on his case. He's still—" Vivienne broke off and sighed instead of finishing her sentence. She looked around at everything in the library, the books and the rug and the furniture. "Thank God for Land's End. It's a refuge. Things are real, here." She gave a short laugh.

Vivienne might look great but she was nervous about something, Mab thought, studying her sister closely.

Vivienne went on in a soft voice. "I don't ever want to lose touch with everything the way Alec did."

"Vivienne, you'd be the last person to flip out."

"Oh, I know. Clancy says the same." Vivienne absently pulled her hair back and then let it fall again around her face. "He wants me to make another movie or do another play right away."

341

"What would you like to do?" Mab asked. "I mean, what besides acting?"

"What *could* I do, is the question. Mab, remember when you got tired of dancing?"

Suddenly, vividly, Mab did remember. The endless *pliés* and *relevés* of her youth, the pirouettes and arabesques, watching the girl in the mirror for hour after hour. She could hear Miss Phipps's voice. "These are steps of *elevation*." She felt her muscles tighten.

"Acting's a lot like dancing, you know," Vivienne went on. "It's endless work. I look back and it seems like a long chain of days—Christ! that's a line from *Uncle Vanya*. Oh, I'm just in a mood. You know me. It will pass." She gave another short laugh.

Mab looked curiously at Vivienne; her sister's face was partly in the shadows and she was sitting very still, in her old way, her beautiful dark eyes staring ahead of her. Her lips were slightly parted. She scarcely seemed to breathe. Was she thinking of Philip? Mab wondered. She wanted to ask Vivienne about the long-ago romance, but she felt that Vivienne should be the one to bring it up. If Vivienne didn't, Mab thought, she would just have to wait and see what happened when Philip arrived.

In the last week Mab had thought almost constantly about Philip. The gambling story puzzled her— throughout the day they had spent together in London, Philip had seemed self-confident and at ease. Mab couldn't picture Philip confused or despairing. If he had doubts and uncertainties, he certainly hid them well. Yet she remembered his asking her if she found life fulfilling. *Do you find the treasures you dig up rewarding enough?* She could hear his low voice and see the wistful expression that fleetingly passed across his face when he asked, "Are Champ and Cypriana happy?" Mab recalled the way he reached across the table at Rules' and took her hand. The memory made her heartbeat quicken, and she cursed herself. She must remember not to think of Philip in that way again.

Vivienne still stared straight ahead, and the silence in the library seemed almost tangible, covering everything like the dust of years lying in layers over the furnishings of a long-deserted room. Speaking of Alec made Vivienne think about her movies, and suddenly she wondered if Philip had seen any of them. The question had never occurred to her before. Had Philip sat in the dark in some London cinema and looked at her, reproduced on the screen in front of him? Had he thought she looked old? Was it strange to him to see on film that body he had once known so well? Or had he never gone near a theater where her movies were playing?

Vivienne realized that her palms had broken out in sweat. She wiped her hands on her skirt and reached for her drink. What had she and Mab been talking about? She had lost the thread entirely. She finished her Jack Daniels.

"I think we should go to bed soon, don't you?" she said to Mab. "And you can sleep late. Cypri and company won't be out until noon. I thought we'd have champagne first and then luncheon around one. The ball is to begin at eight."

Mab rose, putting down her empty brandy glass, and gave Vivienne a kiss.

"I got up at seven this morning and I'm ready for bed," she said. She looked around again. "I love being home."

"I'm glad you're here. Go on up. I'll check with Johnny Mae and turn out the light." Vivienne gave Mab an affectionate smile. "Pleasant dreams."

Mab paused at the bottom of the stairs and put her hand on the shell shape at the end of the banister. She let her hand glide over the smooth wood of the railing as she walked up, studying the perfect proportions of the front hall below.

Upstairs, she found the blue room. It felt strange

to walk across the soft carpet. The bed with its turned-down sheet did look inviting. There were bouquets on both bedside tables and a basket full of blue larkspur on the vanity.

Mab removed her makeup and undressed, breathing in the scent of the swamp honeysuckle coming through the window on the night breeze, mingled with the faint salt smell from the sea. Her nightgown was lying across the foot of the bed. Johnny Mae had unpacked for her and everything was hanging in the closet. Mab looked for a minute at the ball gown she had brought for tomorrow night, checking to see if the wrinkles had already shaken out of it. She had packed it carefully in tissue paper.

As she turned out the lights and climbed into bed, another scent drifted toward her from the side window, a heavy, spicy fragrance—tie gardenia bushes must be blooming. The linen sheets were smooth and silky against her body. Stretching out, she was asleep in minutes.

Downstairs, Vivienne walked back to the kitchen to find the three women just finishing up. The roast beef and the turkeys were out of the ovens, and the ham was baked and ready to be made into ham biscuits. Johnny Mae showed Vivienne the asparagus crepes which were to be heated and covered with lobster sauce for the dinner buffet. The Swedish meatballs, curried shrimp, and chicken croquettes in wine sauce were all prepared and stored in the refrigerators.

"Tomorrow first thing we'll bake pecan cups for your luncheon dessert," Estelle said. "Sue will make the ice cream. I didn't want either made too far in advance."

Vivienne nodded. "Everything looks in good shape," she said. "I'll be down early in the morning. Chooky and Baker will be here about nine. Chooky's bringing some dinner desserts from my sister's. He'll serve lunch. I'll tell him about the wines in the morning. Why don't you all go on to bed?"

They said good night, and Vivienne turned out the lights in the other rooms. She had put bouquets of flowers everywhere. The house was ready. The wood gleamed, and the brass and silver shone. The freshly painted walls were in the old hues, colors that had always seemed exactly right. She wondered who had selected them in the beginning. Probably her great-great-grandmother Eugenia Dane. Land's End had been built for Eugenia; the house had been out of Dane hands for two generations when Bascomb bought it for his bride.

Leaving on the hall lights, Vivienne locked the big doors and walked upstairs. Her room was all rose, rose walls and a rose bedspread and rose satin-covered chairs and sofa. She had tried to match the soft color of Land's End's bricks, a shade of rose that always reminded her of home.

She sat down at her dressing table to remove her makeup. Patting on Pier Auge night cream, she looked critically at her face in the mirror. The rose light bathing her face was a becoming color. She might not look this good in full daylight, she thought.

When she finished creaming her face she went to one of the front windows and pulled back the draperies. The columns of the second-story porch gleamed white in the moonlight. Below her, the lawn was lit from the porch light. Tomorrow people would throng over it. And among them would be Philip.

Vivienne sighed and wondered again if Philip ever thought of her. She tried to stop such thoughts. If she lost sleep over Philip now, she'd look like a hag tomorrow.

Just let the weekend happen, she told herself. Don't try to plan it. Put your mind on something else.

She stared down at the just-cut lawn below and imagined running across it barefoot. In her youth the Dane girls hadn't been allowed to go barefoot anywhere that anyone could see them. She remembered the tickle of pine needles in the woods against the

345

soles of her feet. She had secretly walked barefoot in the woods, but she had never run across the front lawn. Maybe she should do it tomorrow morning, she thought, run over the dew-wet grass. In the back of her mind was a line from some play: "Barefoot all their days, and loved green lawns beneath their dancing feet."

Vivienne leaned her head against her hands and stared out at the grass.

XVIII

Daisy had gone to bed that Friday night not expecting to be able to sleep, and she woke up the next morning surprised to find that she had. Cracks of light could be seen under the blinds at her windows. The house was still. There was no sound from the bedroom across the hall.

Getting out of bed, she went to open a window shade. The sun was shining on the snowball bushes that bloomed in the garden. Scarcely a cloud could be seen in the sky, and the air was cool for June. The weather had turned beautiful the day before.

Daisy grabbed her bathrobe, slipped it on and walked downstairs. The kitchen was deserted. Chooky and Baker were both reporting to Land's End today. Daisy put water on to boil and sat down at the kitchen table, staring at some sparrows pecking sunflower seeds at the feeding station on the porch. In the garden beyond, dozens of birds were singing. She recognized a mockingbird's song. When the kettle boiled, she fixed a cup of coffee and sat with it between her hands, looking out the window at the birds.

The day really had come. She was going to see Philip Alexander in a matter of hours. Last night he had called Champ from Columbia, where he was staying overnight. He had come to America and he intended to marry her. She might shrink in horror before such a prospect, but there it was, and she had to face it. A phrase from the wedding service came into her mind, "In the fear of God." She would be marrying

347

in fear, all right, but not of God. She closed her eyes and said a prayer: "Don't let it happen, please. Let something change his mind." She squeezed her eyes tightly shut and repeated the prayer several times.

"Daisy! You're up already."

Cypriana spoke from the doorway and Daisy opened her eyes, startled. Cypri was standing in her blue satin bathrobe, stretching. Behind Cypri Daisy could hear Champ coming downstairs.

"Champ's going to make us scrambled eggs since Chooky isn't here," Cypriana said. "Isn't this a beautiful morning? Aren't we lucky?"

Champ, in plaid bathrobe and slippers, appeared and greeted Daisy cheerfully. He checked the birds at the feeder and looked into the refrigerator for the eggs.

"Now you may think I don't know anything about this, but I do," he said. "The finest scrambled eggs are achieved by breaking the eggs whole into the pan, and then stirring cream in at exactly the right second."

While Daisy poured orange juice for them all and put on more water to boil, Cypri sat down and yawned.

"It was hard to get up so early," Cypri said, blinking. "But I want to have plenty of time to get ready. And Philip might be here early." She glanced at Daisy. "If I'm not mistaken, he's bringing a surprise for you, Daisy."

No doubt, Daisy thought. There were going to be plenty of surprises this weekend. She said nothing in return. Champ cracked eggs.

Cypriana looked Daisy over. She was pretty, but hunching around huddled in her gray bathrobe, Daisy lacked glamor. Never mind. Inside that gray chrysalis was a butterfly. The dress Cypri had picked out for Daisy to wear that morning was perfect with her blond hair. Philip would be entranced. And tonight, in the strapless white lace gown that Cypri had given Daisy as a gift, Daisy would be both beautiful and bridelike. Cypriana smiled with satisfaction.

348

"How are you feeling today, Daisy?" Champ asked. "Ready for all the excitement?"

The kettle whistled. Daisy carefully measured out instant coffee into mugs and added hot water.

"I'll be glad to see Mab again," she said, not answering Champ directly.

Taking a sip of coffee, Cypri gave Champ a dark look. She wished he'd stop asking leading questions of Daisy. Why couldn't Champ understand that she was trying to bring a nervous mare up to a jump and make her go over? She didn't want spectators standing on the sidelines waving things.

"Don't burn the eggs," Cypri said.

"What? Me burn the eggs? Seems to me you're the one who burns the eggs. Remember the whole dozen that went up in smoke on Chooky's day off last week? You were on the telephone telling Celia Honeychurch the plot of *Carrie*."

Champ chuckled as he spoke. He seemed in a very good humor, Cypri thought. He'd better watch his *p*'s and *q*'s or she'd fix him.

"Here you are, madam." Champ handed Cypri a plate. "Fit for consumption, anyway."

While Daisy poked at her eggs, Cypri wondered if perhaps Daisy should change her nail polish. The light coral color she was wearing wasn't too dynamic. Cypri looked at her own long brown-orange nails with satisfaction. They would be perfect with her dress tonight.

The telephone on the counter rang and Cypri, moving the phone to the table, picked up the receiver. It was Celia Honeychurch. Celia had recently landed one of the Royals, a dumb cousin of Cypri's named Donald, but the course of the engagement was proving stormy, and Cypri was often called for counsel. She usually advised severe measures. This morning she cut off Celia's tale by sharply advising her to tell Donald to stick his head in a commode. "Not until after tonight, though," she added as an afterthought.

"He has to bring you to the ball. It's going to be the party of the century."

Champ ruffled Cypri's hair as he passed behind her chair, and she shook his hand off impatiently, trying to straighten out Celia and drink her coffee and decide about Daisy's nail polish all at the same time.

"Look, Celia, Philip's on his way here already. We should be dressing, Daisy and I. I'll see you tonight, okay? Hang in there." Cypri put down the receiver. "Let Champ stick the dishes in the dishwasher, Daisy. We should start dressing."

It was only nine o'clock, but Daisy didn't argue. She followed Cypri upstairs. She refused to change her nail polish, but she did go ahead and take a bath and fix her face.

"I love that dress on you!" Cypri said, opening the door. Daisy had just pulled on the straight turquoise linen sheath and was adjusting the straps over her shoulders. "That color is sensational on a blond. You look wonderful. Are you ready? Come on downstairs. Do you want a drink?"

"A drink?" Daisy asked, obediently following Cypri downstairs. "At ten-thirty in the morning?"

"Well, I thought, you know, to sort of relax and celebrate."

"You mean to get me drunk so I won't know what's happening."

At the bottom of the stairs, Cypri turned slowly. Her eyes flashed up to her cousin's face as Daisy came down the last step. Daisy gave Cypri as cold a look as she could manage, and Cypri giggled.

"I know all the tricks in your book," Daisy said, speaking softly since Champ was sitting in the sun-room.

Cypri looked at her through her dark lashes.

"Baby, I've got tricks you've never imagined," she murmured, licking her full lower lip.

Daisy flushed all over. She grasped the banister railing. Oh, God, Cypri could always make her do

anything. Anything at all. She felt sick, staring at her cousin. Cypri was wearing a black dress of thin cotton. The low-cut, sleeveless top was trimmed with black eyelet lace, and the skirt fell gracefully into handkerchief points. The black of the dress and of Cypri's long hair made her eyes show up in startling contrast. As Daisy looked at her, Cypri smiled, deliberately letting her dimple come out, and then she pulled Daisy into the sunroom.

"Doesn't Daisy look great?" Cypri asked Champ.

Champ folded away his newspaper, stood up and admired them both. Before anything else could be said, they heard a car drive up the driveway.

"It's Philip!" Cypri and Champ said at the same time.

From the sunroom windows they watched a blue Dodge Charger stop in front. The door opened and Philip emerged.

"We just made *that* under the wire," Cypri said. "Didn't I tell you he'd be early?"

Champ ran down to the car, embraced his brother and heartily shook his hand. When the two men turned and started back toward the house, Cypri was struck by how much taller Philip was, a head taller than Champ, at least. They had the same muscular build, but Champ's sandy hair and engaging grin marked him as the younger brother. Philip's swarthy face and self-confident bearing gave him a more dangerous look, not as open and predictable as Champ.

Cypri pulled Daisy away from the window and out to the front porch. As Philip approached, they could see that he looked less drawn than he had at their last encounter. His eyes were clear, his face fuller. He seemed in the pink of condition, as if, Cypri thought, he had been exercising with dumb-bells every day. He was dressed in an elegantly-cut gray suit and vest, with a white shirt and a crisp blue-and-white striped tie. He gave the occupants of the porch a wide smile as he came up the steps.

"How beautiful you two look," he said warmly.

Cypri put her arms around Philip and hugged him, letting him kiss her on both cheeks.

He released her and turned to Daisy. "My dear," he said. Gently, he took Daisy's hand, held it between his hands for a moment, and then kissed her briefly and carefully on one cheek. Daisy managed to keep herself from shrinking back, and in a second it was all over with.

"Come in," Cypri said, leading the way to the sunroom. "How was your trip?"

They talked about the weather and Eyreville and Philip's flight over, a jumble of topics, and the first few moments went well. Daisy was allowed to be quiet, and Cypri played hostess and manager of the weekend. But then Philip turned to Daisy.

"I've brought you something, Daisy," he said.

Smiling, he drew a little red velvet jeweler's box out of his breast pocket and handed it to Daisy. "See if this fits."

Daisy stopped breathing as the velvet box was pressed into her hand. Everyone looked at her. Daisy had never wanted to perform any action in her life less than she wanted to open the lid of that box.

Inside was a huge diamond ring.

"Oh, how gorgeous!" Cypri cried, jumping up to look over Daisy's shoulder.

Daisy looked up at Philip.

"Cypriana told me your ring size, Daisy," Philip said. "I hope she was right." Philip smiled again into Daisy's shocked blue eyes.

"Oh, I can't—I—" Daisy stopped, looking down at the floor.

"Try it on," Cypri said. There seemed to Daisy to be a menacing note in Cypri's voice. With trembling fingers, Daisy picked up the sparkling ring and slipped it onto the third finger of her right hand.

"Your *left* hand, idiot," Cypri said. Impatiently, Cypri wished she could grab Philip's ring away from

Daisy and jam it onto Daisy's left hand herself. But Daisy slid the ring off again without even admiring it. She fitted it back into the box, closed the velvet lid and looked up at Philip.

"Thank you," she said, as steadily as she could manage. "I'll put it on later. You know, I have to— get used to the idea." She felt herself flushing. Beyond Philip's shoulder, Daisy caught sight of Champ's face. Champ looked puzzled.

Well, that was odd, Champ thought. But Philip's presentation of the ring had been rather public. Perhaps Daisy would have preferred to be alone with him when he offered it. Perhaps Daisy was romantic. Cypri, Champ knew, would not be so picky. She'd grab any jewel she could get her mitts on. With a grin, Champ looked over at his wife. Cypri was staring at the box in Daisy's hand with a deep frown. Catching Champ's look, Cypri tossed her head and restrained herself from punching Daisy in the back. She was vastly annoyed, but she concealed it as well as she could.

"You all know we're due at Land's End," she said, her voice tight. "So why don't we go right on out there? Unless you'd like some coffee first, Philip?"

Philip declined, and Cypri thought for a moment.

"I'll ride with Philip, all right, Champ? He'll want his own car out there. You bring Daisy in the Porsche." Cypri touched Philip's arm and managed a winsome smile. "That is, if you're ready to go now, Philip?"

Philip gave Daisy a glance, as if to say he regretted that Cypri hadn't made a more logical arrangement for the drive. But Daisy was thankful. She had been afraid Cypri would decree that the two women drive out together. Daisy dreaded hearing what Cypri was going to say to her on the subject of Philip's ring. But she just couldn't put it on. She had to forestall that final capitulation. *Surely* something would happen first, and she would never have to wear it.

353

She stuck the box into her pocketbook as they went out the door.

At Land's End, Vivienne awakened to find that she had no time for running over lawns. When she opened her eyes, the bedroom was suffused with the rose light of sunshine striking through the draperies. Looking over at the clock, she saw that it was already eight-thirty. She threw back the sheet and went quickly to pull the curtains open. Sunshine flooded in. A slight breeze was coming from the water, and she could smell the sweet bays at the side of the house. The day would be perfect, she thought; warm but pleasant. Below, the lawn sparkled with dew just drying. At the edge of the lawn, the yellow jasmine vines bloomed brightly, twined in the bordering pine trees on the left of the drive. She took a deep breath and caught the jasmine fragrance on the fresh air. As she stared out, Cypri's yellow station wagon turned into the drive. Chooky, she saw, was driving and Baker sat beside him.

Trying not to think about who the next arrivals would be, Vivienne pulled on a pair of jeans and a shirt and hurried downstairs. Passing through the up-stairs hall she noticed that Mab's door was still closed.

The aroma of coffee and bacon greeted her at the door of the kitchen. Estelle, Johnny Mae and Sue were working already. Baker and Chooky, their arms loaded with pies, walked in just as Vivienne arrived, and there was a chorus of "Morning, Miss Vivienne."

"The coffee is fresh. We've eaten breakfast already," Johnny Mae said. "Would you like your cereal now?"

As Johnny Mae poured her a cup of coffee, Vivienne summoned Chooky to the kitchen table, and asked Sue to help Baker unload the car.

"Chooky, please serve champagne in the drawing room when the others arrive. Take a couple of bottles from the guest-house refrigerator. Then we'll drink the Pouilly Fuisse at luncheon. Just coffee with dessert

unless someone wants a liqueur. There's Kahlua and so on in the buffet in the dining room. Do you remember where the small liqueur glasses are kept?"

Chooky nodded. "Miss Vivienne," he said, "it's sure good to be home. The house looks grand."

"Chooky, thank you." Vivienne felt pleased. "Baker, what do you think? Is it like old times?"

Baker, who had just come in carrying two pecan pies, smiled. "I love Land's End. I'm so glad it's yours again," she said.

Vivienne hesitated.

"Baker, I want your grandmother back here, but I'm not sure it would be a permanent job. I was afraid to ask her to leave the Parkers."

Baker nodded. "She understands."

Johnny Mae brought Vivienne a bowl of hot bran covered with buttermilk and Chooky left to check the supply of glasses. There was to be a bar and several bartenders that evening, and forty bottles of champagne were chilling in the guest-house kitchen.

Vivienne had finished her cereal and was pouring herself another cup of coffee when Mab appeared at the kitchen door.

"Oh, you're up," Vivienne said. "How did you sleep?"

Mab looked radiant. She was wrapped in a cherry-colored negligee and her tipped-up eyes were sparkling. "That bed is great," she said.

After Mab said good morning to everyone, she drank a cup of coffee and helped settle details of the evening, volunteering to supervise the decoration of the buffet table.

"Everything else is set," Vivienne said. "I hope you can just relax and be a guest."

Vivienne felt anything but relaxed herself. The moment of Philip's arrival was approaching fast. She glanced at the kitchen clock.

"Let's get dressed, Mab. They might get here early."

355

"Cypri early? That would truly be an occasion," Mab said, following Vivienne up the stairs.

"You never can tell," Vivienne said vaguely, as if her mind were somewhere else.

Leaving Mab in the hall, Vivienne went directly to her bathroom and ran hot water into the tub, adding an herbal essence to the water that turned it jade green and made the room smell like grass. While the tub filled she snipped off the tops of two Vitamin A capsules and mixed the fishy liquid with some cold cream. She rubbed her face with this mixture and got into the bath. A large glass pitcher of rainwater from the cistern in back stood next to the tub. Vivienne dipped two washcloths into the rainwater and draped them over her face, lying back in the hot water.

As the long moments under the washcloths passed, Vivienne could think of nothing but Philip. Was she actually going to see him? To touch his hand? Or would he shake hands? God knows, they hadn't parted friends. But that was so long ago.

It would soon be over, she told herself. The worst part, the first moment of meeting, would soon be over.

She took the cloths off her face and shampooed her hair. She felt jumpy, no denying that. Rather the way she felt on opening nights. Quickly, she dried off and went into her bedroom.

The sunshine was still streaming in. She blew her hair dry, made up her face, and took a dress from the closet, one she had bought in New York before she left. She had considered having her hair and makeup done for her, but she thought she looked younger when she did them herself. Less professionally perfect, but younger. Even tonight, she wanted to do everything herself.

She pulled the dress on and looked in the mirror. The outfit was very becoming, the shirt a soft ivory cotton petticoat and the top a camisole laced with blue ribbon. She rubbed some blusher on her shoulders and in between the blue laces in front, where the curve of

356

her breasts showed. Then she lingered before the mirror, looking closely for signs of age. But that was silly. Everyone got older. Suddenly, she felt sharply depressed.

In the room across the hall, Mab made up her eyes slowly, brushing on moss green and celery shades. The dress she put on was a thin moss-green cotton with a pleated skirt and a bloused top. At the waist, she tied a large triangular scarf of blue paisley bordered with dark green, arranging it so that the point fell over one hip. It took Mab a few minutes to get it right. When she was finished, she was pleased. It was exactly the sort of dress she liked best, and the soft shade of green contrasted well with her brown hair and eyes.

What had Philip said about her brown eyes? Something about her being all brown when he met her that morning in London; she couldn't remember his exact remark. She had been flustered at the time. She just remembered that he had complimented her. She met her eyes in the mirror, and gave herself a long look. Whatever Philip thought, meeting her today, it could make no difference. She had to remember that. What did it matter if he thought she were pretty? He knew the rest, too, didn't he?

Mab's cheeks felt hot, and she turned hastily away from the mirror, crossed the soft-carpeted floor and went out to the hall. Vivienne came out of her room just at that moment, and they admired one another's dresses before walking together down the stairs.

"Vivienne," Mab said, "has it really been twenty years since you've seen Philip?"

Vivienne was slightly ahead of her, and Mab couldn't see her sister's expression; Vivienne didn't turn around.

"That's right," Vivienne said. The tone of her voice was uninformative, and Mab wished she could see her sister's face.

However, Vivienne briskly led the way into the drawing room. She seemed on the point of pacing up and down. Instead, she walked to a table and rearranged a bowl of roses.

"Damn!" she said.

"What?"

"Just pricked my finger."

Mab wandered over to look out the front windows. Vivienne sucked her finger, then she began to rearrange a few objects on the mantel over the fireplace.

"What are we having for lunch?" Mab asked, in order to say something.

"Oh. Artichokes first. Then crabmeat salad and rice with almonds. And biscuits. Think that's enough? For dessert, Estelle is making Ella's specialty. She got the recipe for pecan cups."

"You don't mean that heavenly—"

"Yes." Vivienne turned and smiled. "That heavenly thing. Pecan cups filled with peppermint stick ice cream and served with hot fudge sauce. I couldn't resist having it once more in my life. Remember Sunday dinners?"

"Do I!"

Vivienne was making perfect sense and yet, Mab thought, her mind still didn't seem to be on what she was saying. Both of them glanced often at the open front windows. Vivienne sat down and got up again.

"Maybe I should check what's happening in the kitchen."

Estelle spoke from the door. "Miss Vivienne? Telephone."

"Oh. I'll take it in the library." Vivienne excused herself and went off.

Mab walked over to the side windows and looked out toward the rose garden. The lawn and garden looked well-tended.

What was it like, to live here again as Vivienne was doing? Mab wondered. Land's End—it had so much to do with things that were over: the lives of their parents, their own childhoods, a way of life that was gone. Land's End seemed to have no link with the future, only with the past. And now they would recreate that past for one elegant weekend, as if Land's End had been restored just for that moment in time.

Mab's thoughts were interrupted as Vivienne came back in, looking annoyed.

"Can you imagine? Clancy called to say *People* magazine is interested in Land's End. He begged me to let them do a story. Really!" Vivienne's tone was indignant. "I gave Clance a piece of my mind. He wants everything I do or say to go immediately into print. Land's End indeed." Her eyes flashed. The color had come up into her cheeks, and Mab laughed.

"You look exactly—" she began.

Before she could finish, they heard a car turn into the drive. They moved together to look out the windows. The Alexanders' silver Porsche was pulling in and a blue Dodge Charger was right behind it.

"They're here," Vivienne said in a low voice. She didn't move. Mab started toward the open double doors.

The cars stopped in the side drive and the guests could be heard coming up the front path. Since Vivienne made no move to greet them, Mab walked into the front hall and over to the screen door. She could hear Cypri's voice as she came up the steps.

Standing beside the window in the drawing room, Vivienne took a moment to compose herself. By the time the group had crossed the porch she was ready to appear in the hall to greet her guests as they came in. Champ held the door for Cypriana and Daisy, and then he and Philip followed.

Philip's initial glance included Mab and Vivienne in a fleeting manner. Before he could speak, the awkwardness of the first moment was dispelled by Cypri flinging herself into Mab's arms.

"Welcome home! Isn't this great?" she said. Cypri seemed in high good spirits. "Mab, don't you love it?"

Vivienne smiled at Daisy and Champ. Finally, when

359

she could avoid it no longer, she lifted her head slightly and looked at Philip.

"How are you, Philip?" Vivienne's voice came out sounding huskier than usual.

For just a moment his dark eyes met hers.

Every detail of Philip's expression at that moment registered on Vivienne. He was older in appearance, but the essential Philip was unchanged; she noticed that in the first second. Her eyes tried to hold his and read them, but he looked immediately away. She was left with only the comfort of knowing that the sight of her older self had not provoked a drawing-back of surprise. Perhaps she could simply thank his damned imperturbable English manners for that.

But what did she expect? It was perfectly possible for one person to feel a hundred emotions when meeting another, and for the other to feel none. Perhaps Philip was thinking about lunch, or unpacking, or where to wash up as he looked around the hall. Vivienne's eyes followed Philip's, and she caught sight of her face reflected in the glass case of the hall clock. She shivered; all her senses suddenly seemed unnaturally keen; some moment lodged in her memory long ago was disturbed by the face in the clock case. Hadn't she once looked fleetingly up at the clock and then at Philip's face, surprising a look of total attention there, as if he were memorizing her features so that his brain could produce a reproduction of her, a holograph? Hadn't she laughed at that intent look on his face, and hadn't he said something nonsensical about the camera in his mind? Something about how it operated on kisses?

Vivienne moved her eyes away from the glass reflection and looked at Philip again. Had he looked at the clock case too, and then hastily withdrawn his own eyes? She almost thought he had. She told herself that she had to calm down, to feel less. But they *couldn't* meet like this, so coolly. Wasn't some sort of acknowledgment due what they had once been to each other? Shouldn't they at least feel a pang?

But Philip stood very still, seemed very composed, there in the front hall of Land's End.

Vivienne's acting talent stood between her and any spontaneous betrayal of emotion. To anyone watching her, she was the epitome of elegant good breeding. Smiling at her guests, she turned and spoke to Daisy. Irresistibly, Philip's eyes were drawn toward her again, but Vivienne was no longer looking at him.

He could take her in a little more calmly now, notice the details of her appearance. He was struck by her air of quiet good humor. It did seem that something more should mark the occasion of their meeting. After the brightness outside, the cool oyster gray-green of the walls inside made Philip feel as if he were suddenly plunged a fathom deep in water. It was hard to breathe. His mind went back to the first time he had seen this hall, over a quarter of a century ago. Then, too, he had felt very much out of his element, as the girl Vivienne led him across what seemed a vast glimmering green space to meet her mother. Hadn't there just been a thunderstorm? Something came back to Philip about raindrops on the windows and the sun coming out; in any case his recollection had a rainy edge. But today, the weather was beautiful, China Dane was absent from the scene, and certainly Philip Alexander was not going to lose his bearings.

Vivienne turned, leading the way across the hall again; from the back, her hair seemed quite the same to Philip, long and dark down her shoulders. The whole party began to move. Philip was scarcely conscious of his legs; he felt as if he were swimming, rather than walking, toward the drawing room. Mab appeared beside him dressed in green, looking like a water nymph. As Cypriana and Daisy paused in the drawing room entrance to exclaim over the finished perfection of the room, Philip turned to Mab.

"You're very cool and lovely, all in sea green," he said. "How are affairs in Chicago?"

As Mab replied to his question, she moved inside the drawing room and seated herself on one of the satin sofas. After an instant's hesitation, Philip took a seat beside her. Mab was smiling at him; it seemed a safe port. The others formed a circle, Cypri sitting in a chair and Champ on a footstool, Daisy and Vivienne sharing the opposite sofa.

As soon as they were settled, Chooky wheeled in the tea cart with iced champagne and a tray of glasses.

"I thought we'd toast the occasion," Vivienne said. Her voice was still throatier than usual, she noticed. She wondered if any of them were curious as to what occasion she meant; perhaps she should have said "our return to Land's End." The smile on her face felt fixed there. She watched Mab take a glass of champagne from Chooky and sip it, looking up at Philip.

"How is everything in London?" Mab asked.

"Very busy. I was lucky to get away," Philip said, presenting only his distinguished profile to Vivienne.

Turning away, Vivienne said to her cousin beside her, "Oh, Daisy, your ball dresses were brought out yesterday; they're hanging in your room upstairs." Vivienne noticed that Daisy looked rather ill at ease. "Cypri and Champ are to be in the back bedroom on the right, and you are across from them."

Since Philip's conversation with Mab had reached a pause, Champ took over. "Philip," he said, "I told the folks that probably you would visit over there tomorrow. Unless you want to run over this afternoon? Of course, they'll be here for the ball tonight."

"Tomorrow will be fine," Philip replied.

They all chatted politely for a few minutes with nothing particular being said, until Estelle appeared in the doorway, to announce "Telephone for Miss Cypriana."

As Cypri left for the library Philip turned again to Mab.

"How many people are coming this evening?"

"Let's see—fifty, sixty, did you say, Vivienne?"

Vivienne looked over at them, pushing her dark hair back with her hand.

"As many as Cypriana can get to come," she said.

Chooky refilled glasses. As he opened a third bottle, Cypri appeared again.

"It was Charles Honeychurch," she said. "I told him Damn the Torpedoes could set up starting at five this afternoon. Is that okay, Viv?"

Vivienne nodded.

"Philip, shall we unload your suitcases?" Champ asked.

"I have just one." Philip looked in the direction of Vivienne without quite meeting her eyes. "Where am I to put up?"

The question hung in the air—was it of any interest to anyone except Philip? Vivienne wondered. Did Daisy want to steal in, in the middle of the night, and cuddle with him? The stiff way Daisy sat on the sofa clutching her untouched wineglass seemed to indicate that his bed would be chaste.

"The cookhouse is now the guest house," she said as if she were making a general announcement. "I imagine Chooky has already brought in the suitcases."

"Oh, I haven't seen the guest house yet," Mab said. "If you're going to show Philip his room, Viv, may I go along?"

"Of course. Anyone else want a tour?"

The others stayed with the champagne, so Vivienne led Philip and Mab through the hall and across the back porch to the walkway. They went up the steps that led to the second-story porch of the guest house, and Vivienne opened the door.

"Oh, I like it! It's lovely," Mab said, looking in.

"It was once two bedrooms, remember? We knocked out the wall."

363

The guest room was now very large. The walls were painted pale brown, and the floor was covered with a thick beige carpet. A brown velvet sofa and chairs formed a sitting area beside a white brick fireplace. Beyond a large gold screen stood a king-sized bed, a dresser and a wall of closets.

"The bath is in there," Vivienne said, waving at a door. "I hope you'll be comfortable."

How strange it was to be showing Philip to a guest room in her house! Through the back windows, the rose barn was in plain sight. Philip had to see it. The three of them stood looking at the room. The draperies and bedspread were in a soft, heavy, woven material of a straw shade. There were yellow daisies in a glass bowl on the low table beside the sofa. Philip's suitcase had been placed on a stand at the end of the bed. And the rose barn was outside the windows. He looked that way, but his expression did not change, as far as Vivienne could tell.

Mab asked Vivienne a question about the rooms downstairs, breaking the silence.

"Oh. A kitchen and another bedroom—Johnny Mae Jones stays there now," Vivienne said. "And that reminds me, it's time for lunch."

She turned, and Mab and Philip went back with her to the drawing room to gather the others. They all moved rather stiffly toward the dining room. Somehow Philip hadn't pictured this part at all, going into the dining room of Land's End, where he had glimpsed Bascomb Dane sitting grandly at the head of the table directing the servants so many years ago. Now Vivienne asked Champ and Cypriana to sit at the ends of the table; she suggested Daisy sit next to Philip on one side, and she took a place beside Mab on the other. Chooky came in with the artichokes.

After a small pause, Cypri asked Philip what the English thought of the President. Philip seized the topic, and politics lasted well into the main course.

Then Champ reported on the current state of Eyreville High's football team.

The white wine had been around several times at this point, and Vivienne had begun to feel more comfortable. It was silly to feel constrained, to keep wondering what Philip was thinking. She looked down the table. Daisy did not say much. Cypri was full of chat.

Mab seemed to listen closely to whatever Philip said—Mab had always been very polite. The luncheon party appeared to be going well, Vivienne thought.

When the dessert arrived, it was acclaimed.

"This is my favorite thing in the world," Cypri said, pouring on the chocolate syrup. "Do they have pecans in England, Philip?"

"There are fewer pecans than there are beautiful southern women," Philip replied. "South Carolina has the exclusive supply of both." He glanced around the table.

"Eat your last pecan cup then, Daisy," Cypri said, looking at her cousin. "I'll have to bring you some pecans when I come to visit London, which will be often." She stressed the last words and glanced from Daisy to Champ. Vivienne and Mab both looked at Philip. He smiled at Daisy.

"There will be sacrifices involved," he said. "Not only pecans, I'm afraid, but, okra, black-eyed peas and—what are those greens? Mustard greens? We've none of those."

Silence fell after his remark.

Daisy did not smile, but Philip seemed undisturbed. With all eyes in the room upon him, he looked at Daisy for a moment longer and then turned back and took another spoonful of peppermint ice cream.

So it *was* true, Vivienne thought. Philip did intend to marry Daisy! She was so surprised to hear Philip confirm it that she sat immobile, merely staring at Champ, who was asking her a question.

Mab looked across the table and studied Philip's face. Philip simply looked pleasant as he ate his ice cream. But he did mean to marry Daisy, Mab thought—he really did. The idea was astounding. It wasn't just a wild notion of Cypri's, then, as Vivienne had said. Philip really meant to marry Daisy.

At last Vivienne recovered. "Excuse me, Champ?" she said.

Champ, looking at Daisy, had forgotten what he had asked. "Uh," he said. "Nothing. Oh, I asked if you could ever get mustard greens in New York?"

"Mustard greens." Vivienne repeated the words without seeming to take in their meaning. If Champ had asked her about the situation in Poland, she couldn't have looked blanker. Champ gave up and looked back at Daisy to study her odd expression.

"You aren't eating your pecan cup while you may?" Champ asked, indicating Daisy's nearly-untouched plate. But she, too, seemed abstracted and didn't answer.

Cypriana wondered that she had fallen in with such a dull lot. What was the matter with everyone! They were just talking at random. She heard Mab ask Philip if marrow, which she had eaten in England, was a vegetable? Philip smiled and confessed he had no idea.

Enough about vegetables, Cypri thought, and spoke up briskly: "What are we going to do this afternoon? We can play golf or tennis. Philip, you can borrow any equipment you need from Champ. Or else we can just go lie around the pool at the club." Cypri looked down the table and was pleased to see that she had gotten everyone's attention.

Philip turned to Daisy.

"What would you like to do, Daisy?"

Daisy was so little used to being singled out and consulted about what she would like to do that she stared back at Philip blankly for a moment.

"Oh, please—do what you like," she managed finally.

"Philip means, Which do you play better, tennis or golf?" Cypri said. "And I have to answer, Philip, that

366

you should choose golf. Unless you like to play tennis in slow motion. All Daisy can do is lob."

"Mab? Vivienne?" Champ asked, "What will it be for you?"

"Are we all going to the club?" Mab asked. "I said I'd decorate the table for tonight."

"We'll take plenty of cars and you can come back when you want to," Cypri said.

Under Cypri's organization, their decisions were made. Vivienne offered to play tennis with Cypriana, and Champ and Mab decided to join Philip and Daisy at golf.

"I was planning tea in the library at four-thirty," Vivienne said. "That will give us enough time afterward to dress."

"I usually need three hours," Champ said. "It takes time to get the shirt ruffles just right."

Cypriana didn't hear this remark. She was looking at Daisy.

"Daisy, come here," she said. "I want to show you something in the library."

As the others went off to change, Daisy followed Cypri into the library with a feeling of apprehension. Cypri closed the door and turned to face her.

"Are you out of your mind?" she asked, spacing each word. Her tone of voice was very sharp. "Philip brings you that enormous rock and you're too good to wear it?"

"Cypri, please." Daisy looked down. She hated to see Cypri's blue eyes blazing at her. "It's just—I just don't want to. I didn't expect any ring. I—didn't want any ring. It's too final."

"Everything is final," Cypri said, emphasizing each word. "Unless you blow it by acting like an idiot. And if you do that—" Cypri paused, suddenly struck by a new idea. "Or wait. Maybe that's it. Maybe Philip is intrigued by the hard-to-get bit." Cypri's eyes gleamed as she evaluated that thought.

Daisy sighed.

"Cypri, everything in life isn't just a scheme to make someone bend to your will. People—"

Cypri's eyes flashed up to Daisy's face. "Don't you dare give me a lecture," she said. "I've had it with you, cousin Daisy." She raised her hand and slapped Daisy hard across the cheek.

"Oh!" Daisy gasped with surprise and put her hand up to her face. As she shrank back, the door of the library opened and Champ stepped inside.

"What are you doing?" he said, taking in the scene. "What—Cypri?"

Tears came into Daisy's eyes and she turned away. Champ closed the door behind him.

"What's going on in here, Cypri? Are you trying to boss Daisy around again? You didn't slap her?" Champ looked angry. Cypriana raised her chin.

"Stay out of this, Champ," she said. "I'm warning you."

Champ walked to Daisy's side. "What is it, hon?" he asked her gently. "Why are you two fighting?"

Daisy shook her head, blinking back her tears.

"It's all right," Daisy said softly. She kept her head turned away so Champ couldn't see her cheek. "It was just something between us."

Champ took Daisy's arm.

"That's not good enough," he said. "Come on, now, tell me what's wrong. Is it something to do with Philip? I can talk to him—"

Champ spoke to Daisy as if he were coaxing a child, and Cypriana's rage boiled over. She longed to smack Champ too, and she barely managed to contain the impulse.

"Oh," she cried, "You fool! Leave Daisy alone!"

"You dominate her too much, Cypri." Champ patted Daisy's arm and tried to see the expression on her averted face. "Daisy has a right to do things her own way. Maybe she doesn't want a big engagement ball or a big wedding." This was a pure guess on Champ's part, but he knew Daisy was extremely shy. "Let her do what she wants, Cypri."

Daisy felt tears come into her eyes again at Champ's words. She wished life were that simple, that they were only quarreling over the size of the wedding. In a moment she'd be sobbing aloud.

Cypri thought that if she watched Champ sympathize with stupid Daisy for one more second she would leap on him and scratch his face. She couldn't endure watching him comfort her dumb cousin and, uttering a cry of fury, she wheeled, tore the door open and rushed out. She didn't see Great-Aunt Martha Austin until too late. Baker had just opened the front door to admit Aunt Martha and Chang, and as they entered Cypri ran full tilt into her aunt.

"Mercy!" Great-aunt Martha spun completely around as Cypriana brushed past to rush headlong up the staircase. Chang leaped sideways, yelped with surprise, and began to bark excitedly. He chased Cypriana up the stairs. Baker grabbed the basket on Great-aunt Martha's arm, saving the two bottles of rare brandy Aunt Martha was bringing out to the house party, but the ring cake baked by Susan, which Aunt Martha was holding in her other hand, was dashed off its plate onto the floor.

"My goodness!" Aunt Martha cried.

Champ saw the collision from the library. He dropped Daisy's arm and sprang to Aunt Martha's side. Upstairs, a door slammed. After a final bark Chang raced back downstairs, tore around the hall once and then nosed the broken ring cake. Daisy watched through the open door as Champ righted Aunt Martha and apologized. Baker took the basket.

"Well I never," Aunt Martha said. "What's going on out here? *She* was in a hurry. I've brought you some brandy, Beauchamp. Where's that brother of yours?"

As she spoke, Philip appeared at the back door. He had changed into white flannel trousers and a knit shirt. He joined them, glancing curiously at Chang

369

eating the remains of the cake on the floor, and greeted Aunt Martha. Leaving Baker to clean up, they all moved into the library.

As they entered, Daisy quickly brushed away her tears. She hoped her cheek wasn't still red where Cypri had slapped her. Surreptitiously, she pinched the other cheek so that the two would match, and then greeted her aunt.

Aunt Martha sat down, accepted a glass of sherry from Champ to recover herself, and looked up at Philip.

"So you're going to marry little Daisy and take her off to England?" she said. "She's used to central heating, you know." She peered at Philip with her bright eyes. "She'll catch cold."

Philip smiled. "I promise to keep her warm," he said, looking at Daisy with a smile. Daisy blushed and Champ grinned.

"I was in England only once," Aunt Martha said. "I stopped there on my way to Belgium to buy tablecloths. King Edward had just died. There was no central heating."

Mab, dressed in a blue madras pants outfit, ready for golf, came through the library door and greeted her aunt.

"You look very well, Mab," Aunt Martha said. She had never clearly understood Mab's job, having confused a curator with a janitor in her mind and come up with a vision of Mab dusting off paintings with a feather duster somewhere in Chicago. Now she solicitously inquired whether Mab was still cleaning pictures.

"Yes, the same job at the museum," Mab answered, smiling.

"Extraordinary you should end up in Chicago," Aunt Martha said. "My uncle Harold was there during the Great Fire. He escaped injury, but came home very shaken. He didn't care for the North. He said, he made the coachman pull up, and he got out

370

and kissed the Mason-Dixon line when he crossed it coming home."

"You know, I think I felt a bit the same, Miss Austin," Philip said. "I was very happy to see Eyreville again."

Aunt Martha turned her attention to him.

"You must come and have some sherry with me while you are here," she said. "You and Daisy. I want to discuss the wedding with you. I plan to give it for Daisy, you know." She glanced at her great-niece.

"Aunt Martha!" Daisy's first reaction was to feel distress at the mention of the ceremony, but after a moment's thought she couldn't help but be touched by Aunt Martha's offer. Aunt Martha had paid for Cypriana's wedding in its entirety, but it had never entered Daisy's head that her aunt meant to do the same for her.

"We will plan it together," Aunt Martha said firmly. "Will it be soon?"

Daisy opened her mouth but said nothing. Mab looked at her, puzzled. Daisy seemed a bit disheveled somehow. Her hair was rather mussed, and she hadn't yet changed her clothes. She appeared somewhat disorganized, Mab thought.

"The sooner we marry, the better," Philip said, his dark eyes on Daisy's face.

Everyone looked at Daisy.

"I like weddings," Aunt Martha said. "Especially outdoor weddings in the summer. Unless it rains."

"We'll visit you tomorrow if we may," Philip said. "Your offer is very kind."

"Daisy is an Austin," Aunt Martha said. "Austin girls make pretty brides. But weddings these days surprise me. At the last one I attended, the bride wore green and climbed down a tree to meet the groom. Extraordinary. Her daughter by her first marriage was the minister who performed the ceremony, and his children by his first and second marriages formed a choir which sang a medley of songs by Rodgers and

Hammerstein. They were divorced again before their first anniversary. Climbed back up her tree, I expect. Charleston people."

In the hall, Chang barked, and Cypriana appeared at the door. Chang padded in, walked over to Aunt Martha and sat down, keeping his eye on Cypri. Cypri had changed into extremely short white shorts and a tee shirt. Greeting only Aunt Martha, she did not look at either Daisy or Champ. In a minute Vivienne appeared behind her, wearing a white tennis dress with a halter top and a short skirt that showed her long legs to advantage.

Aunt Martha rose.

"I'll see you, then, tomorrow," she said, addressing Philip. "Come anytime. Sherry is served at five."

Cypriana looked from Philip to Aunt Martha, but before she could gather what Aunt Martha meant by her words, Aunt Martha was on her way out, Chang at her side.

They all moved in her wake. Cypriana glanced at Daisy's turquoise dress and murmured, "You can change at the club, can't you?" Daisy nodded.

After a short deliberation about who should accompany whom, two station wagons followed Aunt Martha's Lincoln down the road toward Eyreville and the country club.

Mab and Vivienne left the club before the others and returned to Land's End. Vivienne began immediately to direct the laying of tea in the library. Substantial sandwiches and cake and toast should carry them through to a late dinner, she thought.

"How was tennis?" Mab asked Vivienne.

"If you win even one point from Cypri you're lucky. How was the golf game?"

Mab laughed. "Champ and Philip were good; Daisy and I didn't keep score."

Mab declined Vivienne's offer of food, saying she

wanted to get on with decorating the table. Taking just her cup of tea, she went into the dining room where Estelle and Sue awaited her direction.

"Let's see," Mab said. "We can use the long lace tablecloth, and loop it up around the buffet table, like this, and pin up the scallops with ribbons and flowers. Did Vivienne buy the ribbon? Good, just what I told her to get," she said as Estelle showed her lengths of green and yellow. She sent Sue into the garden to cut baby's breath and daisies, and dispatched Estelle to hunt for smilax, to twine around the silver candelabra, the candles on the small tables and the wall sconces.

Mab was glad to have something to do, something to take her away from Philip's presence. It disturbed her to be near him. She had enjoyed watching Philip swing at golf balls, seeing him drive down the fairways with long, competent shots. She had been afraid Daisy would notice her looking at him so often. But the last thing on Daisy's mind seemed to be charming her fiancé. Of course, Daisy was young, and she might simply be shy, but Mab thought that *she* could never have been so long in Philip's presence without at least giving him a smile. Daisy was so grave. Perhaps that was what Philip liked, a female who was reserved and cool. And what else? Mab was surprised at herself. She was actually envious! Well, why shouldn't she envy Daisy? Daisy might have come into their world a poor beaten child, but she had a great deal now— she had youth and beauty and, undoubtedly, physical charms that appealed to Philip. Mab bent her head over her work, wishing she wouldn't have such thoughts. You only hurt yourself by making contrasts, by comparing; hadn't she learned that?

Sue came back with the flowers and Mab directed the making of a long garland to outline the border of the tablecloth. Daisies. How appropriate for decorating Daisy's engagement ball. Mab wondered what it would be like to have an engagement ball. There was a certain heaviness behind her eyes. It surely couldn't be tears?

Estelle arrived with the smilax, and as Mab showed her how to wind the little vines around the candles, they heard the others come in. Vivienne called them into the library.

For a while, Mab kept pinning up scallops, wondering what they were doing in the library. Abruptly, she got up from her knees, scattering daisies at her feet.

"Sue, Estelle, I'll be right back," she said. "I'll just go get a sandwich."

What did she expect to see in the library? she wondered as she walked across the hall. The conversation was about sports. Champ, seated beside his brother, was bringing Philip up to date on American professional football, baseball and hockey. Philip seemed quite interested, his dark head bent toward Champ as he listened. Vivienne was sitting, silent, behind the tea urn, watching Cypri eat a large piece of pound cake. Daisy, at the side table, leafed through a magazine that seemed to have diagrams of electrical circuits in it. Mab picked up a lettuce sandwich and went back to the dining room. Had she really wanted to see Philip for a moment that much? She hated lettuce. She made herself eat the entire sandwich as a punishment. Philip had chosen Daisy, freely chosen her.

Mab's fingers trembled a little as she pinned up the finished garland.

"Oh, the room looks wonderful," Vivienne exclaimed from the doorway.

"It's simple, but it should look pretty tonight," Mab said.

"Mab, you're a genius," Vivienne said. "Thank you. Estelle, I'm going to start dressing now, if there are no problems. The bands will be arriving soon to set up, and the bartenders, too."

"We'll take care of it all, Miss Vivienne," Estelle answered.

Mab put in a few more pins and followed Vivienne up to begin her own dressing. As they went by the library door, Cypri saw them, looked at her watch and swallowed the last of her tea.

"Five-thirty. We ought to start our baths," she said. Daisy obediently followed her out of the library.

Champ turned to Philip, who had begun to read the morning's *Eyreville Times.*

"Like a drink?" Champ asked. "I think I'll have a Scotch on the rocks."

"Thanks." Philip put the newspaper down. "Just some whiskey without ice for me."

"Here's some Jack Daniels. Want to try that?" When Philip nodded his approval, Champ handed him a drink and sat down in a chair with his Scotch.

"To your happiness," Champ said, raising his glass. "Daisy's a fine girl."

He watched Philip's face closely as he said this. The situation, Champ thought, definitely wasn't quite what it appeared on the surface. During the afternoon he had been observing Daisy and Philip together. Philip seemed devoted, and Daisy indifferent at best. In fact she seemed to be actively avoiding Philip, even to the extent of deliberately hitting her golf ball as far as possible from his—if he hooked, she sliced.

Philip's face showed no particular expression in response to Champ's toast. "Thank you," he said quietly. "I want you to know, Champ, that I haven't been near a casino since Daisy and Cypriana's visit. I'm not only patching things up at Downforth, but my gambling is a thing of the past. I intend never to go near a roulette table again."

"I'm glad of that."

Champ paused, still puzzled. He couldn't understand Philip's confidence in the face of Daisy's treatment of him. If Daisy didn't want to marry Philip, it certainly didn't seem to signify with Philip. Maybe, Champ thought, Philip was accustomed to a cool manner in women; English girls had the reputation of being cold

375

and passive. Certainly their own mother turned a cold face to her husband, and she was the only English-woman Champ had known. Perhaps in England all women seemed disinterested in their men. Certainly Champ couldn't blame Philip for *wanting* Daisy. Daisy was extremely attractive; Champ himself had felt certain urges looking at her.

"Daisy had a sad childhood before she came here," Champ said. "You knew that?"

"Mother wrote me a little about it. She lived in a trailer camp down in Texas, I seem to remember."

"China Dane went down and brought her back here when her mother died."

"Oh, yes. Mrs. Dane." Philip's face stiffened and his tone of voice grew cold. The mention of China Dane almost turned him to stone, Champ noticed. That was odd. Most people either smiled or looked sad when they remembered China Dane. Champ studied Philip curiously.

"Do you know what Dad told me at Mrs. Dane's funeral?" Champ said. "Dad was broken up by her death—really affected. He liked China Dane. I think she was one of the few people Dad had ever admired who wasn't a poet. Anyway, I happened to be home—she died in the summer—and Dad insisted I go to the funeral with them. To pay our respects, he said. And on the way to the church he asked Mother if she re-membered the day China Dane came to them and offered to pay for your education."

"What?" Philip's expression changed at last. He looked startled.

"That's what Dad said. I was surprised, too. But China Dane helped a lot of people, I guess. That's why there wasn't any Dane money left except what was en-tailed." Champ looked around the library. "I'm cer-tainly glad Vivienne was able to buy Land's End back."

Philip frowned. Champ's statement made no sense to him. Why would China Dane have offered to give *him* any help? China Dane's sole interest in him had

376

been to prevent him from marrying her daughter; of that he was certain. Champ must have heard wrong. Philip drained his drink. He didn't like to think of China Dane or of any of the events surrounding his departure from Eyreville.

Champ wanted to probe deeper, but he was not sure how to do it. "When do you think you'll get married?" he asked finally.

"As soon as possible," Philip replied. "Unless Daisy wants a big wedding, which I understand takes more time to arrange. I hope I can talk her into something quick and small. An elopement would be the best of all."

Philip's face again resumed its bland expression as he answered, and Champ frowned.

"Elopement? That's an old-fashioned idea. You don't want to rush Daisy, you know," he said. "How old is she? Twenty? Twenty-one? I mean, she's young to settle down."

Philip got up and helped himself to some more Jack Daniels.

"More Scotch, Champ?"

"Thanks."

Philip refilled his brother's glass and sat down again.

"Look, Champ, don't worry about Daisy," he said, smiling at Champ. "She's young; she's rather nervous. I don't think she's accustomed to having a lot of attention paid her. But after we're married, all that will change. I'll make her happy. I've promised her."

"Oh, I'm sure of that," Champ said hastily. So, he thought, to judge from that speech, Philip was aware that Daisy seemed reluctant. Champ waited to hear more, but Philip changed the subject, and though he was not entirely content to let matters lie there, Champ didn't know what else to say. As they discussed doctors' high insurance rates—Philip had read of the recent rash of malpractice suits—Champ resolved to observe Daisy closely that evening. And he'd definitely keep a close watch on Cypri, too. The whole situation bore watching.

Aware that he'd been put through a polite grilling by Champ, Philip had to work not to smile at his brother's obvious confusion about him and Daisy. He was glad Champ cared so much about Daisy. Not the slightest suspicion, obviously, had ever crossed Champ's mind as to the actual role Daisy played in their household. Well, that would all shortly be over. Whatever Daisy's reluctance, Philip was determined to overcome it, and meanwhile he was actually enjoying his mysterious role as Daisy's undaunted suitor. If Champ was surprised at his persistence, what must Vivienne and Mab be thinking? Though when you got down to it neither seemed to care a fig about him—Mab, who could just walk out as she had, or Vivienne, who— but he reminded himself that there was a statute of limitations on painful memories; you didn't have to open old wounds. Vivienne, who—nothing . . . Vivienne, who was presently a famous actress, and Mab the art expert and Cypriana the artful expert at monkeyshines—and there you had the three Danes, as they were, are now and ever shall be. Philip decided he was lucky that it was only a cousin of that trio whom he was marrying. Though Daisy was close enough to being a Dane. She had beauty and guts. He admired her for holding out about the ring. How long would she manage to keep it off her finger, he wondered.

Philip had continued making conversation with Champ as he meditated on their earlier discussion, and he hoped his remarks made sense, though Champ seemed a trifle distracted himself. Finally, Philip turned down another drink and went off to his room. Champ stayed and poured himself a short third Scotch.

Upstairs, preparations were going forward in all four bedrooms. Cypriana, who had finished her bath first, was sitting in front of her mirror in the pale yellow back bedroom—her old room—when Baker ran upstairs carrying two corsage boxes.

"One is for you and one is for Miss Daisy," Baker said, putting one box down on Cypri's dresser.

"I know. I told Champ what kind of flowers to order for me. What did Philip send Daisy?"

Baker peeked inside the other box. "Oh, it's three gorgeous camellias."

"Good. Take them to Daisy and tell her to let Betty Lou pin them in her hair. Betty Lou and Thelma ought to be here any minute to start our shampoos. Oh, and come right back, Baker."

When Baker reappeared, Cypri pulled her blue robe down to bare her shapely right shoulder.

"Baker, I pulled a muscle playing tennis this afternoon. Massage it a minute for me, will you?"

As Baker complied, Cypriana watched Baker's face in the mirror.

"Oh, that feels so good." Cypri sighed. Baker rhythmically squeezed and released her shoulder, and Cypri closed her eyes.

"Baker—" she began, but a knock on the door interrupted them. Thelma from the beauty shop had arrived. Thelma came in full of enthusiasm over the house and all the preparations that were under way for the ball.

"Betty Lou is over with your cousin. Are you ready for your shampoo?" she asked Cypri.

Cypriana pulled her robe around her again, slowly, with a glance at Baker as she did so. "Bring me some sherry, please, Baker," she said. "Ask Daisy if she wants a glass, too. The bathroom's in here, Thelma."

"How do you want your hair fixed?" Thelma asked, lathering Cypri's hair in the wash basin.

"All pulled over to one side. I have some flowers to pin across the back."

While Cypri sipped sherry, Thelma used the dryer on her dark hair and twisted it around a curling iron to achieve curls, which she then swept over to the side.

"That's very becoming!" Thelma exclaimed when she finished. Baker, who was watching, handed her the spray of gold chrysanthemums and yellow rosebuds from the florist's box and Thelma pinned it down the back of Cypri's head.

"Are you wearing yellow?" Thelma asked.

"No. The sales woman called it 'summer gold.' Show her, Baker."

Baker brought out Cypri's dress and Thelma exclaimed. The lightweight material, almost transparent, was dull gold in color.

"I have to stay and see you put it on, even if I miss my supper," Thelma said.

"Fine, but I have to fix my face first."

Under the scrutiny of Baker and Thelma, Cypri applied mauve eye shadow and was outlining her eyes with a dark line when Champ tapped and opened the bedroom door.

"Do you mind if I take my shower now?" he asked. "Don't move, ladies. I won't disturb you."

Champ grabbed his bathrobe and disappeared into the bathroom. Slowly, Cypriana brushed on a brown-orange shade of lipstick and, after an overcoat of gloss, she was finished. Both Baker and Thelma declared that she looked gorgeous. She acknowledged their compliments by smiling until her dimple came out, and then she rummaged in her small cosmetics bag, pulling out the sapphire earrings Champ had presented her on their first anniversary.

"Oh, those are darling! They just match your eyes," Baker said when Cypri had fastened the earrings to her ears.

Baker helped Cypri into the gold dress and carefully tied it for her over her right shoulder. The other shoulder was bare.

"Does your muscle feel all right now?" Baker asked.

"What? Oh, yes. Fine." Baker finished the tie and Cypri smoothed the gored skirt and turned around to face them. Both Thelma and Baker were ecstatic.

You had to give it to Cypriana Alexander, Thelma thought. She was one in a million. The others would have to go some to outdo her.

"Let's go see Daisy while Champ dresses," Cypri said. She applied nearly half a bottle of Enigma to her wrists and temples and then led the way across the hall. The doors of all the other bedrooms were closed. Cypri rapped on Daisy's door, and Betty Lou opened it.

"Look at Daisy," Betty Lou said, sounding awed, and they all exclaimed as they saw Daisy standing in front of the mirror. She turned to face them, crying "Oh, Cypri, you look wonderful!"

"Turn around." Critically, Cypri looked Daisy over. The white lace strapless dress was very becoming. Betty Lou had pulled Daisy's pale hair back from her face and braided it, looping the braid at the back of her head. Philip's camellias were pinned on top of the loop.

"That's perfect," Cypriana said. "Let me see your makeup."

"I used what the salesgirl recommended—brown-gold eyeshadow, and something she called 'star coral' lipstick," Daisy said.

"I love your perfume," Baker said to Daisy.

"What are you wearing?" Cypri asked. She could smell nothing but her own pungent scent.

"It's a new perfume called First. The girl at the cosmetics counter gave me a sample of it."

Betty Lou, Thelma and Baker continued to make admiring comments, and Daisy was pleased. As long as the others were around, Cypri couldn't start in on her about Philip and the ring. The diamond was safely inside the red velvet box in a drawer of the bed table, where Daisy intended it to stay. When Betty Lou seemed about to leave, Daisy asked her to pin the camellias in more securely. Finally, Champ joined them.

"My gosh. You girls look wonderful."

They acknowledged his compliments, Daisy feeling

more gratified than Cypriana. Cypri was still nursing her grudge against Champ for interfering down in the library. Look at the result of it; Daisy's ring finger was bare. However, Cypri couldn't say anything to either Daisy or Champ in the presence of Betty Lou and Thelma. Sourly, she inspected Champ's white jacket and ruffled shirt.

Betty Lou and Thelma had to leave so that Chooky could drive them home and get back to his duties before the guests began to arrive. As the two hairdressers left, Cypri sent Baker downstairs to the garden to pick roses for Champ's and Philip's lapels. Baker returned with one red and one white rose.

"Mr. Philip's dressed and waiting in the hall downstairs," Baker reported. "He looks *so* handsome." She directed this last remark to Daisy.

"Hold still, Champ," Cypri said, poking the red bud into Champ's lapel and jabbing a pin into it. "Now, Daisy, you take the white one downstairs and put it on Philip."

Daisy would have preferred not having this task assigned to her, but she was afraid that Cypri would jab her with the pin she was offering if she refused. Gingerly, Daisy took the white rose.

"Well, let's go down," Cypriana said. "You go first, Daisy."

The sun had just disappeared behind the willow trees and the sky was filled with the pink evening light. Its rosy glow permeated the central hall, even as Johnny Mae lighted the hall sconces.

At the front door, Philip stood looking out at the lawn and the field beyond. Musicians had been running up and down the stairs, and the house was full of bustle. Daisy came down to him with so light a step that Philip didn't hear her, but something made him turn just as she reached the bottom step.

"Daisy, you look beautiful," he said, smiling.

Daisy blushed. She looked behind her, but Cypri

had detained Champ upstairs and for the moment Daisy was alone with Philip.

"This is for you," Daisy said, holding out the rose. "And thank you for the camellias."

"They look lovely in your hair. Will you put the flower in my buttonhole?"

Philip came up close to her. He was wearing a traditional tuxedo, with a black jacket and a shirt with only a single row of small ruffles. Daisy had to admit he looked handsome.

As Daisy pinned in the rose, Cypriana started down the stairs, and Philip looked up, staring openly: Cypri descending was a magnificent sight. The sapphires in her ears did not sparkle half so brightly as her eyes. Cypri loved a good party.

After Philip admired her aloud, they went into the drawing room to wait for the guests' arrival. Champ leaned against the doorway, watching out the front door for a car. Chooky came back in the station wagon, but no one else appeared.

"I wish Viv and Mab would hurry," Cypriana said. "I think they did their own hair; that takes time."

Upstairs, Mab was just finishing her makeup. She had used the light and dark green eye shadows again, and brushed on some blue-red lipstick. Gazing in her mirror, she was pleased. She had never felt quite so beautiful. Remembering Philip's comment about her hair during their evening in London, she had pinned its strands back and covered the chignon with a twist of tiny blue and green silk flowers. The hairdo emphasized her slanting eyes and high cheekbones. Her ball dress had a skirt of pleated chiffon, tiers of the pleats bound in by small bands of green ribbon so that the skirt seemed to mold to her slender body when she moved. The chiffon was a hazy combination of blue and green, the colors shading into each other like the water around a tropical island. The top was very low-cut, with tiny green ribbon straps over the shoulders, giving the illusion that she was fuller in the bust than

383

she really was. She frowned a little, studying her
décolletage. Why didn't she just forget herself tonight
and have a good time? Philip had paid her a great
deal of attention during luncheon and the golf game,
had looked up when she walked into the library
during tea; she thought his eyes had lingered on her
while she stood beside the sandwich tray. She wondered if it was more than polite interest.

Feeling almost daring, she sprayed on some L'Air du
Temps perfume and added a touch of blush to her
cheeks. Then she was ready. It was time to go down.

Vivienne's thoughts while she finished dressing were
far different from Mab's. Philip had scarcely addressed
a single remark to her, and she was angry at herself
for caring. What had she expected? They had parted
in anger and apparently he had never gotten over it.
The more than twenty years between then and now
didn't exist for Philip. Or perhaps they did. Perhaps
Philip found her so shockingly changed, so aged, that
he couldn't bear to look at her. Anxiously, Vivienne
studied her face in the mirror. You couldn't trust people in show business to tell you the truth about how
you looked. Friends always told you that you looked
wonderful, great, better than ever, but it was routine
flattery. She came from an unreal world.

At least, she knew the tricks of that world. Tonight
she had taken a great deal of care with her face, and
she looked back at herself from the mirror with huge
smoky eyes. A grayish-blue shade of eye shadow called
'Silk Suede' made her eyes appear so big. Her skin she
had left pale, without a touch of color except for her
lips, which like her nails were painted in a flame color.
Over the lipstick she applied gold gloss. Running a
final comb through her dark hair, she decided that it
had come out well; it hung long around her shoulders,
and over one ear she had pinned a silk poppy that
matched her flame-colored taffeta dress. The dress
pleased her very much; the minute she had seen it she
had known it was for her. A deep ruffle at the top

384

pulled well down off her shoulders, leaving them bare;
except for the ruffle the dress had simple lines, a tight
bodice and a flared skirt that ended in another ruffle.
Undeniably dramatic, but then she was Vivienne Dane.
Wondering if she were a bit too pale, she added a little
color to her cheekbones and studied the result. Her
eyes looked enormous and the poppy was definitely
provocative. She rose and turned, watching in the full
length mirrors the way her dress swung out at the ruffled
hem. Perhaps Philip would not dance with her, but at
least he would have to look at her on the dance floor.
Suddenly she was eager to go down the stairs and
confront him. She didn't look so old. In fact, she
looked terrific. Hunting amid the perfume bottles on
her dressing table, she found Bal à Versailles. Just the
thing for a ball. She dabbed it on and went to the door.

Outside in the hall, Mab was just going down the
stairs; Vivienne saw her back vanish around the bend.

"Come here," Champ said to the three in the drawing room, from his post in the doorway. "Look at
Mab."

Philip and the girls followed him into the hall. Mab
smiled at them as she came down the steps in her in-
comparably graceful manner. Philip happened to be
directly in the path of her smiling glance. In the light
from the chandelier and the wall sconces the blue-
green of Mab's dress seemed to ripple like water in a
sunlit blue pond.

They were still admiring Mab when Philip looked up.
His eyes widened and Champ followed his gaze. Viv-
enne was coming down the stairs, her head held high.
All the light of the dying day seemed gathered in the
rustling folds of her dress. At the soft sound, the others
looked up, and there was a reverent pause as they
stared at her.

"Oh, Viv, you look magnificent," Mab said, breaking the sudden silence. Vivienne smiled and continued
her descent, conscious that all eyes were upon her. Under the lights the dress glowed as if it were a candle

flame, and the matching poppy lit up her face, making her dark eyes and hair seem blacker in contrast. Champ thought she was breathtaking, and he said so aloud as Vivienne joined them.

Cypri cleared her throat and Champ added, looking around at all four women, "I mean, all of you are breathtaking. Words fail me."

Words had certainly failed Philip. He said nothing at all for a moment.

The gold and flame and white and irridescent blue-green of their dresses mingled as they admired each other's toilettes. Before they had finished, the first car turned into the drive. Neighborhood boys who were parking the cars for the guests hurried out to help, and shortly Mr. Pedicord, the minister, and his wife came up the front steps of Land's End.

For three-quarters of an hour Vivienne, Mab and the two couples greeted guests, passing them from the hall up the stairs to the ballroom where the strains of current hits alternated with fox trots and waltzes. At nine o'clock, and Vivienne saw that most of the guests had arrived, she and Cypriana led the way upstairs. The ballroom was brightly lit, and just as they walked in, the Society Band began to play a waltz.

Philip, who had walked up the two flights beside Daisy, turned and asked her to dance. Daisy could not very well refuse, and Philip swung her away in his arms. He waltzed very well; Daisy felt clumsy and awkward. She had never really mastered the waltz. Philip held her a little closer after a while, making it easier for them to move together, but Daisy would rather have had Philip step on her toes than feel his arm tighten around her.

Across the room, Bob King stopped talking to Nell Rush and simply stared at Daisy. Bob knew the ball was in honor of Daisy's engagement. He had heard the news just two days before; he had come home from college to learn that Daisy was marrying a millionaire, a dashing, handsome millionaire who in the dim past had played halfback for Eyreville High. The damned Alexanders had made it big in this town! With all his heart, Bob wished that Daisy and Cypri had married him and Frank. The Kings were no lower in social standing than the Alexanders. In fact, the Kings had to be judged somewhat higher if you considered only Thomas and Mary and the grocery store. But there across the room were the senior Alexanders, seated on a sofa and talking to Dr. Honeychurch as lordly as if they owned Land's End, all because of Philip's luck in having a rich uncle. Life wasn't fair.

Frank King was dancing with Celia Honeychurch; he didn't know how to waltz but he was capable of a sort of three-four-time fox-trot, and he felt he had to keep in motion. The sight of Cypri in the gold dress had rendered him actually miserable. Wasn't he ever going to get over wanting her? He wondered why on earth she had invited Bob and him. Maybe she liked to watch them suffer.

Wallace Hastings claimed Vivienne for a partner and they danced together under the scrutiny of most of the people at the party. Vivienne's ravishing looks were compared to her sister Mab's.

"They're such different types," Sugar Cunningham said to her husband James. "You can't compare them. They're both beautiful."

"Vivienne doesn't look a day older than she did as Juliet," James answered. "I was in love with her once, remember?"

"You were? How could I remember? I was only seven years old, and all I remember is how I had to beg to be allowed to go to see the play. It was the first time I'd stayed up so late, and I cried all night afterward. Vivienne is such an actress. Did you see *Turn of River*?"

Barbara Rush asked her husband Roland Parker if he remembered the crush Charles Honeychurch once had on Daisy Sykes. Charles, now a bearded guitarist with Damn the Torpedoes, seemed worlds apart from

Daisy now. Still, Barbara noticed that Charles was leaning against the wall with his eyes fixed on Philip's lady.

"In my opinion, Charles Honeychurch has burnt out his brains with hash and heroin. That's what I hear," Roland replied.

"Hush. There are Honeychurches everywhere. Just because Charles wears a beard——"

"Let's get a drink," Roland interrupted her.

The bar at one end of the ballroom was doing a brisk business, and Chooky frequently passed through the crowd carrying glasses of champagne. The party grew jollier. When Damn the Torpedoes came back on the stand even some of the older folks were ready to try rock dancing. Cypri was in her element, and she never ran out of partners from among her former beaus. Bob drank three glasses of champagne and plucked up the courage to ask Daisy to dance. When Bob led Daisy off, Philip looked around for Mab, and found her chatting with his parents. He joined them for a few minutes and then asked Mab to dance.

For a while, Mab and Philip bounced back and forth in silence. Then the Society Band moved onto the bandstand, and Philip pulled Mab into his arms. They moved slowly together across the crowded floor. "Don't let it stop," Mab thought. She had to fight the temptation to squeeze her eyes tightly shut; she made herself take a deep breath and say something. But what? She cast about for a remark.

"It's a beautiful evening," Philip said.

There, yes, that was it. Discuss the weather. "Beautiful," Mab replied. "Not hot," she added after a while.

"You look very lovely tonight." Philip's voice was low.

"Thank you."

It was a sensuous experience to dance with Mab, Philip thought. Her slender body responded to every move of his own so smoothly and effortlessly that they glided about as one. Philip began to feel aroused. He pulled Mab closer.

"Mab, that week you were in England, I was sorry we—that is, I called your hotel several times after— but you were out." Waiting to see what Mab would answer, Philip bent his head down to catch her words.

Mab pulled back slightly and looked up at him in surprise. "You called me?"

"Yes, but I didn't leave a message. When you left so fast, frankly, I thought that I had offended you. Or disappointed you." It took an effort on Philip's part to say those last words, but the champagne he had drunk earlier helped.

Mab's golden-brown eyes were looking expressively up at him. As before, he felt irresistibly drawn to her. Mab's sensitive, undemanding nature and her intense intelligence were deeply appealing. Of course, Daisy was also sensitive and intelligent, but Daisy lacked Mab's air of mystery, her elegant sophistication, her perfect manners. Holding Mab's light body in his arms and feeling her instant, continuous adjustment to his movements, Philip longed to know what had gone wrong in London.

After he spoke, Mab looked up at him for a few minutes as if trying to decide whether to say anything; actually she thought she had heard wrong. They were dancing close to the bandstand.

"Philip," she murmured at last. "Forgive me for mentioning it, but is it true that you are in some sort of trouble?"

"The gambling, you mean? I'm afraid it is—was true. I'm ashamed of it. I can't really explain it. A doctor I've consulted says that when I reached a certain level, life didn't seem challenging any more. Anyway, I started gambling, and gambling was all I lived for. Until the stock market report. Until that morning with you, in fact. The long phone call—my lawyer rang me up to tell me about the report. I had no idea of any serious trouble until that point."

"He called you *that* morning?" Mab was suddenly

short of breath; she could barely make her words audible.

Philip slowed his steps slightly and spoke softly into her ear. They had danced over to the edge of the floor, and she had no trouble hearing him.

"Nothing but drastic bad news could have torn me away from you, I promise you," he said. "I wanted to see you, to explain. When you left like that, and didn't ring up, I thought you wanted to stop things right there, that you had someone in Chicago."

Philip looked down at Mab inquiringly. After a moment she shook her head.

"There's no one in Chicago," she said in a low voice. "I haven't been so lucky."

The music ended.

"You know, I think I'd like a drink," Mab said. Her head spun a bit. She was trying to assess what Philip had said. Did it make any difference? He was going to marry Daisy.

Philip brought her a glass of champagne and stood beside her as the Society Band rendered a version of "Strawberry Wine." Champ danced by with Daisy, and Mab noticed that Daisy seemed more sure of herself, moving around very gracefully with Champ. Daisy laughed at some remark of his. Cypriana whirled past in Frank King's arms—close in his arms, Mab thought. She wondered if Champ noticed, but Champ was busy entertaining Daisy. Hellraiser Cunningham spun past with Vivienne; he was obviously enjoying dancing with the celebrity of the evening.

"Can you still remember your death scene in *Romeo and Juliet*?" Vivienne asked Hellraiser as they circled.

"Don't ask me or I'll perform it right here. Except now that I've got you in my arms, I'm not going to let go. You're more beautiful than ever, Viv."

"You do make a good politician," Vivienne answered, smiling at him. He turned her quickly, so that her dress flounced out, and from the corner of her eye she saw Philip standing on the side of the floor with Mab. Was Philip watching them? Vivienne smiled into Hellraiser's eyes.

"I had to choose between politics and acting," Hellraiser said. "I hope I chose the right road. It's almost unbelievable how famous you are, Vivienne. People ask me all the time if I know you. I used to say in my campaign speeches, 'I come from Eyreville, the home of Vivienne Dane.' And that interested some people in my audience a lot more than my proposals. In the question period after the speech someone would be sure to ask, 'What's Vivienne Dane really like?' "

Vivienne laughed. "I'm afraid to hear what you answered."

Hellraiser grinned. "I told them you were a Democrat, of course."

Vivienne laughed again, and when the dance ended she permitted Hellraiser to get her some champagne. Celia Honeychurch came up to her while she waited, and raved about her dress.

"I want to tell Cypri how stunning she looks, too, but she hasn't once stopped dancing," Celia said. "I never saw such energy."

"She put me away on the tennis court this afternoon, too," Vivienne said. "She never runs out of it."

"It's downright unsouthern." Celia looked around. "This *is* the party of the century, Vivienne. The house looks so wonderful. And all you Danes are so beautiful. You belong here."

Vivienne congratulated Celia on her engagement, and Hellraiser came back. While she sipped the champagne, Vivienne looked around for Mab and Philip. They had begun to dance again. Philip wasn't paying much attention to his young fiancée, Vivienne thought. Daisy was across the room drinking champagne with Champ.

As if Philip suddenly had the same thought, at the end of the dance he led Mab over to Champ and Daisy. Cypriana left her partner and joined the four of them.

"Let's go down to supper soon," Cypriana said. "I'm starved. Daisy, when everyone there has a glass of champagne, I'm going to propose a toast to you and Philip. Announcing your engagement." Cypri spoke very firmly.

Mab looked at Philip. His face betrayed nothing. He nodded gravely. Daisy seemed to shrink a little. The smile faded from her face. She must be nervous, Mab thought. Mab was still trying to sort over what Philip had said while they danced. She felt dazed. So there really *was* a good reason Philip had seemed so disinterested that morning in London. And he thought she had a lover in Chicago. What could that mean? Perhaps she'd drunk too much champagne; she couldn't grasp it. Philip, she reminded herself, was marrying Daisy.

Seeing the family congregate by the door, Vivienne came across the floor toward them. As Vivienne approached, Mab watched Philip's eyes. Philip seemed to avoid looking at Vivienne. He hadn't danced or even spoken with Vivienne all evening. Vivienne in turn seemed not to take any particular notice of him. She included them all in her glance.

"Are we ready for supper?" Vivienne asked.

"Let's go down as soon as this piece is over," Cypri said. "I've worked up an appetite."

"Champ, perhaps we should ask your parents to walk down with us," Vivienne said.

The elder Alexanders were still sitting on their sofa. Mary had enjoyed gossiping about the well-dressed crowd and Thomas had spent the time not listening. He watched the various Dane girls and wondered which one most resembled China Dane. In coloring, it was the eldest, the actress, but in personality he would guess the next one, the art curator, was most like China. Mab had a gentle manner. Thomas wondered what China Dane would have made of her youngest, Cypriana. There was a hot potato. Champ must have his hands full. But Champ was a lively boy himself.

Thomas's musings were interrupted by the call to

supper, and taking Mary on his arm he followed the family members downstairs. The large dining room glowed with candlelight, and the long table with its flower garland was covered with dishes. Sixteen small tables circled the buffet table, each with its own white cloth, yellow candles and bouquet of baby's breath and daisies.

Chooky dispensed champagne from the sideboard as the guests began to help themselves from the buffet. Philip looked around for Daisy, but she was no longer at his side. Wallace Hastings stood there instead.

"Philip, I have been wanting to speak to you," Wallace said, in his stately manner. His hair was whiter, Philip saw, but otherwise his puckish face and dignified bearing was the same as when he had taught Philip to fence during that long-ago summer. "My cousin Laura has asked me particularly, several times, whether I ever saw you. I told her I feared that you had gone to England for good."

Philip smiled. "How is Miss Beltane?"

"Very well indeed. She is still coaching. She left Atlanta for some years, but she is back there now and the theater is flourishing. Laura has many protégés, and high hopes for them, but she still has never found anyone like our Vivienne. It was absolutely the high point of Laura's life when Vivienne mentioned her name at the Academy Awards."

Wallace Hastings paused, waiting for a comment from Philip. But Philip was silent.

"Oh, that's right," Wallace Hastings exclaimed after a moment. "You wouldn't have seen the awards. I forgot you live in England. When Vivienne accepted the Oscar, she said she wanted to thank the first person who encouraged her, Laura Beltane. Laura called me up sobbing for joy."

"Did she?" Philip looked around again for Daisy. The line they were standing in had reached the sideboard, and Chooky handed them both champagne.

393

Wallace Hastings went on talking about Laura Beltane. Mab came by, and Philip stopped her.

"Could I get you a glass of champagne?" he asked. "Where are you going to sit, Mab?"

"Oh, anywhere." Mab looked around, but she didn't see Daisy. Wallace Hastings asked Mab a question about her work in Chicago, and Philip stood listening to their discussion.

Vivienne shepherded the last of the guests into the dining room and then stepped across to the kitchen.

"Johnny Mae, the buffet looks beautiful, just perfect," Vivienne said. "Thank you so much for such a good job."

Johnny Mae looked rushed but triumphant.

As Vivienne crossed the hall back to the dining room, she caught sight of Daisy going out the back door. That was odd, she thought. Perhaps Daisy wanted a breath of fresh air. Both the front and back doors stood open, and the long hall was swept by a light breeze. It was a lovely evening. Vivienne was almost tempted to go out for a moment herself, but Julian Royal caught sight of her from the dining room and eagerly came to lead her back into the midst of the party. He had wanted to speak to her all night, he said, to discuss her renovation of Land's End. As Julian talked, Vivienne spotted Cypriana at one of the tables, eating supper with Champ. Vivienne hoped they would save her a place. She urged Julian to join the group circling the table, and they began to serve themselves.

XIX

What if I just ran away? Daisy thought.

Walking downstairs to the dining room beside Philip, her heart had grown heavier with each descending step. The moment of Cypri's announcement was coming closer and closer. Somehow that moment loomed in Daisy's mind as final, almost as final as the wedding ceremony itself. A public announcement. There were so many people, and everyone would look at her, everyone would expect her to smile. No one would understand what Cypri was doing to her, what Philip was doing to her. No one would understand that she wanted to scream and sob instead of smiling.

Her heart pounded painfully. She had managed to separate herself from Philip at the doorway of the dining room by volunteering to show Barbara Rush the location of the powder room under the stairs. When the back hall was deserted for a moment, she had darted outside, and now she was flattened against the brick wall of the back porch. The porch was dark except for the large rectangles of bright light from the kitchen windows on one side and the dimmer, yellower light from the candlelit dining room on the other. Daisy peered up and down, and then out into the night. Beyond the white porch columns, the ground and the willow trees were silver in the moonlight.

Why not just run and hide in the barn, or keep running over the fields, running until she dropped? In a moment, she would, she thought, she really would, as soon as she caught her breath. She was breathing in gasps.

The bustle of activity in the kitchen and the murmur

of conversation from the dining room came to her through the open back door. The calm, civilized buzz of conversation seemed to carry a message. She would be disgraced forever if she didn't make an appearance in there, a calm, dignified appearance. Think, Daisy, she said to herself. She couldn't go running over fields. It was a mad idea. In a minute, she'd go inside. She'd force herself. If she had a lot to drink, maybe she wouldn't mind the announcement so much. Or maybe she had already had a lot to drink. She couldn't remember. She must compose herself.

She heard Cypri's voice inside ask, "Where's Daisy?"

"I think she was here a minute ago," Johnny Mae answered.

"Must find her." Cypri's voice faded back into the dining room.

Suddenly the back screen door crashed open and a man hurtled through it. Without looking around, he rushed to the edge of the porch. Daisy squeezed herself back against the dark wall of the house as the figure bent over the porch railing and made retching noises. He was throwing up. Daisy made a face. She wondered who had drunk too much. Before he turned around, she ought to go in, go inside and face her fate like a good girl. But as if hypnotized, she stared at the vomiting man.

Before she expected it, the man suddenly straightened and turned. Daisy was surprised to see Charles Honeychurch's bearded face. He looked equally surprised to see a figure in white standing beside the door. With unsteady steps he approached her.

"Who's that? Oh, Daisy. What's the bride doing out here all alone?"

He came so close she could smell the foul odor of his breath and she shrank back along the bricks. She ought to turn and go back inside. Why was she still resisting it? She couldn't do it yet. She wanted to, but she—

Charles looked far gone, she thought. His black tie

396

was askew and his thick hair hung in his face. He reached out to put his hands on her bare shoulders and she jumped with surprise.

"Mind if I kiss the bride?" he said.

Daisy made a cry of disgust and pushed Charles back. She could smell vomit on his breath and make out the unfocused look in his eyes as he came closer again. He pulled her to him and opened his mouth. Suddenly, he was kissing her, his fat tongue poking far back in her throat. She could taste the sweet sick flavor of vomit.

Furiously Daisy pushed at his chest with both hands, but she couldn't budge Charles. He seemed to open his mouth wider; she felt as if the suction would pull her inside the huge slobbering cavern. Her scream was cut off by his powerful, sucking lips.

Daisy's body experienced a revulsion so total that every nerve end seemed to curl up. Frantic, she kicked Charles's shins. She felt one of his hands release the painful grip he had on her shoulder and fumble at her bust. At that, Daisy's whole body convulsed and she jerked so sharply that she actually pulled away from Charles's hold, slamming her head back against the bricks behind her. The pain at the back of her head made tears start into her eyes. Charles had reached his hand inside her dress, and when she flung herself back so violently, she heard the lace tear. She felt as if an electric current had charged through her body. Her mouth was free, but when she opened her mouth and tried to scream, no sound emerged.

Charles stared at her twisted features and fell back a step, releasing her other shoulder. Blindly, then, Daisy shoved at him, turned and clawed for the screen door. She jerked it wide open and fell into the lighted hall. It was empty. Beyond the double doors leading to the dining room conversation was just dying as someone tapped on a glass.

"Attention, everybody, for a minute." Daisy heard Cypriana using her gayest voice to speak the words.

397

The meaning of them didn't register on Daisy. But something—there was something she, Daisy, had to do. Somewhere she had to be. The sound of Cypriana's voice reminded her. Daisy stood up, looking down at herself. Her dress was torn at the front. That was odd. Daisy held the torn part up, hugging herself with her arms. She had to go somewhere and it had to do with a man—but she hated men! Daisy took a step forward and staggered. Men—they had beaten her in her childhood, and now they trapped her and attacked her. . . .

But she had to go into the dining room. Cypri had told her to. Cypri always told her what to do. Daisy slid a little on the polished floor but she hurried forward. She had to be there in time. The Reverend Pedicord was standing just inside the doorway and Daisy slipped into the room behind his ample figure.

The large, high-ceilinged room was completely silent now, the guests in the flickering candlelight watching Cypriana as she spoke. Cypri raised a glass of champagne. In the soft golden light the sparkling wine was the same color as her gown.

"And now I want to propose a toast to Philip and Daisy!" Cypri cried. "Daisy, where are you? Tonight, Philip and Daisy are announcing their engagement."

Philip, standing beside Cypri, smiled and looked around seeking his fiancée. When he spotted Daisy by the door, everyone followed his glance. Reverend Pedicord wondered why they all looked at him, until he realized that Daisy stood directly behind him. With a start he moved aside, giving Daisy a kindly smile as he did so. It struck Reverend Pedicord that there was something odd in Daisy's pose. She was rather bent, and her arms were hugged tightly to her chest.

Suddenly the same realization hit everyone in the dining room. Daisy looked strange. Her eyes were wide and blank. Her face glistened as if it were wet and her hair was somewhat disarrayed—one of the

398

camelias hung askew on the back of her head. Her chest heaved as she breathed.

"Daisy!" Cypriana cried.

Daisy stood silent. They were all looking at her! She had done something—something wrong! She opened her mouth and suddenly her vocal chords worked. She let out a bloodcurdling scream.

As the echo of it died away, the guests stared openmouthed. Daisy closed her eyes; her entire face screwed up into a horrified mask, as if she were on the brink of some terror too hideous to be imagined.

The first person to move was Champ. He was standing next to Cypriana and he sprang across the room to Daisy's side.

"It's all right, sweetie. It's all right," he said in a soothing voice. Daisy began to cry in great tearing gulps, her entire body shaking, and Champ swung her up into his arms.

"I'll take her upstairs," he said, his tone authoritative. He turned rapidly, and Daisy's white lace skirt brushed against the doorway as he disappeared into the hall.

The shocked silence in the dining room was so complete that Champ's steps could clearly be heard mounting the front stairs. The clock in the front hall struck twelve, the faint strokes a counterpoint to the fading footsteps.

"The fireworks in the garden are cancelled," Cypriana snapped.

Cypriana's voice was low, but Frank King, who was standing beside her, heard her. He stared at her, startled. Everybody else seemed stunned, but Frank could have sworn that Cypriana looked annoyed.

The stupid girl, Cypriana was thinking! oh, stupid Daisy! So this was how she chose to end things with Philip. She must have gone outside to carry on and lament her fate until just the moment to make a dramatic appearance and humiliate them all. The thought of Champ upstairs comforting her made Cypri burn with fury. She itched to get *her* hands on

399

Daisy. She would make her rue this night.

Philip stood immobile with shock. He had been smiling as Cypriana made the engagement announcement, and the smile froze on his face. My God! he thought. Daisy has gone out of her mind!

When people in the room began to move uneasily, looking at each other, the import of what had happened suddenly became clear to Philip. Good God, it was his fault. What a piece of misjudgment—he had supposed himself to be helping Daisy, to be saving her, when in truth what he had done was to drive her out of her mind. Shaken, Philip didn't know what to do. He glanced about him, stunned.

Mab was standing next to Philip. Her champagne glass had fallen from her hand when Daisy screamed. It had been like a dream turning into a nightmare. Now Mab studied Philip's expression. He looked bleak, almost despairing.

"Oh, Philip," Mab murmured. She put her hand on his arm. He turned to her.

"Mab," he said softly. "What have I done?"

Mab patted his arm reassuringly. "Daisy will be all right," she said, trying to sound comforting. She felt far from sure herself that Daisy would be all right. What on earth had gotten into her cousin? A memory came back. Mab had seen Daisy this upset once before. At her mother's funeral. Daisy behaved very peculiarly then, too.

Vivienne literally had lost her breath. She'd lifted her glass and looked at Philip as Cypri made the announcement. Everyone in the room had looked at Philip, and then around at each other, wondering where Daisy was, expecting Cypri's announcement to flush her out. The sight of Daisy in the doorway had chilled Vivienne to the bone. Her scream seemed the cry of a damned soul, of someone pushed beyond endurance. Vivienne had suspected before that Daisy might have an unstable nature, but she had never imagined that a public breakdown was in the offing.

Vivienne realized that she wasn't breathing, and she forced herself to inhale.

"Everyone, please," she said as loudly as she could manage. "I'm sorry. I'm sure Champ will—" She stopped. She didn't know how to finish her sentence.

The guests began to talk, asking each other in murmurs, What on earth . . . ? Dr. Honeychurch wondered if he should volunteer to assist Champ, but decided that probably this should stay a family matter. He turned to his wife, intending to say something for the sake of politeness, but for the life of him he couldn't get out a single remark. Daisy's singular scene had unnerved him.

The doctor was not the only one who felt so. A few people managed to carry on. Wallace Hastings regained his aplomb immediately. Having been a theater-lover all his life, he was accustomed to drama, although he seldom met with it in the homes of his friends in Eyreville. He managed to make an innocuous remark to Hellraiser Cunningham, who was also recovering rapidly. Celia Honeychurch regained her tongue and asked Cypriana what the heck was all that about.

"Oh, nothing," Cypriana replied. She had to exercise a tight control over herself to keep from exploding with rage. "Ignore it. Daisy's nutty sometimes. Have some dessert or something."

Slowly, people did move, some to the buffet table but most to the sideboard, where Chooky poured more champagne with a shaky hand, spilling as much of it as he got in the glasses. The various Royals present, all of whom were related to the Danes, felt it behooved them to behave as if nothing had happened, and a kind of chatter at last replaced the shocked silence in the room. Vivienne found Scat Honeychurch.

"Scat, you know, we were going to have more dancing, but now I think we shouldn't," she said. "When people finish their suppers I imagine they'll go."

Scat nodded. "Some scene," he said. "What is wrong with Daisy?"

"I have no idea. I was just wondering if I should go up and see." Vivienne looked around. Her guests were regaining their equilibrium, but the mood was not festive. Philip, she saw, stood with his head down, and Mab was speaking to him. What on earth must Philip be thinking? She wondered if she should go over to him. Before she could, Mr. Pedicord and his wife came up to her. They murmured conventional things about enjoying the party and said they were sorry but they must leave, explaining that Mr. Pedicord had an early service in the morning.

"I hope your cousin will be better soon," Mr. Pedicord added, rather vaguely.

As the Pedicords moved toward the door, Sugar and James Hastings took their place. They said something about having to go home to check on their children. Soon everyone was saying good night and thanking Vivienne for the party. Since Cypriana was also approached by departing guests, she had to swallow her outrage and smile sweetly. Frank stood beside her, for which she was grateful. The Alexanders pressed her hand in silence. Thomas looked as if he would like to say something but couldn't think what; sheer amazement kept Mary quiet. The last thing she had expected this evening was for something weird to happen. She pursed her lips and did not even say good-bye to Philip, but simply dragged Thomas out by the arm.

Bob King finally moved. Bob had been more affected than anyone by Daisy's exhibition; for several minutes afterward he stood at Frank's side simply staring at the empty doorway. At last he came to.

"What do you think happened to Daisy?" Bob asked Frank and Cypriana at the same time that Mr. and Mrs. Bartholomew Rush were saying they had enjoyed the evening.

"Don't ask," Cypri said to Bob, pronouncing the words distinctly as she permitted Roland Parker to kiss her good night on the cheek.

"I'm going to find out," Bob said.

402

Neither Frank nor Cypriana made any comment. Bob walked out of the dining room and into the hall. He had been aware of Daisy's whereabouts almost all evening, and he knew she had not been in the dining room or the other rooms on the ground floor when the guests went in for dinner. He had looked; in fact, he had not gone back into the dining room himself until he decided he couldn't find her.

Now he looked around the back part of the hall, because Daisy had come from that direction. Then he crossed to the kitchen.

Estelle and Baker were sitting at the kitchen table talking to each other in low voices. Johnny Mae, filling the coffee urn, was shaking her head when Bob walked in.

"Baker, did you see where Daisy had been before she came in just now?" he asked.

Baker shook her head. "We were all in the kitchen," she said, "except Sue. She was in the dining room. First thing we knew about it, we heard her scream. Wasn't it awful?"

Bob frowned. "Was Daisy out on the porch?"

"Well, she could have been," Baker said. "I saw someone dash past the kitchen door, but I thought it was a man."

"A man," Bob said. "When was that?"

"A few minutes before we heard Daisy scream."

Puzzled, Bob left the kitchen and walked out onto the back porch. The cars that had been parked in the side field were being brought out by the boys, but there was no activity in the back. The back porch was deserted. Walking over to the porch railing, Bob stared at the willow trees and decided to have a look around. He went down the back stairs.

Most of the guests had now headed for the front porch to await their cars, and Vivienne was kept too busy saying good-bye to check on either Philip or Daisy. When the last pair of guests left the dining room Vivienne looked around, surprised to find the room empty. Philip had gone somewhere. She ought to see about Daisy, she thought, and hurried into the hall and up the stairs. Cypriana was already upstairs, standing before the closed door of Daisy's room.

"Champ, I want to come in there," Cypri said. She sounded determined.

"Please don't right now," Champ replied through the door. "I'm just getting her calmed down, Cypri."

Vivienne thought she could hear Daisy sobbing in the background.

"Champ, I'm here, too," Vivienne said. "Is there anything you need?"

"No, thanks, Viv. Don't worry. I can handle this."

"Really." Cypriana looked furious. She rattled the knob of the door. "Champ, let me in."

"Cypri, you'd just upset her further. Go away." Champ spoke firmly.

"I'll go away, all right!" Cypriana turned on her heel and flounced off, back down the stairs. So Champ was going to keep Daisy to himself, was he? He certainly took an interest in that little airhead, all right. Well, Champ was due for some surprises. Cypri tossed her hair back and ran down the remaining stairs. Frank King stood at the bottom.

"Let's get out of here," Cypri said curtly.

Frank's face lit up. He had no idea what the matter was with Cypri; something was eating her. Whatever it was, he was grateful for it.

"Right away, sure," he said. "My car's parked out on the road. We can leave right now."

Heedless of the people waiting on the front porch, Cypriana walked straight out of the front door, past the Alexanders, and down the front steps. Frank followed her across the moonlit lawn. Fortunately, he had the keys to the Chevvy in his pocket. Bob could walk home.

At the back of the house, Bob poked in the bushes by the porch and then looked in the direction of the barn. From the corner of his eye he saw a figure move underneath the farthest willow tree.

"Wait a minute," he called. Maybe whoever it was had seen what had happened to Daisy. Bob ran down the back yard.

The figure turned out to be Charles Honeychurch. As Bob approached, Charles tried to leave, but his legs buckled under him and he sagged against the willow. After Daisy's desperate push, Charles had reeled backwards and down the steps. He'd heard the scream from the dining room and had managed to make his way to the field, where the Damn the Torpedoes van was parked. But the van was locked tight, and when the boys started driving cars into the driveway Charles had retreated to the shelter of the willows, to lean against a tree trunk and wish the world would stop spinning around. What had made him drink so much? He should have known better than to combine moonshine liquor and uppers. He was in rocky shape.

Bob stared at Charles. He could see in the moonlight that Charles's clothing was messed up and twigs and dirt clung to him. Charles's eyes looked dazed.

"What's the matter with you?" Bob demanded.

"Just had a little too much all at once," Charles replied. His tongue was thick. He tried to focus on Bob's face.

"Did you see Daisy out here?"

"Daisy?" Charles seemed confused. "Why should Daisy be out here? Think she'd come out here with me? No way, man." Charles tried again to leave.

"Just a minute," Bob insisted. "How'd Daisy get her hair messed up? Did you have anything to do with that?" Bob grabbed Charles's shirtfront and pushed Charles toward the shadow of the cookhouse. "What happened out here?"

"I didn't mean anything," Charles said. "She didn't understand." Charles tried to make himself shut up, but his mouth seemed to keep on working despite his

405

effort. "Don't know why she thinks she's so good. The damn Danes give me a pain. Always did. Cypri's a bitch and Daisy's a saint. Right, man?"

"Did you grab her?" Bob shook Charles violently. "If you did, I'm gonna punch you till I drop."

A cunning look came into Charles's face. "One of the nigger boys did it, one of the car parkers," he said.

"What? You mean you saw it? You didn't help her?"

Charles seemed confused again. "I was out at the van," he said. "I saw a struggle. I was too late."

"You liar! Why didn't you come inside, then? Why were you hiding out here?" Bob could contain himself no longer, and he swung his right fist at Charles. It connected satisfyingly. Charles staggered backward, cursing, and then swung in turn. He missed. Charles grabbed Bob and tried to wrestle him to the ground.

"My God," Mab exclaimed, looking out the window of the guest house. "What's happening out there?"

She had just poured a shot of Scotch for Philip, from the small bar in his room. After murmuring reassurances to Philip for several minutes in the dining room, Mab had suggested they leave. They had left by the dining room door that connected with the walkway to Philip's room. Philip was obviously suffering. Once in the guest room, he had sunk into a chair and put his head in his hands. After a few moments, Mab had ventured to suggest a drink.

Through the window beside the bar, she could see the two dark forms swinging at each other.

At her words, Philip looked up. From outside the window, they both heard a faint stream of profanity and a thumping sound. Philip got up to look. The men were right below them, in the shadow of the house. Looking down at the tops of their heads, Mab and Philip couldn't make out who they were. As they watched, the two traded blows again.

"Perhaps I should go down and try to stop it," Philip said.

Even as he spoke, the heavier of the two men

crumpled up. The other stood over him, chest heaving, and then turned and strode out of their view. A moment later, the crumpled figure managed to stumble up and flounder off in the opposite direction.

"What do you think that was?" Mab asked, handing Philip the glass of Scotch. She poured another for herself.

"Someone settling an argument, I guess," Philip said. "God, Mab, what a night. I've been trying to think what I should do." He took a gulp of his drink. "Do you think I should go over and see Daisy?"

Mab didn't know what to answer.

"Maybe not tonight," she said finally. "I'm sure Champ will give Daisy a sedative. She's probably asleep already. I think you should leave her to Champ until tomorrow."

Mab walked over to the fireplace and sat down, and Philip took the chair opposite hers. He sighed. He wished he could tell Mab the truth about Daisy. But that wasn't possible. He couldn't tell Daisy's secret. He was terribly sorry now that he had been using that secret against her. He had certainly been wrong to think that he could help Daisy escape the unhealthy situation she was in. He had behaved stupidly and felt like an idiot. He had used bad judgment all the way. That was a realization that had been brought home to him more than once this year.

Philip stared at Mab with such a miserable expression on his face that she longed to put her arms around him and comfort him.

"Philip, don't blame yourself for what happened," Mab said softly.

"Why not? If I'm not to blame, who is? I forced the engagement on her. Obviously she didn't want it."

"Vivienne said it was Cypriana who was pushing the whole thing," Mab said. "You know that Cypri's close to Daisy." Mab paused. "Philip," she went on, "perhaps I shouldn't say it, but Daisy did something like this once before." Maybe telling him was unfair to

407

Daisy but Philip certainly shouldn't blame himself for Daisy's odd behavior.

Philip looked surprised. "She did?"

Mab nodded. "At Mother's funeral. Daisy tried to throw herself into the grave, crying that it was all her fault that Mother died. Some nonsense. I only bring it up because I remember that Cypri took her home, and by the time we got back to the house Daisy was perfectly all right again. So this may be the same, just a momentary thing. She'll probably be fine tomorrow morning."

Philip looked somewhat relieved. "She was really all right?"

"Just fine. I think she'll be fine."

"God, I hope so." Philip drank the rest of his Scotch in one gulp. He put his glass down on the coffee table. A silence fell between them.

"Mab." Philip said her name into the silence, looking over at her. "This all seems strange to you, doesn't it? I mean, my coming over here, engaged to Daisy."

Mab did not know what to reply.

"Mab, tell me. Why did you run away that morning in London?" Philip actually sounded wistful. "I've wondered about it so often."

"Oh, Philip." Mab rose and paced back and forth in front of the fireplace. She had to keep moving; otherwise she might simply sit down next to Philip, run her hands through his dark hair, and touch his cheek. Locking her hands together, she took a deep breath and said, "I have a complex, I think. It's hard to explain. I don't know if I can."

Philip waited, his dark eyes on her face.

"I mean, it's more than a complex."

Philip still said nothing.

Mab began to cry.

"Mab!" Startled, Philip stood up.

"Oh, my God." Mab felt the tears running down her cheeks and she wanted to laugh at the same time.

"You must think everyone in the world is cracking up tonight."

As Philip came toward her, Mab backed up against the fireplace, tears still spilling from her eyes. It was so impossible. How could she tell anyone the truth? She was trapped with the truth, alone with it; she *knew*. There was something the matter with her and there was no one she could tell.

Gently, Philip took Mab into his arms. She felt his hand caress her hair and her throat. She put her wet cheek against his shoulder, and her tears stopped.

"I thought that night was so good," Philip mummured. "I was falling in love with you."

"Good? You thought it was good?" Mab lifted her head and looked into Philip's face to see if he were telling her the truth. His dark eyes stared into hers.

"I thought *you* didn't enjoy it." He looked searchingly at her, and she felt the blood in her veins heat up; her cheeks flamed.

"Didn't enjoy it? Oh, I did, it was perfect, it was wonderful for me, But the next morning . . . I thought you wanted to get rid of me fast. I thought I was—hadn't been any good in bed. Don't you know what I mean?" Mab's cheeks were burning.

"Good God!" Philip seemed genuinely surprised. "Couldn't you tell that I loved every minute?"

Mab blushed furiously. "I guess I don't have much experience," she said.

"What made you think I wanted to get rid of you? I was rude, I'm afraid, to talk on the telephone, but as I've tried to explain, it really was catastrophic news. It had nothing to do with you."

Mab did not answer, and in a moment Philip kissed her cheeks where they were wet from tears.

"What did you think?" he whispered.

Mab's fingers trembled. She put one hand up to Philip's hair and caressed it tentatively. He turned his head and kissed the palm of her hand. She told herself that Philip really was her friend. He wouldn't lie to her.

"Philip, am I—is there something the matter with me?"

"What?"

Mab felt as if her whole body were blushing. It was now or never, if she was ever going to find out the truth. She forced her words out.

"I think I'm made wrong inside."

"What?" Philip held her very closely in his arms; Mab had to hold her head back awkwardly to see his face. His expression was bemused. "What do you mean?"

Mab was desperate. She could think of no refined way of asking the question. She plunged.

"Am I too big? Is it hard for you to get an orgasm?"

Philip released her a little so that he could look at her face. He seemed confounded.

"Mab, you are the most beautiful woman I can imagine, inside and out. You're heaven to make love to. How could you possibly believe there is anything wrong with you?"

"You mean there isn't?"

"You're perfect."

"But some of the men I've known—" Mab stopped.

Philip's hands grasped her shoulders. "I don't know what sort of men you've known—I can't imagine— but if they didn't adore you they must be mental patients. I can't take one more minute of this." His arms slid around her and he pulled her up to him and kissed her. After a moment his lips parted hers and she felt his tongue in her mouth. Her body relaxed against his. This was right, to be kissing Philip this way. She let her arms slide up around his shoulders. She touched the back of his neck with her hands. She remembered the back of his neck and the feel of it made her close her eyes and hold tightly to him. Philip had made the whole world seem new—or maybe it was the old world but she had been reborn. Philip said she was perfect. But what he said really was nothing; what

410

counted was that he was like her, kind like her, strange like her, nice in the same way, and they were together. Her body seemed to be melting into his. His lips slid across her face. He murmured love words to her, kissing her earlobe and calling her a crazy girl and a darling whom he would like to shake. Her happiness was so great that it threatened to make her cry again.

"There's no way to tell you how happy you are making me." Mab didn't know if she said these words or only thought them; her mouth was locked to Philip's again and he knew, she was sure, exactly what she was thinking. "Sweet," he whispered, slightly lifting his head and kissing the skin of her lips for an instant. She felt his mouth on her eyelids and her brow. He must be telling the truth; he must care for her; it was her last thought before all thoughts became sensations—of being lifted up, of being carried. She saw the chiffon dress on the bed in a watery heap, and as if they sailed in that sea they were naked on top of it, making love. Everything but sensation was suspended. Time went neither forward nor backward there on the bed, it was concentrated in the instant which made them moan and cry out in release and joy.

As he was climbing the stairs with Daisy in his arms, Champ had decided he would get his bag from his room and administer a sedative to her. Daisy was shivering violently, her face still screwed up in a tight mask. Gently, Champ laid her on her bed and went into the opposite bedroom for his supplies. When he came back, he'd closed and locked the bedroom door. He wanted no interruptions until he had some idea what was the matter with his patient.

Turning from the door, Champ found that Daisy had moved; she was crouching up against the head-board of the bed. She stared at him through wide-open eyes as he filled a syringe. When he approached her she shook her head and began to sob again.

"Don't touch me," she begged. "Please don't touch

411

me." Her voice was very strained. She tumbled over onto her face and sobbed into the pillow, heavy sobs which seemed to grow in strength. Champ decided to give her a few minutes. Perhaps she needed the emotional release of her tears. He put down his syringe and stood watching her. A long time seemed to pass. Finally, Daisy's sobs were less intense.

He was picking up his syringe again when he heard Cypri and Vivienne outside the door inquire about Daisy. Champ sent them away. After hearing Cypri's voice, Daisy began to sob harder again.

"What is it, honey?" Champ said at last. "Don't you want me to give you a shot so that you can rest?"

To his surprise, Daisy looked up and spoke, tears running down her face.

"I'm sorry," she whispered. "I'm so sorry. Cypri must be furious at me. But when he kissed me—"

Champ stared at her. As he stood watching her, he had been wondering about her hysteria. He remembered now that she had pulled quite a scene at her aunt's funeral, though he hadn't thought of that in years. Daisy normally seemed very quiet, though certainly well-balanced; only at China Dane's grave had she ever seemed more than just high-strung. Champ frowned.

"Who kissed you?"

Daisy shook her hair back; it had partly come loose from its braid and tendrils hung in her face. She opened her mouth, seemed to think, and then said, "Champ, I don't want to accuse anybody. It was just—a boy who—I was on the back porch and he came out and threw up and then he—kissed me—as if he were going to rape me and—" She broke off, fresh tears gathering in her eyes.

Actually, Daisy now sounded quite rational, Champ thought. He put the syringe on the table and sat down on the bed beside her.

"You mean someone tried to rape you?"

As if his words made her suddenly conscious of her

body, Daisy looked down. She was hugging her arms tightly over her chest, holding up the torn part of her gown. She looked back at Champ. "It seemed like that to me," she said.

"What do you mean? If someone tried to rape you, you must tell me who. The person needs help. He might rape someone else." Champ looked very serious.

Daisy slowly stopped crying completely. She drew her breath and closed her eyes, trying to picture the scene on the porch. What had caused the awful revulsion, the total hatred for Charles that she had felt? The fact that he touched her breast? But that wasn't rape.

She opened her eyes. Champ's concerned face was watching hers. She took another breath.

"You see, I'm not really—normal," she said softly.

"What do you mean?" Champ asked, looking puzzled.

"Well, I'm afraid of men. Ever since I was little, always. My father used to beat me, and then another man—the one who—killed Mother." A few tears came into Daisy's eyes and she blinked them away.

She fell silent.

"Tell me about it, Daisy," Champ said gently.

Daisy shivered. "My father would hit me with a belt," she said. "I used to feel so helpless. I was so terrified of him I could hardly breathe when he was around. And the other man—he was huge, like a giant, and he tried to force me to—do things, and then he'd just hit me in the head when I wouldn't. He knocked me out once. I tried to forget. Truly. I mean, in my brain, I know all men aren't mean, I know they're not all cruel, but I can't seem to control my nerves. Men terrify me. Can you understand?"

"You poor kid," Champ said. He looked at Daisy, all golden hair and skin and big blue eyes. His expression was genuinely sympathetic, Daisy thought. "Maybe you need to get psychiatric help," he said.

After a moment Daisy spoke softly.

"So you see, when—tonight when he tried to kiss

me, it felt to me as if he were attacking me even though he probably wasn't. I think he was just drunk, anyway. And I shouldn't have been standing out there."

A thought struck Champ. "Daisy, sweetie. Are you afraid of Philip too?"

Daisy looked down and felt the blood rush to her cheeks.

"You were going to marry him and you're afraid of him?"

Should she tell Champ everything? Daisy looked up at him. In the light of the bedside lamp, she studied his square, familiar, likable face. He was so good. She *really* knew that. He loved Cypri very much, apparently; telling him the whole truth about Cypri wouldn't help anyone. She was in her present mess because of confessing to Philip, the dumbest move she had made in her entire life. No, it was better to make Champ think she had a different reason.

"I've lived off the Danes almost all my life, Champ," she said. "If I can do something for Cypri—for you—"

"That's nonsense. You can't get married for *our* sakes. Anyway what good would it do us?"

"Well, Cypri said—it might keep Philip from gambling."

"Look, just forget about that. It's your happiness that's important." Champ studied Daisy. Ever since she had come to live in his house, he had wanted to reach Daisy. He knew she had an excellent mind; sometimes when they were both laughing over something Cypri did they'd catch each other's eye almost in comradeship. But Daisy would always withdraw from the momentary contact, shrink back. She had become an intriguing object to Champ; he was happy to begin to understand her. Another thought struck him.

"Daisy, tell me the truth. Are you afraid of me? I mean, sitting right here, right now, are you scared of me?"

Daisy's lips parted.

414

"Think, now. Tell me the truth," Champ said, bending a searching look on her face.

Daisy did think. She *had* been afraid of him, she knew. Was she now? She looked closely at his boyish, freckled face. She remembered all the times Champ had been kind to her. And tonight, he had said, "It's your happiness that's important." No one else had ever said that to her.

"Well—" Daisy said. She was surprised to feel herself start to smile at him. Champ grinned back, pleased.

"You're not really scared of me, are you? Admit it," he said.

Daisy stopped hugging herself and let her arms slide to her sides. Her body felt more relaxed, and she sighed. The torn part of her dress came down, exposing her breast, but she did not care. It felt so good not to be shivering and miserable.

Champ thought she looked very pretty in the soft light. She noticed that he glanced at her bare breast, but his eyes didn't linger on it.

"Shall we play doctor?" he asked softly. He actually looked mischievous. Daisy's eyes widened slightly. Her pupils appeared enormous.

"I'm going to touch your hand, and you tell me what that does to you." Gently, Champ drew his forefinger over the top of Daisy's right hand. She gasped.

"Wow. That much?" Champ grinned again. "What if I touched your hair?"

Daisy blinked, but she held still. With infinite care, Champ reached his hands around her head and found the pins holding the bedraggled flowers. He slid the pins out, pulled away the camellias, and loosened her blond hair from its braid. "I love your hair. It's so thick and it's such a pretty color," he said. He pulled it out and let it fall around her shoulders. He drew back. "Now will you let me dry off your face?" he asked.

As if she were hypnotized, Daisy nodded. Champ's

415

square-tipped fingers carefully stroked her cheeks, as gently as one would touch a kitten. Her cheeks were still damp, and he brushed off the tears and then took her head between his two hands, holding it very carefully.

"So far, is it okay?" He stroked his hands lightly down her hair.

"Yes," she said, only breathing the word.

"You have such a pretty face and body," Champ said softly. He touched her throat. Then he drew back. He looked at her without smiling.

"Would you touch me?" he asked.

"What do you mean?"

"Haven't you ever wanted to be close to someone?"

He picked up her right hand and held it between his palms. "Your hand is cold." He lifted it and before she realized what he was doing, he held it against his lips and then pressed it to his cheek. His cheek felt smooth but hard; she could feel the muscles under the skin. Tentatively, she moved her hand. She touched his ear, and then his hair. It was strange; maybe somewhere deep inside of herself she had been wanting to do that; it seemed to satisfy some instinct in her. It seemed so strange to touch a man. Yet he was, really, just another human being. And he was charming and dear and had always been kind to her, kinder than anyone in the world except Aunt China.

"Would you let me kiss you?"

When he whispered his request, she was anticipating it. She didn't feel quite ready. Yet—it might be all right. She moved a little closer to him. Her finger was on his temple and she could feel the pulse throbbing there. He seemed completely caught up in what they were doing, and suddenly she was, too. She wanted all the new sensations she was experiencing. It was so different to feel desired by a man. It was scary, but it wasn't unpleasant. As his face came closer, he closed his eyes and she closed hers, too, letting her fingers tangle in his hair. His arms held her more tightly. He

416

kissed the side of her nose and then found her mouth. He held his mouth on hers for a long time and she grew breathless and gasped for air when he pulled up his head. He looked into her eyes; apparently what he saw there satisfied him, because he kissed her again.

Daisy was still kneeling. Without knowing how, she slid against Champ, and then they were both lying full length on the bed, pressed together. She touched his back; she liked the feel of his heavy muscles. He stopped kissing her for a moment and shrugged out of his white jacket, letting it drop to the floor. The ruffles on his shirtfront tickled her; as they touched lightly against her bare nipple, she began to feel very aroused. She kissed Champ back and then she whispered his name.

"What, darling?" he whispered back.

He sometimes called her "sweetie" when he addressed her around the house; "sweetie" was a doctor's word, a bedside-manner word; "darling" was different. Somehow it made Daisy intensely happy. It was so new to want a man to care about you; care a little, anyway, for a few minutes.

"I never have," she whispered.

He was kissing her throat and his arms were all the way around her, both hands spread wide against her bare back. He smelled good, she thought, like soap and something else, a clean smell, a doctor's smell.

He said her name. In a way, it was even better than "darling." He lifted her head and looked at her, and repeated "Daisy." Then he added, so softly she almost couldn't hear him, "Do you want to make love?"

"I think I'll die if we don't," she said, and hid her face against his shoulder.

"And you never have?"

She raised her head and looked at him. "Do you mind?"

His gray eyes widened as he stared into her blue ones from an inch away. "Are you kidding? *Mind*?"

"I thought boys didn't like—virgins."

Daisy heard Champ chuckle; when he laughed he could feel his stomach muscles contract against her.

"Well, men don't like them to stay virgins," he said, kissing her temple. "Not when they're beautiful, darling girls like you."

He kissed her on the lips again, and this time when he finished, she was trembling. She wanted him. She squeezed her eyes shut and let him pull off her lace dress. Before he undressed, he caressed her for a long time, until every inch of her skin felt loved. She wanted to caress all of his naked body in turn. From under her lashes, she looked at him as he pulled off his clothes. He was beautiful, muscular and smooth, with just a few brown hairs along the middle of his chest catching the light as he turned to her. He saw her peeking shyly at him and he laughed and caught her against him, and kissed her and lay across her body. They were really making love. She was the girl *on* the bed with him, at last. How strange life was, how ironic; you might as well go ahead and live it, she thought, and not start thinking about the twists and turns that it took. Maybe it all meant something in the end. When Champ finally managed things so that they were locked together. Daisy was rapturously happy. She felt as if she had bubbles in her blood. She called Champ's name, and he kissed her and kissed her, until they were both exhausted and lying back with sweat on their brows, and it was good then, too. It was right, as if something were adjusted that for a long while had been tilted the wrong way.

Champ kissed her hair, and she smiled.

Frank wished Cypri would move closer to him or at least say something. She had flung herself into the Chevvy and ordered "just drive." As he hit the road, Cypri had let her head fall back against the car seat and closed her eyes silent. Since then she hadn't moved. The lights of Dentspur were growing brighter ahead. He wished she'd speak. But it was really wonderful just to sit next to Cypri again, to be able to look over and see her there beside him; it was like a miracle. In the light from the dashboard, her gold dress gleamed and the white skin of her bare arm and shoulder shone like satin.

Frank had been doing a steady seventy and he had to slow down as the outskirts of the little town approached. Cypri opened her eyes.

"Where are we?"

"Dentspur."

"Oh." Cypri closed her eyes again. She was still steaming. She had spent the last half-hour reviewing Champ's transgressions. But that was futile. What she really had to do was cool down and think. Daisy had definitely blown the engagement. Good-bye, Philip. She could kill Daisy. But what if she, Cypriana, took over? What if she just walked into Philip's room and took off her clothes and told him he could have her? She'd straighten him out and run Downforth into the bargain. Champ could go to hell. Champ could have Daisy.

Frank stopped at the first Dentspur stoplight and looked over at Cypri. In a minute she turned her head and stared at him. The palms of his hands broke out in sweat. He felt sixteen.

"I didn't think I'd ever feel this way again," he said. His voice came out sounding husky.

"What?" Cypri's blue eyes were wide.

The light changed and Frank turned into a dark side street. If he remembered correctly, down that way was an old sand pit. He reached it and pulled the Chevvy off into a deserted grove of trees. Beyond the trees, the water in the middle of the sand pit shone in the moonlight. He waited for Cypri to say something.

Cypri was staring out the front window and thinking hard. Should she go back to Land's End right now? Perhaps she should act fast. Just walk into Philip's room. If he were asleep, she could climb in bed with him. Let him wake up and find her there.

Frank thought of what a release it would be to kiss Cypri. It had been so long since he had. He had gone out with plenty of other girls, but not one of them came close to Cypri Dane. She was his girl. He stared at her. Her white skin seemed to illuminate the darkness. A warm, soft breeze coming through the open car window brought him the smell of her perfume—a heavy, dark, mysterious scent that seemed like part of the night around them. The leaves overhead rustled faintly. There was no other sound but their breathing.

On the other hand, Cypri thought, perhaps that would be a bit abrupt. Philip must have thought he loved Daisy; look at the size of the ring he gave her! Some quality in the little simp had made Philip propose. Of course, she, Cypri, had never really used her powers on Philip. And there was tactical value in a surprise maneuver. Still, if Philip liked Daisy's sort of girl, a direct approach might turn him off. Maybe she should cool it until tomorrow, see how the land lay. Or would she lose the chance if she waited? Well, she'd have another night—Philip was supposed to stay until Monday.

She sighed with vexation. She hated having to make decisions.

"Cypri." Frank spoke her name out loud, longing for her to slide over closer to him.

"Oh. Frank." She peered at his face through the darkness. "Why did you stop?"

"Should I say I ran out of gas?"

His sally fell flat. Cypri seemed to have her mind on something else. Frank thought maybe she was worrying about Daisy.

Cypri gave another sigh. "Frank, what do you think of Philip?"

"Think of Philip? I don't think of Philip. Cypri. Honey—" Cautiously he touched her throat, moving a little closer to her and letting his right arm slide across the seat behind her. "I think of *you*," he said.

420

"I think of you all the time, Cypri. It drives me crazy."

Cypriana only half listened to him. Suppose Philip had locked the door of the guest house? Could she climb in a window?

Frank let his fingers wander to the ends of the gold material tied over Cypri's right shoulder. It looked like a square knot. Mentally, he had been untying it all night. Now he cautiously loosened it. The two ends came apart and the material slid down, revealing her beautiful right breast.

"Please," Frank whispered. "Cypri, please. Kiss me."

Cypri felt her nipple contract and she stared down at herself in surprise. Frank's left hand touched her cheek to turn her head toward him. His arm tightened around her and his hand slid down to cover her breast. When he kissed her, her pulse jumped and warmth surged through her body. Frank had always kissed well, she remembered. She let her lips part and her tongue probe into his mouth. What time was it—one or two? She could fool around with Frank and still get back in time to wind up with Philip if she decided to. She let her eyes close and gave Frank a kiss that made his heart pound.

Then she pulled away. "Hey, what is this, high school revisited?" she said. "We're going to *park*?"

"There's a motel back on the highway. I'll get a room."

She caught sight of his face. "Frank, look at me."

"No." He turned his head toward the side window.

She hopped over into his lap and craned her head around to see his face.

"My God," she said. Frank's eyes were full of tears.

"Holy shit, Cypri, don't look."

"Frank. You're crying. What is it?"

"Oh, Cypri." He put his arms around her and locked her against him. She could hear his heart again pounding under her ear. "I'm just so glad to hold you. Oh, God, I don't think I've ever cried before in my life." His voice was hoarse.

421

The steering wheel was poking her in the back and she pulled away to look curiously at him. His emotion was touching.

"Well, let's go to the motel," she said, trying to find the ends of her dress. "Can you find the back part of this?"

Frank tied her back into the gold dress, making a neat square knot, and she kissed his face while he did it. She kept on kissing him while he drove to the Dentspur Motel. He rented a room from a sleepy old lady and led Cypri in the door.

"I may only get one night," he said, closing the door and looking at her, "But you're never going to forget it."

"Really?" Cypri seemed her old self again, the crazy, beautiful kid that he loved. She unpinned the gold flowers and shook out her dark hair. "You kill me, Frank. But don't *really*," she added as he grabbed her. While he kissed her, he untied the knot again and she giggled. "It should be a slip knot," she said. He stripped the dress off and got out of his own rented finery. The bed sagged as they crashed onto it. Cypri put her mind to it; Frank had managed to arouse her in spite of her dilemma and she felt in the mood for sex. Soon she had him gasping for mercy, and she was tingling all over herself. She began to torment Frank, keeping him just on the edge of a climax but not letting him have it. He went crazy. She had forgotten how much fun Frank was. She ought to hunt him up more often. He kept saying he loved her. Once, when he made her scream with delight, she wondered if anyone were sleeping on either side of their room. Oh, well. Too bad. Frank moaned a lot, too.

Finally even her invention was exhausted. Her adrenalin must be flowing, she reflected, because she didn't feel tired, just satiated. She looked at Frank's watch.

"Don't fall asleep, Frank. It's almost four-thirty. I've got to get home."

422

"Home?" Frank seemed dazed.

"Back to Land's End. I've got to turn up there." Suddenly, Cypri remembered her plan to broach Philip. Well, she'd go to Land's End and sack out awhile and then go to work on him. She would manage something. She yawned. "Tie me back up, okay?"

On the way back to the house she sat inside the circle of Frank's arm and squeezed tight to him. He tried to get her to say when she'd see him again. Dawn light was just beginning to brighten the sky as they turned down the road to Land's End. Cypri glanced up at Frank and laughed.

"You look like a playboy," she said. "The cows won't know you." His blond hair was messed and his beard had started to grow. The whites around his green eyes were bloodshot. He grinned down at her and drove up the driveway as far as the front path. All cars were gone from the field and the big house stood silent.

"Cypri, don't say good-bye."

"Frank, I've got to go in."

"No—I mean, I know that. But now, I mean. Don't tell me good-bye, okay? Just give me a kiss and go. And I'll see you, all right? Whenever you want."

When she kissed him he didn't touch her, but simply kissed back as if he never wanted to stop.

She opened the car door cautiously. "Don't shut the door until you're down the road a way," she whispered. "Good-bye," she added, forgetting what he had asked.

He watched her gold dress flash between the porch pillars and disappear, and as she had requested, he didn't close the car door until he got home.

Vivienne opened her eyes as the light grew in the sky. For a moment, she did not have any idea where she was. Her cheek was pillowed on her hand, and her hand rested on something cold and hard. The rock! She remembered. She was down at the river.

She looked around. It was still dark there; the pines were just beginning to be outlined against the sky. The river flowed by below her. A bird began a song, sounding tentative. It was morning. Still dressed in her evening gown, Vivienne had been lying on pine needles with her head on the rock, sleeping. She moved and gasped; she was stiff all over from lying on the ground.

And Philip hadn't come.

Upstairs in the hall at Land's End, after she had spoken to Champ, Vivienne had suddenly known what she had to do. She had hurried directly down the stairs and then down the back steps of the house and across the fields. She hadn't even looked to see if there were lights on in Philip's room. It didn't matter. It was the river she had to reach, their old meeting place. She remembered going the same route so many years ago, over the field and into the pines where the little path led to the rock and the rope swing. Amazingly, everything was exactly the same. The tree still hung out over the water, though there was no longer a rope tied to it.

Ignoring her gown, Vivienne climbed up and out over the river, looking down at the gleam of the moon in the water. The damp smell of the river rose from below and she gripped her hands on the bark of the tree. Crickets were chirping, and on either bank lightning bugs flashed through the undergrowth.

She told herself it meant nothing that Philip had stayed far away from her that evening. Daisy's scene meant nothing either. Philip would come here tonight. He was drawn by the same force that drew her.

Looking at the water flow by below made her feel dizzy. Or maybe the dizziness was the aftereffects of the champagne she had drunk. She was still panting; she had almost run in her hurry. Her sandals were full of dirt, and she pulled them off and tossed them back onto the shore. She was surprised Philip wasn't already there. Maybe he would swim down the river as he had done so long ago, and climb out onto the rock naked in the moonlight, his compact body shining and wet. She imagined his face looking up, looking into the tree for her. I'm here, she thought. She would slide down and fall into his arms.

As sure as I know anything in the world, I know he'll come here tonight, Vivienne thought; the boy she had once known would come. He would have died for her.

Lying full-length on her tree, she let herself remember things they had done together, things they had said—all those things she drew on, in her work, to make her love scenes convincing. She had even looked at Robert Redford and thought of Philip. But truly now, inside the stranger in her house, was that boy still living? *He* would come to her. But was he dead? What was Philip now? a cold, polite dodo marrying a very young girl for his vanity? an obsessed gambler? a self-destructive playboy? He seemed to be all those things. But were they just a shelter for the one inside, a fort in which the real Philip was hiding? Or was he gone completely? Had she killed him all those years ago?

She turned over on the limb and stared up into the sky. The moon was so bright that the stars were dimmed, but if you looked for a long time you could see them, thousands and billions of them up there, and every one in earth's galaxy, and that galaxy just a little knothole in the whole of the universe. She wondered who had first made the word "star" mean a famous person. Had someone in Hollywood thought of it? Or had "star" always meant a celebrity as well as one of those burning far-off fires in the sky?

She was a star. She was a famous star, and all the same she was lying on a tree trunk alone in the middle of nowhere, of South Carolina, waiting, at the mercy of fate. She was like the fisherman's wife who kept demanding more and more of the magic fish, first to be rich and then to be king and then to be pope. Fate had already been more than kind; she had fulfilled all her mother's dreams and ambitions for her—even though too late for her mother to know it—she'd had her moments on the stage, made some good films, a few *very* good scenes, not the ones the critics picked out but some she liked herself, not big scenes but good, neat jobs of work. They'd last. But now, magic fish, give me love.

Would it wash? Could she really love anyone, or anyone really love her?

She thought she heard a twig snap and she stiffened. But time passed and no one appeared. She wished that what was going to happen would hurry up and happen. That way you didn't have to think. You just coped.

Had Philip secretly been searching for the girl he once knew? Maybe he thought that his Vivienne was dead, killed stone cold by what he imagined a star had to undergo, couch casting and psychiatric analyses and face-lifts and drug injections for pep and stringent diets and insane hours and insane directors and the insane life under the California sun. Maybe she *was* dead.

For one thing, she was going to fall out of this crazy tree if her head didn't stop going around. Whoops, old girl, you've had too much to drink and now you might boot the big scene. You'll be the one in the river and your garments will hold you up for a time and then drag you to a muddy death, like we all know who. She leaned far over, daring herself to fall in. But she could swim. And she wasn't a crazy flower-crowned Ophelia, not yet. She did have a poppy in her hair. She reached up and pulled it out and dropped it beneath her and watched the river carry it off. It would go to sea, like Bobby Shafto. Pretty Bobby Shafto. He'll come back and marry me, pretty Bobby—Bobbo—

Would she marry Philip? Jesus, why did she ask herself questions like that? Everything seemed stuck— life seemed stuck and time seemed stuck in a deep, deep groove. She didn't have to think about anything, answer any questions. She was a girl waiting for her demon lover. She just wished things would hurry up and happen. Whatever was going to. Or was anything?

Probably Philip was tucked up in the big bed in the guest house. No romantic jaunts into the back woods for him. What the hell *was* he doing? Maybe in the house telling Daisy to buck up? Daisy. Talk about Ophelia—that scene Daisy played went *Hamlet* one better. The whole engagement might have seemed unreal, but Daisy's frightful cry was right off the wall. Vivienne told herself she really should think that situation out. Why had Daisy done it? Was it simply the only way she could outwit Cypriana, by screaming? Cypri wanted Daisy to marry Philip—that was clear, and Daisy lived with Cypri like a vassal. Cypri had always led Daisy around by the nose, Vivienne knew. Maybe Daisy had to take extreme measures to keep Cypri from getting her way.

Actually, Vivienne thought, that scene in the dining room had left her numb, and she was still numb . . . and a numbskull to be hanging around here. She was tired. After a while, slowly, she groped her way down out of the tree, skinning her right arm slightly as she slid down the trunk. She'd sit a moment and rest beside the rock. She spit on her arm and rubbed it. It wasn't bleeding. She leaned her head against her hand. And that was the last thing she remembered. She hadn't expected she would fall asleep.

Now, it must be hours later. She stood up and groaned. She hurt all over. God, she must have been drunk last night. Drunk and out of her head to expect Philip to come running down here. They were grown-ups now. All grown-up.

She'd better go home before it got lighter. Immensely tired, she picked up her sandals and walked barefoot up the path. It was going to be a lovely day. Many birds were singing now. The sky in the east was full of rosy dawn light.

Come on, Vivienne, she said to herself. Her muscles

felt better now that she was moving. She walked out from the edge of the pines and paused, looking across the wide plowed field. The white columns of Land's End gleamed through the willow trees.

She stood and stared at the house. She had gotten Land's End back. She would get Philip back.

She lifted her chin. Everything came together and made sense. All this nonsense about whether he was or wasn't the old Philip. Of course he was. Whether he came to the river or not. Whether he spoke to her or not. Whether he was rich, broke, obsessed, stupid, old or young, happy or sad, smart or dumb, he was hers and she wanted him. With all of her, she wanted him.

She began to walk rapidly down a furrow toward the house. Her dress whipped around her ankles and the growing light on the horizon turned it to flame as she strode. She began to run. Clouds in the sky caught fire over her head. She ran toward the sunrise, dropping her shoes on the ground so that she could pull up her skirt. She ran faster and faster, not stopping until she had raced up the stairs to the back porch. Gasping, she looked at the guest house. Should she run down the walkway? bang on Philip's door?

In the glass pane beside the back door she caught sight of herself. Her hair was wild, and she was covered with dirt and pine needles. And she was still rather tired, come to think of it. Gradually her breathing slowed. Philip must be asleep. She'd go in and upstairs to bed for a while, and then later in the morning she'd confront him. She looked again at the guest house. He was here, and he was hers. It was just as sure as the sunrise. Whether you cared or not, the sun rose every day; whether you watched or not.

Softly, she let herself into the back door and walked through the silent house to the front hall. She stopped there and looked through one of the small panes by the front door. The ball of the sun cleared the horizon, sunshine bathed her face, and she smiled.

XX

When Champ awoke sometime during the night, he realized he was lying next to Daisy. She was soundly asleep; he could hear her regular breathing. Careful not to disturb her, he inched out of the bed and found his clothes on the floor. A little moonlight coming through a crack in the draperies gave him enough light to pull on his pants and collect the rest of his belongings. With his shoes in one hand, he let himself out of her door and checked the long hall. No one was around. He walked softly across in his bare feet to his own door. It was standing open. Champ went inside and shut the door.

The bed was empty. Where was Cypri? She must have been so upset that she'd gone back to their house. Champ yawned. He dropped his clothes and shoes on a chair, took off his trousers again and climbed into bed. He was very sleepy.

The next sound he heard was an insistent knocking on the door. Finally he came to enough to realize where he was. He was in bed at Land's End and Cypri was now snuggled up against him, fast asleep. It was morning. He moved and Cypri groaned in her sleep. She hated to be disturbed.

"What is it?" he called.

"Dr. Alexander, it's the telephone for you. I'm sorry—your answering service said to wake you." It sounded like Johnny Mae speaking.

It was Champ's turn to groan. His head felt like it needed to be packed in cotton wool. He sat up.

"Okay, I'll come."

Johnny Mae opened the door slightly and spoke in a lower voice.

"There's an extension phone right by your bed if you want to speak there."

"Oh. I see. Thanks." Champ picked up the white telephone beside him. His service had an urgent message for him to call Sugar Hastings.

"I think he swallowed Clorox, but I'm not sure. I mean, he *smells* like Clorox all over—" Sugar Hastings was beside herself.

"Give him some milk, as much as he'll drink. Then take him immediately to the hospital. I'll meet you there and we'll check him out." Champ hung up. Cypri groaned again. He leaned over and kissed her cheek.

"Honey, I've got to go out," he whispered. He wasn't sure whether she heard him or not. She burrowed deeper into her pillow. He found some clothes, wondering if he had time for a cup of coffee. Better get it at the hospital. The house was silent when he came out of the bedroom. Across the hall, Vivienne's door was closed. He hurried downstairs without noticing that Mab's door stood open and her bed was empty.

Champ's Porsche was parked under the window of the guest house, and when its motor started, the sound woke Mab. She was deliciously warm, clasped tightly to Philip, and she lay and listened to him breathing. He was still asleep. She tried breathing exactly when he did. He took long, slow breaths. She wanted to kiss him, but she didn't want to wake him up. She squeezed her eyes shut and just let herself feel happy. They were together. There was nothing wrong with her, at least as far as Philip was concerned! The night had been perfect. She held her breath and let happiness wash through her. Could you be this happy? Her brain felt ready to explode and her skin was all prickly. Philip thought she was beautiful both inside and out. Another wave of happiness washed over her.

Finally she opened her eyes. Blinking, she looked toward the light coming in under the curtains at the windows. Another lovely sunny morning. And what was going to happen? The earlier events of the night before came back to her. Surely Philip's engagement to Daisy was now a thing of the past. So there wasn't any reason why they couldn't—Mab thought of Vivienne. Philip and Vivienne had seemed completely indifferent to each other yesterday. The childhood crush must have been outgrown; neither of them had mentioned it. There was nothing to keep Philip and her apart, once things got sorted out with Daisy. In fact, during her trip to England in February Mab had been offered a job at the Keidel-Hanway Gallery of Modern Art in London. There were wonderful museums in London! She could marry Philip and find a job there.

She let herself have another moment of pure happiness and then she considered the coming day. A lot would have to be resolved. First of all, she didn't want to be seen walking out of Philip's room in broad daylight, wearing last night's ball gown. She looked at the clock. It was seven-thirty. Reluctantly, she gently disengaged herself from Philip's embrace and edged off the bed. He didn't awaken. She padded over to one of the front windows and looked out of a crack in the curtains. Judging from the cars parked behind the house, none of the servants had come back yet—Johnny Mae was the only one who stayed at Land's End. Johnny Mae was no doubt up already, probably working over in the kitchen.

Mab picked up her chiffon dress and pulled it on. She couldn't find the silk flowers that had been in her hair. Softly, she moved to Philip's side and looked at him. Ironic that today, on the first morning she hadn't dreaded waking up beside a man, she was the one who had to leave. But she really should go if she were

431

going to do it without everyone seeing her. She touched the sheet covering Philip's shoulder and then made herself turn away. She decided to go down the inside stairs. That way, she wouldn't have to cross the walkway—she could go under it. She quietly let herself out the door, praying that she was right about Johnny Mae being up already. Mab took the stairs down to a small hall and the outside door, and there was no sign of Johnny Mae.

She darted across under the walkway and then hugged the house, skirting the gardenia bushes, in case anyone might be looking out of an upstairs window. In a moment she was running up the sun-warmed stone steps of the front porch. The front door was open and through the screen door she saw that the hall was deserted. Carefully she opened the screen door and in a moment she had made the stairs. She ran up them soundlessly. All the doors upstairs were closed except hers and she was quickly safe in her own room.

Once there, she was sorry. The bed looked big and empty and lonely. She should have stayed with Philip, awakened with him, not cared what anyone thought. Life was so short. You ought to grab every moment. Should she go back?

She smiled at herself in the mirror. Her eyes were shining. After last night, she really had no doubt of what was going to happen. It was silly to be nervous now. She pulled off the ball gown and found her night-gown laid at the bottom of the bed. She was too happy to sleep, she thought, but she'd crawl in bed and re-member everything that had happened, until the others woke up. They'd all probably sleep for hours. She stretched luxuriously and burrowed into her pillow, and before she could remember half the things Philip had said, she fell asleep.

Johnny Mae had the coffee ready when Estelle and Sue arrived; later Chooky and Baker came in for their breakfasts. In two hours they had the rented tables and chairs all packed away and the dining room ready for the brunch to be laid. Vivienne had suggested that on Sunday Johnny Mae prepare dishes of scrambled eggs and things like kippers and grits and broiled tomatoes and ham biscuits and put them on hot trays on the sideboard. Vivienne said she had no idea when people would get up. Everyone could help himself when he came down.

By eleven the hot food sat on trays waiting, but there was no one about. Johnny Mae and Estelle rested on the back porch and gossiped with Chooky, and Baker and Sue played gin rummy at the kitchen table.

Vivienne awoke at noon. The house was so quiet she could faintly hear the clock in the downstairs hall sound its twelve strokes. Gratefully, she stretched all her muscles. It was nice to wake up in bed and not on the ground. Her head felt all right, too. She had a funny taste in her mouth, but that seemed the extent of the damage that last night had done. She sat up, drew her knees to her chest and hugged them, and then jumped out of bed. She had plenty to do.

While she brushed her teeth she thought about the funny ideas that came into her head. Drinking all that champagne and going down to the river, sitting around down there suffering—what had possessed her? A thought struck her. Perhaps that was exactly the way Philip had suffered, waiting there those twenty-odd years ago thinking she was going to marry him and having her turn up and—well, never mind, she thought. Let the dead past bury the past. She looked at her face in the bathroom mirror. Her eyes were bright and she looked rested and relaxed. There was nothing like knowing your own mind. She wanted Philip . . . or even any old wreck of Philip—whatever was left. She felt excitement just at the thought. If she touched him—

At the thought of touching him she whirled and ran back into the bedroom, almost laughing out loud. She grinned as she looked through her closet. What should she wear? The sundress she'd taken to New

433

York for the Sally Berman show was hanging there and she grabbed it. That was it. She put on white sandals with tiny crisscross laces and tied the dress over her shoulders, not too tightly. When she bent over, the tops of her breasts showed. Her hair was still clean from last night, and she brushed it until it snapped with electricity. She didn't feel like putting on any makeup, but she did put a little blue around her eyes. Her face was glowing; she didn't need another thing. Except maybe a very springlike perfume. She hunted amid the bottles on her dressing table.

When Daisy woke up, she couldn't remember what she had been dreaming except that it had been something very strange. She sat up to look at the clock, but it wasn't where it should be, and then she remembered that she was at Land's End. The clock on the dresser said twelve-fifteen. My God, she had slept! For a moment she felt disoriented, and then she remembered the entire night. She drew her breath in. Champ was gone; when had he left? And oh, my God, what a mess there was to straighten out. Charles Honeychurch, the scene in the dining room—Cypri—and—Daisy blushed —Champ. He was so nice to her last night. She wasn't a virgin! Suddenly she was physically aware of that fact. So much had happened!

She hopped up and ran over to open the curtains. It was a gorgeous day. The lawn and fields were bathed with sunshine, and a slight breeze was blowing from the ocean, bringing the smell of the water and the mingled scents of what seemed like a thousand flowers. She breathed it in to the bottom of her lungs. Oh, Land's End—she loved it. She decided to take a quick bath before she dressed; turning from the window, she went into the bathroom humming. Everything had to be straightened out, but things were so much better than they had been.

Now, why did she think that?

Daisy paused, in the middle of pinning up her hair.

Things were better—did they seem so because she didn't have to marry Philip? No, she thought in amazement. That wasn't it. It was that she had made love with a man. With Champ! She was—normal; or anyway, bisexual like Cypri was always telling her. She had *liked* making love with Champ. That was amazing. Maybe she'd like it with other men. Maybe she really could leave Cypri, leave her self-imposed bondage. A new world lay ahead, full of fantastic possibilities. She felt actually in high spirits. She, Daisy, was happy.

She submerged up to her chin in the tub and scrubbed herself, and afterward she brushed her teeth for a long time and then gargled. She remembered how revolted she had felt by Charles's kiss. It seemed to have happened ages ago, to someone else. She felt fresh and new.

While she brushed her hair, she stared at herself in wonder. The girl in the mirror looked confident. She *could* leave this damaging relationship with Cypri. She could just walk out. It would mean nothing to Cypri. Cypri had Champ and anyone else she wanted. Champ was such a darling. Daisy actually felt envious. Cypri had Champ and she—Daisy—

Daisy's thoughts stopped right there, stopped and seemed to hang on the edge of something. The brush in her hand remained suspended in the air and a strand of her hair settled back against her head after the stroke she had just given it. She, Daisy, had what? Motionless, she waited for the thought to form. Of course. She had Philip.

Philip. Her blue eyes widened, and she looked into the depths of the mirror, searching the eyes of the girl there. Philip wanted to marry her. He really did. Whatever would it be like to make love with him? Could she ever do it? Her heart seemed to beat heavily as she let her thoughts race on. Would Philip be like Champ? Champ was really wonderful. And Philip was also gentle and kind, so far as she could judge. She had hated Philip for trying to help her. But now, did she still hate him? What if he turned out to be like Champ?

Why, Philip was glamorous and rich, and he wanted to take her off to live a fairy-tale life in London. And —her thoughts ran on quickly—if she married him and they were happy and he rebuilt his life, it would pay Cypriana and Champ back for everything they had done for her!

The hairbrush fell to the carpet. The soft thud it made seemed symbolic of the way things suddenly fell into place. For a moment, Daisy sat rigid and cautious, her mind exploring all the corners of the new idea. Was this it? Was this the way out? Out of her relationship with Cypri, out of a life that she had never lived to the fullest? She really couldn't be sitting here, feeling this sudden burst of utter joy, could she?

Carefully, she reviewed the situation. Philip wanted her. He had come over from England to get her. He was determined. All right, he could have her. And she wouldn't go unwillingly, sullenly. She'd make him happy! It might really be possible.

She had to trust herself and judge for herself. Should she start out by making such a drastic decision? Yet her hand was forced. She must tell Philip either yes or no this weekend, and everything was set up for it to be yes. If she fooled around about it, he would go back to England and she would lose what was possibly the happiest future she could have. Possibly. But she should risk it! She thought again of Champ and then of Philip, who so tenderly had told her he would wait for her, not push her but help her. Her mind was made up. She had actually made a decision for herself, she was operating on her own, and she felt like shouting with happiness. The life ahead of her suddenly seemed a wonderful challenge.

She jumped up, zipped herself into a blue denim jumpsuit and came back to the mirror for some lipstick. Her heart was beating hard and she saw in the mirror that her eyes were sparkling. She had never looked better in her life, she thought, or felt better either.

For a moment she lingered to look at herself, and then she went over to the bedside table, took out the red velvet box, and slipped Philip's ring onto the third finger of her left hand.

When she opened her door, the hall was deserted and the house downstairs quiet. She felt shy about being the first one down, so she closed her door again, deciding to wait until the others had gone downstairs. She sat down on the loveseat in a patch of sunshine, and admired the sparkling facets of the diamond.

Cypriana woke up vaguely remembering Champ's leaving. Had he gone to the hospital? She had heard him talking. What time was it now? She looked over at the clock. Why, the day was half gone! Her mind flew to Philip. He was probably already up. And what was she going to do?

Well, first she was going to take a shower. All that lovemaking with Frank had made her sticky. Then she was going to put on her blue halter and skirt, her most becoming outfit, and go downstairs and think of some way to get Philip alone. And after that . . . she smiled.

Hurrying frantically, in just ten minutes she left the bedroom, dressed in the sexy halter. She ran into her sisters in the upper hall. Vivienne was admiring the strapless rose-print sarong that Mab had donned for brunch.

"We were just about to go downstairs," Mab said. Mab was looking exceptionally radiant, Cypriana thought. Why, her face was positively glowing, for some reason. She must like being home.

Cypri looked around the upper hall. Daisy's door was still closed. "How's Daisy?" she asked.

"You—I thought you'd know," Vivienne said. They all looked at Daisy's door. "What does Champ say?"

"Oh, Champ went out at dawn on a call. I didn't get to speak to him. He stayed with Daisy a long time, and I was asleep when he came in, I guess." Cypri lowered her voice. "Maybe she doesn't want to come out." She would like to check on dumb Daisy, Cypri thought, but she didn't want to take the time right now. She was dying to go downstairs and see Philip.

"Well." Vivienne looked at Daisy's door with a puzzled expression. "I don't know what we should do; I'm not sure we should disturb her at all. There's brunch downstairs—let's see if Daisy comes down. Maybe she's still asleep. We can wait and ask Champ what to do."

Mab followed the other two downstairs, feeling that she couldn't be totally sure of anything until she saw Philip smile at her. That final reassurance. After that, everything would work out—Mab was positive of it.

They walked into the dining room through the double doors just as Philip stepped in through the door from the walkway. Looking quite handsome in sports jacket and gray flannel trousers, he quickly crossed the room. He greeted them all, smiling and saying good morning and what a beautiful day.

Everyone said hello, and Johnny Mae began to pour cups of coffee. Mab could scarcely bear to look at Philip without wanting to touch him. He sat down at the table. Mab helped herself to eggs from the sideboard and sat down next to him. Cypri, depositing herself across the table, stared at Philip over the rim of her coffee cup.

Philip spoke first. "Have you seen—" he began, intending to say *Daisy* when Daisy herself bounced through the double doors into the room.

"Good morning!" she said. "Oh, you're all here. I'm glad." She glanced at Johnny Mae and then went on. "I want to tell everyone right away how sorry I am about last night."

Her words fell into an absolute silence. Everybody in the room felt startled. Daisy appeared as chipper as a blue jay. She smiled. She didn't seem to mind that they were all staring at her.

Cypriana saw the ring first. Her mouth fell open.

438

Philip heard Mab make a small sound of surprise, and when he followed her gaze, he saw the ring for himself. Vivienne looked wonderingly at Daisy's changed appearance. Suddenly Vivienne, too, caught the wink of light on Daisy's finger, and like the others she stared unbelievingly at the engagement ring.

Daisy went on: "What happened last night—I know it was awful; it must have looked awful. Had you just announced our engagement, Cypri? You must have thought I was mad. But I was out on the back porch just before. And someone came out there and"— Daisy stopped and swallowed. She looked somewhat embarrassed, but she spoke cheerfully enough—"I thought he was attacking me. I mean, he kissed me and tore my dress, and I tried to scream, but I couldn't. I just shoved him back finally and tried to get away. When I got here"—Daisy looked around. She was standing right in front of the very spot where she had cowered the night before—"I guess I was hysterical. Can you all forgive me?" She looked straight at Philip as she said the last words.

"*Well*," Cypri said. Her tone was outraged. "We all know Miss Pure Daisy shouldn't be kissed!"

Mab was startled by Cypri's bitchy reaction, but actually Cypri spoke for them all. Daisy ignored Cypriana, walked to the sideboard to get a cup of coffee from Johnny Mae, and carried it over to sit on Philip's other side.

Philip appeared blanker in expression than even an Englishman could hope for.

If the house had burned down around her, Mab couldn't have moved. Vivienne stood at the sideboard with a spoonful of scrambled eggs suspended in the air. Cypriana sputtered.

"I guess you know, Daisy, we're all disgraced. Not one soul will forget the party at Land's End to the finish of time around here," Cypri said. "And it's all your fault." She stared across the table at Daisy, hoping to see her cringe.

439

"I said I was sorry," Daisy replied calmly. She looked up at Vivienne.

"Don't—worry about it," Vivienne managed to say. Her voice came out sounding very peculiar.

Daisy turned to Philip. "When are we supposed to go to Aunt Martha's?" she asked.

"Aunt Martha's." Philip repeated the words. Their meaning did not seem clear to him.

"Yesterday you told Aunt Martha that we were coming over to talk about our wedding." Daisy tried to sound casual. She wondered if Philip had noticed that she was wearing his ring. She wanted to make it crystal clear that she was now a willing fiancée. Maybe Cypri hadn't noticed the ring yet, either. Surely Cypri was going to be happy about it when she did.

"I think Aunt Martha wants us to get married outdoors. Maybe we could have a ceremony at Gardens." Daisy glanced out the side window, through which she could see part of the garden at Land's End. Perhaps Vivienne would offer to let them be married here. But Vivienne said nothing. "What would you like?" Daisy asked, a little more shyly, looking at Philip. "You know, my grandmother was a Royal, and the Royals usually let any of their kin use Gardens."

Philip did not know where to look or what to say. When he didn't answer immediately, Daisy thought that probably she had made a sufficient point. She glanced around. "Where's Champ?" she asked, noticing his absence.

Vivienne managed to put the spoonful of eggs on her plate and to sit down at the far end of the table. Her legs felt weak. What did it signify, that Daisy had on a ring? she asked herself. She looked over at Philip, but he didn't look at her. He had picked out a particular spot on the wall to scrutinize, and he was chose to keep staring at it.

"Champ's exhausted from treating a rape case," Cypriana said. Her tone was tart. "If that's what you claim to be." Cypri's temper was high. She had made

440

up her mind to have Philip for her own now, and crazy Daisy wasn't going to get him!

"Philip," Cypri said, turning her eyes on him, "I promised your parents I'd take some pictures of you, and I want you to come with me right now, right after we finish breakfast."

As she spoke, the front doorbell rang. Since Chooky had driven to Crosstree to pick up the Sunday papers, Estelle delegated Baker to go open the front door.

Baker found a very thin young man with curly dark hair and big brown eyes standing on the front porch. He was wearing blue jeans and a western shirt. Baker cautiously opened the screen door.

"Yes?" she said.

"Great Scott! Nefertiti!" The young man stared at her.

Baker blinked. "I beg your pardon?" she said. Who is this? she wondered.

"You're magnificent! That skin—that—do you know *your* roots? Partly a Dane, for sure. You look just like Viv. Only less earthy. What's your name?"

"My name?" Baker was bewildered.

"You have a name, haven't you?" The young man took Baker by the arm. He talked fast, like a New Yorker. "Or do they just number you down here?"

Baker tried to pull away. "I'm Baker Browning," she said.

"Okay. That name's okay. You're officially discovered, Baker Browning. I'm going to shoot a black epic and you look like a star. A black Vivienne. What a great set this is!" The young man looked up at the high ceiling of the hall. "The minute I saw this place I knew I could use it. I'll bet there are still slave cabins out in back."

He squeezed Baker's arm and she tried to pull away again. This was a crazy man! The telephone in the library rang. "I have to answer the phone," Baker said.

"Never mind the phone. What's in here?" He started pulling her toward the drawing room.

441

"Mister, let me go!" Baker raised her voice. She heard footsteps on the front porch, and to her relief, Dr. Alexander came in the front door. The telephone kept ringing. Champ stared at the young man.

"Hello," Champ said, with a tentative air.

The young man was looking into the drawing room. "Fantastic!" he said to Champ. "Maybe we can get all the descendants of your slaves back here for a huge reunion. The place is intact. What material!"

"This man is nuts," Baker said to Dr. Alexander.

"Isn't that the phone?" Johnny Mae asked coming into the front hall at that moment.

"Look, I don't quite know who you are," Champ said to the man.

"Oh. I'm Alec Markowitz."

"Alec Markowitz!" Champ knew that name and he grinned.

Johnny Mae gave the three of them a funny look and went into the library to answer the telephone. It was for Vivienne. As she went back to the dining room, the new guest was still raving, this time something about the purity of concept of the house, and Baker had stopped pulling away and was looking at him with big eyes. Baker knew who Alec Markowitz was, all right. He had made Vivienne Dane famous.

In the dining room, the last few minutes had been spent eating—or, in Mab's case, pretending to eat. She was finding it difficult just to breathe. Daisy intended to go through with the engagement, with the wedding! She seemed to want it. But how did Philip feel? Did he still want Daisy, after all he'd said last night in the guest house? She longed to know what Philip was thinking. In a moment she was going to crack wide open and say something. She clenched her hand under the table.

"Telephone for Miss Vivienne. And some man's arrived," Johnny Mae said from the door.

"What?" Vivienne was totally distracted. She had

442

been staring at a broiled tomato on her plate as if it were a crystal ball and could tell the future.

Johnny Mae repeated the message. What was the matter with everyone this morning? The one who acted oddest last night, Daisy, was the only one who seemed to have her wits about her today. The others were taking turns at acting strange.

At that point Champ led in Alec Markowitz, who still clutched Baker's arm so that they made a threesome, Alec in the middle. Vivienne was stupefied at the sight.

"Hi, Viv," Alec said airily. "You stay right here," he ordered Baker, backing her against the wall. "I don't want you out of my sight." He walked over and kissed Vivienne on the cheek. "I love your house, Viv. It's perfect. Wait till I talk to Bernie Silverman in Hollywood! We can probably start shooting next month."

"Alec!" Vivienne finally uttered his name. "What are you doing here?"

Even Philip swung his gaze to Vivienne as she spoke. Her throaty voice was vibrant, and her dark eyes, wide and staring in her pale face, made her look as if she were seeing a ghost.

Alec gave a nonchalant wave, looking about him. "Love the dining room, too," he said. He measured the ceiling with his eyes. Then he looked back at Vivienne. "Honey, I owe my recovery to you. It happened as soon as I saw you at Havenfield. I just had to play that scene with you one more time, I guess. After your visit my head straightened out. Cipes said artists sometimes have depressions like mine, said a withdrawal like that is often a very creative period for them. It's like their brains are switched off for a while. Rests them up. Anyway, it took me a week to convince the folks at Havenfield that I felt fine. They finally let me go. Then it took me three days to track you down. What a place this is! I just found out about the big hit *Roots* made, and I was

443

thinking on the flight down, I'll do a black epic for my next picture. And here's the star already!" He waved at Baker. "She opened the door."

Alec looked around the table. Mab, Daisy and Cypriana all stared at him in fascination. He looked closely at each one in turn.

"Good God, it's a nest of them," he said. "I feel as if I'm at the Miss America pageant. Are you all Danes?"

"Alec. It's—they're my sisters." Vivienne could barely speak; she was still in a state of astonishment. "Cousins."

Alec poured himself a cup of coffee and ate some eggs right out of the bowl. "Nothing like fresh eggs," he said. "Look, Baker, don't run away. I want to sign you up. I've gotta call New York and the Coast. Where's the phone? Are the slave cabins still in back?" He peered out one of the back windows.

Hearing that, Johnny Mae threw up her hands and retreated to the kitchen. Estelle gave her an inquiring look. Johnny Mae just shook her head and got out a bottle of bourbon. She was pouring a nip for both of them when Alec stuck his head into the kitchen for a look.

"Fantastic," he said, and made for the library.

In the dining room, after Alec followed Johnny Mae out, Champ looked around, gave Daisy a grin, and poured himself a cup of coffee.

"You're certainly all quiet today. Sugar Hastings's little boy drank some Clorox for breakfast this morning. He's fine now." Champ put some kippers and ham biscuits on a plate and sat down to eat. Some silent moments passed. No one seemed interested in Sugar Hastings's little boy.

"Viv." Alec stuck his head back inside the dining room. "It's Tom Clancy on the phone. He claims he's been waiting an hour for you. I told him how great this place is and he said *People* mag wants to write it up. Maybe it would be good publicity for the movie.

Anyway he refuses to get off the line and let me call the Coast until he's spoken to you."

Maybe she should just stand up and scream a blood-curdling scream like Daisy, Vivienne thought.

"Alec, *what* are you talking about?" she said. Finally she found the strength to get up from the table. "*What* movie? Land's End is not going to be in *People* magazine or in any movie or in anything."

She walked out into the hall and Alec followed her.

"Aw, now, Viv, don't be that way. Think of the drama this place has seen. Slaves sold away from their families. Babies born to girls who were raped—what stories!"

Alec went nattering on as Vivienne turned into the library and picked up the telephone.

"Where'd you come from, Borneo?" Clance said. "Look, I just spoke to Alec. I was calling to tell you that he'd recovered. I'm too late, I guess. He certainly got down there fast. How is he?"

"His usual raving lunatic self," Vivienne said.

"Sounds like he's got a great idea," Clance said, a bit tentatively. "What's this about he's found a star already?"

"Clance, do you mind if we don't discuss it right now? I have a house full of guests."

"You sound funny. Are you okay? Do you need protection? Want me to come down? Don't let Alec fox you. I could get there tonight."

"If anyone else comes down here we'll run out of buttermilk. I'll call you back later. I've got to go."

"Okay, but promise—"

Alec was hovering over her, and when she hung up he grabbed the phone. He took a little book out of his pocket and started dialing a long number. Vivienne finally had a delayed reaction to the sight of him. Alec was *out*. He was well. She didn't have to feel guilty for a minute longer. Unless she gave in to her impulse to kill him.

"Don't you promise this house to a soul, you idiot,"

445

she said menacingly into his ear. She couldn't stay to hear his conversation—she was dying to get back to the dining room to see what was happening.

She had not missed much. Cypriana again had mentioned taking Philip's picture, but Champ laughed at that.

"Better let me take his picture, Cypri. Remember how those shots for the Christmas card came out? You always jerk the camera."

Cypri remembered all over again that she hated Champ. She gritted her teeth. However, she couldn't waste time inventing cruel tortures for him. She had to think of some other excuse to get Philip off alone. While her mind raced, Estelle came in and spoke softly to Daisy. "Miss Daisy, Bob King is here to see how you are."

"Oh." Daisy blushed. "That is nice of him. Did you tell him I'm fine?"

"He's on the back porch."

"Maybe I should tell him. Excuse me a minute." Daisy looked around the table. As she left the room, Mab tried to stir from her lethargy.

"So that's Alec Markowitz," she said. "I wonder if he should be running around the countryside? I mean, do you think—" She paused.

"I think he's still nuts," Cypri said. "He probably *escaped* from that loony bin." But remembering Alec's admiring look at her, she added, "I guess they're all crazy in Hollywood."

Baker was still standing where Alec had placed her. Suddenly she wondered what she was doing there; she sidled out the door as Vivienne came back in.

"Would anyone like a drink?" Vivienne asked. "I think I might have something." She headed for the bar.

"Is that guy okay in the head now?" Cypriana asked.

"He's normal for him." Vivienne found the ice bucket.

Daisy came back in and sat down next to Philip again.

446

"Guess what? Bob found the—the guy who was on the back porch last night, and he beat him up," she said to Champ.

There was a pause.

"Well, *who* was it?" Cypriana asked. "Why are you so mysterious?"

"I don't think Daisy has to tell us," Champ said. "If Bob got him, that's enough."

"That's too much, if you ask me. Did *you* get beaten up for every pass you ever made?" Cypri said. "You'd have lived in the hospital." She glared at Champ.

Daisy wondered why Cypri sounded so hostile. She stared at her. She could look at Cypri now without feeling her usual sensations. It was amazing. She could scarcely believe it, but suddenly she didn't physically want Cypri at all. After all these years. It *was* amazing! Those desires were gone—she would infinitely prefer Champ. Daisy looked over at Champ, blushing slightly.

When Vivienne reached the bar, she changed her mind about having a drink and opened a can of soda instead and poured it over the ice. She wondered what they were going to do next. Cypriana had been more or less in charge of planning the activities of the weekend. She looked at her sister. But it was madness to think of golf or tennis or, for God's sake, badminton on the lawn. Not with so much hanging in the balance. Was Philip going to keep up this pretense of his engagement?

"Philip, are you going to Aunt Martha's?" Vivienne asked the question abruptly, not giving herself time to think first. She just plunged before she lost her nerve. She stood absolutely still and looked directly at Philip as she spoke.

He raised his eyes to hers. He looked terribly strained, she thought. Mab watched as their glances locked. Cypriana and Daisy both watched tensely, too. Only Champ was relaxed. He glanced at Daisy and noticed that she was wearing Philip's ring. Well, how about that?

447

Philip didn't immediately answer Vivienne, and Cypriana jumped up from the table.

"Philip can't go right now," she said. "He has to—uh"—desperately she cast about—"to go to his parents' house. I'll drive him, okay? We'll go right now."

When Philip didn't move Cypri added, "Come on, Philip. We'll take the Porsche." It was a bit crude, but the best she could manage for the moment.

"I'll come, too," Daisy said. "Then I can explain to the Alexanders about last night."

"No, there isn't room in the Porsche. Besides, what would you tell them? That a kiss at midnight turned you into a pumpkin?" Come on, Philip, hurry, Cypri thought; pick up the cue and let's get out of here. But Philip was still looking at Vivienne. She seemed to have hypnotized him.

Philip only half-heard Cypri's voice. He was trying to imagine what Vivienne could mean by speaking so directly to him, by forcing him to look at her face, to look at it and see that it was older and different and yet that her eyes were the same. He wished he could read the message there. What was happening? The room suddenly seemed full of confusion, beautiful women gathered around a table; he had an odd sense of having lived through it before, not here, not at Land's End, but those nights in London, where the wheel spun and the cry "No more bets!" echoed softly through the rooms, and everyone gambled. He had found a kind of peace there, or anyway a substitute for despair. But why the despair?

Cypriana moved directly in front of him, speaking again, forcing him to look from Vivienne to her; he could not read Vivienne's eyes anyway. He had come to Lane's End to show Vivienne his indifference. He had been prepared for her indifference. There was nothing between them now, and Vivienne probably just asked her question as his hostess: "Are you going to Aunt Martha's?" The words were simple enough, the meaning simple—yet once Philip looked away from Vivienne's face he longed to look back. Would she still be gazing at him?

Afraid to test her, he fixed his eyes on Cypriana, thinking again how much she resembled Vivienne. He had been struck by the resemblance at her wedding . . . he could remember exactly how Cypriana had walked down the aisle in the candlelight, how Champ had run to meet her. It occurred to him that he had doubly paid the price for that wedding, a high price to see his younger brother marry a Dane. The actual money of course, agreeing to help with the financial end of Champ's affairs, making it possible for him to marry without waiting or hardship. But there had been an emotional price too, the price paid in his youth. The scheme to send him to his uncle had cost him Vivienne. The scheme had made him rich and yet according to his psychiatrist had given him nothing he wanted or valued, only a compulsion to lose his money . . . had he ever told the doctor about his brother's wedding? Had he described the ice-blue bride, the satin-garbed bridesmaids, the roses and the candles and the ceremony that sanctified their union and let them live together the way he had once dreamed of living with his own love?

He wondered if, after all, he hadn't figured out, on his own, the wellspring of his discontent. Was it the wish to rewrite the past? How did you, then, do that? He thought you didn't.

His eyes traveled from Cypriana's face to the faces of the others; he was still not listening to what was being said. Vivienne stared straight ahead of her. Mab looked at him with her tilted eyes shining and a slight, encouraging smile on her face. Daisy was wearing his ring—

Daisy! He looked again at the ring on Daisy's finger. Was he honor-bound to Daisy? He thought he was. Over his tea table in Mayfair only a few days ago, Vivienne and Mab had seemed so remote—worlds away—and Daisy the one who needed help. Last

449

night he had told Mab he loved her—Daisy had seemed far away then. But now! Suddenly, the moment he had looked forward to, seeing Mab, having her beside him again, the happy moment he had been anticipating when he stepped through the door to the dining room was not going to come up so easily. Something was going on in this room, something none of them fully realized yet. Philip didn't want to realize it. He gave his attention to Daisy; she was speaking.

"Look, Cypri, we can take the station wagon," Daisy said, as if patiently trying to soothe away an inexplicable mood in her cousin.

"Oh, shut up!" Cypri shouted.

Champ sat bolt upright in his chair.

"Hey, what's eating you?" he said to Cypri.

Her fury boiling over, Cypri turned on him. "You can shut up too," she cried. "I've had it with you, Champ. I'm leaving you."

"What?" Champ stared at Cypriana.

Cypri wished this were Arabia or somewhere, so that she could just yell, "I divorce you!" three times and be free. Her blue eyes flashed from Champ to Philip. There. Now Philip would know he could have her. He did look at her.

They all did. Cypri was a magnificent sight. Her breast heaved with wrath, and the red color staining her cheeks contrasted with her black hair, making her look like Snow White just restored to life and ready to kiss the prince.

Alec Markowitz appeared in the doorway to say something, but froze at the sight of Cypriana's stance. What a bosom! Apparently some sort of family fight was going on. Alec thought, Dolly in the camera slowly . . . now, give me full face—hold it . . . now back out slowly, slowly.

Mab put her hand on Philip's arm.

"Philip's not going with you, Cypri," Mab said steadily.

"Who are you to say?" Cypri's head lifted even higher.

"Look, Philip's our guest. He can do what he wants to do." Mab turned her eyes on Philip's face.

Daisy stared at Mab's hand resting on Philip's arm. What did that mean? Mab was smiling. As Philip looked from Cypriana to Mab, he wore a strange expression, a look that seemed to say he was on the spot and didn't know what to do. Mab's hand on his arm must mean something! Mab, like Aunt China, Daisy knew, was always very correct in her behavior. Mab wouldn't touch Philip possesively like that unless there was reason to. What if the two of *them*, Mab and Philip—

"Mab." Daisy made herself speak. "Do you and Philip—do you—are you—" Daisy bogged down. She stared at Mab's unmoving hand.

"Yes," Mab said, her voice clear. "Philip and I—"

Mab left it at that, longing for Philip to corroborate her words, to put his hand over hers.

Cypriana's mouth sagged open. Well, of all the nerve!

Slowly, Daisy drew off the diamond ring. Gently she laid it down on the dining room table.

"I had no idea," she said softly. "Philip, you don't have to go through with our engagement. I never knew why you wanted to marry me in the first place, and anyway, I think I'm really—cured."

Cypriana in surprise fell back a step. Her act was over. Everybody in the room looked at Daisy.

Pan, Alec thought, then use a wide angle and get them both in, now close-up on the blond.

The sight of the diamond ring lying on the dining room table stung Cypri back to life.

"Philip," she said, "I'm in love with you." It was terrible to do this in public, but time was running out. To her surprise, Philip appeared not to hear her.

He too was looking at the ring on the table.

451

"Daisy," Philip said, his eyes traveling up to her face again, "you're sure?"

Daisy licked her dry lips and spoke quietly. "I would have married you and—and really tried. I might be—I think I'm all right now." The blood came up into Daisy's cheeks, and her blue eyes probed deeply into Philip's dark ones. She tried to get her message across to him by telepathy, thinking hard, *I'm all right!* Surely he could tell by her blush what she meant. "I know you wanted to help me, Philip, and I'll never forget that," she added. "But you're free."

Slowly, Philip looked from Daisy to Mab. Mab's hand tightened on his arm. Soundlessly, he said her name.

"Well, Philip?"

Cypriana spoke commandingly again, and Philip, startled, looked up at her. What a fantastic bitch, he thought. She really was larger than life. "Are we going?" she said.

"Going?"

"To your parents."

For one second, Philip was tempted to agree and get up and leave with Cypri. It was a way out of there. From the corner of his eye, he could see that Vivienne's face had turned dead white. She looked like she might faint. She was white, white like the girl who had sat so many years ago at the kitchen table of Land's End staring at him. With an overwhelming urgency he suddenly wanted to say. *Vivienne, couldn't we start again, couldn't we make it come out better?* Even as he thought that, he was struggling with another thought. He couldn't endure an instant's glance at Mab. She still clutched his arm tightly, and she had every right to expect him to respond; there was last night between them and a rapture so compelling, a personal bond so tight—

If he left with Cypriana, if he just rushed out . . . how good it would feel to stand up, to move! Not to sit here in the middle of the confusion which he himself had created. What did Vivienne want? *Him*? Was it possible?

Vivienne stared at Philip, and she could not believe she was taking so long to tell him she needed him. This morning it had seemed so simple; why was she letting other things get in the way, agents, directors, family squabbles, chit-chat over Daisy's state of health, Mab quarreling with Cypri, plans for visits to Crosstree? It was the way things usually happened, Vivienne thought, a thousand little things delayed and delayed the important matters, the important things like picking the petals off a daisy to see if you were loved. That was the important matter, the thing missing from her own life—she had no love, only love remembered, the way you remember music after you leave the concert hall. It plays in your mind but it is not really heard again. . . .

A sentence darted through Vivienne's brain. She heard the words *She could have been a concert pianist*. Who had said that? About whom? Why did she think of it now? But the disembodied sentence provided the impetus she needed to speak, as if it pulled a trigger in her mind.

The voice that had thrilled millions had never brought quite such a response from the nerves of her listeners. Vivienne's words seemed to vibrate in the air.

"Philip, in the name of God!"

Philip's eyes swung from Cypriana's face to Vivienne's, and this time he could read the dark eyes. They blazed at him from her white face; he rose, every muscle in his body taut. His facial muscles were so tense that they hurt; they felt like iron chords beneath his stretched skin. For a moment he resisted any action, with no thought at all in his mind—the time lag between Vivienne's words and his realization of their meaning. She was demanding their reunion, after so many years of separation. She was demanding the ending that belonged to the beginning.

453

He heard an anguished sound, and he did not know whether it came from his lips, or Vivienne's, or Mab's, but Vivienne stretched her hands out to him and without thought, he covered the distance between them and caught her hands in his. His arms went around her and he felt her arms clasp him.

In his amazement, Alec forgot to point his imaginary camera. No one else moved. Mab's hand which had been on Philip's arm remained extended out into space as she stared blankly at Vivienne and Philip.

They made no sound. Vivienne's eyes were closed; Philip's head was turned away from Mab and she couldn't see his face.

Mab longed to throw herself on the two of them and pry them apart. Only an instinct for self-preservation kept her from it. Her heart did not seem to beat, and she felt that if she attempted movement, the strain would be too much and she would die.

Quietly, Daisy moved to Mab's side. She thought Mab looked as if she might lose consciousness. Where was Champ? Daisy looked around for him. He was still sitting at his place at the table, and his face was a study. Ever since Cypri publicly offered herself to his brother, Champ had been in a strange mood. The thought of beating Cypri had seized his imagination. He could almost hear her cries for mercy, and he longed to hear those cries. He stared at his wife with blazing eyes.

Daisy looked back at Mab. She was alarmed by what she saw. She wondered if she should put her arm around Mab. "Mab?" she said.

Mab drew a breath at last. She still looked at Philip and Vivienne clasped in each other's arms. She couldn't see his face and she did not want to see Vivienne's.

Mab dropped the hand that had been on Philip's arm, the hand that so foolishly still was stretched into space. She stood up. She had lost. She must leave, walk out with every bit of dignity she could summon.

She cried to herself for help, and from the ancient past she heard Miss Phipps's voice: *You only give them your beauty*.

She had to attempt to move, even if her heart didn't beat, even if she did die on the spot. She was not conscious of anyone except Philip and Vivienne in the room; nothing besides them seemed to be in the room except the doorway. She had to get through it.

Mab turned and started for the door. What an exit! Alec thought. Keep the camera on her now, move with her. He stared from the doorway as Mab approached. Her face was composed, masklike. She had become a dancer concentrating totally on her dance. Her light footsteps made almost no sound.

Alec fell back before Mab as she reached the doorway. He saw her move regally into the hall, and mentally he photographed it all.

Mab walked as far as the stairs in the hall. Then her legs suddenly went weak and numb, and she clutched the shell shape of the end of the banister and hung on. It was over, she told herself; she was out of the dining room.

The brightness of the day outside shone through the open front door, and the radiance blurred as tears filled her eyes. The front hall reminded her of something—what was it? She tried to think. The front hall seen through tears—where on earth? Then she knew. It reminded her of "Interior at Petworth," Turner's strange masterpiece. Where Philip had—

Mab bent over the banister. The pain in her head was severe, and her chest felt tight. There were little flutters of some sort in the hollow of her throat. Why was it frightening to feel this way? The answer came—because it was familiar. These were familiar symptoms. She was always the loser at this game. It was infinitely worse this time, but the feeling was the same, just more intense.

She clutched her hands on the banister so tightly that they ached. Don't think about last night, she told herself, even as the thoughts came. Had Philip only been pretending that he was happy to make love to her? Oh, she told herself hastily, he *couldn't* have been pretending. Why did she think it? In frustration, Mab wanted to hammer her hands against the wooden shell. She shouldn't let even the tiniest suspicion form. But suppose Philip had lied to her? Suppose last night had been just a lie, and she was still locked up with her problem?

An image formed in Mab's mind. Locked up with her problem, the way a reflection is locked up in the mirror. All outward beauty and perfection, the girl in the mirror, but no feelings. Perhaps her problem was not her inner dimensions at all, but the fact that she had been letting the girl in her mirror do the living for her, and not lived life herself.

Mab drew a breath, surprised at the thought. Her mind went on working. This kinship she felt with Philip, this idea that they were the same—was it the compulsive aspect of Philip's nature which she recognized? Her dancing had been compulsive in her youth . . . maybe even now, her devotion to art . . .

Mab let her tears run unchecked, managing not to sob violently. While part of her mourned, the odd thoughts that had just come into her mind took on a radiance. When she closed her eyes, the thoughts were almost visual, small flecks of hope like fallen bright leaves that glow on a wet path on a dark day, beckoning you on into an ever more beautiful forest. Where would such a path take her, supposing that she followed it? What would she find if she left Arthur . . . perhaps took the job in London?

Mab wiped the tears from her cheeks. She sighed. It was dreary, curing yourself. Much nicer to have a mother to do it, a mother soothing away life's hurts. Or if your mother were dead, a substitute like Arthur Windsor. But suppose you had nobody. You *could* do it yourself, and just—go on.

In the dining room, Cypriana grew bored by looking at Philip and Vivienne hugging each other. What was this all about? They loved each other? She had heard they used to go together, back a million years ago. Well, what a shock. She let her gaze slide over to Champ. Wow! He looked mad. Cypri sucked in her underlip and looked around for a napkin to dry off her hand. Something red was all over it. She must have put it into the plate of boiled tomatoes when she reached behind her for support.

"Cypri, I want to talk to you." Champ's voice was very quiet and somehow deadly. Cypri's eyes widened.

"Well, how about later?" she said, starting to move toward the door. Alec Markowitz was standing there; maybe she could start a conversation.

"Now."

Champ got up, took Cypriana's arm in a firm grip and marched her out the door. Daisy followed them, brushing past Alec. Champ's back was rigid. He walked Cypri through the hall and right past Mab at the staircase without stopping.

Mab was still bent over the newel post. Daisy touched her arm.

"Are you all right, Mab?"

Mab straightened and gave her cousin a small smile.

"Daisy," she said, "Let's go into the library and have a drink."

Agreeing at once, Daisy turned and headed with Mab across the hall. Daisy was vastly puzzled by Philip and Vivienne's embrace in the dining room; she wondered if Mab could explain. It seemed that Mab was not the only one who had been involved with Philip. So many amazing things had happened in the last twenty-four hours that Daisy could scarcely feel surprised at Vivienne—or anything else. In fact, she felt only the urge to sit down and stare into space for a while.

In the dining room. Alec was the sole observer as

Philip and Vivienne kissed each other. They were both barely able to breathe from excitement. It made the kiss rather an awkward one. Philip lifted Vivienne up in his arms afterward and managed to carry her through the outside door to the walkway. Alec was left to size up the dining room furnishings and help himself to some Jack Daniels from the sideboard. Bernie Silverman was due to call him back any minute to discuss the film. And where was that girl, Baker? Alec took his drink and went across to the kitchen. Baker was sitting at the kitchen table. Alec sat down beside her.

"Kid, you've seen the last of a kitchen," he said.

"What happened in there?" Baker asked. "We're all wondering."

Alec cocked his head to one side. "I guess," he said, "Viv has found something she's been looking for, for a long time. Still, I wouldn't take it too seriously. I'll have her back in a movie within a year. But not until I make the one with you."

"Honest?"

"Come on into the living room and I'll tell you about it."

Baker thought it a bold move, but after a moment she got up from the kitchen table. Anyway, Estelle and Johnny Mae were out in the guest house having juleps.

Upstairs, Champ relinquished his plan of punishing Cypri and simply pushed her onto the bed. He made love to her instead, with a violent intensity even greater than Frank's the night before. Cypri squirmed in pleasure and had to bite the pillow to keep from hollering.

"Oh, Champ," she whispered to him, "I'm so glad you didn't let me leave you. I really do love you."

"I think I hate you."

"Champ." Cypriana opened her blue eyes wide and looked reproachfully at him.

"But I'm condemned to you," Champ said, kissing

her face. "Condemned. And condemned men eat hearty meals—"

Cypri put her hand over Champ's mouth and hushed him, and his arms tightened around her.

*   *   *

Vivienne's body was tense, flooded with the sensations of fullness and warmth, but her mind was at rest. As she drew closer and closer to physical happiness, she thought of the way she and Philip had been drawing closer and closer to each other too, through the hours since they had first met in the hall at Land's End; a warmth spreading through the air from one to the other; invisible filaments tightening between them even if they never spoke or looked at each other.

She lay on the bed in the guest house with Philip and she could not have told who was more avid. Both of them muttered incoherent things, touched all the familiar places. Philip pulled her hand up beside her head and put his palm against hers, pressing it, pinning her hand to the bed while he kissed her breasts. For a minute, Vivienne resisted; she tugged to free her hand, almost panicked, but Philip did not release her, and then she accepted him. His expression was intent as he touched her in a way which pulled her to a peak of sensation. Vivienne moaned and Philip laughed and she closed her eyes and it was the times in the barn and the van and the river bank and she was young with Philip lying on top of her and his breath in her ear.

Vivienne sighed, bathed in sweat. All the events of her life seemed to have brought her to this point, where she could feel and not pretend. Philip asked her nothing, whether she was happy or not. He knew through touching her skin, through her pores and her lips and her whole body, knew because they had fashioned one another long ago, and those first kisses had shaped them for each other.

Lying with his body against Vivienne's, Philip could finally comprehend the impasse through which he had lived. Now that he had managed to reach the other bank of the chasm, a great deal was clear. He had identified his present success with his past unhappiness. He had tried to get rid of his money as if by doing so he could change the past. His mind went back to the darkness and the river, to his pain and horror at the way it had turned out, pain over losing Vivienne, horror at the realization that he was capable of rape and fury. He remembered running through the night crashing into trees. Pain at his loss. Perhaps his sensations when he lost at roulette had been similar, in a way had been like touching Vivienne for comfort in the dark.

Vivienne was here now. Tenderly, Philip kissed Vivienne's long hair, drawing it across her face. He was healed. Vivienne had forgiven him. She said it; he knew she had forgiven him. She had been lonely, too.

He drew her hand up to his lips and kissed it, uncurling her fingers from whatever she gripped. She had seized a handful of the pillow with her free hand as he kissed her; then her hand had struck something soft and she had grasped that. He saw a flash of blue and green as he kissed Vivienne's palm, and suddenly he realized what she had been holding. Lying beside the pillow were the blue and green silk flowers Mab had worn last night in her hair.

Mab.

Dear God, Mab. Philip closed his eyes. Oh, God, he had made Mab a loser. He had made Mab feel exactly the same sensations he had felt himself long ago, when he lost Vivienne. He knew Mab loved him. And he loved her. She didn't deserve pain. He had made Mab a loser, and he knew a loser's sensations in gambling, in life. He identified with Mab; not only in that way but in all ways, Mab with her delicate character. She was so sweet to love! She stirred him in every way,

460

and now she was going from him, floating past on a current which took her away. . . .

Philip pictured the deft manipulation of the stacks of colored chips in the croupier's hands, those hands which flashed out and arranged one's life in such a practiced manner—you win, you lose—with the stacks pushed here and there in an instant, directed by the winning number on the wheel. The croupier's hands were without compassion.

Philip thought of rising and going to find Mab. Mab whose flowers were in his bed. But what could he say to her?

He opened his eyes, and seeing Vivienne's face so close, he covered her lips with his mouth and kissed her. He wanted to stop himself from remembering the cold London dawns and walking home from the casino. He would never do that again; why was he thinking of it? He had won, hadn't he, and not lost?

The intriguing adventures of the daring, beautiful, captivating shopgirl they called

A novel by
Josephine Edgar

Coming in April from Warner Books

"Abrim with action and outrageous romance . . . a delight!"—Jennifer Wilde, Author of *Love's Tender Fury* and *Dare To Love*

"This rags-to-riches romance set in late Victorian London is delightful . . ." —*Library Journal*

"An indisputably appealing romance . . . Head and decollete shoulders above others." —*Kirkus Review*

Duchess

by Josephine Edgar

It had been a cold afternoon and Leeds lay under a pall of low grey clouds, creating a light more like November than late April. There were only fifteen minutes before the London Express left and Betsy Holder, waiting by the barrier with a small carpet bag containing all her possessions, was filled with anxiety.

Where was her friend, Viola?

Supposing she had changed her mind? It was not possible. It had been Viola's idea entirely that they should leave their local jobs and take positions in London. Betsy had waited nearly an hour. The carriages had been gently shunted along the platform. The mailbags had gone in. The guard with his flag and lantern had arrived along with the dining car attendants, and for the last fifteen minutes the passengers had begun to stream through the barrier. The engine, enormous, black and green and gold, emitting hoarse, steamy shouts like a harnessed dragon, had been coupled up. But Viola was not there.

What **would** she do if Viola did not come? She had given in her notice at Hardcastle's. Should she go to London alone? The thought terrified her. She would never have taken such a step on her own. Viola had received references for them from Mr. Hardcastle. Viola had written to Dwyer & Netherby Ltd., Emporium for Ladieswear, Outfitters & Haberdashers to the Nobility and Gentry, of Oxford Street, London. In fact Samuel Hardcastle had also written personally to Arthur Netherby about them, thus securing Viola a position as second sales in the gloves, with Betsy as junior sales in the same department.

Betsy was very small, just five feet tall. Under her plain black straw hat, her straight hair of the nondescript colour known as "mousy" was drawn back into a small tight bun. She wore a shabby navy blue costume, and a grey shawl about her narrow little shoulders to keep out the cold. Her usually pink face was white with anxiety, and her large gentle grey eyes behind her metal-ringed spectacles were clouded with anxious tears.

She watched the passengers streaming through the barrier. A tall young gentleman in an Inverness cape passed, smoking a cigar, followed by a manservant shepherding two trolleys of luggage, complete with gun cases, a polished racing saddle and a bag of golf clubs. The young gentleman was so handsome, in spite of the fact that his nose had, at some time, been broken, that it was difficult not to notice him. He strolled on without even turning his brilliant blue eyes to see if his possessions were following him, leaving his manservant to cope with everything. Betsy envied him. He looked so pleasant, unhurried, so indolently self-assured, as though he was quite sure the train would wait for him. Then she saw Viola.

Although she was only a working girl, Viola was

like the handsome young gentleman who had just gone through the barrier: you had to notice her. She was tall, her new brown straw hat was topped with the defiant cluster of yellow buttercups, and her cloud of shiny, waving hair was a vibrant, burnished auburn. She was just twenty-one and very beautiful. Betsy adored her—her friend and protector. Viola apparently was scared of nothing, Betsy of everything. She had lived under Viola's wing ever since she had been apprenticed into the gloves at Hardcastle's when she was fourteen. She had gone to "live-in" there straight from the orphanage. She was told she was lucky, training to be a "shop-lady" instead of going into domestic service, especially at Hardcastle's, for Mr. Hardcastle, though a sharp man, did not try to save money by half-starving his "living-in" staff as did so many shop-keepers.

Betsy raised her arm to wave frantically to her friend, and then she saw whom she was with, and her eyes widened and her white cheeks reddened. Viola was with Mr. Samuel Hardcastle.

The rumours about Viola and Samuel Hardcastle had flown round the shop, and Betsy had refuted them as indignantly as a little hen bird defending its young. Mr. Hardcastle, they said, was sweet on Viola, and his wife had found out, and **that** was why Viola was leaving for London, and why he had been so generous with references and written personally to Mr. Arthur Netherby.

He stood by Viola, talking to her very earnestly. Not a very tall man; very respectable in his frock coat and shining top hat. It seemed to Betsy that the hard face, which had always so terrified her when he came round the department, was contorted, as though at any moment he might break down and weep. Betsy was shocked. As she watched Viola put her hand on his shoulder, and with a warm smile bent down, for she was half a head taller, and kissed him full on the lips. When she raised her head, he touched his mouth with his gloved hand and then looked at it, as though he expected the kiss to be something tangible that he could see on his glove, like a butterfly. Suddenly he thrust his hand into his breast pocket, drew out a packet and pushed it into Viola's hand. Turning away, he plunged blindly through the crowds towards the entrance of the station.

As Viola turned, she saw Betsy, and walked towards her, smiling. A porter was wheeling her small trunk and valise. She did not hurry her long graceful stride, her slender hips swaying, like some tall and lovely flower bending in a summer breeze. "Betsy!" she said. "Where the heck have you been? We'll have to hurry. Let the man take your case."

Betsy, swallowing her indignation, snatched up her carpet bag, unwilling to let it out of her hand, and followed in Viola's wake, puffing as she trotted along the platform.

* * * * * * *

"Mr. Lyttelton, they are just making the first dinner call. His lordship presents his compliments and says if the young ladies would care to join him too he would be—ahem—honoured."

Matthew was staggered. Jimmy did not even know the girls. Remembering James' reputation as a blood at school he opened his mouth to refuse for Viola, but realized she was not under his protection and he had no real right to do so. He looked at her helplessly. She looked at Betsy.

"Well, my Betsy, what shall we do? Eat our brawn sandwiches or have dinner with a lord?" Her long eyes widened mischievously, and she asked, "I suppose he is a **real** lord? Not a circus one like Sanger?"

"Lord Staffray," said Jevons coldly. "The son of the Earl and Countess of Louderdown."

"Well, Betsy?"

"I **couldn't!** I can't!" Betsy was in a real flutter of fear. "Don't ask me to, Vi. I'd be scared."

"I have already accepted," said Matthew, "but I assure you, Miss Holder, no harm shall come to you . . . you would be under my protection."

"It isn't that, sir, thank you. I just don't **want** to go. I'd be dropping everything, and couldn't say a word, I'd much better just have my sandwiches here."

"Miss Corbett?"

"I'd be happy to accept," Viola said grandly. "Would you pass my hat down from the rack, please?" Jevons did so. She took out a small hand mirror, tidied her hair, set the pretty hat on straight, and skewered it into place with an amber-headed pin. She picked up her gloves and handbag and rose, settling her skirts, twitching her brown velvet lapels straight.

Jevons led the way along the corridor, grinning to himself and thinking there were not many flies on this young piece. A filly who would give the master a run for his money, no doubt about that. Matthew followed Viola's long, swaying, graceful back, the yellow buttercups bobbing high on her head. He spoke in her ear.

"I met Lord James at Rugby. You won't talk about the Low Ayrton school, will you? I . . . well, at school I always said I had a tutor when I was small."

She nodded understandingly.

"And I won't say anything about you . . ." he promised.

The gold-green eyes were grave and questioning. "About my mother, you mean? Her scrubbing floors?

And about the father I never had? Don't worry, Mr. Lyttelton, I don't mind if you do." Her smile softened consolingly. "Young Matthew," she said, "you haven't altered. I'll tell you about me. I'm honest with honest folk, and the others can go hang themselves. And I know you're honest too."

Matthew was covered with confusion—and was a little ashamed. Viola was full of such baffling contradictions.

Jevons was waiting ahead holding open the door to the dining car. They could see the rose-shaded lights, white napery, the silver and the uniformed waiters, and James rising from his table to greet them, his bright blue eyes fixed hungrily on Viola.

He stepped forward, shook hands formally, then took her arm to lead her to the table. Her eyes were just level with his mouth. It was a bonny, inviting mouth, made for kisses and laughter, and she had an impulse to lift up her head and kiss his lips. Meeting his eyes she knew he knew what she was thinking and her creamy skin glowed for an instant with rose. Confusion was a new experience. She was filled with a heady excitement. They were like two beautiful tropical birds, sparring and displaying themselves until the precise moment for mating arrived.

James was entranced with her. He thought her a real little ripper and not in the least affected, without any of the high-toned pretensions of the actresses and expensive tarts he amused himself with. She made the girls of his own class fade into innocuous puppets by comparison. As he and Matthew settled in their seats, Matthew beside Viola, himself opposite, he set out to exert all his charm.

* * * * * * *

The two girls looked up at the large forbidding doorway, black-painted, with dirty brass and unwashed steps, and a feeble gleam of gaslight showing through the fanlight above the door.

"Well, here goes," said Viola, and tugged on the bell pull.

After a pause, footsteps could be heard shuffling along the stone hallway inside, and the door was opened by a thin, slatternly girl, wearing a grubby apron and a cap from which long strands of wispy hair escaped.

"Yes, ma'am?" she said.

"Is this the assistants' hostel for Dwyer & Netherby?"

"Yes. Will you be the two new ones, then?"

"It looks like it."

"Will you come in. I'll get someone to take your bags." She peered curiously at the two contrasting figures. Viola, so tall and assured, Betsy peering nervously round her friend. "It's too late for dinner. Saturdays we finish at seven."

"Thanks, I've eaten. How about you, Bet? You've only had sandwiches."

"I'm all right."

"A cup of tea or cocoa?" suggested Viola.

"Tea would be grand."

"Mrs. 'Arding, the 'housekeeper, don't allow no cups of anything after nine o'clock."

Viola took a sixpence out of her bag, handed it to the girl and said, "One cup of tea. And show us where we have to sleep."

"All right, miss. I'll do me best. It's against the rules, but I'll do me best. Come this way."

She took a candle from the hall-stand, lit it and led them up the tall, narrow stairs, the mahogany rail winding above them. A smell of dust and boiled cabbage pervaded the house. On the first landing, the servant girl, who told them her name was Sal Perkins, stopped and indicated a door with a dull glass panel behind which gleamed a feeble jet of gas. On the door painted in white were the letters W.C.

"There's one on each floor," she said.

"What luxury," said Viola gravely. "And how many ladies sleep on each floor?"

"Fifteen. Five to a room. Some of the senior ladies, first sales, like, sleep out."

"I'll bet," said Viola. She thought of Sam Hardcastle's hostel in Leeds with the decent coal fires, good plain food, comfortable beds, and the piano in the rest room.

"Let's see our bedroom."

It was one of two big rooms in the front of the house. There were five narrow iron bedsteads made up with unironed cotton sheets and grey army blankets. The floor was covered with linoleum. Five slim wardrobe cupboards and two wash-stands lined the walls, and beside each bed stood a yellow varnished commode on the top of which stood a candlestick and beneath there was a cupboard which contained a chamber pot. The curtains drawn across the windows were of a dull dark red rep. Sal Perkins lit a single gas jet, turning it carefully down to a small blue flame.

"Mrs. 'Arding," she warned, "expects you to be very careful with the gas. The other ladies is out until ten thirty, it being Saturday."

Viola sat on one of the beds. It was extremely hard. Betsy was nearly in tears. Compared with this, Hardcastle's in Leeds had been a palace.

"Better get that tea," said Viola. When the girl went out, she said cheerfully, "I see what Matthew Lyttelton meant when he said the food might not be very good. If it's as good as the sleeping accommodation, I reckon we'll starve to death, love."

"Oh, Vi," wailed Betsy, "it's terrible. It's not even clean. I wish we hadn't come. I wish I was back at Hardcastle's."

Viola rose, turned up the gas to a full flare, illuminating the room, in defiance of the as yet unknown Mrs. Harding.

"Don't give up yet. When Sal comes up with your tea, give her this sixpence and tell her to fill our hot-water bottles. Mine's in my case, right on top. I'm going down to visit that extremely modern convenience on the landing."

Viola picked up her bag and went downstairs. She opened the W.C. door, bolted it, and once again turned up the meagre gas jet to a full flare. Then she opened her bag and took out the envelope Sam Hardcastle had given her when they had parted and opened it. Bank notes—fivers. Twenty of them. A hundred pounds. Enough to keep her for a year—protection against a rainy day. Sam had been a champion friend to her. She placed the money back into her bag and went up to the dormitory. Sal meantime had brought the tea for Betsy and was turning the gas down again.

"You'll get me skinned, miss, if Mrs. 'Arding sees the gas burning like this."

"Turn it up again," commanded Viola. "And if the housekeeper objects, you tell her to see me about it."

Sal, open-mouthed, did as she was bid. The new saleslady had an authoritative air, which would not be gainsaid. And with it a smile that warmed the girl's starved heart.

"I'll get the hot-water bottles filled for you," she said, and vanished down the stairs.

On the way she met some of the young members

of the staff coming in from their Saturday night out, and said, "The new one for the gloves has arrived. A proper young Duchess, she is." The name stuck, and remained with Viola all the time she worked at Dwyer & Netherby's and followed her throughout her life.

* * * * * * *

The great bed dominated the room, a gilded swan holding the draped brocade curtains, the bed end was curved cream gilt shell.

Viola went slowly forward, twitched back the dust cover. Beneath was a brocade bedspread. She pulled that back, exposing the bare mattress and down-filled pillows. She turned, her eyes wild with excitement. She crossed the door with her slow, swaying, seductive gait, closed it, locked it, walked back to the bed. Before James's astounded and entranced eyes she took off her hat, sent it whirling, pale bronze feather fronds twirling like a Catherine wheel, to the other side of the great bedroom. She pulled the pins out of her hair and let its magnificent length ripple down about her shoulders, sat on the edge of the bed, took off her shoes, threw them aside, then stretched out her arms to him.

"Viola!" He was shocked, tormented, then, suddenly caught into her mad reckless mood, he went across, took her in his arms, laid her back on the unmade bed, began, expertly to unhook the high lace collar and the skin-fitting, boned bodice, while she lay back looking at him, smiling, mocking, abandoned.

"I may never be a duchess," she whispered, "or a countess, or a lady—perhaps not even just a plain Mrs.—but this is the first time for me. So, James my lord, if it's going to be, then it's going to be on the Empress's bed."

There, in the brocade jewel-box of a room, these two splendid and mutually obsessed creatures made love through the late summer afternoon. There James ravished her through the initiation of pain into a superb fulfillment. There was neither fear nor shyness nor embarrassment between them; they taught each other, claimed each other, calling forth heights of joy which neither of them was ever to forget or experience again.

* * * * * * *

During the days that followed James and Viola lived intensely, locked in their own private world. Recklessly he insisted that they stay on at Staffray House until the time came for him to leave London, and when Viola protested that his mother would be outraged, he said his mother was in Italy and would not know.

"People will tell her."

"Who?"

"Servants, people in the square."

"And if they do? It will soon be forgotten. She will be angry, but she will forgive me, as she always does all my scrapes."

Viola, lying deep in the bed with his smiling face against her breast, could very well believe it. She too would forgive him anything.

They had a cook, a housemaid, a footman and the ubiquitous Jevons to serve them in the house and Carson to drive them out anywhere they wished. Viola could guess what these servants were saying, but it did not worry her: she was lost in her own illusion that these few weeks were an eternity of happiness. At some future time they would both look back upon their conduct with bewildered amazement. Perhaps with deep regret. But not yet. For them there was neither past nor future, only the wonderful, passionate, extravagant present.

Viola thrived in the atmosphere of luxury, blooming like a rose in June, a tawny, silken rose. She gave her orders with charm and authority, as though she had lived in a big house all her life, delighting James and the servants—all of them, that is, but Jevons, who watched her with veiled insolence in his hard, predatory eyes.

The season was nearly over so far as the fashionable world was concerned, and the houses round the square were emptying. Word went round the mess that young Staffray had found himself a real beauty, and if in the restaurants, at race meetings and theatres, ladies passed them with averted eyes, his fellow officers buzzed around Viola like bees round a honey pot. She was the toast of the town, always surrounded by an entourage of smart young soldiers, and her nickname, Duchess, was on everyone's lips, bandied in club, mess-room and drawing-room with shocked disgust or wild admiration.

James showered gifts on her. He delighted in spoiling her. He was proud of her unerring natural taste, and to see her in beautiful clothes. He loved to show her off. He had a young, proud man's pleasure in knowing that every other man who saw her envied him. He hired horses and took her riding in the Row, delighting in her quickness to learn, the strength of her long slim wrists, adoring her in her skin-fitting habit, the little hard hat veiled over her fiery hair.

Sometimes they did not get up until midday, lying in each other's arms in the blue brocade room, then they would go out to lunch at the Cecil or the Savoy, a bonny couple, beautifully dressed. In the afternoons they would drive out to a race meeting, or take a punt to Cookham and laze and laugh the summer hours away.

Through the little pubs round Belgrave Square where the grooms and footmen went, the scandal slid from mouth to mouth, out into the country to the great houses, so that in smoking-rooms men guffawed, and in the drawing-rooms ladies whispered together in hushed tones, clamping into warning silence if any unmarried girl were present.

"What a terrible thing," they murmured. "Poor Lady Louderdown! His poor **dear** mama!"

Herbert Netherby heard the news from one of his favourite young gentlemen in the haberdashery. He told his sister. There had been many other occasions when Arthur Netherby had noticed an attractive assistant in his emporium, but Herbert had never felt that they were a danger—until Viola came.

He saw the scandal as his chance of a kill. This would finish off any chance that imperfinent bitch had with his father. One evening, when Arthur sat silent and preoccupied at the head of the dining table, Herbert told him what had happened. Arthur regarded his son coldly. His protuberant eyes were filled with dislike. To him Herbert was not only a nelly but a whining sneak as well.

"**And** living with Lord Staffray openly at Staffray House," he faltered before his father's frozen stare. "A **common** shopgirl! What his lady mother would say if she knew, I **can't** think! Everyone in the shop is talking about it now. Why, she had the impudence to send a maid in for gloves and handkerchiefs on Friday. To be charged to his lordship. I think it would be as well, sir, to dismiss that little friend of hers, a stupid little thing anyway, **all** thumbs—and then so far as we are concerned, the whole thing will be over and done with . . ."

"It is disgraceful," exclaimed Emily. "It will give the store a bad name if it was known you ever employed such a woman!"

Arthur Netherby slammed his hand down on the polished table. He glared at his offspring. He remembered Viola's fresh young beauty, now, it seemed, lost to him forever, and they appeared to him more dessicated, more like their dreary martyr of a mother than ever before. Carping, life-hating. When he spoke they both shrank at the tone of his voice.

"I do not wish to hear anything about this matter. And as for you, Herbert, perhaps you would keep your mind on your work at the emporium, and not go round gossiping and mincing like a girl apprentice. It is for me to decide whom I shall dismiss."

He rose, threw down his table napkin and strode out of the room.

"Well!" exclaimed Herbert. "The old brute! I was only trying to help!"

"What is the matter with him?" wailed Emily. "He's drinking so much. He's out every night after dinner. He never goes to church now. Huggins says that in the kitchen they say he's **in love** with this awful woman. Herbert . . . **supposing** this young lord gets tired of her, and Father brings her back here?"

"Don't let your imagination run away with you," said Herbert crossly. The boy assistants he drank with in the local pubs were talking along these lines. "Not that this Staffray **won't** get tired of her. All men get tired of **that** sort of woman. I mean, what do they have? But Father has too much sense to bring such a woman home . . . but, I tell you, Em, I wouldn't like it even if he set her up somewhere . . . she's the kind that might really rook him . . ."

If he had followed his father out of the house that night he would have been even more alarmed.

Arthur Netherby went to Belgrave Square and stood outside Staffray House, looking up at the tall facade from the far side of the road. The great plane trees in the square cast heavy shadows between the gas lamps and his dark-clad figure could hardly be seen. He knew the store was buzzing with gossip about Viola, but pride had not allowed him to question anyone about her, least of all Herbert. But now, at least, he knew where she was.

It was nearly nine o'clock when a carriage drew up and the door opened, sending a brilliant shaft of light under the columned portico and across the steps. He saw the golden boy and girl, hand in hand, come out of the house. James, so tall and fine and handsome in his evening clothes, the tall hat tipped back on his crisp brown hair, Viola with pearls round her long white throat, and a greenish orchid in her red hair, matching the colour of her chiffon gown. It was so hot that the long opera cloak of flame-coloured taffeta banded with Valenciennes lace was thrown back, displaying her low cut decolletage, her beautiful shoulders and bosom rising from a froth of frills. Even her shoes were green, the buckles glittering as she ran down the steps.

Both of them were completely unaware of the world around them. They had eyes only for each other. They were consuming time, drawing every sensation from every hour of every day, every vibrant touch, look, every burning caress, every abandoned moment, into themselves, storing memories against their coming parting.

Arthur hailed a hansom and followed them to a restaurant in the West End. He hung about outside, jostled by the crowds, the target of every street-walker, standing like a beggar, waiting for her to come out. He followed them to a music-hall, and sat in the stalls watching Viola sitting in the front of a box, the stage lights illuminating her beauty as she leaned towards the stage, watched the shadow envelop her as from time to time she whispered to James, and kissed him softly behind her fan. She seemed to have a new beauty, radiant and almost unearthly.

Arthur Netherby watched and burned with a monstrous jealousy, her remoteness from him, her intimacy with her young lover, destroying his sanity.

* * * * * * *

The journey through France seemed interminable. Viola lay in her berth, her face and jaw aching where Arthur had struck her. He had never struck her face before—he had been too careful of her beauty. But that night his anger seemed to have released an almost homicidal storm.

In the eight weeks of their marriage he had alternately petted and humiliated her, alternatively insulted and praised, tormented and then pleaded for her affection. He wanted to reduce her to a doll woman, to kill her spirit and her pride. Once she had laughed at him and the memory had rankled deeply. Part of his wish to marry her had been a morbid longing to have her in his power so that he could punish her for that indifference and mockery. He loved to cause her pain, because pain was the only sensation his exhausted body could give to her. She had pleaded, she had argued, she had even tried to charm, please and tease him into some kind of normal affection. But it served no purpose. A doll beauty for everyone to admire in public; in private a frightened suppliant begging for his mercy. She could be the first but she could not be the latter. Every inch of her stubborn North-Country spirit rebelled.

His impotence had been manifest from their first night together in Paris, and she had learned he took tablets in an endeavor to stimulate himself. She managed to hide her pity and disgust. She told herself many married women suffered and concealed such treatment, and she was now his wife. But the sickening alternatives he wanted, the kind of services he told her could be bought at the houses he frequented in St. Giles, left her frozen with horror. She was a whore, he ranted, and a poor one at that.

After the ball he had ripped the exquisite white and blue dress from her, the glittering beads spitting round the room like hail-stones.

At last he had left her alone, telling her to get the **femme de chambre** to help her pack, as they would catch the early train to Le Havre.

During the journey he watched her ceaselessly. She wore a thick veil to hide the bruises along her brow and cheekbone. She was apparently calm. She did not cry. She should cry—all women did. His first wife always had. Emily cried when he was angry with her, and he often reduced the women who worked for him to tears. He had even reduced Herbert to snivelling pleas. But Viola did not cry. When he had taunted her with the fact that he would never permit her to see Staffray again she had quietly agreed it would be better for them all.

He hated the dignity with which she bore his treatment. She reminded him of the grand, rich women customers who came to his store, who patronized him with a vague graciousness and whom he would like to see grovelling for mercy.